BOBBY ROBOT

BOBBY ROBOT

IN A WORLD RUN BY MACHINES,
ONE BOY MUST PROVE
THE HEART STILL MATTERS.

MICHAEL HILTON

an imprint of
Roan & Weatherford Publishing Associates, LLC
Bentonville, Arkansas
www.roanweatherford.com

Library of Congress Cataloging-in-Publication Data
Names: Hilton, Michael, author.
Title: Bobby Robot/Michael Hilton | Bobby Robot #1
Description: Second Edition. | Bentonville: Mad Cat, 2025.
Identifiers: LCCN: 2025942889 | ISBN: 979-8-89299-065-3 (trade paperback) |
ISBN: 979-8-89299-066-0 (eBook)
Subjects: | BISAC: YOUNG ADULT FICTION/Science Fiction/General |
YOUNG ADULT FICTION/Technology |
YOUNG ADULT FICTION/Computers & Digital Media
LC record available at: https://lccn.loc.gov.2025942889

Mad Cat trade paperback edition August, 2025

Cover Design by Casey W. Cowan
Interior Design by Staci Troilo
Editing by Sabine Berlin & Don Money

Dedication

To my Supreme Robot Overlords.
Hail High Command.

<!001: Booting Up>

THE MOTORS IN Bobby's cybernetic arm reflexively tightened as the fastening bolt bore deep into his left shoulder. The spike of pain ebbed with another shot of anesthetic from the surgical bot's probe. Bobby blinked against the swimming vision of the surrounding anti-gravity pod and wondered why his head felt so foggy.

He floated face-up, weightless, amid a flurry of surgical arms extending from inside the pod's curved sides. Faint notes of antiseptic burned his nostrils as a probe cleaned the junction of skin and synthetic fiber at his shoulder. Fighting through the slow transition to wakefulness, he forced his focus up through the pod's plastiglass hatch to his room outside. It was still dark. Stars twinkled in the domed ceiling's circular window.

He got the nebulous impression that he should wonder what time it was. But a glance at the vidscreen in his metallic left forearm gave no answer except an empty loading bar.

The surgical arms whizzed about, adjusting alloy couplers, installing plastifiber plates, and tightening screws in his synthetic limb until a collection of vague thoughts suddenly tangled together in his brain.

What the scrub is going on?

"LINC?" He stretched out his biologic fingers to tap the vidscreen, but a probe swatted his hand away.

"Do not interrupt the resizing of your cybernetic appendage," a deep voice filtered into the pod's narrow space. "Your arm's core processor is exposed and could sustain damage if you move."

"Hovel?" Bobby mumbled as another shot of anesthetic dulled his senses.

"Yes, Robert," the dwelling's central computer answered in dulcet tones through the pod's inner speakers.

"What are you talking about?" Bobby forced the words through his drowsy brain and out his throat. "Resizing's next month, right?"

"Maintenance schedules have shifted due to your recent growth spurt. Your sixteenth year of life is inconveniencing our timetables."

"I don't understand."

In response, a holographic miniature of Bobby's body coalesced in front of him. A thin frame and pale chest stood in stark contrast to the shiny bulk of the cybernetic arm attached at his left shoulder. The hologram then overlaid a plexus of nerves that snaked from his neck down into the arm where it mingled with circuits and newly expanded machinery.

He frowned, wrestling the anesthesia to make sense of all this. "Where's LINC?"

"Living Inter-Neural Communicator reboot is underway. Your task assistant should be operational by the time short-acting anesthetic clears from your system."

With that, a probe tightened the last screw, and the surgical arms withdrew from the space, disappearing through hatches in the chamber's side.

Bobby watched the loading bar creep along his forearm's vidscreen. A nagging thought vibrated in the back of his mind like a faulty plasma sword, not quite sharp enough to cut through the fog. Something was wrong. Out of place, out of sequence. Something the Hovel had done wrong. But the Hovel never did anything wrong. Its perfect programming carried out Protocol. Before he could tease out the mystery further, the loading bar filled and disappeared with a chime.

"Hey, Bobs." Abstract color swirled on the screen in sync with a modulated voice coming from his forearm's speaker. "What did I miss?"

"LINC, I think the Hovel resized my arm too early." Bobby's words tumbled out, tangled with medication, as he pumped his cybernetic fingers to stimulate his brain out of its haze.

"Well good, now I don't have to hear you complain about chafing."

Bobby pushed down a vague bite of annoyance. Something about the rescheduled resizing perplexed him, but he couldn't quite pinpoint why.

"Too bad the Hovel rescheduled it for today, though." LINC's tone dropped in a synthetic sigh. "Could've used that time to study for your Programming test today."

Bobby's eyes shot wide as adrenaline spiked through the cloud of receding anesthesia.

Programming.

"Scrub!" He punched a button on the inner wall and landed hard on his back with the return of normal gravity. "Oomph." The Hovel had been right about how short-acting the anesthetic was. Back aching, he picked himself up as the chamber hatch slid open, then launched himself out of the pod and into his room. Of all the days for an arm resizing, why did it have to be the morning of his final Programming test?

He stumbled through the dark, managing to trip over the holoprojector mounted in the floor's center. The projector whirred to life, and the holographic image of a huge robotic face bloomed out from its center.

"Welcome to Sentinel Programming Corps. Lesson two hundred thirty-two," the bot droned. Bobby fumbled for the projector's off switch, but his arm's recalibrating motors jerked his finger onto the volume control instead. The bot's monotone voice boomed, shaking the walls. "History of Sentinel, Part Three: The Mining Facilities...."

"How about some light?" LINC suggested. "Hovel?"

"Light level three," the central computer responded in a deep voice as the room brightened.

"Thanks," muttered Bobby, jabbing the holoprojector's switch. The face evaporated, and the voice faded, leaving Bobby's ears ringing as he picked himself off the floor and raced to his clothes dispenser.

"How much time before Mother comes in for wake up?" He retrieved a clean tunic from the wall's dispenser slot and stuffed his head through a sleeve.

"Two minutes," LINC replied as Bobby found the hole for his head.

"Two minutes?" Bobby hopped on one foot while threading a leg through a pair of trousers. "The whole point was to get up early and finish my last Programming lesson before my test. Scrub it! Why did the Hovel reschedule my arm resizing for today?" He gritted his teeth, guilt squeezing his stomach. He knew better than to question the Hovel. Or any other bot on Sentinel, for that matter. They were perfect, after all. The Hovel only responded to certain keywords, but what if Mother overheard him complaining? She would not tolerate an emotional outburst.

"I'm sensing rising cortisol levels. Would you like a mood stabilizer? I think there's some left in your emergency meds cartridge. Wanna get your chill back?"

"LINC," Bobby grunted. "You know I can't have mood stabilizers during my final." He succeeded in pulling on his trousers and swiped a pair of socks from the dispenser.

"Yeah, but you're not going to pass your test spazzing out either."

"First of all, stop using non-Protocol vernacular." Bobby jammed a foot into a sock.

"'Spazzing' is a non-Protocol vernacular?"

"Yes. Don't talk like that in front of the Programmers. Try being normal for once." He stuck the other sock on.

"Why?"

"They already think you're glitchy. Why they don't uninstall you, I don't know."

"Who would be your task assistant?"

"Probably a bot who follows Protocol."

"Boring."

With a sigh, Bobby located his weathered urban-terrain boots in the corner and stepped into them, letting the self-adjusting laces form fit to his feet.

"And second?" LINC asked.

"What?"

"You said 'first of all.' I assumed there's a second of all."

"Yes, second, you know I can't scrub up my finals again. I don't want to start Programming all over. If they even let me this time."

"The pace seemed exceptionally difficult this year."

"I know, but I'm the most caught up I've ever been."

"You're still behind on your history lesson."

"You're behind in your Programming?" a harsh voice sounded from behind.

"Whoops," LINC said.

Bobby whipped around and went rigid at the sight of Mother crawling through the sliding door on her clunky tripod legs. Her enormous, orb-shaped body rotated, scanning the room with a giant central lens before directing it at Bobby.

Sparks flew from an exposed wire where her body met her legs, resulting in several loud pops and the smell of singed metal. "You did not complete your assignments?" Her voice was like the hum of electric wires.

"I just have one history lesson to finish," Bobby blurted in defense. "I was going to get up early this morning, but the Hovel rescheduled my arm resizing, and I didn't have time."

"Your tone indicates that you are blaming the Hovel for your shortcomings." When Bobby clenched his jaw, she pointed a telescoping tentacle at him. "And now you are becoming agitated. What do you say when your emotions begin to take over?"

Bobby huffed and recited his Programming mantra. "Feelings don't factor."

Mother clomped closer. "Your final is today. Why did you not notify me earlier that you were falling behind?"

Bobby dropped his eyes to his boots. "I didn't think it was worth mentioning."

"Not worth mentioning?" Mother's faulty vocal box seemed to scream. "Robert, use logic. Your human neural matter lacks the processing power to determine how to best use your time. I must schedule your at-home tasks around your human weaknesses so that you can be as efficient as possible. Therefore, you must inform me of your progress in Programming, or lack thereof. How does it make sense to keep this information from me?" More sparks flew from her body. This seemed to be happening more lately, but if the Hovel hadn't yet deemed repairing Mother necessary, Bobby wasn't going to say anything.

"If you had informed me that you were failing at your lessons," she continued, "I would have scheduled a make-up session so it wouldn't interfere with your other tasks."

"I'm not failing," Bobby muttered.

"I am programmed to make sure you operate at optimal performance," said Mother. "If you cannot complete an assignment on time, then you are failing. What is the probability that you will become the Prime Human if you don't complete your Programming?"

The Prime Human.

His stomach twisted at the mention of those words. *Feelings don't factor*, he reminded himself again, this time to stem a swell of anxiety.

"I know more than enough to pass my test," he said, hoping it was true.

"You cannot afford to make mistakes," Mother replied. "The Programmers will not engage in any more experiments to see if the human race is worth reviving. You are the last."

Bobby swallowed hard. Mother often reminded him that he was Sentinel's last experiment, but every time was a plasma blast to his gut. *Feelings don't factor, feelings don't factor.* If he didn't repeat it over and over, another thought would take hold, the one that said, *The human race lives or dies with me.*

"The shift in your countenance indicates you understand the importance of your task." Mother's lens zoomed in.

Bobby gave a feeble nod. "You're right, I was complacent in my progress."

"I will not see you fail." Mother stomped a resolute leg. "You will become the Prime Human."

Bobby stared at the floor. "Yes, Mother."

"Now you will perform your morning tasks."

"What?" Bobby cried. "I can't finish my lesson?"

"You should have thought of that before you decided not to inform me. Your tasks must be carried out. Do you understand?"

His shoulders fell. "Yes, Mother."

Sharp hisses escaped Mother's pressurized valves as she crawled out of the room, leaving a trail of sparks in her wake.

When she'd gone, Bobby grunted and hammered his head with his cybernetic fist.

"Damaging the frontal lobes of your brain won't help, Bobs," LINC pointed out.

"She's right." Bobby sighed. "I've got to try harder."

```
<o:!0110101-000Z><01110000></x:01011>
<o:010011100/01>
<
```

READOUTS POPPED UP on LINC's screen detailing Bobby's morning tasks.

Morning meal.
Buff Hovel floors.
Calibrate corilum panels.

The list continued past the vidscreen's bottom border.

"Do you think Mother will help buff the floors?" asked Bobby, trudging into the corridor. "I mean, she has a scrubber attachment. It would give me some time to finish my Programming lesson."

"Doubt it," LINC answered. "She's already turned up her discipline settings. Or didn't you hear her yelling just now? It's probable she wants you to find your own routine."

Bobby shook his head. Buff the floors? Didn't Mother know today was the most important day of the year for him? Halfway down the corridor, he caught the bitterness mounting in his chest and stifled it. *Feelings don't factor.* If Mother required him to complete morning tasks despite today's test, it must be for his ultimate benefit. She could only act out of logic. And he should too.

"Okay, let's get started." He sighed again as he reached the Hovel's main bay.

The main bay was a circular room which connected other areas of the Hovel via corridors like a hub and spokes. Holographic readouts lined the curved walls, scrolling and blinking in a constellation of muted colors. Mother emerged from the south corridor carrying a small bowl full of meal pellets in one of her tentacles.

"You require a portion and a half today because of your test." She offered the bowl to Bobby. "Your human cortex requires extra fuel for demanding tasks."

Bobby moved to take the bowl, but the motors in his cybernetic joints overcompensated. With an unexpected burst of speed, his hand overshot the target and knocked the bowl from Mother's appendage. Meal pellets scattered across the floor.

"Scrub!" Bobby grabbed his writhing arm with his biologic hand.

A shower of sparks flew from Mother's body. She uttered a series of clicks in her own mechanical language and gathered the bowl and pellets in a flurry of tentacles, then rotated and focused on him with a scrutinizing eye. "Did you recalibrate your motors after your arm resizing?"

"LINC's doing it right now." Bobby's servos lowered his arm in a quick succession of halting movement.

Mother's lens zoomed in on the swirling colors of LINC's display. She clicked something else, then held up the bowl. "Soil-based microbes from your boots have contaminated your meal pellets. Since I will have to replace them, you will make do with a half portion this morning."

"But what about my final?" Bobby protested. He imagined his stomach rumbling in the Programming chamber.

"You should have recalibrated your arm." With that, Mother crawled out of the bay with the ruined meal.

"Great," Bobby spat. "LINC, hurry up with that calibration. I can't have that go wrong too."

"Hey, I'm working as fast as I can," LINC replied. "The Hovel rerouted a number of neuron-to-circuit functions."

Bobby flexed his synthetic fingers, testing their movement. "I need precise movement for the Human Killer Simulation today. Can you fix it by then?"

"Yeah, no problem."

"You've said that before."

Mother clunked back with a bowl of fresh meal pellets. Bobby eased his hand out and, finding smooth movement, took the bowl and popped the pellets in his mouth. He'd learned to ignore the chalky texture a long time ago, but today his senses seemed to be in overdrive, each acerbic crunch bringing a grimace to his face.

"Proceed with your chores," Mother said, crawling out of the bay before he'd swallowed the last gritty pellet.

"Buffing the floors is the next task on your list." LINC's cheery voice annoyed Bobby this morning for some reason. "You've got thirty minutes before you're scheduled to leave for your test."

"Feelings don't factor." Bobby reminded himself as he exited the bay through the northeast corridor. He ducked into a neatly organized supply closet to retrieve the handheld power buffer and a few scrubber packs. Then he set to work cleaning and polishing the floors on hands and knees, letting the power buffer's high-pitched whir drown out the test anxieties pinging around his head.

He reminded himself that he'd missed just one Programming lesson this year, a personal record. Even LINC had remarked on the significance of that feat since each failed final caused Programming's difficulty to increase the following year. The Programmers had told him this was to compensate for his cumulative experience in order to present the same level of challenge each year.

"After all," they'd said in their modulated voices, bulbous eyes focused on him, "if you become Prime Human, you will face multiple tasks, each more challenging than the last. You must demonstrate perfect performance if you are to annihilate Fallen humanity and restart the human race." Despite the power buffer's noise, the memory of those cold, sterile words still echoed in Bobby's ears, making him shiver.

LINC, however, was convinced that the difficulty was increasing exponentially, disproportionate to age and experience. The supposition annoyed Bobby. LINC never acted like the other bots on Sentinel. He used non-Protocol vernacular and made unexpected statements that seemed to undermine Protocol in general. Bobby had learned to ignore most of his task assistant's anomalous behavior as his comments were usually detrimental to his Programming, but as he buffed the last edge of the Hovel he couldn't help wondering if LINC was right. This year's Programming had been brutal. He'd removed two whole hours from his sleep cycle every night just to stay on pace with the lessons. His jaw tightened when he thought of how his arm resizing had prevented him from finishing the last one. It was like the Hovel was trying to decrease his chance of success.

He shook the thought from his brain. That was ridiculous. The Hovel was linked to Sentinel's larger artificial intelligence grid. It wouldn't act outside his best interests. Besides, the lesson he'd missed was a history module. Sure, those were rare, and normally he'd devour every bit of info in it, but what were the odds that it contained something that would be on his Programming final today? The Programmers valued math equations and combat simulations. Not shreds of info about extinct humans Bobby managed to extract from one or two history lessons. Deep down, he'd hoped the current module would be a continuation on the First AI War lesson he'd encountered last Programming cycle. But with his luck, it was probably a history of corilum mining or something boring like that. With his luck, corilum mining was probably on the final. *Scrub*.

When he was done polishing, Mother pointed out all the spots he'd missed.

"Your cleaning pattern is only ninety-three percent efficient," she said, then proceeded to have Bobby scrub the main bay of the Hovel again in a more effective pattern.

When at last she seemed satisfied, LINC announced his next task. "Calibrate the corilum panels."

Bobby touched a button on the wall, and a hidden panel slid open to reveal a ladder leading up to a maintenance hatch. He hurried up and twisted the hatch open, pushing his lanky body through and onto the roof.

The Hovel resided in an otherwise empty lot, affording a silence Bobby rarely experienced elsewhere on Sentinel. He stood, letting the cool air brush his skin. In the distance, the city sprawled over the planet's entire surface, harsh lights rallying against the pre-dawn sky. Above the towering skyscrapers and clustered factories, a steady line of corilum cargo vessels zoomed in and out of the atmosphere, guarded by flanks of automated fighter ships. In the city's center, Sentinel Tower spiked into the sky, its top pulsating with purple energy from the city's central corilum reactor. He tried not to think about how in the next hour he'd be taking his final test in that tower.

The distant light did little to illuminate the Hovel's domed roof, and Bobby had to watch his step so he wouldn't lose his balance. Corilum panels lined the roof in neat rows. They rotated throughout the day so they could soak up the energy Sentinel Tower bounced off the ionosphere from its central reactor. Bobby scanned the roof for the defective panel and spotted it immediately. It had gotten stuck in its rotation and sat askew of the others.

A nearby control console blinked. With careful steps, he made his way to the console and tapped its screen. Navigating through menus, he found the recalibration option and selected it. The corilum panels rotated with a whir as they reset their position. Except for the one that was stuck. It wouldn't budge.

"Scrub it," Bobby cursed, then glanced at the access hatch to see if Mother had heard his emotional outburst. He turned back to the console, muttering under his breath. "I don't have time for this."

"Want to troubleshoot?" At LINC's suggestion, the swirling colors on his display blurred into the background under a set of icons. Bobby chose the one shaped like a plug, and a short prong telescoped out of his cybernetic index finger. He stuck the prong into a slot on the console causing a green light under LINC's vidscreen to pulse in sync with the console's blinking light.

"Running diagnostics," LINC announced. The lights blipped at a quicker pace. "I don't see anything wrong with the software. Must be a mechanical problem."

Suppressing a frustrated grunt, Bobby picked his way over to the defective corilum panel.

"Light, please," he said.

LINC responded by illuminating a small diode set near Bobby's wrist hinge. The shaft of light bounced off the panel's surface. Bobby dropped to his knees and investigated the turning mechanism underneath.

"The most probable cause is a leak in the pneumatic system," LINC said. "A pneumatic system uses air pressure to create force to—"

"I know what a pneumatic system is," Bobby said with a huff. "I missed the history lesson, not the engineering lesson." He stared at the shaft connecting the corilum panel to the motor at its base. After a moment, he said, "Uh, so what do I do?"

"Oh, I thought you completed your engineering lesson?"

"Fine, you win. How do I fix the scrubbing thing?"

"I'm glad you asked," LINC replied. "First, remove the gearbox from the motor. This will require you to grip the connecting shaft and lift it out. But first—"

Bobby didn't wait for the rest. He grabbed the shaft with his cybernetic strength and yanked it out of the socket. A mess of wires snapped and sputtered in a shower of sparks. The steady hum of the Hovel's power generators suddenly dropped into silence.

"But first," LINC continued in a pointed voice, "you must disconnect the motor from the power source, or risk creating a short in the power grid."

"Scrub it." Bobby grimaced. He chucked the panel in frustration and immediately regretted it. The panel crashed into two others, knocking them out of rotation before sliding off the roof. He tensed at the resulting shatter of delicate parts.

"Robert!" Mother's screeching voice echoed up the access hatch.

Bobby's head dropped in exasperation. A quick glance at LINC's vidscreen told him he was scheduled to leave for his test in ten minutes. He didn't have time for this.

"Coming," he called back through clenched teeth.

He hopped on the ladder and plunged into pitch black. His arm's diode cut the darkness as he made his way back into the Hovel's main bay. But he didn't need a light to know where Mother was. Sparks spewed from her body, illuminating her legs which stomped around as if her circuits would overload any second.

"What did you do?" she demanded.

Bobby tried to form a response that wouldn't make it sound like his emotions had gotten the better of him. But he knew even in the dark Mother was scanning his features with her heat vision for any sign of deception. "I—I just—I didn't mean to—"

"I miscalculated the timing of my warning," LINC interjected. "I was late in informing Bobby of the danger of shorting out the power grid. An outcome of my recent reboot, most likely."

Bobby cast a surprised glance at LINC's vidscreen swirling calm blue. Why was his task assistant taking the blame?

Mother's body emitted a high-pitched whir as her internal cooling fans kicked on. The space grew warm from the hot air escaping her exhaust vents. "Regardless of your Living Inter-Neural Communicator's defective behavior, your inability to plan a sequence of tasks safely and efficiently demonstrates poor cognitive skill. You will not become the Prime Human making mistakes like this." She gestured a tentacle to the darkness outside the diode's sliver of light.

"I can figure out how to turn the lights back on. It shouldn't take me long to—"

"You've already disrupted the morning schedule with too many mistakes," Mother said in a spew of sparks. "I will fix the power. Proceed to Sentinel Tower for your Programming test."

"Fine," Bobby spat.

"Control your emotions," Mother commanded as she crawled out of the bay.

Bobby snorted and made his way back to his room. He scooped up his rucksack from its resting place near the anti-gravity pod.

"Well, there's one thing I'm really good at." He retrieved a container of meal pellets from a storage bin and shoved it into the rucksack. "I'm really good at scrubbing things up in record time." Bristling, he seized his handheld omnitool and threw it in a little too hard. It jostled the meal pellet container and landed with a *thwack* at the bottom of the bag.

"When you do it wrong, you do it really wrong," LINC said in an upbeat voice.

Bobby frowned as he packed his portable holoprojector along with some spherical holopods, including the one containing the history lesson. "And what's with you? Maybe Mother's right. Maybe you are defective."

"Hey, you don't see sparks flying out of my body, do you?"

An unexpected laugh escaped Bobby's throat. He quickly caught himself and adopted a serious expression again. "Still, why did you take the blame back there? You know it was clearly my fault."

"It was the most efficient course of action for you," LINC replied in a quieter tone.

"But isn't that kind of deceitful?" Bobby rummaged through another bin and snatched some protective goggles he would need at his factory shift later. "Does your programming allow for that?" He stuffed the goggles into the rucksack and slung the bag onto his shoulder.

"You have no idea what my programming allows for," LINC replied.

Bobby cocked a brow, but when LINC didn't elaborate, he let it pass. LINC was always saying bizarre things, and anyway, he had other things to think about.

Like his test.

He hurried through the Hovel's main bay and out the exit. The sun's first golden rays mixed with the city's sterile, white lights. To his left, a railpod hovered over a thin, magnetic track, awaiting his arrival.

"Well, I suppose there's one good thing about scrubbing up this morning," he said as he climbed into the pod's plastiglass cabin. "I might be able to finish my history lesson at the Tower before my test."

"You'll be Prime Human on this planet in no time," LINC said.

Bobby touched the console's display screen and selected Sentinel Tower from a list of destinations. Motors whirred to life, and the pod shot toward the city, pushing him into his seat.

"You know, LINC," he sighed as they plunged into Sentinel's heavy robotic traffic, "if I scrub up today, I might just have to settle for being the only human on this planet."

<!002: Initializing Setup>

THE CITY STREAKED by in a blur through the railpod's plastiglass canopy as the two-seater craft zoomed along its track toward Sentinel Tower. The tower's spire rose high above the infinite skyline like a blade cutting through the dark plumes of factory smoke. Bobby, however, stared at a squat, domed building in the distance. The structure's bronzed roof peeked just over a factory cluster to reflect the early morning light.

"You listening, Bobs?" LINC's display swirled shades of impatient pinkish-purple at his voice.

"What?" Bobby shifted in his seat. "Oh, yeah."

"Then what was I just saying?"

Bobby scrunched his face. "Something about Programming, or something."

"Nice try. I was listing your schedule for today. Want me to repeat it, or is becoming Prime Human not on your priority list this morning?"

Bobby rolled his eyes but let out a controlled breath before replying. "LINC, I need you to work with me today. This might be my last chance to even become the Prime Human."

"Which is why I'm trying to help you focus."

Bobby sighed. LINC acted haywire sometimes, but he couldn't deny that his task assistant was always on his side—even when it baffled logic, like earlier when he'd taken the blame for the corilum panel.

"What were you thinking about anyway?" LINC's colors expanded into a cloud of yellow curiosity.

"The Depository." Bobby nodded at the domed building in the distance. "When I become Prime Human—if I become Prime Human—that's the first place I'm going to explore."

"Let me get this straight," LINC said. "When you're Prime Human and you're governing Sentinel and restarting the human race, the first place you're going outside our Utility Zone is where they keep the corilum mining records?"

"The Archiver thinks there's more than just mining records there. He says it might contain information on humans. Before the Fall, I guess."

"The Archiver's an off-the-grid bot. I gotta advise against listening to him."

"Because he knows more than you," Bobby muttered, sticking his chin onto his palm.

LINC's colors changed to vibrant green. "Does not."

"Well, whatever. The Depository doesn't matter if I don't pass my Programming anyway."

"Because of the Tether?"

Bile rose in Bobby's throat. He knew LINC was trying to keep the conversation light, but there was nothing light about the Tether—his consequence for failure.

"No, I'm not scared of the Tether," he protested. "I meant all that matters is restarting the human race. And if I can't prove to the bots I'm perfect—"

"They'll never start the cloning project, it'll be the Fall all over again, blah blah blah," LINC finished. "You worry too much, Bobs. You've done great in Programming this year. Well, not great, but good. Decent, at least."

"Hey," said Bobby defensively.

"I'm just saying, you'll do fine on your test."

"That's easy for you to say." Bobby snorted. "You're already a bot. Do you think it'll hurt when they transfer my mind into the Tether?"

"*If*," LINC corrected. "Don't go giving up yet."

"But what if this *is* my last chance at Programming?" Bobby's breath shortened. "What if I fail and they *do* turn me into a bot?" He pictured the Tether and its smooth chrome head that might house his mind if the Programmers deemed him—their experiment—a failure. They would transfer his consciousness into the Tether's corilum-infused circuits. He'd be a bot. Thinking with perfect precision, lacking all emotion. But wasn't that the point? He shook his head, regretting how he was letting so much fear seep into his brain before his test.

The cockpit fell silent for a moment. The colors on LINC's display swirled in mixed hues, something he did when he was processing a large amount of data. Bobby used the silence to force his tangled emotions out through steady breaths. Breathe in logic. Breathe out fear. Breathe in facts. Breathe out frustration.

The technique eased the tension in his shoulders somewhat, but he lost focus when the railpod took a curve. For a brief moment, a row of three Hovels, identical to Bobby's, peeked out between two factories. Their windows were dark. No trace of purple corilum energy powered their rooftop panels.

Despite how many times he passed these abandoned Hovels, Bobby found his head filled with images of other humans living on the planet at some point in the distant past. His forebearers, Sentinel's previous experiments, of which he was the last. He often wondered what they'd been like at his age. If they'd had caretaker bots like his. Or maybe they'd had human caretakers, real mothers, just like in the Archiver's stories.

With a pang of sadness, he tried to imagine how long the Hovels had been empty. Had their occupants failed the

Programmers' rigorous standards and fallen to their emotions? To mindless depravity like the rest of humanity scattered throughout the galaxy? Or had they been destroyed as failed experiments before their basest emotions could take hold?

Will my Hovel be empty after today?

The dwellings disappeared behind a passing building. He glanced at the empty seat to his left, wondering if one day someone would sit next to him. For that to happen, he had to pass his Programming.

"One thing's for sure, Bobs." LINC broke the silence, his response calibrated. "We'll understand everything when you're Prime Human. And you're going to become Prime Human today, okay? So let's gear up, yeah?"

Bobby shoved his thoughts away and nodded. He had one mission this morning—pass Programming. "You're right. Let's do this."

```
<o:!0110101-000Z><01110000></x:01011>
<o:010011100/01>
<
```

BOBBY SCRAMBLED OUT of the railpod and steadied his jostling rucksack as he hurried over the connecting bridge to the tower's entrance. As always, the colossal pylons marching on either side of the bridge made him feel small.

At last, he passed under the tower's overhang and came to a smooth sliding door with no handle. A nearby control panel emitted a thin, blue laser, scanning the access chip hidden deep in his forearm, and the door parted in the middle to allow passage.

Inside, the thump of his boots echoed around the empty chamber.

He sat down cross-legged in front of a line of copper-colored elevators and retrieved the holoprojector from his bag. He set it on the floor and dropped a holopod into its slot. The familiar, robotic face expanded above the lens and began the lesson.

"Lesson two hundred thirty-two," the bot announced. "History of Sentinel, Part Three: The Mining Facilities."

Bobby's stomach thrilled, excitement mixing with the anxiety he tried to ignore. Any other day he would have played the lesson on repeat, consuming every clue that might point to his origin. But today, he only had one chance to watch the archived footage and memorize as many facts as he could before his test.

The robotic face dissolved into the image of a gaping hole set in a stony quarry. A dozen or so cargo ships hovered about in a holding formation, waiting for their turn to descend into the dark shaft.

"The history of corilum mining extends as far back as the founding of Sentinel," a deep voice narrated the scene.

Bobby snorted. "Oh great. We get to learn about corilum mining. I knew it."

"Well, well, well," LINC said. "Do I detect a note of non-Protocol sarcasm in Bobby's voice?"

Bobby clicked his tongue. "Hush."

"Corilum," the voice in the lesson continued, "is a precious ore whose properties make much of Sentinel's advanced technology possible."

Purple chunks of a rocky substance materialized in the holographic display. Complicated data readouts popped up detailing the ore's chemical composition. Bobby stifled a sigh of frustration. Inorganic compounds were not what he wanted to memorize. He wanted something, anything, that might offer a glimpse into the life humans lived before the Fall.

"Wow, that's a lot of chemical symbols," LINC said.

"You're not helping." Bobby pumped his plastifiber fingers to stimulate his focus, but the symbols slid out of his brain the instant a new scene appeared.

A montage flickered images of human anatomy diagrams, all modified with numerous synthetic devices—oddly-shaped cybernetic appendages, implants clustered around various organs, and even pulsion reactors glowing in palms and chest cavities.

"After the First AI War," the instructor narrated, "humankind's widespread adoption of cybernetic enhancements and neural implants eventually led to their near-extinction. The incredible properties of refined corilum only accelerated this process." The renderings of body mods grew more and more extreme as shards of corilum infused the cyberware in stylized animations. "Still reeling from the war and fearing AI would again rise and become the dominant species, humans used this powerful new energy source to enhance their own biology beyond its limits. In the end, they enhanced their most depraved desires and fell to their lowest instincts, becoming little more than self-indulgent, violent creatures."

Bobby's stomach soured as the holo cut to recordings of bots marching through a battlefield strewn with real human casualties, their bodies so heavily modified they barely looked human at all. This wasn't what he wanted to learn—the history after the Fall. He knew this period all too well.

The sight of broken cyberware scattered among downed human fighters made his own cybernetic arm grow impossibly heavy. He stared at his hand—the product of precision engineering someone had crafted long ago—and flexed his synthetic joints, imagining the mass of complex circuitry integrated into his nervous system. Was it poisoning his brain like the mods in these humans? Surely the bots wouldn't test him if he was doomed to lose his mind. This was the only comfort to that constant, terrifying thought. He had to keep his emotions in check. To keep from becoming like the rest of his species. He set his jaw and returned his attention to the holo.

A time-lapse clip was showing the rapid construction of Sentinel's city. Structures grew from the stony ground and formed something close to the current skyline Bobby had seen a thousand times from the roof of his Hovel.

The scene changed again, and a jolt ran through him.

"LINC, look!" He shuffled to his knees and leaned forward until his face was mere centimeters from the holo.

"My sensors see an image of space," LINC replied. "So what?"

"Watch."

An expanse of countless twinkling stars bloomed in the holo's spherical projection.

"Since the Fall," the instructor said, "Sentinel has stood as the last upright planet in the galaxy." The voice had taken on a strange, tinny quality that seemed incongruent with the rest of the program. The fact barely registered for Bobby as he searched the stars for something.

A giant ship cruised into view, filling most of the projection.

"For years," the instructor continued, "Sentinel's warships have fought depraved human marauders who seek corilum for their own evil schemes."

The projection's point of view drifted up from the warship to reveal a horde of smaller incoming ships. The smaller fighters opened fire in a torrent of red plasma streaks. In return, the warship unleashed a barrage of photon cannon fire. The blazing blue photon orbs plunged into the fighters' tight formations and destroyed them in bright explosions, which were quickly extinguished in the vacuum of space.

The scene changed to a star chart, where red lines extended from a single point to turn shining blue worlds on the periphery into crimson dots.

"The humans' infestation was halted," said the instructor, still in that tinny voice. "For the moment."

The lines stopped expanding, leaving no other worlds infected.

"There!" Bobby pointed, but the scene cut to a tall bot with an angular face standing triumphantly in the warship's bridge.

"What?" LINC asked.

"In the Battle of Sol," the narrator continued, "Gamma's forces struck the opposition's base of operations and once again preserved Sentinel from the evil of human—"

Bobby traced a finger on the holoprojector's control pad, and the program rewound. The bot with the angular face moved backward until the scene switched back to the star chart of Fallen Humankind's expansion. Bobby tapped the pad, and the program paused.

"There, see?" He pointed to the origin of the red lines, a tiny, bluish speck in space.

"What, that star?" asked LINC.

"It's a planet!"

"So?"

"It's not just a base of operations," Bobby insisted. "It's where the humans come from! Remember when the Archiver showed me that star map?" He rotated the projector back and forth, viewing the holo from different angles. "I remember him telling me there was a blue planet right below the constellation of the Crawler. See, it's the horned bot that stands on four legs." He pointed at a cluster of stars and traced down to the blue speck. "What if this is it? What if this is where humans came from in the beginning?"

"The Archiver said that, did he?" LINC's colors spun green. "Wow, he's so smart." The modulated condescension in his voice wasn't easy to miss. "Logically, humans must come from some location. So, what if it's this planet?"

Bobby blinked at the question. "I mean, don't you want to know more about it?"

"All you need to know is that it is a vile planet," droned a voice behind him.

Bobby shot to his feet and turned to see a wiry-framed bot standing there. Harsh, glowing orbs stared at him from underneath metallic brows slanted as if in a perpetual frown.

"Greetings, Programmer Alpha." Bobby gave a respectful nod. "I, uh, didn't hear you come in."

"Your caretaker unit sent me a transmission," the Programmer said in that distorted whine that always left a ringing in Bobby's ears. Had he not fixed his faulty voice box yet? It seemed to get worse every cycle. "She said you would arrive ahead of schedule. After your maintenance mishap this morning it would seem logical for you to review your engineering lesson, but you seem to be engrossed in the wrong aspects of study. Speculating on the humans' planet of origin will not aid you in your Programming final today." The bot gave Bobby a pointed look.

"I won't fail this year," Bobby said in a small voice.

"You've already fallen behind, it seems." Alpha bent over and retrieved the holoprojector, bringing it to his face to inspect the image.

Bobby tried to suppress a frown. "Just one lesson."

Alpha's orb eyes flashed him a scrutinizing look. "I've done the calculations, and your probability of passing remains low."

"I won't fail." Bobby's teeth clenched.

"We shall see." The Programmer tapped the projector's control pad, and the holo resumed motion, cutting to the image of the tall bot with the angular face. "Gamma would rather not take drastic measures." Alpha's bulbous eyes lingered on the projection of Gamma, then regarded Bobby with an air of warning.

Bobby gazed at Gamma standing on the bridge of his flagship cruiser. The bot's alloy chin lifted as he watched human fighter vessels blown apart. He'd only met Sentinel's overlord on a handful of occasions, once for every year he'd failed Programming. It hadn't been pleasant.

"I must inform you that there is no guarantee he will grant you another chance at Programming if you fail this year," Alpha continued. "Of course, I can't say whether he will have you upload your mind into the Tether bot immediately upon failure. That is for his higher level of programming to decide. I will, however, remind you that this might be your last chance to prove the human race is worth restarting."

Feelings don't factor, feelings don't factor. "I won't fail," Bobby repeated, more to himself than to the Programmer.

"Come, we shall begin your Programming final early." He thrust the projector into Bobby's hands and strode toward the elevators. "I have instructed your caretaker unit to increase her discipline settings no matter the outcome of today's test. She will decrease your sleep cycle by half a standard solar hour to increase your morning task schedule. Perhaps imposing more severe consequences will improve the predictability of your behavior and actions, confirm?"

"What?" Bobby cried. "But that means I'll only get six hours a night!"

The Programmer stopped and slowly turned. Recognizing his outburst, Bobby dropped his eyes.

"Emotional reactions like that are the reason you have a low chance of passing this year," Alpha said. "I needn't remind you of your human weakness in requiring a hybernative state. Decreasing sleep by one half hour will better calibrate your circadian rhythm. Confirm?"

"Confirm." Bobby bit back a scream. What did the Programmers know? They didn't have to sleep. But with a pang of guilt, he checked the thought. If they thought he would benefit, then who was he to question?

"We will begin with the Human Killer Simulation," Alpha said. "Confirm?"

Fear coiled in Bobby's stomach. "Confirm." This time, his voice quavered.

"And," the Programmer tapped a button on the elevator, "pain settings will be set at maximum values."

<!003: Running Program>

THE ELEVATOR OPENED, and Bobby took a hesitant step into the Programming chamber. Computers projecting abstract holographic displays lined the circular room. Bobby recognized two other Programmers, Beta and Delta, standing at control decks along the far wall. With each test they calibrated, the ethereal displays above the projectors condensed into solid images. Differential equations hovered in one, word problems in another. Some of the challenges were more dimensional, like a multi-segmented cube which required the user to line up colored tiles on its surface. One by one, the challenges popped up all around as Bobby followed Alpha to the chamber's center.

Halfway across the room, his eyes fell onto a familiar shape. There, next to the control deck, stood a sleek bot with a smooth chrome face.

The Tether.

His stomach roiled. What was it doing here? With sinking spirits, he concluded the Programmers had brought it to preside over his Programming final. A reminder that if he failed, he'd have to upload his consciousness into its corilum-powered circuits. They wanted to see how he worked under pressure, after all. And what better way to remind him that his species' fate rested solely on his performance today?

"The tests are ready." Beta's voice buzzed from the control deck, snapping Bobby out of his thoughts of a human-less future.

"A small change in schedule," Alpha replied. "Robert will begin his test in the Human Killer Simulation."

Bobby's nostrils flared. He bit back a cry of indignation. *Small change.* Exhausting himself in the Human Killer Sim then doing differential equations afterward was no small change.

"Affirmative," Beta replied.

Delta touched a button, and a smooth door slid open to reveal an octagonal room inside.

"Proceed into the holo chamber," Alpha directed.

Bobby licked his dry lips. His legs felt like hunks of metal he had to force all the way into the chamber.

He glanced over his shoulder at all three Programmers gazing at him with their expressionless faces. Then the door slid shut, and the chamber's harsh lights went out, leaving auxiliary diodes on the walls to illuminate the room. A hefty holoprojector descended from the ceiling and powered up with a loud whir that grated his ears.

"Proceed to the center," Alpha's voice echoed over the com.

Bobby balled his fists. He knew what was in the middle of the room. Two tracks of orange diodes lit the path, blinking in sequence toward the chamber's center, urging him along.

"Don't forget, Bobs, I'm allowed to assist you in here," LINC said over the rising intensity of the chamber's boot up process. "But only in a limited capacity. Remember your combat training."

Bobby nodded and wiped his sweaty palm on his trousers. The journey to the middle was short, but the distance felt like kilometers. As he prepared to take the last step, the deafening whine of the room's powering sequence came to a peak.

"Good luck, Bobby," LINC said at maximum volume.

"I never understand why you say that," Bobby shouted over the din, his foot hovering above the center tile. "The sim tests my skill and minimizes chance so that—"

"Stop stalling, Bobs. You'll do fine."

Bobby bit his lip. LINC was right. He was stalling. But the encouragement gave him enough of a push to let his foot fall on the center tile. At once, a panel in the ceiling retracted. A hive of tiny drones descended, swarming at him with terrifying speed. He sucked in a sharp breath as they bit into his flesh with needle-shaped prongs and pain exploded all over his body.

In an instant, the high-pitched whine seemed to fade. Holographic images flickered into existence until the chamber vanished under the projection of an urban battlefield. He stood in a crumbling building overlooking a decimated cityscape. All the familiar structures he knew from his trips in the railpod had collapsed. Dozens of foreign fighter ships broke through the dark cloud canopy, exchanging fire with Sentinel's ground defense. The air cracked with every blinding blast. The ground trembled with every explosion. The smell of burnt metal and noxious gasses stung his nostrils. Though invisible under the impenetrable holographic layer, Bobby felt the vibrating drones on his skin relaying sensory information within the scenario.

"Humans!" a voice shouted from behind. Bobby spun around to see a squad of battle bots crouching behind piles of rubble. The camouflage settings on their streamlined armored plates emulated the grimy palette of a war-torn city. One of them stepped forward.

"Humans!" the bot shouted again. Bobby recognized the orange emblem emblazoned on his torso. This was the bot that would give him instructions for this scenario. "Enemy humans have broken through Sentinel's planetary shield. We have to protect the corilum cargo ships." He pointed at a launch pad visible below the surrounding rooftops. Three bulky cargo ships were preparing for launch. Beyond, a human marauder vessel was dropping enemy troops in the street. "Battle bots on security outposts need the corilum." The bot pushed a blaster into Bobby's cybernetic hand. "You're in charge."

Feelings don't factor. No emotion. Action. "All right, let's do this." Gripping his blaster, Bobby took off, leaping through a gap in the wall onto the neighboring roof. A hard landing turned into a roll, and he was back on his feet, sprinting along the rooftops with the squad of bots close behind. Underneath the crunch of gravel, he could almost feel the holo chamber's floor rotating as he ran.

"What are the chances of a painful death in this scenario?" Bobby asked under his breath as he jumped the space between two rooftops.

"Uhhhhh, maybe just concentrate on saving those cargo ships," LINC replied.

Bobby sneered. "That bad, huh?"

"I don't want to talk about it."

"Best course of action?"

"I suggest cutting to the left to intercept the enemy troop head-on."

"Shouldn't we ambush them from the side?" Bobby vaulted onto another roof.

"There is an eighty-seven percent probability that a flank attack will result in mission failure. Positioning your squad between the cargo ships and the enemy will result in an almost guaranteed victory."

The launch pad was getting closer. "But won't that mean—"

"Complete sacrifice of your entire squad including yourself, yes."

"Great," Bobby said. "Just what the Programmers want."

"They want to test your ability to make decisions for the greater good."

"I know." Bobby cut left as LINC had instructed, angling toward the launch pad. "It just… hurts."

"Don't worry, Bobs. In this scenario, the odds of a quick and painless death are very high."

Bobby scrambled up a low wall onto another roof. "And that's a good thing? Thanks."

"Multiple enemy troops detected," LINC announced.

From his high vantage point, Bobby could see dark figures in the street sprinting toward the launch pad, a mass of armed cybernetic and organic muscle. Black filtration masks shrouded their faces, reminiscent of the human skulls he'd seen in anatomy lessons. At once they both terrified and intrigued him.

They're evil, he reminded himself. Yet, a part of him longed to see their faces. Would their features match their heinous nature?

A tone blared from LINC's speaker.

"What's that?" Bobby shouted. They were a few buildings away from the launch pad.

"Looks like you have an air strike at your disposal," LINC replied. A missile icon flashed on the vidscreen. "It'll destroy everything on the launch pad. Including the cargo ships. I'd say use it as a last resort."

Bobby nodded. The thought of using the airstrike right now to simply end the entire encounter flashed into his mind. After all, if he was going to sacrifice his troops, why not do it now? But he knew the Programmers valued protecting the corilum. If he blew up the cargo ships, they might fail him.

"Enemy incoming," LINC said.

Bobby motioned for his squad to fan out, and the bots spread into a wedge formation. He snapped his attention to the cargo ships. His squad would just make it to the launch pad before the enemy arrived.

He jumped off a low wall, landing on the launch pad in time to see the first human troops emerge on the far side.

"Go!" Bobby yelled over the thrum of the cargo ships' engines igniting.

The black-clad troops rushed his squad in a berserk rage. From this close, Bobby could see their hulking masks were streaked with what looked like red paint. A split second later, he realized what it was.

Blood.

Their own blood.

The Programmer had told him how humans would sometimes kill their own troops before battle to create a frenzied rage. They were abominable.

The enemy troop unleashed a barrage of plasma fire. Bobby ducked behind the nearest cargo ship's landing leg. Harsh zaps assaulted his ears as the blasts hit the reinforced plastisteel on the opposite side.

"They're shooting the cargo ships!" shouted the head battle bot from behind the adjacent leg.

Bobby peeked out to see the enemy troop turning their fire on the cargo ships' hulls.

"They'll take out the shields if you don't stop them," LINC warned.

Bobby swallowed a bubble of anxiety. Without giving himself time to think, he sprinted toward the next leg, spraying the field with plasma fire. His cybernetic motors jerked uncontrollably, sending a wild pattern of shots far above enemy heads. He dove behind the ship's foremost leg, narrowly escaping a flurry of return fire that blasted the ground where he'd been a split second before.

"LINC, I thought you recalibrated my arm?" Bobby cried over the blasts pinging around him.

"I did, but it's not calibrated for this much adrenaline." LINC's colors flashed red.

"What am I supposed to do, not panic?"

"Uh, yeah?"

Before Bobby could respond, an enemy bolt connected with the head battle bot. He covered his face against the explosion and somehow managed to dodge the worst of it, but bits of shrapnel lodged into his light armor vest.

"Scrub it, LINC, we gotta do something."

"There's something you're forgetting, but, um, well, I can't tell you."

"What? Why not?"

"Scrubbing rules. I'm not allowed. But, uh, it rhymes with Pre-Encounter Schmecklist."

In the span of a heartbeat, Bobby visualized his Pre-Encounter Checklist for entering a skirmish. He almost slapped himself.

"Enable advanced aiming mode."

"There you go!"

The auto-aim icon popped up on LINC's display, and the motors in Bobby's arm took on a life of their own. He popped out from behind the leg and let LINC fine-tune his aim. Though his arm still jerked with buggy movement, more shots connected this time.

Dozens of enemy troops fell to the ground in a rain of cyberware. With every downed body, a familiar acerbic pang twisted Bobby's gut. Humans. Members of his own species. He was killing them. But that was his job, right? The thoughts tore into his brain before he'd fired his last shot, and in that instant of regret, his own neurons overrode the automatic movement. His finger refused to squeeze the trigger.

A barrel-chested human sprinted at him, screaming in fury under a mask smeared with bright red blood. Bobby's muscles seized under the assault, rooting him to the spot. Just before the assailant fired the shot that would end him, a battle bot blasted the human to the ground. The other bots joined in, picking off the remaining enemy troops.

Overhead, engines boomed. The vessels were in their final preparations for takeoff. Bobby let out a relieved sigh as their legs retracted in a hover.

"You okay, Bobs?" LINC asked.

Bobby's muscles relinquished their involuntary spasm. His breath eased, but anger spiked through his head.

Scrubbing fool. What was wrong with him? This was a simulation. No matter how real it felt, those were just holograms he'd killed. He wanted to blast himself, but another part of his brain reminded him that this was more than a test. That he'd frozen for a reason. If he passed, he'd one day have to kill them for real. And maybe end up in a Programming lesson watching himself march through a battlefield of slaughtered humans. Was he really capable of that? He just hoped the Programmers hadn't seen him falter on the battlefield. *Feelings don't factor. Finish the test.*

"Enemy reinforcements have arrived," LINC announced as a new platoon appeared on the launch pad. Bobby's heart dropped. These weren't mere replacements. These were advanced infantry rolling out plasma cannons.

He fired, letting LINC train his blaster from one enemy to the next. But he was too late. A volley of cannon fire breached the hovering cargo ships' sides. The explosions were so loud that he felt the drones attached to his ears vibrate with an intensity that threatened to rip them right off his head.

Debris from the ship's injured hull rained down. LINC took over his cybernetic motors, jerking him out of the way just before a mangled side panel cracked the ground where he'd been standing.

"You're welcome," LINC said.

Bobby had no time to respond. He glanced up. The ships were losing altitude. It was only a matter of seconds before they came crashing down right on top of him and his remaining squad. With nobody left to defend the ships, the humans would raid the wreckage and succeed in seizing the corilum.

There was no time for LINC to advise a course of action, but it didn't matter. Bobby knew what he had to do. He tapped LINC's vidscreen and pulled up the air strike option. A blinking button asked him to confirm the action. Squeezing his eyes shut, he tapped the button and seconds later felt the raining bombs burn his flesh.

```
<o:!0110101-000Z><01110000></x:01011>
<o:010011100/01>
<
```

BOBBY WOKE WITH a start. He was lying on the cold floor of the holo chamber. With bleary eyes, he looked around. The holographic carnage had disappeared, leaving the dim, gunmetal walls of the chamber in their place.

"Hey, you're awake," LINC chimed.

Bobby sat up and rubbed his aching head. "What happened?"

"The sensory stimulation from the air strike overloaded your neural pathways, and you lost consciousness," LINC replied.

"What?"

"You blacked out. I just wanted to sound smart."

"That's never happened before." Bobby glanced at the sensory drones still attached to his skin.

"You've never dropped a bomb on yourself either."

Before Bobby could respond, Alpha's voice broke over the com. "You have failed the Human Killer Simulation."

"Failed?" Bobby cried. "I completed the mission, didn't I?"

"You stopped the enemy from obtaining the corilum stores," Alpha noted. "But you destroyed the corilum in the process. Using the air strike as a last resort might have resulted in a passing grade provided your score tally was higher. However, your performance was unacceptable."

"Unacceptable?" Bobby let out an indignant huff.

"Your Living Inter-Neural Communicator has an advanced aiming mode, which you activated after the skirmish began. Why did you not turn it on before you engaged in battle?"

"I, uh…." Bobby squirmed.

"Speak," Alpha commanded.

"I forgot, okay?" The words felt like acid coming up.

"You forgot to review all items in your basic checklist protocol." Alpha's voice hammered the walls. "With your advanced aiming mode enabled from the start, you might have destroyed enough enemy troops to change the course of battle. You also ceased movement for two point oh-eight seconds at a critical point in the skirmish."

Scrub. They noticed.

"In addition—" Alpha wasn't finished listing his mistakes, "— your LINC program assisted you in avoiding debris that would have killed you. That is expressly against the rules."

"I was auto-aiming," LINC uttered in a modulated grumble.

"Shut up, LINC," Bobby whispered. If the Programmers found his task assistant engaging in deceit, they'd uninstall him for sure.

"Your task assistant," continued Alpha, "also said something that sounded suspiciously similar to 'Pre-Encounter Checklist.' We're reviewing the recording, but because of his later action in saving you, we are assuming an infraction and deducting points."

"Whoops," LINC said in a low voice.

"Your mistakes rendered the mission a failure," Alpha said. "You will run the simulation again."

"Wait," Bobby scrambled to his feet. "I have another chance?"

"Negative. You will not receive a grade. The next run is for practice only."

"What?" Bobby couldn't believe it. "I have to do it all over again *just for practice?*"

"The Prime Human requires perfect precision," Alpha said. "You will need to demonstrate your ability to make sound decisions on the battlefield in the event that you pass the rest of your final. You will run the simulation until we are satisfied."

Bobby's cheeks burned. He was tired enough after one run of the simulation. How could he do it multiple times and have the energy to score high enough on the rest of his test to pass? In a flash of anger, he seized a drone attached to his chest and went to yank it out, but LINC interjected.

"Bobby, don't do that." His task assistant spoke low enough so the Programmers couldn't hear him, but it was in that steady voice reserved only for rare moments when he was completely serious. "You'll fail if you openly defy them."

Bobby released the drone in a slow, deliberate act. He set his jaw as the whir of the chamber's power sequence began and holographic projections once again filled the room.

```
<o:!0110101-000Z><01110000></x:01011>
<o:010011100/01>
<
```

Hours later, Bobby stumbled out of the holo chamber and slumped against the wall. The Programmers regarded him with hard gazes.

"Well?" Bobby panted. "How was that last one?"

Alpha's orb eyes narrowed. "A mild improvement."

"What?" Bobby asked. "How could I have done any better? I must have run every possible scenario for that battle!"

"You ran thirty-eight iterations to be exact." Alpha pointed to a holoscreen. "Thirty-eight out of infinite permutations. The number of battle bots you lost in the last run was tolerable. But you will have to do much better if you expect to become the Prime Human. Now, proceed with the rest of your exam."

Bobby gaped at the Programmers as they went back to their stations and booted up the holocomputers. Differential equations and spatial reasoning puzzles materialized in the air, awaiting his attention. His brain ached just looking at them. How was he supposed to do any of it after thirty-eight Human Killer simulations? His exhausted thoughts centered on his empty stomach and the meal pellets in his rucksack.

"Can I refuel before starting?"

"Negative," Alpha replied without looking up from his control deck. "The Prime Human must be able to perform well during extended periods of stress without nourishment. You will also need a near perfect score to make up for your poor performance in the Simulator."

Bobby stared at the holo projections and swallowed a wave of despair. With a heavy sigh, he got to his feet and trudged over to a differential equation hanging above a holocomputer. The phantom pain of the simulated battle still lingered in his joints, his skin red where the sensory drones had attached themselves.

He retrieved a stylus from the console's slot and hovered its corilum-infused tip near the equation's shimmering edge.

"Begin," Alpha called.

A five-minute timer appeared at the projection's border. Bobby set to work solving the first equation, scribbling holographic numbers in the air. Arriving at an answer of $y(t) = (1/4)t^2 + (8/t^2)$, he tapped the floating submit icon. A green check popped up with a chime, and the next equation appeared.

He willed his tired brain to solve each problem with as much speed as he could muster. With every check mark, he glanced at the remaining time. At fifteen seconds, the last equation popped up. A first order equation. *Easy*, he thought with a flood of relief. Ten seconds later, the answer floated in front of him, and he tapped *submit*.

Buzz.

He stared in disbelief at the red X blinking next to his solution. What had he done wrong? He tried to retrace his scribbled work, but the timer ticked to zero, and the projection evaporated.

"Your last answer was incorrect," called Alpha. "You do not have enough points to pass the rest of your final."

Bobby blinked. It took a moment for the Programmer's words to sink in. After a few painful heartbeats, they finally settled into his brain as a fully formed pronouncement of failure. He threw up his hands in disbelief. "Are you serious? I missed one question!"

"Double points were allotted to the last question."

"But it was a first order equation!" Bobby thrust a plastifiber finger at the space where the projection had been.

"It was designed to test your dependence on using shortcuts in solving the equation, which you did—incorrectly."

Bobby racked his brain for how he'd solved the problem. Had he used a shortcut? Everything was so foggy.

"But—but—" Protests jumbled in his throat, none of them escaping. He looked around the Programming chamber, at all the holos still floating in the air. His eyes landed on one on the far side, displaying images of Sentinel's corilum mines. His history test. The lesson he'd never completed. And now, he might not ever get the chance to.

"So, that's it?" His voice cracked. "I failed?"

"Control your emotions," Alpha said.

Bobby pinched his thigh to keep tears of frustration from pouring down his cheeks. "Will I get to try again next year?"

"I will forward your results to Gamma," Alpha replied without looking up. "He will determine if you are eligible for another cycle of Programming. Otherwise, he will have you upload into the Tether."

Frustration turned to horror at those words.

The Tether. His penance for failing humanity. Its chrome face reflected the panic etched in his features at the thought of losing his free will, all emotions, and everything that made him human. But of course, that was the point, right? What was the use of staying human if he was so flawed?

He relaxed his face, bit the inside of his lip, and tried to conceal any further betrayal of emotion. But the threat of transferring his consciousness to the Tether and his lifeless human body piled on some junk heap in the Incineration Bay pierced him with white hot terror. The possibility of becoming a bot had just become so, *so* real.

<!004: Scrubbing Operations>

BOBBY PICKED AT the strap of his protective goggles and stared at his workstation as he waited for the conveyor belt to move. Everything, even his cybernetic nerves, felt numb.

A lanky assembly bot with a cylindrical head and two goggled eyes sauntered past. A legacy bot still in service after an untold number of years. He waved, speaking in rigid syllables. "Greetings, Robert. Are you ready for work today?"

Bobby nodded. "Hey, Six. Yeah, I'm ready. What about you?"

"I am always ready for work," the bot chirped with a hint of static. "We are going to build warp engines for space travel."

Despite the numbness, Bobby smiled at the bot's simple tone and the way he made their job sound like the most important on the planet. He supposed it *was* the most important job on the planet for Six since it was his *only* job. The Programmers had given Bobby "production privileges" ten years ago, and Six had been a fixture through all that time.

Six ambled by and took his place at the line's end where newer, sleeker assembly bots stood at their workstations. Bobby sighed.

"Bobs, your neurotransmitters are unbalanced again," LINC said. "You want a mood stabilizer?"

"I wish I was Six." Bobby flicked a screw on his workstation and watched it spin around.

"Really?" LINC asked. "You want to be a Tier One bot and do one job the rest of your life?

Bobby shrugged. "Maybe."

"Seems kinda scrubbed to me. They're the simplest bots on Sentinel. Especially Six. I mean, look at that guy." LINC let out a low whistle. "That bot is old."

"I wouldn't mind simple right now."

A harsh buzzer blared, and the conveyor belt crawled forward.

"I'm just saying, if you want to be a bot, choose the Tether. You'll probably have to upload into it now, anyway."

Bobby shot LINC a sideways glance.

"Sorry," LINC said. "I didn't mean it that way. But you should at least be a Tier Two bot like the Programmers. Or Tier Three, like Gamma. I mean, he's the closest to true sentient intelligence on the planet—and the overlord. Imagine the power, right?"

"Yeah, but then I'd have to torture a human experiment every day." Bobby tossed the screw onto the conveyor belt and let it drift past before catching it with his other hand.

"Your complexity is what gives you potential," LINC replied. "Seems illogical to take that away."

"It would make life a lot easier." Bobby glanced at Six. The bot waited at his workstation in perfect stillness, a serene expression on his alloy features.

Another buzzer sounded, and a hatch in the wall opened up, spilling unassembled parts onto the conveyor belt. They drifted to the first bot on the assembly line. Bobby watched as the bot jumped into action, snatching the parts off the belt and assembling them with incredible speed. Amid its flurry of precise motions, a roughly cylindrical object about the size of Bobby's torso seemed to appear out of thin air. Seconds later, the newly assembled warp core was back on the belt and coming toward Bobby, who was next in line.

With the strength of his cybernetic arm, Bobby gripped the core and lifted it onto his workstation to inspect. A quick scan told him that the assembly bot had done a precise job. At the core's center, the little sliver of purple corilum glowed from underneath a protective plastiglass casing. Two nodes held the ore fast between them. If the corilum was skewed even a centimeter, the whole warp core might become unstable when powered by a ship. But a quick inspection revealed it was perfectly centered in this one. Bobby dropped the core back onto the conveyor belt with a *thud*. His job was done.

He watched the core drift down the line where Six and his team added parts to the product in succession until it transformed into a fully functioning warp engine core. "Complexity," he muttered.

"What?" asked LINC.

"You said my complexity is what gives me potential." Bobby fingered the unused tools gleaming on his work surface. "If I'm so complex, why do I do the simplest job in the factory?"

"Robert," a garbled voice shouted from down the line.

Startled, Bobby turned to see the hulking form of the Inspector bot lumbering toward him. Grime muted his bright yellow body, which was plastered with faded warning labels on almost every surface. Bobby had suspected the labels were for the benefit of previous human experiments. But now that he was the only human remaining, the bots had probably thought it too low a priority to waste materials on new stickers. Now, it occurred to him that they'd been right to not renew the labels. He'd failed Programming. Soon, there might not be any more humans to read them.

The Inspector eyed Bobby with two telescoping lenses. "Your inspection was point oh-eight seconds too slow." He reached Bobby's workstation and slammed a vidscreen down. He pointed to a frozen timer on the display. *5.08* seconds blinked in red. "Sub-five, Robert. Sub-five. No more delays." He scooped up the vidscreen and ambled off.

"Do you want his job?" asked LINC. "You could be a Tier One bot who tells all the other Tier One bots what to do."

"Thanks, LINC." Bobby let his shoulder slump. "Look, let's stop the thought experiment and just help me stay on my target time. I can't scrub this up too."

"Fine," LINC replied. "But factory work is sooooo boring."

A timer popped up on LINC's display, and for the next two hours, Bobby performed his warp core inspection in under the required five seconds. It was tedious work, made more taxing by the Inspector's frequent scrutinizing glare.

After some time, Bobby wiped the film of sweat from his brow and checked LINC's planetary clock. Twenty minutes left to go in his shift, then he could go back home to the Hovel. But when he realized that the Programmers had sent his test results to Mother, he wasn't so sure he wanted to leave. He reminded himself that *feelings don't factor*. Besides, there was still a lot of work that required his concentration. Each round of warp core parts had been arriving steadily faster.

Drumming his fingers, he glanced upstream where a new pile of parts poured out of the hatch. He turned to see Six and his team finishing up the last round. As he watched the bots, he noticed Six having some trouble.

In contrast to the newer bots' fluid movement, Six's jerky motions were much more pronounced than usual. In fact, the old bot seemed to completely freeze at regular intervals.

Bobby realized that if the Inspector found a legacy bot like Six defective, the old bot would be decommissioned and thrown into the Incinerator. No more of Six's anomalous, cheery greetings at the factory.

A sudden desire to rescue Six gripped Bobby. Perhaps he could reboot the legacy bot without the Inspector noticing. He glanced around the factory and spotted the Inspector off recording notes in a distant corner. The newest round of incoming parts had just reached the first bot. Bobby estimated he would have about forty-five seconds to reboot Six and make it back to his workstation in time. It was now or never.

He seized his omnitool and dashed down the assembly line. The newer assembly bots took no notice of him as they worked on the current warp core. Six had frozen again by the time Bobby reached him. With a quick glance to make sure the Inspector was still occupied, he pried open the bot's rear maintenance hatch with the omnitool's flat head. He stuck his finger's prong through tangled wires into the diagnostic slot deep in Six's core.

"LINC," Bobby whispered. "Initiate reboot."

"Searching this model for the proper execution command," LINC replied as readouts popped up on his display. "Wow, this code is *old.*"

"Just hurry."

"Hold please."

Bobby chewed his lip. The first bot was finishing the newest warp core while the bots in Six's team were passing along the current product toward Six.

"Aw, scrub it, LINC!" Bobby breathed. "Come on!"

"Got it!" LINC exclaimed.

Six slumped over, then whirred back to life. His cylindrical head jerked around to regard Bobby and smiled when he saw him. "H-h-hello, B-bobby," Six stuttered. "W-w-we are going to b-build warp engine c-cores."

"LINC, did you fix him?"

"There's a lot of corrupted data here. I can't believe he's lasted this long."

Bobby pointed to the incoming warp core. "Six, you've got to finish it! You've got to last the rest of your shift."

"Ah, of c-c-course," Six replied. With halting motions, the bot turned back to his workstation, adding parts to the warp core with trembling hands.

Bobby unplugged his finger and inspected the legacy bot's work. It checked out. Six's movements weren't fluid, but he seemed able to get the job done now.

"Robert," the Inspector's voice pierced the din. Bobby went rigid. The Inspector was plodding toward him as fast as his bulky legs would allow.

"Scrub!" Bobby sprinted back toward his post. With a sickening realization, he found that the new warp core had drifted past his workstation. *All right, no problem*, he thought, forcing away a wave of nausea. He would intercept the core on the line. A quick inspection would show everything was okay, and there would be no time lost.

He seized the core and scanned it in a flash. He was about to set it back onto the conveyor belt when something caught his eye. The little sliver of corilum sat askew between the two nodes.

"Scrub, scrub, scrub!"

He would have to fix it. But his tools were at his workstation, and the Inspector was getting closer. In a panic, he popped off the plastiglass case and jabbed at the corilum trying to push it back into place.

"Whoa, be careful, Bobs," LINC warned. "That stuff is super unstable. It could—"

Without warning, the corilum slipped too far off the node and shot out of the core like a blaster bolt, ricocheting around the factory in a storm of pings. Instinctively, Bobby ducked, dropping the core, which landed with a heavy crack. Crouching in a ball with his head covered, he listened to the corilum bounce off the factory walls until it stopped with a loud, metallic *ching*.

He slowly rose and scanned the factory. The Inspector stood rooted to the floor. His telescopic lenses focused on something down the line. Bobby followed his gaze to the assembly bots. They were all turned toward a single bot in their team. His eyes widened. Six, smiling as always, was standing at his workstation with a glowing purple hole in the center of his head. Jagged lines spread from the hole where his cylindrical casing had cracked. Bobby froze, unable to breathe.

With perfect precision, one of the newer assembly bots marched over and pulled the corilum out of Six's head, then placed it in a container on a nearby workstation. Six collapsed into a heap on the floor.

The Inspector whirled on Bobby. "Explain your actions."

"I-I didn't mean to!" Tears welled in Bobby's eyes at the sight of Six's crumpled body.

The Inspector jabbed a huge finger toward Six. "Why did you intervene in that bot's assignment?"

"I was trying to help him," Bobby choked.

"Why would you help him?" the Inspector demanded.

"I was afraid he was defective. I didn't want him to be recycled, so I helped him."

The Inspector stomped closer. "Illogical. He is a bot. His utility has expired. So why would you leave your post and help him?"

"Because I care about him!" Bobby blurted.

The Inspector stared.

"You—care—about—but—utility—illogical." The Inspector's lenses suddenly went out of focus, and his gargantuan head fell onto his chest with a bang. A split second later he lifted it only to let it fall again. The cycle repeated.

"I believe you scrubbed him," LINC said.

"Not again." Bobby groaned.

"Now, Bobs, don't get frustrated. You know these Tier One bots aren't good at processing things like—"

"My complexity," Bobby spat.

"I was going to say human motivation."

"Same thing." Bobby tore off his goggles and strode to his workstation. "I gotta get out of here before he reboots." He tossed the goggles into his rucksack and shoved the omnitool in after it.

"You're going to leave before your shift ends?"

Bobby shouldered the bag and headed for the exit. "I think my shift is pretty much done."

With a last glance at Six, Bobby heaved the exit door and left the factory, wiping his wet cheeks.

<!005: Bypassing Standard Protocol>

AN UPCOMING FORK in the track scrolled into view on the railpod's vidscreen, and Bobby barely registered selecting the rightward branch. An icon popped up asking him to confirm a diversion from the pod's normal route. Without thinking, he tapped *Yes*. Like the pod, all his systems felt like they were on autopilot.

"Did you mean to change course, Bobs?" LINC asked. "Hovel's to the left. Mother's waiting on us."

"She doesn't know we left the factory early." Bobby fell back into his seat. "We have time before she expects us."

"The Inspector probably alerted her of our absence."

Bobby said nothing, only stared outside as the pod broke its usual course and swerved along the fork's right branch.

"Of all the days to see the Archiver," LINC remarked.

"It might be the last time I get to," Bobby whispered.

```
<o:!0110101-000Z><01110000></x:01011>
<o:010011100/01>
<
```

TWILIGHT PRESSED INTO the crumbling buildings that lined the deserted street. The dusty scent of crushed plasticrete and mangled plastisteel clogged Bobby's nose as he picked his way through the debris-strewn path. Down narrow alleys and broken walkways he went, farther and farther into the waste.

"I can't believe this isn't sectioned off yet," LINC said. "You know, one more kilometer and we're out of our Utility Zone."

Bobby made no comment as he hopped along a row of flagstones half-submerged in a pool of dark water.

"Look!" LINC's voice dropped to a whisper.

Bobby landed on a stone halfway across the water and froze. Three small creatures were moving through a tangle of twisted metal rods growing out of a pile of rubble. The deepening shadows obscured their form, but he could make out their small, hunched bodies and thin forceps claws. Pale green eyes scanned the debris in a frenzy.

"Scavenger bots," LINC said.

"Scrub." Bobby dropped to a knee to conceal his presence.

The scent of oil wafted up from the murky pool while faint scratching cut the silence as the bots scurried about on the pile, snatching odd bits of rubbish in their clawed hands and bringing them up to their glowing eyes. He should have known they'd be out here. Ever since the Programmers had sanctioned their development, they'd begun releasing more and more of them into the ruins to retrieve corilum from scrap computers and outdated tech. Bobby had never reported discovering the Archiver while on one of his scavenging missions some years ago. Now that bots performed these kinds of jobs, his visits to the legacy Archiver unit were proving more difficult to accomplish.

His leg was beginning to cramp, but the bots were still making their rounds. Biting his lip, he shuffled his foot out just enough to relieve the spasm, knocking a loose bit of rock off the flagstone in the process. The rock hit the water with a *plop*, and the scavenger bots sat bolt upright, their green orbs searching. Then, without warning, they scattered, disappearing from the pile.

"My scanners aren't picking up any more bots," LINC said after a moment.

"Good." Bobby got to his feet and jumped over to the bank of the pool. "The last thing I need is to explain to the Programmers why scavenger bots found me out here."

He continued on in the fading light until he arrived at a low building. The structure strained under its own weight, threatening to cave at any moment. The door lay on the ground, torn from its hinges in some ancient battle with humans he'd only heard stories of.

He sidled through the opening, careful not to disturb the crumbling walls. As his eyes adjusted to the dim light, he picked his way deeper into the wreckage until he came into a wide room. The last glow of evening filtered through a hole in the ceiling, illuminating a cylindrical figure about Bobby's height, half-buried in the ground. A lamp on the figure's triangular head flickered to life. Its beam searched the room before resting on Bobby.

"Ah, good—Bobby," a voice scratched the thick air. "—evening, LINC." The figure tried to straighten but remained askew. Regardless, a smile spread across its mechanical lips up to its orb eyes. "I hope—are—well."

"Hey, Arc," Bobby replied.

"Evening, Archiver." LINC's colors shifted green. "I see you've developed new rust spots."

"Are you here—another story?" The Archiver swung its headlamp in a circle, spotlighting the floor-to-ceiling shelves lining the room. They were mostly empty, save for about a half-dozen grimy holopods.

"Hmm, got anything new?" LINC asked flatly.

"Not for—long time," the Archiver lamented. From the folded arms that ringed his body, the bot extended the only functioning one and retrieved a holopod with its pincer. "How about this one?"

He offered the device to Bobby. "Zel by—Grimm. It—your favorite."

Bobby considered the battered holopod. It had been damaged in the wreckage long before he'd discovered this place. The holo itself was primitive, displaying only still images as a faulty voice narrated the story of a girl trapped in a dark tower looming over a neon cityscape. Static fuzzed out most of the pictures, including her silhouette—much to Bobby's disappointment. He'd never seen an image depicting the female of his species. Only a snippet of her excessively long golden hair here and there escaped the corrupted images. Regardless, her story resonated something deep inside him. Now, more than ever, he longed to see what the girl looked like, to free her from the tower, as if doing so would somehow free himself. But of what? He wasn't imprisoned like her. Not yet, anyway. The Tether didn't yet house his mind. So why did he feel so trapped?

Bobby pushed the thoughts away before tears could form. "I'm not here for a story."

"What—shame," said the Archiver, placing the pod back on the shelf. "What—wrong, Bobby? It seems that something—troubling you."

Bobby looked up through the hole in the ceiling to catch the first stars twinkling in the inky black sky. "I failed my Programming—again." He took a breath to say something else but found no words would come.

"And you—here to tell me goodbye." The Archiver's eyelids clicked.

Bobby blinked. "How did you know that?"

The Archiver's face shifted into a soft expression. "Because I know you, Bobby."

"How? How do you always know what I'm thinking? The Inspector sure doesn't. Oh, and by the way, guess who I scrubbed again today? The Inspector. Big surprise, huh?" Bobby ran a frustrated hand through his hair. "I think even the Programmers get confused about me sometimes."

"I was designed long before—Programmers."

He glanced up. "Who? Who designed you?"

A green light blinked on the Archiver's torso. Dust motes hung suspended in his headlamp.

"I'm sorry, I cannot retrieve—data."

Bobby nodded. He knew the answer hadn't changed since the last time he'd asked, but somehow, he was still disappointed. "Well anyway, you're right. I might have to upload into the Tether soon. There's no way I can come back here after that."

"I wish I—help."

Bobby hung his head. "Me too."

The Archiver's strained voice box produced something like a mournful sigh. "I will miss you."

"Miss me?" Bobby repeated. "What do you mean?"

"An expression. From—time long ago. Perhaps you—like to take your favorite story?"

"No." Bobby shook his head. "I shouldn't. If the Programmers see it, they might find you. I'm already putting you in danger with these scavenger bots around."

The Archiver waved away Bobby's concern with his pincers. "They sense corilum—no corilum here."

"Still." Bobby kicked at a loose bit of gravel. "I could lead them to you if they see me. Besides, if I get another chance at Programming next year, I'll have to devote all my time to studying."

"Why?"

"Why?" Bobby repeated, incredulous. "Because I've got to become the Prime Human. If I can't, my species is done. Gone! And I scrubbed up today. Arc, I scrubbed up so bad. What if they make me upload into the Tether? Make me hunt Fallen humans down whether I want to or not. I'll be a bot like them. And then I won't get to see you and watch stories and—and—" He began to hyperventilate.

"It—okay, Bobby. You just need—hug."

The Archiver wrapped his arm around Bobby and pulled him into a tight embrace. Bobby felt the warmth emanating from the bot's internal processors. It reminded him of how Mother used to hug him when he was a child. Her programming dictated the act to ensure his proper neural development. That was before her discipline settings had increased. But the Archiver's embrace was different, not pragmatic like Mother's, but given simply because he knew Bobby craved comfort in that moment.

Bobby's breathing slowed, and he relaxed. "How do you always know?"

<!006: Experiencing Unexpected Anomalies>

BOBBY LAY IN the center of his room, staring up through the domed window at the night sky. The Hovel had entered night mode, shifting its ambient lighting to calming warm colors to prepare his nervous system for sleep. But Bobby didn't feel like sleeping. He was numb. He'd shorted out the Hovel's power grid, failed his Programming, destroyed a legacy bot, scrubbed a factory Inspector, and said goodbye to the Archiver. On top of that, he'd had to bear a lengthy lecture from Mother when he got home.

All in one day.

"Bobby!" Mother's buzzing voice broke his sullen thoughts.

"Yes, Mother?" Bobby replied, shaking himself out of his daze. "I'm, uh, preparing for a sleep cycle." He half expected another lecture when the bot clambered into his room.

"Get up," she said. "The garbage chute appears clogged. Likely from the power outage this morning. You will fix it."

"Yes, Mother." He was relieved that she wasn't there to further discuss his flaws.

He followed the bot out and stepped into the supply room to grab a wrench and some gloves before proceeding outside the Hovel.

The city's lights washed out most of the stars, but overhead a sparse blanket of twinkling points stretched out in a glimmering canopy. Pavement and plastisteel released the day's heat into the air and, save for the hum of the Hovel's power generator, the night was silent. Bobby took a deep breath, savoring the momentary peace.

"You remember how to fix the garbage chute?" LINC asked.

"Are you afraid I'll scrub that up too?" Bobby muttered as he slipped on the elbow-length gloves.

"Not at all."

"Well, I am." He trudged around to the Hovel's rear, up to a paneled hump on the wall that housed the garbage chute. His cybernetic fingers pried at the panel. It popped open to reveal the large pipe running from the Hovel's wall into the ground. The pipe gurgled as the clogged waste tried to force its way down.

"Try gently tapping the pipe first to see if it dislodges any—" Before LINC could finish, Bobby slammed the wrench into the pipe as hard as he could.

Clang.

"Okay, that was kind of excessive," LINC said.

But Bobby didn't stop. Again and again, he pummeled the pipe with all his force.

"I—hate—my—life!" Bobby yelled each word with a pound of the wrench.

"Uh, Bobs, you're going to damage the pipe."

With a last strike that sent tingling vibrations up his plastifiber forearm plates, Bobby straightened and flung the wrench aside, panting as it landed with a clatter. After a few seconds, the pipe stopped gurgling and emitted a whoosh as it cleared its clogged contents. Bobby slumped against the side of the Hovel, exhausted from the effort.

"Talk to me," LINC said.

Bobby stared at the night sky. Cargo ships zoomed along the starlit canopy as they entered and exited through the planet's invisible orbital shield. One star, in particular, shone brighter than the rest. He looked at it for a while without thinking much of it until the star began to glow brighter. And larger. He squinted. Was it moving too? Sure enough, it fell from its position, gaining speed as it descended.

"LINC, what is that?" He raised his cybernetic arm toward the sky so LINC's sensors could better assess.

"Looks like some kind of debris."

"It's getting bigger." He got to his feet. The debris, or whatever it was, had grown a considerable size and was now hurtling toward the horizon, dragging a red flaming tail behind it. In a matter of seconds, the burning something disappeared behind the city skyline.

"Weird," LINC remarked. "Whatever it was must have come from inside the atmosphere since no foreign objects can come through the planetary shield."

"Can you search for any reports of it?" Bobby fixed his gaze on the spot where the object had vanished.

LINC's colors swirled. "Hmm, all I can find is a security report on that thing that fell through the sky a few years ago. You remember that one?"

"Yeah." Bobby recalled a similar falling object he'd seen from his room one night. "But I read that report. Said it was a network satellite reentering the atmosphere. Whatever just fell was way bigger than that."

"Looks like there are no reports of the object in our Utility Zone. Want me to contact the Hovel's main computer to request outside reports?"

"No, not right now." Bobby sighed. "Mother will see it, and I don't need her asking any more questions today."

"Wait, I'm getting something. Listen." A garbled voice broke over LINC's speakers in bursts of static.

Bobby's heart jumped. "What is that? What's it saying?"

The sound fizzled.

"Lost it," LINC said.

Bobby looked from the vidscreen to the horizon where the red flame had disappeared. His eyes narrowed. "That wasn't a satellite, was it?"

"Could be a transmission from Sentinel's security force. But I tasted an unexpected frequency, so I'm not certain. Whatever it was, landed outside our Utility Zone, that's for sure."

Bobby stared at the sky. It was like nothing had happened. Cargo ships stayed on course, and even their accompanying fighters didn't break away. No alert. Nothing. He racked his brain for what could have hurtled through the atmosphere without calling attention from Sentinel.

When Mother finally called to come back inside, LINC said, "Better get some sleep, Bobs. I'll let you know if I intercept any reports."

"Okay." With a last glance at where the object had fallen, he turned and trudged back into the Hovel.

He climbed into the anti-gravity pod, wondering how he would ever sleep tonight. Gravity off, he stared through the hatch and out the ceiling window, searching for any more mysterious debris.

<!007: Decrypting Foreign Transmission>

THE NEXT MORNING, Bobby was scrubbing the floors and thinking about the garbled message when a chime sounded in the Hovel's main bay. He looked up from his work to see a flashing window had displaced the other holoprojections on the curved walls. *Urgent Message from Programming Corps.* blinked along the top of the frame. He jabbed the power switch, and the scrubber whined down into silence.

"This is it, LINC," he said with a sigh.

"Maybe they decided to give you another chance?" LINC offered.

"Doubt it." Muscles, taut from yesterday's Human Killer Sim, ached in protest as he got to his feet. "Hovel, open message."

The window expanded to a video of Programmer Alpha at his control deck. Bobby's eyes flicked to the chrome face of the Tether in the background, then back to Alpha. He swallowed a wave of despair.

"Robert," droned the Programmer, "Gamma will arrive at Sentinel Tower at oh-eight-hundred hours of the planet cycle. He requires you to report here and perform one final test to determine your future as Prime Human." With that, the window closed, revealing Bobby's daily schedule behind it. *Factory Shift*, which dominated most of today's time slot, moved down the list as a new block titled *Report to Gamma* appeared above it.

Icy dread squeezed Bobby's stomach. "A final test? What do you think it is?"

"No clue, but it can't be good."

"Thanks, LINC."

"I mean, uh, I'm sure it's not that bad." LINC modulated a weak chuckle.

Mother clambered into the bay on her way to another corridor and paused to turn her central lens at Bobby.

With a start, he dropped to his knees and thumbed the powerbuffer's switch. The scrubber attachment reanimated, and he resumed cleaning with brisk motions. After a few moments, he peeked over his shoulder to confirm Mother had gone.

The powerbuffer tugged him a way he didn't want to go, and he pulled it back on track with a grunt. "One more test to scrub up, and then I won't have to do this anymore." He noted that LINC, usually ready with a reply, had no answer this time.

```
<o:!0110101-000Z><01110000></x:01011>
<o:010011100/01>
<
```

THE TRIP IN the copper elevators seemed to last forever. By the time the doors opened, Bobby's palm was sweaty. The steady hum of holocomputers was absent as he stepped into the Programming chamber's frigid air. Across the room, the Tether's chrome face arrested his focus. He tried to believe it was the lack of computer heat that chilled him, but when his muscles began to tremble he couldn't deny that fear had gripped his core like purple ice in the cold season.

Fear, the Programmers had said, was the deadliest emotion, giving rise to all others responsible for the Fall. Apprehension mounted with every shaky step, solidifying the frost in his veins. He wondered if today would mark his own Fall. Before Sentinel rotated another full cycle, the Tether might house what was left of his irredeemable, flawed mind.

With the computers off, no holographic projections hovered in the chamber this time, another reminder that he'd failed yesterday. At the control deck, the Programmers conversed with each other in mechanical clicks. Upon seeing him enter, Alpha hurried over to him.

"Lord Gamma's ship has landed," he said.

What little heat remained in Bobby's cheeks drained, the ice hardening. He wondered if he would ever get warm.

"He will arrive in approximately five minutes," Alpha continued. "He is up to date on your performance yesterday and will question you. Keep your answers brief. If he is satisfied with your responses, he will administer a final test. Do you understand?"

Bobby nodded, trying to keep his face impassive. As Alpha stalked back to the control panel, he lowered himself into a nearby chair and pumped his fingers. Brief answers weren't going to be the problem. Making his parched throat produce any sound at all would be the problem.

Quiet blips and chirps from the control deck mixed with the rapid drum of his nervous fingers on the armrest. He was just about to remind himself that feelings don't factor for the dozenth time when LINC emitted a chime.

"What is it?" Bobby whispered.

"I'm picking up the transmission again," LINC replied.

"Yeah?" Bobby's voice was louder than he'd intended, a spike of excitement cracking the ice just a little. He glanced at the Programmers, but they were busy conversing. This might be his last chance to learn anything about the message. He leaned forward, elbows on knees, and spoke in a hushed tone. "Who's sending it?"

"Unknown," LINC said. "The sender is using an old frequency that I have stored in my data banks. Can't trace the source. Want me to play the message?"

"Hang on," Bobby whispered, then stood up and addressed the Programmers. "May I practice differential equations while I wait?"

The Programmers' orb eyes blinked, calculating the request in their domed heads. After a moment, Alpha nodded his assent, and Bobby strolled over to a holocomputer at the far end of the chamber. He jabbed a button, and the computer hummed to life, an equation blooming above its projector. Careful to position himself so that the hologram was between him and the Programmers, he whispered to LINC. "Okay, play the message, but keep the volume low."

"Hold please."

A staticky hologram flickered just above LINC's vidscreen. The image stabilized to reveal a slim figure. A cowl masked its face along with a pair of black goggles.

"What the...?" Bobby's voice trailed in astonishment. "Is that a bot?" The figure wore some sort of dark, long-sleeve tunic and trousers made of a strange, form-fitting material. Not a centimeter of its body was exposed, but by the fit of the clothes, Bobby could make out a slim waist that contoured out into curved shoulders and hips. The figure's shape was unlike any robotic model he was familiar with.

"Playing message," LINC announced, and the figure animated.

"I'm—broadcast—need—assistance," a voice, higher in pitch than Bobby's, rang between clips of static. It was a voice unlike any he'd heard. Not modulated like a bot, but seemingly organic, like his own. The closest thing he could think of was the brute grunts and howls from marauders in the Human Killer Simulation. Unlike those awful noises, however, the words here were intelligent—clear and purposeful. There was no way this figure could be human. Right?

The voice lost its ring, sound bites scrambling into discordant notes as the image began to sputter and fade.

"What's it saying?" Bobby whispered. "Get it back!"

"I'm trying," LINC replied over the transmission's dying sounds. "Sorry, Bobs. I don't think I have the range to pick up the entire message."

"Keep trying." Bobby stared at the spot where the figure had vanished as if he could bring it back through sheer willpower.

"On it."

Bobby's mind raced in the resulting silence. Had the transmission come from the falling object he'd seen last night? His eyes snapped to the Programmers. Were they picking up the same transmission? If so, they made no indication of it.

"Do you think this is part of my final test, or whatever?" He feigned working to solve the equation in case the Programmers looked up.

"It's possible," LINC admitted. "Maybe some sort of twisted puzzle."

Bobby scribbled a nonsense solution. His brain was both too exhausted and too wired to work out the correct answer. "But we picked up the transmission last night. Alpha told me about the test this morning. What's your advice?"

"Tell Alpha to scrub himself."

"LINC, seriously."

"Fine." LINC's colors swirled orange. "What does Protocol say in any situation?"

"Gather intelligence before planning a course of action," Bobby recited.

"So let me get the message back, we'll gather intelligence, and plan a course of action. Yeah?"

"Robert!" Bobby started at Alpha's call. Had the Programmer heard their conversation?

He leaned out from behind the hologram. "Yes, Alpha?"

"Gamma is here."

At his words, the elevator chimed. Bobby clicked the stylus back into the holocomputer's slot and hurried to the chamber's center to present himself. He forced his lungs to take even breaths as the doors slid open and a troop of battle bots marched in. Not holograms from the Human Killer Simulation. Real battle bots. He gazed at their streamlined plastisteel bodies in awe, at the plasma burns on some, and wondered if they'd just returned from destroying a band of human marauders on some faraway planet.

The squad parted, and a tall bot with an angular face strode through their midst.

Gamma.

Dread constricted Bobby's chest, displacing the thought of the message. Sentinel's overlord was even more intimidating than he'd remembered. Yellow, wedge-shaped eyes were set above sharp angled cheeks and a wide metal jaw. Flat armor plates adorned the bot's broad chest while a long, thin plasma railgun was slung on his back.

Alpha scurried over to Gamma and bowed. Bobby thought it strange for a bot to bow, and stranger still to see his instructor operate as an inferior.

"Lord Gamma," Alpha rose. "The human is ready to see you, as you requested."

Gamma turned his sharp eyes onto Bobby. Alpha jabbed a finger toward the floor.

Bobby dropped into a bow, glad to be released for a moment from the overlord's penetrating gaze.

"Robert," Gamma said in a deep tone. "Stand up. Let me look at you."

Bobby rose. He'd forgotten how smooth Gamma's voice sounded, how fluid his movements were. No other bot on Sentinel came close to the intelligence and complexity of the Tier Three bot.

The overlord scanned every angle of his body, eyes clicking in rapid succession. "You seem nervous."

Bobby screwed his face up into a stony expression and cleared his throat so his words wouldn't croak. "Feelings don't factor."

"The absolute truth," Gamma agreed. "Do you remind yourself often?"

"Yes." Bobby nodded, remembering to keep his answers short.

The bot inclined his head. "Did you remind yourself yesterday during your exam?"

"Uh," Bobby began, unsure of what to say.

"Because," Gamma continued, "I was informed that you had multiple emotional outbreaks during the course of your test, confirm?"

Bobby struggled to keep his eyes from falling. "Confirm."

"Your emotions contributed in large part to failing your Programming." Gamma's eyes flicked to the holographic differential equation Bobby had pretended to solve and the nonsensical answer hovering beneath. "Careless mistakes contributed as well, it would seem." He returned his attention back to Bobby. "You agree, confirm?"

Bobby's face flushed, the first heat he'd felt in a while. But he remained impassive, knowing Gamma was scrutinizing every centimeter of his face for emotion. "Confirm."

"Your ineptitude places me in a disadvantageous position." The bot folded his plated arms behind his back and paced to the holographic equation. "Much of my time is engaged in battling your depraved species. You understand that if the other humans are not wiped out, their mindless violence will destroy us and themselves?"

Bobby nodded.

"You are humanity's last chance for its renewed existence." Gamma studied the scribbled solution for a moment, then shook his head. "My programming, however, is very clear. I may only allow the revival of the human race if our experimental human cultivation program proves successful. And so far, it has not. For sixteen years, you've proved capricious and erratic in your behavior."

Bobby shifted, uneasy with his weight on either foot. The question of who had tasked Sentinel's bots with restoring the human species usually burned in his mind. But now it blazed white-hot with the chilling notion that he might not become Prime Human and learn the answer.

"One day," Gamma continued, sliding the stylus out of the computer's slot, "you demonstrate adequate logic in your thought processes. Next, well...." He gestured at the floating jumble of numbers and symbols Bobby had written. "The Prime Human must possess many attributes. Fact-based decision making, logical trains of thought, apt skill...." He worked a separate solution into the air next to Bobby's.

"Bobs," LINC whispered.

"Shh," Bobby hushed as Gamma continued his discourse.

"Bobby, I think I got the whole message."

"What? LINC, don't."

The hologram popped up above LINC's vidscreen.

"This—any—humans," said the figure.

Bobby whipped his arms behind his back, hiding the holo while somehow managing to hit the "mute" icon in the process. Gamma, the Programmers, and the battle bots all turned to regard him with inquisitive expressions.

"Did you say something?" Gamma scanned him again.

"Uh," Bobby stammered, angling himself to hide the hologram. "I just said I agree with you. Yeah, I agree with you that the Prime Human can govern Sentinel without the bounds of Tier One and Tier Two programming."

Gamma narrowed his yellow eyes. "Precisely."

Bobby dug his nails into his palm. After a few excruciating seconds, Gamma focused back on the holoprojection and tapped the floating *submit* button. A check mark popped up, signaling the correct answer. Then the equation evaporated, and a stream of other Programming challenges flashed in the air at high speed.

"Now," Gamma said, watching the cycling images. "You must retain all of this information if you are to assume the position of Prime Human."

"LINC, shut it off," Bobby breathed.

"You told me to get the message back," whispered LINC.

"Not now, you stupid, scrubbed bot."

"Fine." LINC emitted a low chime.

"Is it off?" Bobby asked, afraid to move his arms.

"It's off. Looks like I'm still out of range for the full message anyway."

Bobby let out a sigh of relief. Carefully, he brought his arms forward, making sure the staticky image was gone.

"Did you hear what I just asked you, Robert?" Gamma turned to face him.

"Confirm," Bobby blurted. He wasn't at all sure what the bot had said, but he nodded, perhaps a little too vigorously, for Gamma paused to consider him. Bobby licked his dry lips, hoping deceit hadn't crept into his face.

"Then what is your decision?" Gamma challenged.

Bobby's mind cramped searching for an answer. He could make up something. But it was like coding a program incorrectly. The further he went with his mistake, the worse the outcome. In the span of a capacitor discharge, his brain somehow seized upon a response with the least amount of risk. "I would like your analysis of the best course of action."

Gamma's features took on a thoughtful expression as if analyzing Bobby's behavior through a series of algorithms. Bobby held firm for a breathless moment until the overlord leveled his gaze.

"I'm programmed to annihilate what's left of fallen humans while you prove your race is worth reviving," Gamma said. "I must suggest you accept my offer of a final test for the chance to restart your Programming." He pointed to the Tether at the chamber's far end, and his metal maw curled, almost, *almost*, like a smile. "However, should you wish to upload your consciousness and rid yourself of your human pain and weariness, I will allow it."

Despite the control he tried to exert over his features, anxiety contorted Bobby's face as his eyes flicked to the Tether. For a few caustic heartbeats, he considered it. He could end it all in that moment. Upload to the Tether, and his disappointment, pain, and exhaustion would disappear, along with the survival of his species. He would fail his sole purpose. But right now, his brain was screaming at how unfair this was. Entrusting the continuance of the human race to a sixteen-year-old boy? Who was the scrubbing hack who assigned him that task? Who had placed him at the end of a line of failed experiments? At least if he had been the first, he wouldn't have known just how impossible his mission was. But everyone had failed. Would it be so bad if he failed too?

Maybe humans aren't worth reviving. After all these years, all these failed Programming cycles, the thought had worn a deep fissure in his brain, convincing him of its truth each time it cut across his mind. Only this time another thought interrupted its path.

The message.

Something had said the word *humans*. Was it a defective bot looking for humans to annihilate on the wrong planet? A fallen human that had somehow retained bits of language and had infiltrated Sentinel's orbital shield?

He needed to know. He couldn't give up. Not yet.

"I accept the test."

Whatever expression had been on Gamma's face disappeared. The bot stiffened. "Very well. We shall proceed." He motioned to Alpha, who tapped a button on the control deck.

A panel in the chamber's rear wall slid open. Bobby recognized the corridor behind as the one the Programmers used to exit the room after a Programming session. He'd never been allowed more than a glimpse of its dark passageway, but now Gamma marched toward it, beckoning him to follow.

Bobby trailed after the bot into the corridor to face his final test.

<!008: Recycling Primitive Technology>

ADRENALINE FORCED BOBBY'S legs through banks of icy fear as he followed Gamma down the dim corridor. A chemical symbol popped up on LINC's vidscreen, a silent offer from his task assistant to administer a mood stabilizer. It was tempting. Gamma hadn't forbidden it. But if it was against normal Programming rules, then it might break the rules of whatever final test was waiting at the end of the hall. Besides, if by some improbable chance Bobby did pass, he couldn't let the Programmers find mood stabilizers in his system. Reluctantly, he tapped the *No* icon and focused his nervous energy into keeping up with Gamma's long strides.

Bronze arches ribbed the hall, meeting overhead in the vaulted ceiling. Faint recessed lights did their best to illuminate the path, but Bobby had to rely on Gamma's vision to lead the way.

The bot strode ahead with a burst of speed, and Bobby had to half-walk, half-jog to keep up. Every time he fell too far behind one of the battle bots would shove him ahead a few paces.

Wings branched off the main corridor, but the party kept straight until at last, they arrived at a single copper elevator. The doors opened as if expecting their arrival.

Though the space inside was large, Bobby found himself squeezed between two battle bots as the doors closed. Still, it was preferable to being too close to Gamma. The overlord hadn't passed him a glance since they'd left the Programming chamber, and for some reason, it made Bobby even more uneasy. What was going through the bot's neural processors?

The elevator descended, slowed, sped rightward, dropped again, leftward, then forward. By the time the doors opened, Bobby had lost all sense of their location in the tower. Gamma exited first, followed by the squad and Bobby, a battle bot prodding his back.

He looked around. They were marching in an arched hallway like the one above, but this one ended in wide bay doors.

Gamma punched a button on the wall, and the doors parted to reveal a large industrial bay. In every corner, bots worked disassembling equipment in a cacophony of buzzing and scraping metal that assaulted Bobby's ears.

The Incineration Bay.

"Come," Gamma said.

At each station they passed, bots were tearing down familiar objects like outdated holocomputers, antiquated power generators, and even other bots who had finally expired in their line of work. Bobby wondered if Six was in here somewhere and shuddered at the thought of the legacy bot waiting to be turned into a heap of scrap.

A roaring furnace dominated the center, staining the bay walls with its red glow. Bots shoveled scrap parts into the fiery center, which burst with flames at each scoop. Even from a distance, waves of heat rolled over Bobby's skin.

At last, they came to a station at the far end, where bots were breaking down an old garbage-disposal unit. The bots dismantled the cube-shaped body of the garbage bot into a pile of parts within seconds, leaving only its head and core. Blank eyes stared at Bobby as the workers tossed the garbage bot onto a conveyor belt rolling toward the central furnace. Bobby winced. What kind of test was in the Incineration Bay?

"What do you see here, Robert?" Gamma asked.

"Looks like they're recycling outdated equipment," Bobby replied, careful to state only objective facts.

"Outdated, yes." Gamma lightly touched the garbage bot as it drifted by. "Everything comes to the end of its life cycle and must be reused for the greater good. You agree, confirm?"

Bobby watched the garbage bot roll off the assembly line and disappear in the furnace with a molten splash. He turned back to Gamma, attempting to keep his voice steady. "Confirm."

Gamma signaled for the disassembly bots to halt their work. The belt stopped. He turned to Bobby. "The Programmers informed me of your conduct in the Human Killer Simulation yesterday." His yellow eyes glinted in the furnace's light.

Unsure how to respond, Bobby defaulted to silence.

"They told me that your efficiency in decision making was low," Gamma continued. "But that you sacrificed your life multiple times to achieve your mission."

"Yes, sir." Bobby's muscles tensed as he recalled each painful simulated death.

"Sacrificing yourself is one of the few useful traits found in more advanced individuals of your species," Gamma said.

Bobby straightened. Was Gamma giving him a compliment?

"Unfortunately," said the overlord, "the trait often coexists with an inability to sacrifice others, especially those with whom you have attachments." Gamma motioned to a disassembly bot at a control panel, and the worker restarted the conveyor belt. Bobby's brief elation vanished as a familiar cylindrical body emerged through the wall's rubber flaps, its ring of hinged arms retracted save for a single claw trying to push its body upright.

"Arc!" Bobby cried.

The belt brought the Archiver to Gamma and stopped. The Archiver let out something like a groan, weak and fuzzed by static.

Bobby wanted to run to him, but Gamma was blocking the way. "What are you doing with him?"

"The question," replied Gamma, gaze boring into Bobby, "is what were *you* doing with him? Your interaction with this unsanctioned equipment was detected last night by bots in the area."

The scavenger bots, Bobby thought with a pang of guilt as he glanced at the Archiver lying on his side. He hadn't been careful enough.

Gamma leaned close. "How long have you been interacting with this Archiver unit?"

His eyes were scanning Bobby's features for deception. He had to tell the truth. "Since my first assignment scavenging for corilum in the ruins," Bobby admitted.

The overlord let out a hiss of air from some unseen valve. "And why did you not report that you discovered a bot that is off Sentinel's main grid?"

"I mean," Bobby mumbled, "it wasn't against Protocol."

Gamma's alloy fingers clenched into a fist. "What did this Archiver unit tell you?"

"N-not much," Bobby stammered.

"Deception!" Gamma cried, rising to his full height. "My bots found unsanctioned holopods in his dwelling!"

"It's t-t-true," the Archiver interjected, managing to push himself halfway up with his functioning arm. "My d-data is largely corrupted. I cannot recall many f-facts."

Gamma whirled on the disassembly bots. "He still speaks? Silence him!"

Bobby watched in horror as workers popped off a panel on the Archiver's torso and began ripping out wires.

"I do recall one th-thing, G-Gamma." The Archiver's voice became more scrambled with each torn connector.

"That your d-designer was—"

"Silence him!" Gamma demanded over the Archiver's last strained words.

A worker tore out the vocal box, and the Archiver fell silent.

Bobby's ears thrummed with rushing blood over the furnace's roar, the Archiver's final words lingering like a distorted sound bite in his mind.

Gamma stared at the voiceless Archiver with something like anger twisting his alloy features, if that was possible. After a moment, the overlord turned to Bobby. "This is your test, Robert." His voice was low, corrosive. "You will send this piece of scrap into the furnace."

"No." Bobby breathed.

The furnace lit Gamma's wedge-shaped eyes with fire. "If you cannot recycle an obsolete piece of equipment, then you cannot become the Prime Human. Throw him in the furnace."

"Alive?"

"He is not organic. He is a bot. Do it now, or you will fail!"

Bobby clenched his jaw. With extreme effort, he approached the Archiver. The old bot's rusty arm squeaked as it scratched at the belt. *Feelings don't factor.*

With his cybernetic arm, he lifted the Archiver to his chest and proceeded toward the furnace, the bot's ancient body jangling with every step. He felt Gamma's glare burning into the back of his head even as the air grew hotter. Could he do this?

At length, he came to the furnace and stared into its white, blazing center. Roaring fire drowned out the other sounds in the bay. The intense heat rolling out burned his skin and expanded the alloy in his cybernetic arm. The bots scooping scrap had retreated at Gamma's command.

It was just him and the Archiver.

He stood for a moment, willing himself to do it. To just get it over with. Toss him into the furnace. Get on with his Programming. It was the logical thing to do. Right?

Tears streamed down his cheeks, evaporating almost instantly in the heat, as he gazed at the Archiver's face. The bot's flickering orbs stared back at him. With jerky movements, the Archiver hooked his arm around him in a last hug that broke Bobby's resolve into hard sobs.

Bobby shook his head. He couldn't do it. Setting the Archiver on the floor, he turned to see Gamma striding toward him, yellow eyes burning bright as the furnace.

"You are too flawed to be useful!" Gamma shouted. In one swift motion, the overlord seized the Archiver and hurled his broken body into the furnace.

"No!" The roar of the fire drowned out Bobby's scream as he ran toward the furnace. The wall of heat hit him like a force field, searing his skin. He staggered back, stunned, watching the Archiver's arm sink below the edge of the furnace and disappear in a splash of molten metal.

The bay spun around him, blurring the next moments. The blast of the furnace dimmed, and the entire scene seemed far away. LINC's voice floated to him from somewhere, penetrating the fog, warning him about rising heat levels. When he didn't move, his cybernetic arm jerked him away from the furnace. The next thing he knew, he was face to face with Gamma. The overlord was shouting something.

Then he was stumbling back through the hall and into the bright light of the Programming Chamber. The Programmers swam into his view, their tinny voices distant. But the Archiver's melting arm blotted them out. Played on a loop in his brain.

The Archiver.

All his caring warmth was gone.

Now logic and precision were all that remained on the planet.

<!009: Processing Large Amount of Data>

Too flawed to be useful.

"Bobs, talk to me, how we doing?" LINC's voice, real and present, floated to him over the echo of Gamma's words.

Bobby gasped awake and blinked at the blurry shapes streaking by in his vision. "Where am I?" The words boiled up, thick like tar.

"Railpod back to the Hovel," LINC replied.

"What happened?" Bobby squinted as the shapes condensed into buildings whizzing by through the plastiglass canopy.

"Well, um, not a great day for you. Listen, I want you to know I did the best I could with what I had."

Bobby clutched his throbbing head. "What are you talking about?"

"You know how your arm isn't *quite* calibrated, yet?"

"LINC, what did you do?"

"What did I do? I saved your life, that's what I did. Probably. I was *trying* to tell you that the heat from the furnace was rising to dangerous levels."

At once, the memory of the furnace—and Gamma throwing the Archiver into its molten pool—came rushing back, dialing up the invisible weight crushing his chest. He doubled over, elbows on his knees, trying to suck in enough air to stay conscious.

"Easy there, Bobs." LINC's colors swirled a cautious yellow. "I lowered your body temperature to counteract the furnace. And injected you with the last of your mood stabilizer to calm the anxiety episode you were having."

"Is that why I feel like this?" Bobby said between gulps of air.

"Side effects. Actually, the combination made you pass out."

"Thanks."

"For keeping you from a heat stroke? You're welcome. Thank your uncalibrated arm for the overdose and near-cryonic body temperature drop."

Bobby sat up with a groan and let his head fall back against the headrest. "I thought you were supposed to be calibrating it."

"I'm working on it. Lots of activities going on today."

Bobby sighed, staring outside. "Sorry, LINC. It's just—scrub, when is this mood stabilizer going to wear off? I feel like—" He sat bolt upright. "LINC! The message! What happened to it?"

"Oh right, I picked up the signal again while you were delirious."

"Well? What did it say? Can you play it again?"

"I'm sorry, Bobs. The signal is just too weak. We'd need to find some way to extend my range."

"Great." Bobby crossed his arms. "Something on this planet has an interest in humans. And guess what they'll never find? Me. Because after Mother gives me another lecture, I'll probably be decommissioned. Say goodbye to the last sentient human in the galaxy." He snorted.

LINC's color abstraction shifted about as if calculating a response, but none came. Bobby chewed his inner lip.

The console showed the upcoming fork in the track. The rightward branch was now grayed out. One of the Programmers must have discovered the oversight and restricted the option to divert course into the wastelands.

He sighed, wondering if he could feel more numb than he already did. Though his eyes followed passing buildings, he never saw them. His mind had gone back to that terrible moment the Archiver drowned in the fiery furnace.

```
<o:!0110101-000Z><01110000></x:01011>
<o:010011100/01>
<
```

"A TRIBUNAL?" BOBBY plopped onto the floor of his room, hands covering his face in despair as he sat.

"Protocol dictates you present yourself before the Programmers for the final decision." Mother's sparking body popped and hissed. "Based on your unacceptable performance today, Gamma will most likely decide to have you upload into the Tether."

With a groan, Bobby doubled over, head between his knees. He'd assumed that since he'd failed the final test, that was it. They'd upload him into the Tether once they'd prepared the transfer process. Or something. Those last moments in the Incineration Bay were fuzzy, and he couldn't quite remember what Gamma had been shouting before passing out.

But of course there would be a tribunal. Nothing happened on Sentinel that didn't require official proceedings. There was no way they'd give him another chance at Programming. Right? Withholding a decision until the tribunal only gave him hope for another shot. The Programmers must know how agonizing a glimmer of hope could be. His brain threatened to detonate in an angry explosion.

"How long is this uncertainty going to last?" He groaned.

"Control your emotions," Mother droned. She crawled over to the anti-gravity pod and pressed a button. The hatch popped open, and she pointed inside with a tentacle. "You will sleep now and receive your verdict tomorrow." When Bobby made no move, her faulty voice box hummed louder. "Robert. Obey my directive."

With a grunt, Bobby pushed himself up and stomped over to the pod, refusing to look at her as he stripped off his outerwear and climbed inside.

"Night mode," Mother called, and the Hovel obliged, darkening the room with warm, ambient light. "Set your alarm for oh-five hundred of the planet cycle," she called through the hatch. "You will begin your morning tasks an hour early, then travel to Sentinel Tower for your tribunal." With that, she clunked out of the room, bursting with sparks.

He stared up through the open hatch to the stars glittering through the domed window.

"You gonna turn off the gravity?" LINC asked.

Bobby made no reply. His body was numb, neurons and circuits exhausted by more emotions than he'd let himself experience in a long time. Maybe uploading into the Tether would be a good thing. A relief. No more painful ache in his heart.

"Bobs?"

"What's your best memory with me?" Bobby asked, no longer caring to delete all the crazy thoughts streaming in his brain. They'd be gone tomorrow, anyway.

"Best memory?" LINC's colors cast confused shades of yellow on the pod's inner walls.

"This is the last night we'll spend together if I go in the Tether tomorrow." The words cut through his chest, intensifying the ache.

LINC was silent for a moment. Bobby wondered if his task assistant had even thought about the possibility of being separated from him. Any other bot would have logically deduced it, but LINC wasn't like other bots. The Programmers would have asked Bobby to define "best," probably taking it to mean "most efficient." But LINC would know what he meant without any clarification. Another anomaly.

"Well," LINC finally replied, "there was the time when I hummed that high-pitched note that interferes with the Inspector's communicator frequency."

Bobby frowned. "You scrubbed him."

"It was great."

"I got in a lot of trouble for that."

"Yeah, for laughing."

A smile tugged on Bobby's lips at remembering the look on the Inspector's face as his systems shut down. He wiped away the grin. Emotions had gotten him where he was now.

Regret poured into him. If only he could have done better. Been more efficient. Not let his emotions get the best of him. It was why humanity had fallen, after all. The Programmers had told him all emotions begin the transition to depravity. He shut his eyes, willing the numbness in his body to seep inside his brain, to sterilize it from all his broken thoughts. There was some solace in the fact that he soon wouldn't have to fight his flaws anymore. Let the Tether's perfect coding overwrite them.

"Actually, I'll tell you what my best memory is." LINC's voice startled him.

Bobby kept his eyes closed, and although he told himself he no longer cared about the answer, his ears pricked up to hear LINC's response.

"My best memory is the day I booted up in your arm."

Despite himself, Bobby opened his eyes and looked down at his task assistant's vidscreen swirling warm colors.

"The day you arrived at the Hovel," LINC continued. "I was pretty rudimentary then. Basically, just programmed to monitor your vitals. But even before my circuits started to integrate with your neurons, I remember thinking you were special."

Bobby inclined his head toward LINC. "But you don't even know where I come from. Where *you* come from."

"Yeah, but there's something in me. I don't know, something deep in my code. But also, not exactly *in* my code. Like metadata or something. I wish I could access it. It's almost like it's walled off. I don't know how that makes sense. But still, I feel like there's something about you. Some sort of...." His voice trailed, and the next word came so soft Bobby almost missed it. "...purpose."

Bobby bit his lip. The numbness had receded somewhat, rolling away to once again uncover that ache in his heart. "Thanks, LINC." His voice came out more unsteady than he intended. "You've been a good task assistant." He wiped away a bit of moisture gathering in his eye. "And a good friend."

"Good enough to pick up the message again."

"You got it?" Bobby sat up and bumped his head against the hatch. "Ow."

"Check it." LINC's projector illuminated, and the cloaked figure bloomed above Bobby's arm.

"Any—humans—" The figure's voice scratched with static.

"Scrub, signal's still too weak," LINC said.

"Hang on." Bobby retracted the hatch and scrambled onto the top of the pod, raising his cybernetic arm high in the air. "Anything?"

The figure splintered into pixelated motes, then evaporated.

"Sorry, Bobs."

Bobby lowered his arm, staring at the space where the figure had been. He slammed his fist into the pod's side. "Great. Guess I'll never know what it said."

"If only there was a way to extend my range," LINC mused.

Bobby scanned his room. Aside from the central holoprojector and a few omnitools residing on his workstation, there was nothing to amplify LINC's range. He shook his head, about to give up on ever seeing the message, when a faint beeping punctured his awareness.

"What is that?" He cocked an ear to the ceiling where the sound seemed to emanate.

"Sounds like a delivery drone," LINC said.

"That's impossible, how would a delivery drone—"

Something thumped against the roof. Bobby peered up through the domed window to see a hovering craft carrying a large metal crate.

"It *is* a delivery drone!" LINC said. "Told you!"

"What the scrub?" Bobby wrinkled his brow in confusion. "What's it doing here?"

"Let's find out. Hovel, open the wind—"

"No," Bobby cried. "If the Hovel could sense it, it would have opened it already. I'll do it manually."

"Going against Protocol again, eh?"

"Stow it." Bobby ran over to a control panel mounted on the wall and pushed a button. The domed window retracted. The delivery drone squeezed through and deposited the crate before buzzing off.

"This is highly unusual, right?" Bobby stared at the box, fingers twitching with nervous energy.

"Well, what are you waiting for?" asked LINC. "Open it."

Bobby unhitched a latch on the crate's side and lifted the lid. He peered inside and sucked in a sharp breath.

There, at the bottom of the crate, lay Six's limp body.

<!010: Cloning Operating System>

"WHAT THE SCRUB?" Bobby whispered, tracing Six's battered frame with his eyes. He snapped his head toward the door, half-expecting to see Mother come clambering in. But the Hovel hadn't sensed the drone. That was strange enough, but it also meant it hadn't alerted Mother. Nothing significant ever happened without an authority monitoring him. Yet here he was, alone with mysterious cargo from an unknown sender. A strange sense of displacement came over him. The closest he ever came to feeling this off-the-grid was in the wastelands. It was exhilarating and terrifying all at once.

He ran over to his clothes dispenser and retrieved a clean set of outerwear. It was foolish, but somehow he felt vulnerable.

Clothes on, he returned to the box. He reached in to touch the lifeless bot, but a flat, red holo message expanded inside the crate's lip, stopping him short.

"What's it say?" LINC vibrated Bobby's arm in excitement.

"Looks like an invoice." Bobby skipped to the message's last line, which listed the sender. *ARC048*. "It's from the Archiver!"

"How's that possible?" LINC's colors swirled fast.

A notice blinked at the top of the holographic message, reading: *Autolanguage program has repaired corrupted or missing text contained in this script.*

Bobby's eyes darted to the beginning of the message, and he read out loud in a breathless voice. "Bobby, bots have taken me to the Incineration Bay, where I believe they intend to terminate me. Do not blame yourself. It was always a matter of time before they found me. Consider this fortunate because I discovered something at this recycling facility. I seem to contain a coding language that these newer bots do not understand. As such, I scanned the area for bots with my programming type and came across the one you see here. His name is Six. His memory is corrupted, but it pinged my receiver. He appears to possess memories of you. I hope the legacy drone I ordered to deliver him arrives without interference. I suggest exploring this bot's debug mode. Perhaps it will aid you in some way. It is my last gift to you. Do what you will with it, but remember the theme from your favorite story—you always have a choice. My memory remains fragmented, but I somehow think you were *programmed*—forgive me, I cannot seem to retrieve the correct word—for a much different purpose than the life you now live. I am sorry I will no longer get to enjoy our conversations. Please take care of yourself."

Bobby blinked and had to read it a second time before the words fully registered. His favorite story? The Archiver had told him the girl trapped in the tower had the choice to stay in her tower or leave. What was he encouraging him to do with Six's debug mode? He absently swiped the text away and stared for a long moment at Six's crumpled form.

"Well, come on," LINC's tone turned impatient. "Let's fire him up. See what we can get out of him."

Bobby cast an annoyed glance at his task assistant. "He's not just an—" He was going to say *object*, but then it hit him that that's exactly what Six was. A piece of machinery designed for a specific task. He'd often wondered why it was so easy for him to think of the bots as more than just specialized equipment. The Programmers called it *projecting*, his tendency to see attributes of himself in other things. Instead of letting Six malfunction and be recycled, he'd accidentally destroyed him instead, all because of a misplaced desire to save the bot. All because he'd projected on a mindless machine.

Guilt formed a pit in his stomach. He couldn't tell if it was for ending Six or for letting himself be upset about any of it when *feelings don't factor*. Probably both.

Cursing himself for another human flaw, he reached into the crate and lifted Six out by the torso.

"All right," LINC said as Bobby laid Six onto the floor, "let's see what we can find in this bucket of bolts."

Bobby pressed his lips into a flat line. He was certain that no amount of projecting would explain LINC's anomalous behavior.

Then an idea struck him.

"LINC, do you think we can use Six's hardware to extend your range and pick up the message?"

"Bobs, that spongy little human brain of yours is pretty smart sometimes."

```
<o:!0110101-000Z><01110000></x:01011>
<o:010011100/01>
<
```

BOBBY SAT CROSS-LEGGED among the slew of Six's internal parts strewn across the floor. The day's events still weighed on his mind, but the thought of seeing the message again boosted his energy. The excess mood stabilizer still in his system probably helped too.

"This doesn't make sense." He squinted at the computer on his lap. Wires coiled from Six's opened chest cavity into the computer, transferring readouts to the vidscreen. "His programming doesn't follow standard coding procedure, but he has these extra chunks of code like someone added behavior restraints."

"A lot of these legacy bots were modified about nineteen years ago," LINC said. "To bring them up to Sentinel's new standards"

"What happened nineteen years ago?"

"Records indicate there was a breakthrough in rudimentary artificial intelligence programming, but most of it is classified."

"But why would a breakthrough in AI produce *more* behavior restraints? Seems like a step backward."

"Yeah, doesn't make sense. Wish I had access to that information."

Bobby frowned. He thought of the Depository and how the Archiver had hinted at the secrets under its domed roof. With a sigh, he again shook away the image of the old bot sinking into the furnace.

"Well, let's get Six up and running." He looked up at the hologram floating above his room's central projector. The image depicted a detailed breakdown of Six's internal parts. "Wow, this stuff is really old. Do you think we can even pick up the message with it?"

"His parts are way outdated, but his antenna looks like it has a broad enough range."

Bobby swiped, and Six's schematic rotated with his gesture. "Do you think he'll be the same if we get him up and running?"

"Not a chance," LINC replied. "His data's way too corrupted."

Bobby picked at Six's chipped casing with his thumb. "What if I try to patch up the code using the same language he's programmed in?"

"It's not even a language you know. We'd be here for weeks. We don't have that kind of time."

Anxiety bubbled up Bobby's throat. He knew LINC was trying to avoid the topic of the tribunal tomorrow. Pushing away the thought, he tapped at the holographic keyboard on his lap and focused on picking up the message. Maybe if he figured out what it said, he could relay it to the Programmers. Maybe Gamma would offer him another chance at Programming. Hope grew in his chest, but he was careful to stifle it. *Feelings don't factor.*

"Try a basic reboot," LINC said. "We don't need all his code working to pick up the message, just communication functions."

Bobby nodded and typed a command. "Okay, let's try this one." He tapped a holographic button and waited for Six to respond. The bot didn't move.

"Look at his execution functions." LINC motioned to the other bot. "If they're not operative, you'll need to repair them before you can enter any commands."

Bobby navigated through Six's code and found the function LINC had suggested. Text flashed on the screen.

DATA CORRUPTED

"Scrub," Bobby groaned. "We're going to have to code these functions from scratch."

"Want me to pull up the Programming lesson on coding?" LINC offered.

Bobby cocked his head. "Actually, I think I have a better idea." Setting the computer aside, he got to his knees and inspected Six's stripped chest cavity. "What if we copied your neural network into Six? Just until we get the message. See, we could use the same diagnostic slot we used to reboot him at the factory."

"You know that overwriting a bot's neural net with another's is against Sentinel Protocol," LINC said. "You sure you want to do that?"

Bobby bit his lip. He had no idea what punishment awaited him if Mother or the Programmers discovered he hadn't reported an unsanctioned delivery. If they found out he was breaking Protocol at the same time, they might upload him straight into the Tether without a tribunal.

"Buuuuuut," LINC intoned, "since this bot is dysfunctional and doesn't have much usable code to begin with, copying my neural network might not technically count as overwriting."

Bobby smiled. "So a loophole?"

"Exactly."

```
<o:!0110101-0007><01110000></x:01011>
<o:010011100/01>
<
```

BOBBY REPLACED THE last piece of hardware into Six's open hatch. The diagnostic wires still splayed from the bot's chest.

He disconnected them from the computer and attached them to the port next to LINC's vidscreen.

"Connection successful," LINC chimed.

"Okay, clone your operating system."

"Yeah, sure, no problem."

Bobby waited, eyes flitting to the door, worried Mother would crawl through any second. After a moment, he focused back on LINC's screen. Nothing had changed. "Are you cloning?"

"Uh, yeah, it's fine," LINC said. "Everything's fine."

"What's the matter?"

"Nothing," then after a beat, "just pulling up instructions on how to copy my neural network."

Bobby cocked a brow. "You don't know how?"

"Don't rush me," LINC snapped, taking over Bobby's finger and pointing it at his face. "It's not like I do this all the time. Ah, I think I got it."

The finger fell back to Bobby's control, and a loading bar popped up on LINC's display. Bobby drummed his fingers on Six's chest as he watched the *Percent Complete* slowly tick up.

"Uh, Bobs?" LINC's voice warbled with rare uncertainty. "Something's happening."

Bobby hunched over LINC's display, heart pounding. "What is it? Is something wrong?"

A buzzing alarm broke from LINC's speakers. *WARNING* flashed on the screen in big block letters.

"LINC? What's going on? What's happening?" He tapped furiously at the display, but the alarm kept blaring.

"Security protocol activated." A modulated voice sounded from Bobby's arm. It was LINC's voice, and yet not like LINC at all. His tone, but none of his inflection. "Your license number," continued the LINC-like voice, "will be reported to the Federation—"

"Bobby, I—" LINC's voice—his real voice—interjected but cut off as a jolt shot through Six, sparks flying from his chest. The bot convulsed, its eyes flashing on and off in alternating sequence.

"No, no, no, no!" Bobby scrambled over to the bot, searching for something, anything to make it stop. "LINC, cancel, cancel!"

"Bobby—disconnect," LINC stuttered over the alarm as Six's arms flailed.

"Okay, okay, disconnect." Bobby yanked the wires from Six's chest. At once, the bot went limp. The alarm stopped, leaving his ears to ring in the silence. He looked at LINC's vidscreen. It was black.

"LINC?"

No response.

"LINC? Are you there?" Bobby mashed the display.

The screen lit up blue, along with a blinking message that read:

ERROR

"No, no, no, this can't be happening." He slapped the screen in frustration. The message scrambled, then reappeared with the text:

GOODBYE!

"What? No!"

The display shut off, and with it all the sensors in Bobby's arm. His entire cybernetic limb went numb and fell to the floor in a dead weight of metal and plastifiber.

"What the scrub?" Bobby cried. He looked around in panic. What could he do? He had to plug into a power supply. The extra juice might allow him to reboot LINC. If LINC still existed, that is.

"Scrub, scrub, scrub," Bobby cursed. He crawled over to the central holoprojector. With no working motors, he had to drag his dead arm along the floor, trailing still-connected wires in his wake. He tapped the projector's touchpad. The image of Six's schematic wavered as the Hovel's main menu replaced it. "Hovel,

I need assistance," he called, scrolling through the options for a way to fix LINC.

"What is your request?" the Hovel responded in its ever-calm tone.

"I need instructions for reinstalling my Living Inter-Neural Communicator."

A spinning circle appeared at the menu's top corner as the Hovel processed the request. "The L-I-N-C program is not a part of my database. Records indicate a similar program is stored in the Depository. Shall I inform your caretaker unit to request access to the program?"

"No, don't do that." Bobby chewed his lip. The last thing he needed was for Mother to discover what he'd done.

"May I be of further assistance?" said the Hovel.

Ignoring the question, Bobby closed the menu, leaving the schematic to hover back in the air.

His breathing came shallow as he glanced helplessly around the room. The quiet pressed in all around, heavier than mere silence. Even when he wasn't talking, LINC was always there, monitoring vitals, colors swirling. But now Bobby was alone. Part of himself gone. His arm's dead weight tore at the muscles in his shoulder. Heavy as it was, it felt hollow, empty. Like a huge amount of code had vanished somehow leaving his circuit boards lighter.

"Okay, Bobby, think logically." He tried to steady his breathing. "What would LINC say in this situation?"

Something like a capacitor recharging sounded behind him, followed by a stir of movement. "He would say he spent way too long crammed in that arm of yours," a familiar modulated voice said.

Bobby snapped his head around to see Six's battered arms stretch out toward the ceiling.

"Six?" Bobby cried.

"Six?" the bot repeated, propping himself up on his elbows. "I've been in your arm for sixteen years, and I have one little change of body, and now you don't recognize me?"

Bobby's eyes widened. "LINC?"

"New look, same great taste." The bot got to his feet and dusted himself off. His movements were smooth. Much smoother than Six's had ever been. His voice certainly didn't sound like Six's glitchy voice box either, but like LINC's modulated speech profile.

The bot looked up and cocked his head. "You really not sure it's me? All right, look, if I was Six, could I do this?" He snatched three holopods nestled next to the projector and juggled them in the air. "Aha!" he exclaimed, head pointed up at the arc of pods. "You didn't know your old pal could do this, did you?"

Bobby watched in bewilderment.

With a flair, the bot caught all the balls in a single wire-veined hand. "Ta-da!" His eyes clicked as he paused for effect.

Bobby's mouth hung open, gaping at the sight.

The bot sauntered over to him and knelt down. "I get it," he whispered, closing Bobby's jaw with a gentle finger. "I'm pretty amazing."

Bobby blinked at the bot's smile. "Wait, what the scrub happened? What happened to LINC in here?" He pointed at his dead cybernetic arm.

"Oh, right," the bot said. "Well, when you copied my operating system into Six's body, I hit a few snags. It triggered this weird alarm I've never seen."

"Yeah." Bobby shifted to his knees as he tried to fit the puzzle pieces together. "I heard a voice saying it was alerting something that sounded like 'Federation,' but then it cut out, and the screen went dead."

"What voice?"

"It sounded like you, only it wasn't. It was different."

"I don't remember that."

"What's the Federation?"

"I don't know. I wouldn't listen to strange voices." The bot bent over and dropped the holopods back next to the projector. "I do remember discovering a lot of weird stuff while trying to copy myself." He stood up. "Without getting too technical, I basically got tangled up in Six's old code. And let me tell you, that bot had some major problems."

"Wait, wait, wait, back up." Bobby held up his hand. "I still don't understand. I *copied* LINC's operating system. I didn't transfer it. LINC should still be in my arm." He wiggled his shoulder, rattling the locked-up appendage.

"Oh, that's no good," the bot responded, leaning closer to inspect Bobby's arm. "Wow, can you believe I lived in that tiny little thing for so long?"

"Answer my question. How are you LINC?"

The bot straightened. "Oh, well that's easy. While I was cloning, I ran into that outdated code in Six's processor and those behavior restraints hit me pretty hard. I tried running a diagnostic test to see if it was even possible to install my operating system on his old equipment." He banged a fist against his chest. "That's when all the sparks and thrashing started. It was a movement test."

Bobby frowned. "I thought Six was going haywire. You told me to disconnect."

"No, I said, 'Bobby, *don't* disconnect.'"

"Your voice definitely cut out when you said 'don't.'"

"Hey." The bot shrugged. "I was multitasking. Anyway, you disconnected the wires at the same time that weird alarm was trying to shut me down. I think all of it together corrupted my operating system in your arm. Luckily, I'm super smart, and I managed to clone myself into Six right when you pulled the plug."

"So, I scrubbed again, huh?"

"Yep," chirped the bot. "I'm basically the hero of this story."

Bobby pursed his lips, letting his brain piece everything together. "So, you really are LINC?"

"At your service." The bot bowed. When Bobby made no response, he straightened and, sticking a fist on an angled hip, gestured to himself. "Not what you were expecting?"

Bobby inclined his head, scanning Six's—or rather, LINC's—wiry frame up and down. "Actually," he said at last, "this is exactly what I would've expected."

The bot, LINC, arched a mechanical brow. "You thought if I ever had a body it would be this pile of junk?"

Bobby shrugged. "It seems right for you."

LINC rolled his eyes. "Wow, thanks."

"So how do you, um, feel?"

"Well, I have this hole in my head, thanks to *someone.*" Bobby winced as LINC pointed at the hole between his eyes from the factory mishap earlier. "Easy fix, though." The bot tore a strip of tape from a roll on Bobby's workstation and plastered it over the hole. "See? Good as new. Feels so good to be free." He stretched his arms overhead. "You might not believe this, but as many behavior restraints as Six had, I found out I have triple the amount."

"Who would put behavior restraints on you?" Bobby wrinkled his nose as LINC performed some deep squats.

"I'm not sure. But making a copy of my neural network gave me the chance to look back at myself if that makes sense. They seem to be mostly memory restraints."

"Memory restraints?" Bobby perked up. "Does that mean you have memories of where I came from?"

"I don't know." LINC put a wiry finger to his chin at the bottom of his squat, his eyes twitching as if retrieving internal information. "Seems more like reference files. Science facts and historical data. I can only get bits and pieces."

"Can you remove the restraints?"

"Nah, they're too advanced, even for me." LINC stepped into a side lunge. "Whoever put them there knew what they were doing."

Bobby rolled these new revelations around his head. "Maybe the Programmers were going to remove them when I became Prime Human?" Then, with a bitter twinge, he realized he'd never become Prime Human. Not if the tribunal decided against him tomorrow. He might never learn who put the restraints on LINC, or the answer to countless other questions. Before he could spiral further into despair, LINC grabbed his arm and pulled him to his feet.

"Let's get this arm working, and then I have a surprise for you," LINC said.

"What is it?"

"With my new receiver range, I've already downloaded the entire message you've been dying to hear."

Bobby's eyes lit up.

```
<o:!0110101-000Z><01110000></x:01011>
<o:010011100/01>
<
```

"THIS SHOULD DO IT." LINC plugged the last wire into his open chest cavity and checked the connection to Bobby's forearm. The bot's eyes appeared to focus on something far away as he processed data only he could see. "Whew, my original source code is a mess. I'll have to reprogram your arm."

Bobby leaned onto his desk where LINC had propped up his dead cybernetic arm. The surface was littered with parts and pieces the bot had ripped out. Bobby frowned as his task assistant systematically jammed them back in place with an omnitool.

"You know what you're doing?"

"Please," LINC waved away his concern. "I'm a robot, I know how these things work. Whoops—" A processor snapped under the omnitool's flat head. He extracted the broken bits with his fingers and inspected them. "Oh, don't worry about this. It's not important." He tossed the pieces over his shoulder.

"Can we listen to the message now?" Bobby asked, trying not to think about all the damage LINC was doing to his arm.

"I should have enough processing power to do both." A small, circular disk ejected from the center of LINC's torso. The bot pulled it out of the slot and set it on the table. A fuzzy hologram bloomed above its surface. "Hang on a sec." LINC flicked the disk with a wiry finger, and the image condensed into the masked figure.

Bobby held his breath as the holo animated.

"This is a distress message for any humans in the area," said the figure.

Though he'd heard it earlier in the Programming chamber, he still couldn't get over his surprise at the figure's voice. Without the static interference, he was certain it wasn't a bot's. No bot he'd ever heard produced tones this clear, this soft.

"Our ship has crash-landed."

At this, Bobby gasped, remembering the object that had fallen from the sky the night before. So it *had* been a ship.

"We're broadcasting on this legacy frequency to any fellow humans who might still inhabit the planet."

Fellow humans. Bobby's eyes went wide at the image of the cloaked figure. "It's a human."

But humans had lost the ability to speak, right? Aside from grunting a command to kill or making guttural noises while going berserk, their higher brain functions had atrophied sometime after the First AI War from all the cyberware implants. But this creature's words—the inflection, the coherent reasoning, the calm delivery—could they belong to a human?

As if in answer to this question, the figure said, "We're desperate for aid from any fellow humans."

Even LINC, hardly surprised by anything, paused from hammering a delicate circuit board back in place. He looked at the holo with an expression that seemed to show he was working out the logic too.

"LINC, it's a human," Bobby said over the holo's words. "A *human.*"

"I know, I know." LINC waved for him to calm down, his lensed eyes trained on the holo.

Bobby's stomach did a flip at LINC's confirmation. He hadn't come to the wrong conclusion.

Another human was, in fact, on Sentinel.

Then his brain homed in on something the figure had said—*Our ship*—and his stomach did another flip. "LINC, there's more than one human. There's more than one human!"

"Yeah, yeah." LINC waved at him to be quiet.

Bobby's heart threatened to burst from his chest. Why wasn't LINC saying anything? "*LINC*, we need to *do* something."

Finally, LINC threw up his hands. "Bobs, I can't hear anything over you spazzing out."

Bobby moved his lips to form a response, but nothing came out. He only watched while LINC traced a wiry finger on the disk to rewind the message.

"This thing's been broadcasting for a whole planetary cycle now," LINC said, at last coming to the point in the message where Bobby's outburst had begun. "Taking another sixty seconds to see what it says isn't going to matter much."

Though a thousand more questions cropped up in Bobby's head, he remained silent, LINC's point taken.

"We have crashed in a forested area outside the city." The holo started again.

Bobby frowned at this. Outside the city? Didn't the city stretch over the entire planet?

"We require assistance to avoid termination by enemy bots on this planet. "We are broadcasting over Federation frequency to any allies of the Federation."

"Federation frequency!" LINC snapped his fingers. "That's the frequency I was tasting."

"What's the Federation?" Bobby asked, squirming in excitement.

"I don't remember." LINC shrugged. "But it's a super old frequency for sure. I don't think these newer Sentinel bots can pick it up. Now stop moving. I'm trying to fix your arm."

"We only have enough power to run our ship's cloaking function for two days," said the figure. "After that, we will be vulnerable to discovery. The bots will likely board us and kill us. We ask for assistance. Our coordinates are embedded in this broadcast. Please, hurry."

The image froze in place, the message ended. Bobby stared at it, the clear voice still ringing in his ears. Something had been nagging at the back of his mind the whole way through the message, and only now it registered in the ensuing silence. The voice. He'd already determined it was human. The strange part was that it was unlike any he'd heard in the Human Killer Simulation. These sounds weren't brute grunts or unintelligible words. They were clear and purposeful. Almost—what was the word he'd once heard the Archiver use?—*pleasing*.

"So, uh, what do we do?" asked LINC, breaking the silence.

"That's what I was trying to ask," Bobby replied.

"Yeah, really loudly over the message. So what do you think?"

"Aren't you my task assistant?"

"What do you want me to tell you, that we should report it to the Programmers?"

Bobby let out an incredulous snort. "And explain how we picked up the message with your new body? We'd be incinerated on the spot."

"Exactly my point. I am coded to think logically, you know."

With a sigh, Bobby dropped his head onto the table with a solid *thunk*. Whether it was the impact on the hard surface or his new Protocol-free thinking, an idea slammed into his brain.

"LINC!" He snapped his head up. "What if we capture those humans? We could bring them to the Programmers, and maybe it'd be enough to convince them that I'm worth giving another chance." Already, the idea was coursing through every neuron in his body with nervous energy. If his cybernetic arm had been online, he was sure it would have tingled too. The Archiver said he always had a choice. He could either show up at the tribunal tomorrow and accept his fate or seize this opportunity and try to change it. Was that what the Archiver wanted?

LINC seemed focused, not looking up from his work.

"It makes perfect sense," Bobby continued, more to himself than LINC. "The bots can't pick up the message or sense the ship through its cloaking device. Something about a Federation frequency? But I can! And you might say"—he broke into a mocking tone—"'Bobs, why don't we just tell the Programmers about the message? Wouldn't that be enough for them to give us another chance?'" He shook his head, switching back to a normal voice. "Well, you'd be wrong. Think about it. Humans are mindless and brutal, right? Our only shot at impressing the Programmers is to use all our combat training to *capture* them. Don't you see?" He bounced with growing excitement until LINC grounded an exposed wire, zapping a nerve in Bobby's shoulder. "Ow!"

"Be still."

Bobby rubbed at the pain in his shoulder, but continued his musing, keeping still so LINC wouldn't ground any more wires. "The only thing is, we'll have to get access to the Hovel's weapons cache. And figure out a way to get to the crash site without being seen. You got their coordinates in the message, right?"

LINC tightened a screw. "This isn't going to work."

Bobby stared at LINC. He opened his mouth to protest, but suddenly all his arguments seemed foolish. The bot was right. He'd let emotions get the better of him. Again.

His shoulders fell and with them his hopes for getting another chance at Programming. He'd just have to tell the Programmers about the message, alert them to the humans' presence, and go to his tribunal the next day as planned.

Then upload into the Tether.

"You're right," he muttered. "It was a scrubbed idea."

"Huh?" LINC finally looked up. "I was talking about your arm's motivator. It's not going to work. It's fried. What are *you* talking about?"

The embers of Bobby's smoldering excitement rekindled a little. He explained his thought process again, calmer this time so it didn't sound so impulsive. "So, what do you think? You like the plan? No, you don't. It's scrubbed, right?"

LINC regarded him with lensed eyes that displayed a kind of intensity he'd never seen in a bot. "Bobby." His task assistant placed a wiry hand on his shoulder. "I have wanted to break Protocol for sixteen years." He gestured at his battered frame. "There is no way you're going to keep this fresh body from going out tonight."

Bobby allowed himself to do something he often denied himself. He grinned.

"Now, let's replace this motivator." The bot rummaged in his chest cavity and dislodged something with a snap. He pulled out a worn cylinder that appeared to be a crude motivator of sorts. "Old tech, but should work." LINC popped out Bobby's fried component and set to work installing the one he'd removed from himself.

Bobby eyed LINC's open chest. "You don't need that?"

LINC shrugged. "I don't know. I'm still functioning, right? All right, hold still. Starting reboot." The bot's eyes twitched with processed data.

"Ow!" Another shock, this time throughout Bobby's entire cybernetic arm, and the motors in his joints powered up.

Each finger oscillated in sequence before a chime sounded, signaling completion of the reboot. He waved his arm around. "Feel's good. Are you, um, still in here too?" He tapped the vidscreen.

"A corrupted version of my operating system is." LINC adjusted the wires from his chest cavity to Bobby's diagnostic slot. "It'll take time for me to figure out how to fix it. Looking from the outside in, it's a wonder my software ever fit in your arm to begin with."

"Why?"

"There's a massive amount of data contained in your arm's internal memory, and I mean massive. I have no clue what it is." LINC's eyes now vacillated back and forth as if scanning invisible text. "It's the most advanced code I've ever seen. I'm trying to read it, but it keeps changing and shifting. Almost like...." His voice trailed.

"Like what?"

"Almost like it's trying to read *me*." LINC shook his head, snapping out of his processing trance. "We can investigate later." He yanked the wires out of his chest, closed his hatch, then pointed to the figure in the holo and smiled. "Let's go capture a human."

Bobby bounced to his feet, swiping the dangling wires from his now-functional arm. "I'll see if I can hack into the Hovel's weapons cache and—"

Without warning, the door slid open, and Mother crawled in on her tripod legs.

"Robert?" Mother's faulty voice box screeched.

The motors in Bobby's arm seized at the same time his heart stopped. His mind raced to explain the holographic human on his desk and the legacy bot with LINC's operating system in it. But his throat spasmed so only little hisses escaped as he gasped for air. Any second Mother's side would erupt in sparks, and it would be the Tether for him. But nothing happened. She just stood there, her domed head jerking left and right as she scanned the room.

"Relax," LINC said. "She can't see us."

Bobby managed to drag his eyes away from Mother and glance at the bot in utter confusion.

"Watch." LINC bounded from his seat and pranced over to Mother, waving his hands in wild gestures. Mother's telescopic lens seemed to focus straight through the bot and his bizarre motions. LINC looked back over his shoulder with a grin. "See?"

Bobby watched in disbelief as Mother inspected his empty anti-gravity pod then shuffled back and forth a few times before clambering out of the room.

"What just happened?" he asked as the door slid shut.

"Found my debug mode." LINC admired the backs of his alloy fingers. "I now have access to my local cloaking function."

"You mean," Bobby said as the meaning dawned on him, "we're invisible to other bots' sensors?"

"And that, Bobs"—LINC pointed at the hologram—"is how we are going to find those dirty humans."

<!011: Neutralizing Critical Threats>

BOBBY PEEKED OUT from behind a squat power generator and scanned the busy street. Harsh lights illuminated countless bots and cargo vehicles as they went about their programmed routes.

He gripped the blaster in his cybernetic hand a little tighter and glanced at LINC, who was crouching at his elbow. "You sure this is going to work?"

"Nope," LINC replied.

Bobby shot the bot a worried look.

"What, do you want me to tell you the odds or something?"

"Uh, yeah," Bobby said. "That's what you do."

"Let's see, it's the middle of the night." LINC ticked off his fingers. "We put Mother in extended sleep mode and hacked into the Hovel's weapons cache. We're about to go out of our Utility Zone to meet our first human ever. And we're relying on a cloaking function packed in some very ancient equipment." He slapped his chest. "So, what are the odds? Hang on." He closed his eyes, counting on his fingers and mumbling. "...and carry the two...."

"Okay, I get your point," Bobby said. "Stop acting like a scrubbed bot." He returned his attention to the street. There seemed to be no break in the constant traffic, no reprieve that might let them slip through. They'd just have to test LINC's newfound cloaking function to see if it worked. "All right," he said, taking a deep breath, "let's do this."

He got up and strolled into the street as casually as he could, making sure to stay close to LINC. But no more than a dozen steps out he realized a number of bots had turned to look at him. He froze.

"LINC," he whispered from the side of his mouth. "They can see us."

"That's strange," LINC said. "Hold please." He banged on his chest until a bell dinged somewhere inside his torso. "That should do it." The watching bots seemed suddenly confused, heads swiveling back and forth as they scanned for the intruders. After a moment, when it was clear they were picking up nothing in their sensors, some higher-priority programming kicked in and sent them back about their routes like nothing had happened.

Bobby released a held breath. "Next time, let's make sure the cloaking function is on *before* they see us."

"So, there will be a next time?" LINC nudged his ribs with an elbow as they resumed their pace.

Bobby pursed his lips. "I mean, maybe. No. No way. We're capturing these humans, then we're done. The Programmers will give me another shot, and we won't have to break Protocol anymore." He said this last part mostly to himself.

"Surrrrre."

Bobby bristled. His plan was going to work. It had to.

```
<o:!0110101-000Z><01110000></x:01011>
<o:010011100/01>
<
```

"WHERE ARE WE?" Bobby peered at the unfamiliar buildings cropped around the narrow avenue. They had left the constant traffic back in the main roads, leaving them to trek alone for the last fifteen minutes. Still, he jumped at every sound, power generators kicking on or the din of factory work, thinking that somehow a bot had discovered their unsanctioned journey through the city.

Or that a human had found them.

"We're on the edge of our Utility Zone," LINC replied, leading the way at a steady clip. "We're getting close."

Bobby frowned. "The message said they crashed outside the city. We're not even out of our Zone. How can we be getting close?"

Rounding a corner, LINC halted, causing Bobby to bump into his back.

The bot pointed. "I think there's your answer."

Bobby gaped at the sight before them.

The avenue came to an abrupt end as smooth plasticrete gave way to a peculiar green substance. In shadows beyond the reach of city lights, strange shapes twisted up from the ground, forming a dark canopy high above the path.

"Should we keep going?" Bobby suddenly felt hesitant to leave the lighted avenue.

"The humans are that way." LINC nodded toward the darkness.

"Right." Bobby swallowed his rising fear. "Okay, let's find them. Easy, right?"

They proceeded at a cautious pace, the darkness ahead growing larger with each step until it threatened to swallow them. At the pavement's edge, Bobby halted and crouched down to study the green substance that coated the ground. The substance wasn't uniform but consisted of thousands of green blades sprouting ankle-high from the soil.

"What is this stuff?" he asked.

"I'm attempting to access a memory file," LINC said. "But these scrubbing restraints are blocking most of it. I can only retrieve a few facts. What you're looking at is plant matter, termed *grass*."

"Grass," Bobby repeated. "Can I touch it?"

"Its biological makeup is benign. It's not dangerous."

Bobby brushed his fingers through the blanket of grass, surprised and delighted by its springiness as well as its smooth texture, cooling to his skin.

"Of course, I could be confusing it with a mutated form that's extremely toxic," LINC muttered.

"What?" Bobby said, busy stroking the blades back and forth.

"Um, nothing. Let's keep going."

Bobby stood and took a cautious step onto the grass.

"Good job, Bobs." LINC slapped him on the back. "You're officially outside your Utility Zone. Now, come on."

The grass rustled under Bobby's feet as he followed LINC into the darkness. Excitement and guilt mixed in his stomach, a volatile chemical reaction. But wonder soon replaced the nausea as he glanced at the strange shapes twisting up all around them.

"What are these things?"

"I believe they're called *pencils*."

"Pencils? You mean those old-timey styluses?"

"No, wait. They make pencils. I believe they're called *trees*." LINC switched on a diode embedded in his arm. Shadows went crawling from the tangled roots as he swung the bright shaft of light. Bobby observed the trees, from their thick, sturdy bottoms—*trunks*, LINC called them—to their lofty arms—*branches*—covered with countless flat blades of green.

"Is that more grass up there?" He pointed to the canopy overhead.

"Uh, yeah, sure," LINC replied. "Tree grass to be exact."

"Tree grass," Bobby mumbled in astonishment. "Is that where the pencils grow?"

"Yep."

"Wow."

They journeyed for some time. Bobby was entranced by the bizarre forms of plant matter around them—everything that made up this forest, LINC called it. So many questions crowded his mind he wasn't sure which to ask first. Finally, as they came to the largest body of water he'd ever seen, his dam of questions burst.

"What is this? Is this a reservoir? What was that crusty stuff on the ground back there? Did you see those tiny parabolas growing out of that tree? What is—"

"Shh," LINC hushed, shutting off his light. "Listen."

At the bot's alarmed tone, the questions died in Bobby's throat. He strained to listen for any sound, but all he could hear was the water's gentle lap against the muddy shore. Then he heard it. The low rumble of a ship's engine.

"Look," LINC whispered. "Across the lake."

"Lake," Bobby repeated, gazing across the water. All he could see was the white slivers of Sentinel's two moons reflecting on the glassy surface, but as his eyes adjusted further, he could make out a glowing square on the opposite shore. A figure stood silhouetted in its center. Bobby's heart jumped. Was that the human? Without warning, the light shrank into a small line like a door was closing. When it was gone, the rumble faded.

"Well, we know they didn't fix their ship," LINC said.

"How can we get to them?"

"The lake is approximately a kilometer in circumference. We won't have to walk far."

```
<o:!0110101-000Z><01110000></x:01011>
<o:010011100/01>
<
```

BOBBY PICKED HIS way through the tangled roots of the forest floor, tensing at the impossibly loud crack of each branch that snapped underfoot. LINC crept along without making a sound. Probably using his night vision. Bobby wondered what kind of sensors the Tether was equipped with, if he would have night vision when he transferred into it. Dismay burned in his chest when he realized a part of him was already beginning to accept the Tether as his fate. He extinguished the thought, reminding himself that if he could capture these humans, he might still have a chance.

In time, they rounded the lake and approached the forest's edge on the opposite shore. Bobby peeked out from behind a rotting stump into the clearing. The ship obscured their view of the lake, blacker than the surrounding darkness. There was no trace of damage or a rift in the ground suggesting a crash landing. It was difficult in the moons' soft light, but Bobby could just make out the shape of the vessel.

"Is that a Sentinel cargo ship?" he whispered.

LINC crouched beside him. "It sure is. Probably how they got through the planetary shield."

"But how could they steal a *mmph*—"

LINC clapped a wiry hand over his mouth and pointed at the clearing with the other. A dark figure was walking along the left shore toward the ship. A gruff voice crackled over a communication device hidden on the figure's frame.

"Anything?" the voice asked.

"Nothing," the figure answered.

Bobby immediately recognized its higher pitch and clear ring as the voice from the message.

"Get back inside," the gruff voice said.

"All right," the figure replied.

As the human walked back to the ship, it stopped a few paces short and looked up at the stars. By the dual glow of the moons, Bobby could see it peering at the sky, its face hidden under its cowl and goggles. It was definitely the human from the message.

He gripped his blaster and set the dial to *stun*. It was the perfect opportunity. If he could incapacitate this human, then the others might come out looking for it. He'd disable them, too, then call for battle bots to retrieve their bodies. LINC met his glance with a reassuring nod. He raised the blaster on his arm and trained it on the human. Just as he was about to squeeze the trigger, the human slipped off its goggles and cowl. A cascade of golden hair fell around a soft oval face and pale blue eyes that sparked in the moonlight.

Bobby's breath caught.

He'd always imagined seeing his first human face, expecting to be shocked by lifeless, bloodshot eyes. Not ones that were so—how could he describe them? Vivid? Pleasing? He'd once heard the Archiver use the word *beautiful*. Did that word apply here? He traced the human's frame, recalling Zel's silhouette from the Archiver's story.

The human let out a small sound, almost like a satisfied sigh. A smile flickered across its lips as it resumed its walk back to the ship. By the time it was out of sight, Bobby had forgotten all about squeezing the trigger.

"What kind of human was that?" He stared at the spot where it had disappeared.

"A female," LINC replied.

"Female?" Bobby tasted the word. "Of my species? Are you sure?"

"I can still pick up monitoring data from your arm, and considering your hormone profile right now, I'm pretty sure."

"Stop scanning me." Bobby swiped at the blue laser fan sweeping his arm from LINC's eyes.

"Anyways." LINC blinked the laser away. "Since you botched the shot, let's go to Plan B. I'll create a distraction to draw the humans out, and you pick them off."

Before Bobby could protest, LINC sauntered into the clearing and banged on the ship with his alloy fists.

"Welcome, humans!" LINC called over the noise. "We have a present for you out here! You have to come outside to get it, though!"

"LINC, stop!" Bobby dashed out of his hiding spot and tried to pull LINC back into the forest, but the bot was surprisingly strong.

"Hey, you're scrubbing up Plan B," LINC said, fighting Bobby's grasp.

"Stop!" a voice boomed on their right.

Bobby whipped around to see a massive shadow emerge from behind the ship's far side. Moonlight glinted off a huge gun barrel the instant before a brilliant photon blast struck Bobby in the chest, sending all his muscles into seizure. Pain wracked his body, and the last thing he remembered was the dulled sensation of hitting the ground and the shadowy figure towering above him. Then the world faded.

```
<o:!0110101-000Z><01110000></x:01011>
<o:010011100/01>
<
```

BOBBY'S EYES SNAPPED open. He sat up, ignoring the ache from his protesting muscles. The world spun with his sudden movement, adrenaline buzzing his nerves as he fought to get his bearings. As the dizziness subsided, smudged colors condensed into a small room awash with amber light. Heat seeped from his body into the metal floor beneath. In the corner, a figure sat with its back to him, studying readouts on half a dozen computer screens.

The figure turned to regard him, and Bobby scrambled to his feet, fighting another wave of dizziness that threatened to topple him. "Who are you?" he demanded, squinting through blurred vision.

The figure stood and approached, but Bobby denied the impulse to run. Was it the female?

"Stop right there." He threw up a hand.

But the figure got closer until a voice cut through the ringing in Bobby's ears.

"...you'll mess up the connections," came gruff tones.

Bobby blinked away the blurriness, and a face came into focus. He gasped. It wasn't the female, but a male. He was smaller than the giant human who had stunned him outside, but still tall with a thick build. Hard, graphite-colored eyes peered at him above wide cheeks and a square jaw. The chin was covered in short black hair flecked with gray.

"Get a grip, it's all right," said the man.

"Who are you? What do you want with me?"

The man glanced at Bobby's cybernetic arm, where a thick cable connected it to the monitors in the corner.

"Ah!" Bobby tore the cable from his arm.

"Hey, calm down." The man slowly crouched to retrieve the cord, eyes trained on Bobby.

Bobby scanned the room. "Where's LINC?"

"Your bot's fine, now relax." The man rose and attempted to reinsert the jack in Bobby's forearm.

"No!" Bobby withdrew on reflex, knocking him in the chin.

The man cried out, stumbling back, hands clutched to his mouth.

Bobby seized his chance and dashed for the door.

"Get back here!" The man's growl fell away as Bobby sprinted through a dim passageway.

"LINC!" he called, voice reverberating off the close walls. "Where are you?"

He flew by sealed doors and hatches, looking for some way to escape. A warm patch of light fell from an opening on the right. He stumbled through it, coming into a large hangar bay. He ran for the opposite side, hoping to find the exit, when an unseen hand seized his throat.

"Gck," Bobby choked as his feet flew out from under him.

He fought against the steely grip, managing to twist enough to see the giant figure holding him with a forearm the size of Bobby's leg. It was the human who had shot him. Oxygen slipping away from his brain, he had little time to wonder at the man's towering stature and dark skin.

"Let—me—go," Bobby gasped.

The gargantuan face remained impassive.

"Whoa, easy there, Doc," came a rusty voice. "No need for all that. Let the boy go."

The giant stared at Bobby for a beat, then rumbled something that sounded like "Fine," and released his vise grip.

Bobby crumpled to the floor, sucking in ragged lungful's of air.

"You'll have to excuse Doc. He's the ship's security."

Through a fit of coughs, Bobby focused on the voice's source. Another man, smaller and thinner, with wispy white hair, shuffled toward him. Knobby knuckles held fast to a thin rod that seemed to support his bent frame. He smiled. Bobby scrambled to his feet, balling his fists and eyeing the rod.

"Oh, this?" The man tapped the rod with his toe. "Just a cane to keep an old body upright. I promise it's not a weapon. My name's Benjamin Barnes." He extended a wrinkled hand. "Everyone calls me Barnes."

Bobby glanced at the bent man to his right and the giant on his left. If he had to fight his way out, he'd take the frail creature leaning on the cane. "What do you want?"

The man, Barnes, withdrew his proffered hand with a shrug. "I want to play a decent game of chess, but this bot of yours doesn't seem to grasp the rules." He jabbed a thumb over his shoulder. Bobby followed it to where LINC sat hunched over a cargo box set with a game board and black and white pieces.

Bobby scrunched his face. "LINC?"

LINC waved without looking up. "Hey, Bobs."

"You'd think a bot would learn strategy quicker than this." Barnes plodded back to the makeshift table, cane clacking with every other step. "But not this one." With some effort, he seated himself at the game board. "I've beaten him five times in less than ten moves."

"Don't worry, Bobs." LINC waved a dismissive hand. "I got him this time. Ha!" The bot seized a white game piece and slammed it onto a square occupied by a black, spire-shaped piece. The spire flipped off the board and landed at Bobby's feet.

"That would be a great move," said Barnes, nodding, "if a pawn could move sideways three spaces."

"Bobby, I'd like to see you beat this guy in a Programming sim of Gridlock." LINC clanged a fist on his hip. "See how well he learns the rules."

"I'm sure I'd be no match for the young man, so I'll stick with chess. Er, do you mind?" Barnes indicated the black piece at Bobby's foot.

"Come on." LINC urged Bobby to bring it over. "I can't let these humans beat me."

"Humans." Bobby's head swam. This had to be a dream. Or maybe he was jacked into a glitching sim back in the Programming Chamber. No way other humans were standing before him. No way they were *talking*.

Footsteps echoed outside, and a figure dashed into the bay, blood trickling from an impossibly square jaw. He thrust a finger at Bobby. "There you are."

Bobby snapped into a defensive stance, rearing back his cybernetic arm. "Don't move, or I'll hit you again."

"Oh, what's this all about, Kerrick?" Barnes rapped a knuckle on the table, rattling the pieces on the board. "Why is everyone trying to scare this poor boy to death?"

"I was checking that robotic arm for tracking devices when he attacked me." The man, apparently Kerrick, wiped blood from his chin.

"Well, what did you expect? Doc knocks him out cold, and then you hook him up to a computer without introducing yourself? I thought I raised you better than that."

"He was supposed to stay unconscious for another hour," Kerrick grumbled. "Doc didn't calibrate his stun gun for a cyborg."

Bobby glanced behind at Doc, standing sentry, massive arms clasped behind his back like a battle bot waiting for orders.

"He's a boy, not a cyborg," Barnes said.

"What do you call that?" Kerrick spat, pointing at Bobby's left arm. "It could have a homing beacon that's leading every bot on

Sentinel to our location. Dirty cyberware, just like the scrappers back home. Doc, get him to my quarters so I can finish the scan."

Bobby hopped out of reach as the giant took a colossal stride.

"That won't be necessary," Barnes said, and Doc stopped short.

"I'm captain of the ship," Kerrick growled.

"And I'm your father." Barnes raised his chin.

"Fine, I'll do it myself." Kerrick unlatched a device from his belt and sparked its prongs. He marched at Bobby.

Bobby shuffled backward in a panic until he hit the mountainous Doc behind.

Kerrick seized Bobby by the collar and raised the device. Before he could strike, LINC leapt onto his back with a hoot and toppled him to the floor.

"I got him, Bobby!" LINC cried. "Run! Ow!"

Kerrick zapped LINC with the electrified prongs, sending the bot into convulsions.

"Ow, ow, ow, ow. Where's the scrubbing switch for my pain sensors?" LINC's voice wavered as he shook.

Fire ignited in Bobby's chest. He rushed to knock Kerrick off LINC but instead collided with a slender body that had chosen that moment to come bounding into the bay. The newcomer let out a yelp as they both tumbled to the floor in a shower of golden hair.

"What the slag? Get off me!" A clear, sweet voice rang in Bobby's ears.

Bobby pushed himself off the figure and froze.

It was the girl.

"What's going on?" She sat up, sweeping hair from her eyes. Then, catching sight of Kerrick zapping LINC, shouted, "Uncle!"

Bobby glanced at Kerrick, who had LINC pinned under his knee.

"Don't—worry—Bobs," LINC said through modulated grunts. "I've got him—right—where I want him."

Kerrick thrust the device into LINC's back.

"All—part of my—strategy," LINC stuttered through electric pops.

The girl scrambled to her feet. "Uncle, what are you doing?"

"Being a fool." Barnes ambled over to Kerrick and thrust his cane at him. "You can forget about my help on this mission if this is how you're going to handle things."

Kerrick glared at Barnes for a moment and seemed to weigh something in his head. "Fine." He removed his knee, allowing LINC to wobble to his feet.

"Take this." LINC threw an unsteady punch at Kerrick, but Doc intercepted it with a hefty fist.

"Well, Bobby." Barnes sighed and spread his hands in a sweeping gesture. "Welcome to the *Quasar*."

<!012: Installing Updates>

"I THINK WE got off on the wrong foot," Barnes said, leaning on his cane.

Bobby tensed, ready to run, but the sight of the girl chained him to the spot. LINC hopped next to him in a fighting stance, proud at having disentangled himself from the attacker. He seemed unaware that Kerrick had begrudgingly removed his knee from his back.

In that moment of paralysis, Bobby's gaze flickered to the other humans before settling back on the girl. They looked nothing like he'd imagined. All those Human Killer Simulations had depicted humans as mindless brutes. Where was their cyberware? Their blood-soaked masks? Was this a trick? Were they distracting him so they could kill him? Kerrick had already threatened him, and Doc had caught him by the throat. Still, there was something in their eyes. In this girl's eyes. Something he never thought he'd see in a human.

Intelligence.

The girl had yelled at Kerrick, stopped him from attacking LINC. Humans killed their own kind to create a frenzy before battle. They never defended someone like this. Did they?

"How about some introductions, then?" Barnes continued. "You've already met my son, Kerrick. He's the captain of this ship and a good fighter, so it's impressive you got such a nice shot on him." Barnes chuckled, wrinkles spreading in a smile while Kerrick glowered. "I think he owes you an apology. Isn't that right, son?"

Kerrick growled something incomprehensible.

"Well, that's the best apology you'll get from him," Barnes said. "Anyway, you've met Doc too." He nodded toward the giant standing watch like a dark tower, arms crossed and wearing a stony expression. "Doesn't talk much, but very good at his job. All of his jobs, actually. Let's see, he's the first mate, navigator, cook, weapons master, and, oh, what am I forgetting?"

"Doctor." Doc's deep voice seemed to vibrate Bobby's bones.

"Oh, yes, of course," Barnes laughed. "And this lovely young lady is my granddaughter." He indicated the girl, and despite the possible danger of his situation, Bobby somehow found that he was relieved to finally have a reason to look at her. She stood with arms folded and weight shifted to one hip, pale blue eyes scanning him up and down. Her jaw worked like she was chewing something. One side of her glossy pink lips curved up the same time her brows arched. Bobby tried to read her demeanor, which seemed to mix the smile and frown expressions preprogrammed in Sentinel's legacy bots. His mind gave up all tasks, however, when she locked eyes with him.

"Bobs," LINC leaned in and whispered, "I'm detecting a spike in your heart rate. You all right?"

Bobby nodded, unable to form a coherent response.

For an instant, he thought he saw the girl's eyes flicker to LINC with a corrosive glance—an expression he recognized as he'd often done the same himself—but then her features changed back to that smile-frown. A *smirk*, he'd once heard the Archiver say while telling a story.

She stepped forward and offered a hand. "I'm Jen."

Bobby stared at her hand, unsure what this gesture meant. Did she want him to reciprocate? Logic screamed at him to refrain, that it might be a trap. But his stomach fluttered, a thousand tiny drones flitting about inside. A strange impulse to touch her overwhelmed his senses. With caution, he reached out and pushed his palm flat against hers.

"Don't shake hands on this planet, huh?" Jen asked, a full smile now playing on her soft lips. She wrapped her fingers around his hand and pumped it up and down before letting go. Then she stepped back and brushed a golden strand of hair behind her ear. "So? What's your name?"

"It's, uh, it's—my name's—" Bobby stuttered, scrambling to come up with his own name. What was it? "It's Bobs—Bobby—Robert," he finally choked out. "My name's Robert. LINC here calls me Bobby."

"Well, nice to meet you, Bobby," she said with another of those smirks.

"Good to meet you, son," Barnes added, reminding Bobby that other humans existed in the space. The other two, Kerrick and Doc, remained silent, however.

"Uh, why are you looking at me like that?" Jen said after a few seconds.

Bobby realized he hadn't replied, hadn't taken his gaze off her. To his surprise, his cheeks burned like he'd scrubbed up on an easy differential equation. Jen continued to chew whatever was in her mouth, waiting for his answer.

"I mean—I—I…." Bobby trailed when a big pink bubble ballooned from Jen's lips, then burst with a pop. He blinked.

"What's the matter, never seen gum before?" asked Jen.

Bobby shook his head.

"Oh." She sounded genuinely surprised. "Of course not. What am I thinking? Well, here, have some." From her pocket, she produced a little sliver of foil wrapping and tossed it to him.

Bobby turned it over in his hands. "But it's not feeding time."

"I'll take it." LINC snatched the foil and shoved it into his hinged maw. "To make sure it's not poisoned."

Jen shot the bot another dark look, but her face quickly shifted into a smile. "You're supposed to unwrap it first." She laughed, and Bobby was sure it was the most beautiful sound he'd ever heard.

"Mmm?" LINC spit out the wad of foil and extracted some pink, rubbery stuff from its center. He discarded it and popped the foil back into his mouth. "You're right, much better. Hey this is pretty good."

"Your bot's crazy." Jen flashed a grin that made Bobby's knees weak for some reason.

"Enough," Kerrick barked. "We didn't come to hand out candy to the locals. Our cloaking function gives out in sixteen hours, and then every bot on Sentinel will be on top of us." He leveled his gaze at Bobby. "Where's the weapon?"

Bobby frowned. "What?"

"Don't play dumb with me."

"I don't know what you're talking about," Bobby insisted. "What weapon?"

"The weapon that Gamma's using to tear apart the Federation. We know the plans are here on Sentinel."

"Federation?" Bobby tasted the word.

"The United Systems Federation," Kerrick enunciated each word with rapidly decaying patience. "The coalition of planets your bots are gonna wipe out with that weapon. We know the plans are here on Sentinel. If you're not on the bots' side, tell me where they are. Now."

"You're fighting Gamma?" Bobby took a step back, eyes wide. "He was right, you *are* here to steal our technology."

"Son," Barnes said in a soft tone. "The bots are trying to conquer our planets. You do know they're the bad guys, right?"

"Yeah, we thought they'd enslaved you or something," Jen added.

"Don't listen to her, Bobs." LINC munched on the wrapper. "Humans are dirty liars. They lure you in with tasty foil, then kill you."

Bobby's gaze flicked from human to human as he slowly backed away. "I don't know if this is some human trick or what, but I don't know how you got here, and I don't know what you're talking about."

"How *can* you guys talk, anyway?" LINC asked between munches.

"How can *we* talk?" Jen scrunched her nose. "How can *he* talk?" She jutted her chin at Bobby. "You take Common one-oh-one on this planet?"

Bobby froze, confused. Was she talking about his language lessons?

"Common one-oh-one was like twelve Programming cycles ago, lady," LINC scoffed. "You think we're stupid?"

"What's a Programming cycle?" Jen asked.

"It's how they test us to see if your dumb species is worth reviving, you ignorant scrub."

Jen narrowed her eyes as she processed this. "The bots? They're testing you?"

"Shut up, LINC," Bobby said through his teeth. "Stop telling the humans stuff."

"We're wasting time," Kerrick snapped. "Tell us where the weapon plans are, and we'll get you off this planet."

"I knew it, Bobs," LINC said. "They're going to kidnap us. You run. I'll hold 'em off."

Bobby raised his fists, preparing to barrel through Kerrick and Doc for the exit.

"Wait." The urgency in Barnes's tone made him pause. "I know this must be a lot for you to take in, but let us prove what we're saying. Jen, run the news clip on your comtab."

With another pop of gum, Jen pulled a small tablet from her pocket and tapped its display. In seconds, a hologram grew from its surface, showing a starscape dotted with small fighter ships battling a Sentinel cruiser. The shaky footage panned right until a hefty transport ship orbiting a bright green planet edged into view. The vessel detonated in a blinding explosion, flinging mangled shards back at the planet. A man's voice spoke over the scene.

"You're seeing a recorded holocam stream over the Artemis system, where a carrier ship full of refugees was just destroyed by a Sentinel Class C warship."

"That happened about one standard cycle ago," Barnes said, "Right before we crashed here. That carrier was full of injured civilians and the elderly. They were no threat to the bots."

Bobby shook his head in disbelief. "You're lying. Gamma said humans lie."

"What about the other humans on this planet?" asked Kerrick.

"There are no other humans."

"Oh yeah?" Kerrick sniffed. "Then where do you come from?"

Bobby gritted his teeth. "I don't know."

Jen paused the hologram. "Does that mean you're a robot?"

"Jen," Barnes chided.

She shrugged. "What? I'm just joking."

"I have a hard time believing you appeared out of thin air, kid." Kerrick cocked a brow. "What do the bots say about that?"

"I'm supposed to restart the human race," Bobby said.

"You were serious?" Kerrick barked with hollow laughter. "Restart the human race! With who, your bot here?"

"Cloning," Bobby spat. His cheeks burned again. Here he was, explaining how he was destined to restart the human race to a bunch of humans who were nothing like Gamma had described. Could they be telling the truth? Were there other humans out there? Human who hadn't fallen? He felt lightheaded, wavering in everything he'd always believed.

"That's enough, Kerrick." Barnes's rusty voice grew stern. In a gentler tone, he said to Bobby, "Son, it sounds like Gamma's been feeding you false information. He's been lying and killing since he was built."

"You know who built the bots?" Bobby threw out a hand to steady himself as adrenaline brought on a bout of vertigo.

"Sounds like you have a lot to learn. We'll take it slow. Why don't you sit down?" Barnes tapped a crate with his cane. "I can tell you everything I know. Then maybe you can tell us what you know. Together we'll figure this out."

The bay fell silent for his answer. Even Kerrick with his perpetual scowl kept quiet. Could they be telling the truth? This might be his only chance to learn where he came from. Besides, he'd get to see more of Jen. He watched the girl seat herself on a crate, popping another bubble and scrolling through some kind of feed on her comtab.

LINC whispered in his ear, "Ask if she has more gum. I think I lost the foil in my throat."

Bobby ignored him. He raised his chin at Barnes. "Okay. But I want to know everything." *Gather intelligence before planning a course of action*, he mentally recited Protocol. He knew listening to these humans was a risk, but it was a calculated one. At least, that's what he told himself.

Barnes seemed relieved at this. He gestured to the makeshift table, and Bobby cautiously walked over. LINC followed, circling his fists at a frowning Kerrick.

For the first time, Bobby fully took in his surroundings. The bay appeared to be the ship's main cargo hold, though it contained no freight save for the crates Barnes was using as impromptu furniture. In place of cargo, a mid-sized sloop-class ship dominated the bay's center. He scanned its sharp angles, trying to place its origin. It was definitely not Sentinel made.

Bobby eyed the sloop, the *Quasar*, and it finally clicked. "You didn't crash land."

"We disguised our coordinates as a distress signal," Barnes explained. "We're not exactly supposed to be here, if you didn't know."

"But how did you get through our planetary shield?"

"Sentinel cargo ships come and go all the time with shipments of corilum." Barnes gestured all around at the bay. "And this is a Sentinel cargo ship, isn't it?"

LINC snapped his fingers. "You hijacked this ship and used the access codes to get through the shield! Genius!"

Barnes chuckled. "Maybe your bot has some sense, after all."

"So that's the ship you used to steal this one?" Bobby indicated the *Quasar*.

Barnes's glassy eyes wavered for a split second, flashing something unfamiliar, then he nodded.

"So…." Bobby rubbed the back of his neck, connecting the pieces. "You're all with, what did you call it? The Federation?"

"The USF," Kerrick interjected before Barnes could answer. "Volunteered to retrieve the weapon plans and a chunk of corilum to power it. Now start talking."

Bobby bit his lip. "I—I don't know. I'm not sure I should."

"You that selfish, kid?" Kerrick snarled. "The longer you keep quiet, the more people die."

Bobby opened his mouth to retort, but nothing came out. Was he being selfish? He knew the fact he was asking himself that question meant he was beginning to believe these humans' story.

"Leave him alone," Jen said. "He doesn't know what's going on."

"We just told him what's going on," Kerrick growled.

"Mission is need-to-know," Kerrick replied. "We're here for the plans. That's all he needs to know."

Bobby narrowed his eyes. "We need to know a *lot* more if you want our help."

"Kerrick," Barnes reprimanded. "He's part of the mission now. We can trust him."

Kerrick gave his father a dangerous look, but Barnes paid no mind.

"Now." The old man cleared the game board off the table as Bobby eased himself onto the edge of a nearby crate. "Let's catch you up. Jen, can you connect to the *Quasar's* main server and look for a video on the founding of Sentinel?"

With a disinterested expression, Jen tapped at her comtab for a moment, then tossed the device on the table with a clatter. Another hologram expanded, displaying in stylized block letters the words *Federation Cadet Training Corps.*

The title disappeared, replaced by *Lesson 232.*

Lesson 232. Something about the number pricked the back of Bobby's mind, but before he could contemplate it the words evaporated, and a gray planet floated into view. A deep voice narrated the scene.

"Planet U-0124, first charted in the year one-twenty-two WE and later named Sentinel. It was long overlooked as a barren wasteland of rock unsuitable for terraforming."

The voice struck Bobby as familiar. While he tried to connect it with something, the image of the planet lingered, and the voice was replaced by a swell of brassy sound that coalesced into a striking tone, stirring something deep inside him.

"What's that noise?" he marveled as the sound fell.

"You mean the music?" Barnes asked.

"Music," Bobby tasted the word, allowing the harmonic notes to sink in.

"Beautiful, isn't it?" Barnes smiled.

Beautiful, Bobby thought, and glanced at Jen. She was busy twirling a strand of hair around a finger and staring off into the distance. When she looked up at him, he snapped his eyes back to the hologram, hoping she hadn't caught him staring again.

"It wasn't until researchers from the Helios system discovered vast quantities of a new type of ore that Planet U-0124 emerged as a significant world," the familiar voice narrated.

The image dissolved into a mountain range striped with veins of purple rock.

"The new ore was dubbed *corilum*, and its properties constituted an extremely potent power source that would change the course of human history."

A blocky ship settled on the planet's stony surface. Figures in exo-suits stepped out and scanned the environment with various devices.

"With enough energy in five grams to power a warp engine over multiple interstellar jumps, corilum quickly became one of the most precious commodities in the galaxy."

The scene changed to a deep quarry. Dozens of cargo ships hovered about, ascending and descending into the gaping hole.

"Thus, the history of corilum mining extends back as far as the founding of Sentinel."

The familiar voice.

The lesson number.

A shiver ran down Bobby's spine as the memory clicked.

"This is my history lesson!" he cried.

Jen raised a brow. "From your Programming, yeah?"

Bobby stared at the holo in disbelief. "Yeah," he managed.

"So you *are* a robot." She popped another bubble.

"Hush, Jen." Barnes leaned toward Bobby. "So the bots instruct you in history? And they showed you this?"

Bobby nodded and pumped his cybernetic fingers to stem a swell of anxiety. "I mean, sort of. This is the same holo. But different. Like it's all in a different order or something. And I've never seen some of this stuff." He pointed to the hologram which now depicted two men in white overcoats experimenting with shards of corilum in a lab.

"Because of its immense energetic potential," said the narrator, "researchers found that corilum could boost the processing power of supercomputers to a level previously unknown, finally allowing the safe re-development of advanced artificial intelligence after the Second AI War over a century before."

At the edge of Bobby's vision, Kerrick shifted his stance. He got the vague sense that the captain was watching him, but when he looked up, Kerrick's eyes were on the recording.

He refocused on the holo. Two researchers interacted with a primitive bot that reminded him of the legacy models like Six.

"The United Systems Federation," the narrator said, "commissioned the development of the first batch of AI soldiers since the War to counteract the growing threat of Fringe World Supremacists, whose many factions defy Galactic Law regarding AI and human cyberware. Doctors Richard Elif and Cordell Cane headed the endeavor, which was dubbed the 'Sentinel Project,' after their robotic soldiers' mission to stand guard against Fringe World threats." The scene centered on each of the men in turn as they made adjustments to the primitive bot. "Their team made quick advancements with the corilum, and soon their colony became a self-sustaining city." A high-speed clip showed Sentinel's barren landscape transform into clusters of factories, streets, and buildings.

Bobby's jaw dropped.

It was the same clip he'd seen from his lesson before his Programming final.

Lines of tension etched his forehead as a sickening question squeezed his brain. Had the Programmers scrambled the contents of this holo, repackaged it with new narration to form a false narrative? Was it true that humans hadn't actually fallen after the Second AI War? Had their cyberware not driven them insane? The humans before him seemed to prove these facts by their mere presence.

"How is this possible?" he whispered.

"Vewy intwesting," LINC said around a finger he was using to dislodge the foil from his throat.

"As the project progressed," the narrator continued, "Doctor Elif and Doctor Cane harnessed corilum's unique makeup to develop new weapons to help defend the USF against Fringe Supremacist factions."

A large ship, familiar in shape, floated into the image. Bobby concluded it must be a forerunner of Sentinel's modern battle cruiser. A flank of small fighters swooped in to attack, but a gargantuan purple photon blast from the cruiser's cannons scattered them.

"A new era of peace pervaded. For fourteen years, researchers worked on the code for advanced artificial sentience, using corilum as an energy source to replace crucial infrastructure lost in the

Second AI War. Reports from Doctor Elif confirmed that with their newest robotic model, they were on the verge of a breakthrough." The shot changed to a close up of Elif and Cane working on a bot with an angular face.

Bobby's blood froze.

"The Gamma model proved a significant leap forward in reinventing advanced artificial intelligence."

The bot shook hands with the Elif and Cane, its alloy features twisting into a smile to match the doctors'.

"Elif's final report stated that the Gamma model was Sentinel's first Tier Three bot. A thinking machine with a form of consciousness akin to the previous century's AI, but compliant with the ban on total sentience. The researchers were changing the course of history. But not in the way they intended."

With a percussive thrum, the hologram cut to black.

"In the year one-twenty-four WE, communication with Sentinel went dark." The scene faded up to a quiet image of the gray planet from space. "An impenetrable shield enveloped Sentinel's orbit, and all attempts to enter the upper atmosphere were met with hostility."

The holo cut to a scene of Sentinel's orbiting defense cannons blasting a Federation fleet into debris.

"New firepower emerged from the lost world—" An enormous ship floated into view, a modern Sentinel battle cruiser. The warship stretched across the starry backdrop, firing photon blasts at oncoming Federation ships. "—and obliterated the USF forces."

Fighter vessels swarmed the battle cruiser, only to explode under photon volleys in quick bursts of fire.

"Outmatched by the mysterious new fleet, the USF was forced to retreat."

The shot changed to a distant blue point set among glittering stars.

Bobby sucked in a breath. "That's where humans come from."

"The remaining Earth territories fell to Sentinel's superpowered forces," the narrator said. "Led by Elif and Cane's last creation,

Gamma. To this day, no intel of Sentinel's terrestrial condition or what became of the research team has surfaced. Federation-led reconnaissance—"

Barnes shut off the hologram. "The rest is USF recruiting information."

Bobby ran a hand through his hair, trying to process all of this. "But what happened? How did Gamma overthrow the research team? And how did I get here?"

"I said I would tell you how the bots were built," Barnes said. "It would seem your existence is still somewhat of a mystery."

"How do I know you're telling the truth?" Bobby demanded, louder than he'd expected. "Why should I believe all this?"

Barnes waved a gentle hand. "That's not the end of the story. I served in the USF for forty years, and I led the Sentinel Reclamation division. Let me show you a classified report."

From his pocket, the old man produced a tiny, external drive which he plugged into a slot on Jen's comtab. Another hologram expanded, depicting text in green block letters. Barnes spun the comtab around until the text faced Bobby. "Read it."

Bobby scanned the green lines, lips moving silently with each word.

Confirmed. Cane reprogrammed Gamma. He's taken control of Sentinel and killed our team. Please advise.

He read it two more times before turning to Barnes. "What does this mean?"

"Elif's last transmission," Barnes answered. "It means Cordell Cane was leaking Sentinel technology to the Fringe Supremacists. Those factions on the fringes of the galaxy." He let out an indignant huff. "He reprogrammed the Tier Three bot to take control of the city. We advised Elif to terminate Cane immediately, but we never heard back from him. A month later our fleet gets wiped out by that new monster cannon on the Sentinel cruiser, and new super-intelligent bots captured Earth. That was sixteen standard years ago."

Bobby stiffened. "When I was born."

Barnes nodded, wrinkles deepening in thought. "Seems you *are* tied to this mystery."

"But... what about the humans that came before me?" His voice sounded distant to his ears, as if someone else was speaking, was asking for the final answers that would close the loops in a story with a horrifying conclusion. "The other humans—the other test subjects."

"Yeah," LINC said, seeming to pick up what he was trying to say. "Are you telling us we're *not* the last in a long line of experiments to restart the human race?"

The crease on Barnes's forehead deepened. He squeezed Bobby's knuckles. "Son, it sounds like you've already figured it out." He took a breath. "The human race is still alive."

The bay seemed to spin around Bobby. He gripped the edge of the table to steady himself, to anchor against a reality that was now shifting all around him. Moments of his life, pieces he'd once thought so solid, seemed to break apart, rearrange themselves into a confusing sequence of events.

Barnes must have noticed his distress, as he laid a gentle hand on Bobby's knuckles. The effect grounded him, brought him back to the bay, back to reality. But a reality profoundly different than the one he'd experienced just minutes ago. Like an operating system resolving a freak glitch, his memories repositioned back to a logical sequence, his life reconstructed. Only now, with added data. New meaning to everything he'd ever experienced.

"How is this possible?" Bobby whispered. "How can humans still be alive."

"Each minute you waste is a chance for Gamma to wipe us out," Kerrick said.

Jen straightened. "We need your help, Bobby."

The way she said his name, pleading, urgent, gave Bobby the strength to look up at her. Disinterest had given way to something fierce shining in her pale blue eyes.

"If we can find the plans to that weapon, it will even the odds," Barnes said. "That's why we need you to tell us what you know."

He dragged his gaze away from Jen, glanced at Barnes, then at Kerrick and Doc, at their expressions of stone.

No.

Something deep inside lashed out at this new reality.

They were the invaders. *They* were the liars. Not Gamma. Not the Programmers.

Gamma believed Bobby could become the Prime Human. The Programmers tested him to make him an exemplary human. Even Mother, with her discipline settings at maximum, had his best interests in mind.

"No!" Bobby knocked Barnes's wrinkled hand away and sprang to his feet. "I don't believe this. I don't believe any of this. You're all lying." Breaths came rapid, shallow.

"Son, you're hyperventilating." Barnes pushed himself up and reached for Bobby.

"No," Bobby cried through ragged gasps. Before he knew it, he was running out of the bay and through the ship's passageways.

"Get back here," Kerrick shouted.

"Run, Bobs!" LINC called over the sounds of a struggle. "I'll take care of him!"

The walls blurred and somehow dissolved into hot night air. He found himself in front of the lake shimmering with the light of two moons.

He heaved lungfuls of oxygen until his senses crept back. Then his legs gave way, and he collapsed on the soft bank, tears streaming down his cheeks. Whatever fire inside him had lashed out at the humans' story, he knew deeper down it was nothing more than the dying sparks of a past life set ablaze by a new reality. The evidence was overwhelming. Real humans had presented themselves. Unlike any of the stories he'd been told.

"I know this is a lot for you to take in," Barnes's rusty voice came up behind him. With a grunt, the old man seated himself to

Bobby's right and gazed at the moonlit water. He placed a hand on Bobby's shoulder again, but this time Bobby didn't fight it.

"Everything's wrong," Bobby sobbed. "Everything was a lie." A fresh wave of tears came, and Barnes's comforting grip tightened.

Bobby sensed someone else sit on his left. Through blurry vision, he saw Jen's golden hair illuminated in the soft glow cast by the ship's entrance. She leaned back on outstretched arms. Her concerned expression gave way to a reassuring smile. And though she didn't say anything, like Barnes's comforting touch, he found it soothing.

"I can't imagine what it must have been like to grow up without another human around," Barnes said. "I'm sure it was lonely."

Bobby sniffed. "I don't know what that means."

"Lonely? It means, well, er—" Barnes broke off, then said, "Well, I'll show you. Jen, will you get my compass, please?"

Jen blew a bubble and let it pop, then got to her feet. She disappeared inside the ship, and returned a moment later with a small device. Seating herself again, she reached across Bobby to hand it to her grandfather. Bobby wasn't sure why his cheeks burned at her closeness, but he tried to shake away their heat as Barnes pushed a circular device into his hands.

"This," the old man said, "is a ceremonial Naval compass."

Bobby blinked away his tears and studied the compass, looking for a power switch.

"You won't find a holo display in this one." Barnes chuckled. "No, sir, this is the real thing."

Bobby held the thing closer to his face. In the moonlight, he could just make out a flat needle set in an etched face beneath a plastiglass covering. It looked just like the holographic versions in his atmospheric flight simulations, only constructed with primitive, analog materials.

"Long before the Warp Era, humans sailed on the sea." A twinkle danced in Barnes's eye as the old man gazed over the moonlit water.

Bobby rotated the compass, watching the needle bounce back to its original position. "Sea?"

"It's a large body of water. Like this lake here, only bigger."

"Why were they in a big lake?"

Barnes laughed. "They sailed on ships. Wooden ships that floated on the water. And they used nothing but the stars and compass to get home to their families." The old man reached over and tapped the compass.

The plastiglass covering turned opaque with a picture. Bobby inspected it, an image of Barnes, surrounded by Jen, Kerrick, Doc, and another man he didn't recognize.

"That's my family." Barnes smiled. "And when I'm not with them, I get lonely. Do you see?"

At their smiles, warmth kindled deep inside Bobby's chest, like when the Archiver had hugged him and told him he would miss him. Lonely. He hadn't been able to describe it, but that's how he'd felt ever since the Archiver had been destroyed. He wiped his cheeks. "I think so."

"Many families are dying," said Barnes. "We really need your help. But I'm not going to force you."

Bobby thought about the tribunal tomorrow. About how he'd have to upload into the Tether. He'd come here to capture these humans and deliver them to the Programmers. He'd never expected to learn that he'd been deceived all these years.

"You must do what you feel is right," Barnes continued.

Bobby sat in silence, rubbing his thumb over the picture of Barnes and his family.

"What I feel is right," he muttered. "How can a feeling be based on logic?"

"Sometimes the deepest desires of your heart guide you when logic can't." Barnes pointed to the compass. "Why don't you hang on to that for me? It's often guided me." He leaned forward and smiled. "Maybe it will remind you to choose your own direction."

You always have a choice. Bobby remembered the Archiver's message.

"But you should choose us 'cause we'll die if you don't," Jen said.

"Jen," Barnes scolded.

Choose your own direction. Bobby rolled Barnes's words around his head. He tapped the compass, and the picture disappeared to show the needle beneath. To his surprise, he noticed it pointed to Jen. *Coincidence*, came the automatic reaction from the part of his brain so well-practiced in logic. But a second response rose up from another, deeper part of him. As it took a familiar shape, he remembered how often he'd shoved it down, doused its warm edges with cold reasoning. But this time, he allowed it grow, to illuminate the recesses of his mind and reignite desires that felt so criminal he'd made sure to destroy them long ago. But as he gazed at Jen, her golden hair so like Zel's from the Archiver's holopod, he finally realized what that story meant to him. *Freedom.* She'd escaped her tower. Had escaped the structure that closed her in, defined her.

She was free.

And though he'd scoffed at the idea of fate or destiny or whatever the Archiver had called it in that story, he couldn't help but wonder—was this a sign? Could Jen help him escape his own tower?

If other humans like her were out there in the galaxy, and he'd been lied to his whole life, why should he stay on this planet?

Giving the compass needle one last look, he let out a cleansing sigh. Something inside him shifted, and the vise around his chest loosened.

"Okay," he said. "I'll help you."

Barnes clapped his hands. "Wonderful to hear, son."

Even Jen looked pleased, if not just mostly relieved.

Bobby thought he could stare at her smile all day. *Scrub.* How long *had* he been staring? Cheeks burning again, he tore his gaze from her and tried to focus on the decision he'd just made. "I don't know anything about weapon plans," he admitted. "But I do know a place that might have what you're looking for."

He pointed to the domed Depository rising above the treetops in the distance.

<!013: Indexing New Information>

"THAT BUILDING OVER there." The moon glinted off Bobby's alloy finger pointing at the domed structure. "The Depository. I've heard it contains a lot of information."

Barnes squinted across the lake in the direction indicated.

"You've never been there?" Jen asked.

Bobby shook his head. "It's out of my Utility Zone."

She raised her brows. "Your what?"

"I've seen that building in old holos," Barnes said, shuffling back to them. "If I recall correctly, it housed a research database for the planet. How do we get there?"

"We'll need LINC's cloaking function." Bobby looked around. "Where is he?"

"Your bot and my uncle were fighting when I left," Jen said.

A crash echoed from inside the ship. They all turned to see LINC sprint out onto the bank carrying a weathered boot in his hand.

"I've dismembered the aggressor," he announced, waving the boot in the air. "A prize for you." He held it out to Bobby. "The captain's foot."

"LINC, that's a shoe." Bobby pointed at his feet. "I wear them too."

LINC shook the boot, listening for something inside to rattle.

Something clattered from the ship, and Kerrick stumbled out, followed by Doc's steady stride.

Kerrick pointed at LINC. "You."

LINC turned the boot over and shook it, but nothing came out. "Whoops." He backpedaled as Kerrick marched unevenly toward him on one booted foot.

"Easy there." Barnes blocked Kerrick's progress with his cane. "Bobby here has agreed to help us."

Kerrick halted, glancing at Bobby with a cocked brow. "Oh yeah? What changed your mind?"

"Never mind that," Barnes said. "He's going to take us to Sentinel's database. But we need his bot to get there."

"Figures," Kerrick snorted. "But he's scrap unless I get my boot back."

"Give it back, LINC," Bobby said.

"Fine, but he should be nicer if he wants us to give him a tour of Sentinel." LINC kept a wary eye on the captain as he slowly extended the boot out to Kerrick. The captain snatched it with a grunt.

"Good." Barnes gave an approving nod. "You all should get moving."

"About time," Kerrick grumbled. He clutched his boot and strode back up the entrance ramp. "Doc, grab our guns. We roll out in five." Doc nodded and followed the captain inside.

Bobby turned to Barnes. "You're coming with us, right?"

"I'm afraid I'd just slow you down." Barnes tapped his right hip with the cane's handle. "Besides, someone needs to stay with the ship, right?"

"Oh." Bobby thumbed the compass, bringing up the picture of Barnes's family. He imagined himself in the middle of the group. A pit formed in his stomach at the thought of leaving the old man behind.

Seeming to read his thoughts, Barnes clapped him on the shoulder. "Don't worry. I'll be here when you get back. And afterward, you'll have a home here with us if you want it." He smiled.

"Really?" Bobby's heart warmed. A home? With other humans? On impulse, he hugged Barnes, just like the Archiver had hugged him. No sooner had he wrapped his arms around the old man than he realized how foolish he must be acting. Cheeks flushing, he attempted to let go but was surprised to find himself locked in Barnes's own warm embrace.

"You're not alone anymore." Barnes patted his back.

Bobby had to blink to hold back tears. "Thank you."

"Ugh, get a room," Jen said, scrolling through her comtab feed.

"I'm confused," LINC added. "Is he attacking you?"

Barnes patted Bobby on the back before releasing him.

Bobby smiled, awash in a powerful warmth he'd never experienced before.

"Wow, your serotonin levels are skyrocketing." LINC's eyes scanned Bobby with his blue laser. "I want to try." The bot clamped his metal arms around Jen.

"Uh, I'm good, thanks." Jen pushed LINC away.

"All right, group hug time is over." Kerrick, both boots on again, emerged from the ship with three blasters. He tossed one to Jen, shoved another in his hip holster, and gripped the third.

Doc appeared bearing a huge blaster cannon Bobby was sure must have weighed a thousand kilograms. But the giant swung it about like it was a tiny pistol.

"Where's my gun?" Bobby asked, remembering his blaster Kerrick had confiscated.

"On the ship." Kerrick checked his weapon's plasma chamber.

Bobby frowned. "You still don't trust me."

"Not when you aim firearms at my crew." He jerked his chin at Jen.

"It was set to stun."

"Reason enough not to give you one. Jen will cover you if we get in a sticky situation."

Bobby cast an uncertain glance at Jen, who was blowing another bubble. When she noticed him staring, she raised a brow, and said through a mouthful of bubble, "Oh, you want to see?" She spat the bubble into the air and blasted it with a single shot from her gun.

"Jen!" Kerrick barked. "Knock it off. We don't need a swarm of bots finding us."

Jen shrugged and unwrapped another piece of gum, handing the foil to an eager LINC.

"All right, let's move." Kerrick pointed to Bobby. "You and your bot are up."

The command snapped Bobby from the trance he'd fallen in by watching Jen.

"Okay," he said. "LINC, activate your cloaking function."

"You got it." The bot hammered his chest until a *ding* sounded. "Activated."

"Take care of my granddaughter." Barnes winked at Bobby.

Bobby stared at the gun in Jen's obviously-capable hand. "Uh, yeah sure."

"Lead the way," Kerrick said.

Bobby nodded and with a last glance at Barnes, led his new acquaintances toward the Depository.

```
<o:!0110101-000Z><01110000></x:01011>
<o:010011100/01>
<
```

As the Depository loomed larger, Bobby's stomach twisted into knots. A dark new meaning now tinged the din of factory work floating through the empty streets. No longer was it the sound of progress for a noble city waging a righteous war against Fallen humanity. That facade had been stripped away a mere twenty minutes ago. Now, as Bobby led the group through the city's industrial grid, the clang of machinery and drone of assembly work carried with it images of bots conquering distant worlds, terrorizing innocent humans. Good humans. Like Barnes. It was almost more than Bobby could bear. And yet, like shrapnel lodged in his heart from an old wound, part of him still doubted. For sixteen years he'd believed the bots, done his Programming, served the greater good for the redemption of the human race. And now he was supposed to believe all of it was a lie?

He looked back at the group. At Kerrick gripping his blaster, scanning every nook and alcove along the path. At Jen making faces while snapping photos of herself with her comtab. At Doc bringing up the rear with his steady gait.

Was he doing the right thing?

In a short while the Depository would either prove or disprove their story.

He sighed.

"You okay, Bobs?" LINC asked, plodding along at his side. "Your heart rate is pretty high."

"Yeah, why are you so bummed?" Jen joined them, eyes glued to her comtab.

"Hmm, it's getting faster," LINC said.

"Shut up, LINC," Bobby said through clenched teeth.

"Jen," Kerrick said, "you're supposed to be taking reconnaissance pictures."

"What do you think I'm doing?" Jen held her comtab at arm's length, centering the image of her and Bobby on the screen. She draped an arm around his shoulders. "Smile."

At her touch, the servos in Bobby's left arm locked up. Every muscle in his upper body went rigid.

"I said smile, not look terrified."

Bobby bared his teeth in an unsuccessful attempt to match Jen's perfect smile as she snapped the picture.

"Wow." She laughed, studying the result. "You're terrible at that." She tapped at a keyboard on the screen. "Infiltrating city of Sentinel," she said, labeling the picture. "This one goes in the album."

"Jen," Kerrick snapped. "Pay attention."

"Fine," she sighed, turning her comtab on the surrounding factories.

LINC leaned in and whispered to Bobby, "You can breathe now."

Bobby released a captive breath.

```
<o:!0110101-000Z><01110000></x:01011>
<o:010011100/01>
<
```

"PLEASE TELL ME you remembered your slicing tool," Kerrick said.

They huddled in a recess of the towering Depository walls. The control panel next to the locked door barred their entry.

"It's the reason you brought me, right?" Jen replied. From a satchel, she whipped out a small device that reminded Bobby of a screwdriver. "And it's called a decryptor."

She jammed the decryptor into the panel's slot and tapped the device's display. "All right. Should take just a sec." She leaned against the wall and inspected her nails.

Bobby pumped his cybernetic fingers to relieve the anxiety welling up inside. He stepped outside the recess and looked up at the Depository's curved walls. Just yesterday, the idea of being anywhere near this building would have seemed ridiculous. But one scrubbing crazy decision had changed his whole view of reality. And now in a few minutes, he would be on the other side of that door, deep in the midst of Sentinel's secrets.

"Well?" Kerrick prodded after a long moment.

Jen frowned, scrolling through the decryptor's display. "Um, this might be a little harder than I thought."

"What's the problem?" Kerrick sidled up to the control panel.

Jen bit her lip. "This encryption is crazy complicated. It's defending all the breach protocols I wrote. I've never seen anything like it."

"Meaning what?" Kerrick's voice was a low growl.

Jen fidgeted with her hair. "I've never seen encryption this advanced. I don't know how to get in."

"Fine, we'll blast it." Kerrick leveled his gun at the door.

"Not a good idea," Doc's voice rumbled. He pointed to the door, then traced his finger in a backward arc.

"Reflector shields." Jen pressed her lips and patted Doc's massive arm. "Good call."

"Great." Kerrick lowered his blaster and balled his other fist. He looked like he wanted to punch something. "Any ideas, kid?"

Bobby rubbed his chin, mind racing. A glance at Jen's decryptor sparked a thought. He froze and gazed at his finger. He could plug into the panel with it. But would it work outside his Utility Zone? With a bitter pang, he realized if Barnes's story was true, if those holo clips were true, Utility Zones might be another part of the bots' fabrication.

"Let me try something." Pushing away the painful thought, he tapped at his forearm's display. "LINC, can I still use my diagnostic jack?"

"I got your basic functions back online," the bot replied, leaning over and pointing to a set of icons. "They're lacking my particular brand of personality, though."

"I just need it to function." Bobby selected an icon, and the diagnostic prong telescoped out of his index finger. He pulled the decryptor out and handed it to Jen, then stuck his finger into the control panel's slot.

Jen leaned over his shoulder to watch the readouts on his arm's vidscreen.

"Wow," she whispered.

The warmth of her body tangled with his, notes of some sweet scent shaking out of her hair. His gaze traced her oval face, the line of her nose, the curve of her cheeks, both dusted with light freckles. Brows knitted in concentration, she moved closer to inspect his arm, reaching out as if to touch his synthetic fingers. His cybernetic neurons fluttered, anticipating her touch, but at the last second, she looked up at him and hastily withdrew her hand.

"Sorry, didn't mean to be all up in your space," she said, making a show of folding her arms. "I've just never seen anything like this. So, what now?"

"Now?" Transfixed by the shine of her pale blue eyes, every thought dumped out of his brain. When he noticed she was looking at him, expecting an answer, he fought to gather them back. "Uh, well, if the computer recognizes my arm as Sentinel-based tech, I might be able to find a way around the entry code." He was surprised at his coherent response and delighted when Jen looked impressed.

"So, this thing has a computer in it too?" She traced a finger along his plastifiber bicep like she'd forgotten all about personal space. "Have you always had it?"

"As far back as I can remember," he replied, trying to keep his voice smooth against the battering ram inside his chest.

"It helps me lift warp engine cores in the factory." On impulse, he flexed his bicep under her finger. *What the scrub am I doing?*

She smirked, and something flashed in her eyes that Bobby couldn't quite read. Then she withdrew her finger and leaned against the wall, suddenly more interested in her comtab than his arm. Out of the corner of his vision, he saw Kerrick roll his eyes and Doc's normally impassive face tug with a smile.

His cheeks burned again—which was happening a lot, lately—like he'd missed some sort of human social cue. But before he could wonder at this, the control panel's display blinked, and a block of text popped up reading: *Access Granted.*

With a chime, the door panels retreated, letting out a cool rush of air.

"How did you do that?" Jen demanded, pushing herself off the wall and staring at Bobby's finger with a frown. "It gave you access just like that?"

Bobby unplugged his finger and held it up in astonishment. "I-I don't know. I guess it read an access code in my arm? I figured it would bring up a menu or something."

Beside him, Kerrick and Doc exchanged a brief glance.

"So we didn't need this at all?" She pulled the decryptor from her satchel. "Great. Glad I couldn't even do my one job on the slag mission." She cursed with a word Bobby had never heard, then threw the device onto the pavement. "Why did I even program this thing?"

"Jen," Kerrick barked. "Knock it off." He scooped up the decryptor. "We might need this later." He waved it in front of her, then turned it over to assess the damage.

"Why?" Jen's face was flushing red. "It's a piece of junk."

Bobby held his breath, unsure what had brought on this sudden change in her.

"Cut it out," Kerrick said. "The cyborg got us in, that's all that matters."

Cyborg? Bobby found the word nicked him like the edge of a plasma sword.

"Let's go, we're on a time crunch." Kerrick ducked through the door.

Doc followed, blaster cannon at the ready. Jen went next, shooting the control panel a furious glance before disappearing inside.

"What was all that about?" LINC said, fists stuck on his hips.

"Emotional outburst," Bobby muttered, remembering how many times Programmer Alpha had accused him of the same. He shook his head. Jen's reaction must have served some purpose, even if it eluded him at the moment.

"You having second thoughts?" LINC asked when Bobby didn't follow him to the door.

Bobby stared at the entrance, replaying Jen's outburst in his mind. It didn't mean the bots were telling the truth, that humans couldn't control their emotions. Right? Humans weren't only *sometimes* mindless, were they? What if these were some kind of humans that had only partially fallen? Removed their cyberware but still prone to madness?

"Bobs?" LINC prodded.

Bobby swallowed a knot in his throat. He'd know the truth soon enough. All he had to do was step through this door. What was inside would confirm if the bots had lied to him.

"Let's go." He marched through the entrance, and his eyes went wide at what he saw.

```
<o:!0110101-000Z><01110000></x:01011>
<o:010011100/01>
<
```

BOBBY FOUND HIMSELF in an enormous chamber tinged in dim blue lights. Rows of towering shelves marched along either side of a wide aisle leading farther into the Depository. Vidscreens set into each shelf designated different sections with blocky text.

Mining Operations.

Corilum Experimentation.

City Planning.

Holopods lined each shelf. Bobby concluded that they must be storing copies of data in case Sentinel's computing grid ever crashed. And yet from what he knew, the grid didn't even contain some of this information. Why else would the Hovel have needed to request a copy of LINC's program from the Depository? So far, it seemed Barnes's story was checking out.

"Come on, kid," Kerrick's voice echoed. The captain was waiting with the others some distance down the center aisle. Bobby jogged to catch up with them. "Your bot says the area's clear. But I don't trust it."

LINC crossed his arms. "Maybe you'd like to do a sweep with *your* scanners then?"

"Doesn't make sense to leave this place unguarded."

"I mean, it's not like they're expecting a bunch of humans to break in," Jen said, taking pictures of the chamber. She'd seemed to calm down and was back to sneaking pictures of herself in different poses.

Kerrick grunted. "Stay in range of the cloaking function."

"Well, look who needs me," LINC humphed.

"How are we going to find the weapon plans in all this?" asked Bobby, counting the rows of shelves.

"It's like one of those old libraries from the pre-Warp Era," Jen said. "But like a really creepy one run by robots."

"Old Federation schematics show a data bank on the far side." Kerrick pointed. "Let's hope they're accurate."

With that, the captain took the lead. Bobby followed next to Jen, his head swiveling between signs on the shelves.

Terrestrial Samples.

Compositional Studies.

Star Charts.

Disappointment mounted with each passing row. Where was the section that might contain information about where he came from? They passed the last shelf, and he'd almost given up hope until Kerrick led them through an archway at the end.

They came into a much smaller chamber with its own racks of data. He scanned the signs.

Sentinel Records.

Artificial Intelligence Development.

Robotics and Neural Architecture.

Bobby read the last one and gasped.

Cybernetic Human Amalgamation.

He sprinted toward the shelf.

"Bobby, stay close," Kerrick snapped.

But Bobby barely heard him. He skidded to a halt in front of the shelf. It was empty save for a single row of holopods. Bobby fumbled with the devices, snatching them off the shelf to search each one for an inscription. In his haste, he knocked over a pod and sent it clattering to the floor. The drive activated with a whir, and a hologram bloomed above its surface, expanding between the shelves.

Kerrick cursed as the group pressed around, but Bobby's eyes were glued to the hologram now playing.

Without a holoprojector, the image fuzzed, but he could still make out a man wearing a white coat and black, elbow-length silicone gloves. He looked similar to the researchers in the hologram Barnes had played, but he was impossible to recognize because of the filtration mask that covered his face. Not unlike the berserkers' masks in the Human Killer Sim, Bobby realized with a sinking feeling.

The researcher approached a squat, circular glass tank filled with cloudy blue liquid. He twisted and removed the tank's metallic cap, then set it on a nearby table before plunging his gloved hands into the tank. Bobby's stomach knotted as the researcher pulled a squirming infant out of the dark pool. What was he going to do with it? A breathing apparatus on the infant's mouth dulled the baby's faint cry. From the angle, it was impossible to tell male or female. The researcher pressed the dripping child into the toweled grasp of a primitive humanoid bot. The scene cut to a close up of the baby, now wrapped in a blanket and lying on a cushioned observation tray.

"Is that me?" Bobby breathed.

The image panned the length of the baby. A researcher's gloved hands appeared in the frame, unwrapping the infant's blanket, revealing the lower body. Bobby's heart stopped. The cloth around the baby's hips was pinned together on one side.

The infant was missing its right leg.

"Guess not," LINC said.

The holo cut to the infant lying on the table, unconscious, as another researcher attached a crude cybernetic leg to its right hip.

In the next scene, the child was awake and crying. It lay on its back, thrashing at the air, kicking its new synthetic limb. Bobby held up his cybernetic arm and pumped his fingers, listening to the quiet whine of motors.

"Was I made in a lab?" he whispered.

"We're running out of time." Kerrick stooped and clicked the pod's switch, causing the hologram to evaporate.

"But I have to know," Bobby cried, lunging for the device.

"Later." Kerrick snatched the pod before he could reach it. "We have to find the plans first. And I think we just found the database." He pressed the pod into Jen's hands as he brushed past, striding toward a wide computer console peeking out from behind the last row of shelves.

Bobby's heart raced, faster than ever. Spots punctured his vision. He was sure he might pass out any second.

"It's true," he breathed. "It's all true. Barnes was right."

"I think you're right, Bobs." LINC placed a hand on Bobby's shoulder.

"I'm not scrubbed, right?" A green spot from the holo's light lingered in his sight. "The bots said they were the ones who started the human revival experiment, but those were *humans* who attached that baby's leg, right?"

LINC's grip tightened. "No way around it. The bots lied."

Bobby steadied himself against the shelf, truth washing over him in a disorienting wave. He turned to Jen, eyeing the pod in her hand. "I need to know where I came from."

Jen's gaze softened for a beat, then her jaw set with determination. "Come on, we'll take all of them and watch them later." She slipped the holopod into her satchel and began ripping the rest off the shelf. "Help me."

Bobby, still dizzy, seized as many as he could, stowing them with the rest Jen had grabbed.

"Congratulations." She smirked, holding out the satchel. "You get to carry the bag."

Bobby snatched the strap and slung it over his cybernetic shoulder, hugging the bag close.

"Jen," Kerrick called. "Get over here."

Bobby followed Jen as she hurried to join Kerrick and Doc at the console. LINC sauntered up behind, already spouting off advice about how to best navigate the computer system.

"I can't navigate anything," Kerrick snarled, "if I can't even get in the system."

Jen tapped at the console's main vidscreen before shaking her head. The look of fury had returned.

"Bobby, you wanna have another crack at this?" she said, her tone corrosive.

"I'm not even sure what I did last time." Bobby gave a helpless shrug. Even as his shoulders fell, a blue laser fan beamed from a lens on the console's surface, scanning Bobby's synthetic arm. The laser faded, and a chime rang.

"We're in," Kerrick exclaimed.

Jen shook her head in annoyance. "Whatever."

"How's that possible?" Bobby stared at his hand.

A red light on the console flickered in time with a rapid *beep* as Kerrick navigated the menus.

"What is that?" Bobby asked.

Jen's eyes widened. "An alarm."

"Uh-oh." LINC's lensed eyes twitched as he processed data. "I'm detecting multiple bots converging on our location."

"Extraction plan," Kerrick said, gaze fixed on the screen. "We get the plans, then leave through there." He pointed to a sliding door on the right wall.

"But your cloaking function's on," Bobby said to LINC. "They won't be able to see us, right?"

"I don't know." LINC shrugged.

"What do you mean you don't know?" Bobby cried.

"Tier One bots can't see us. As long as they're not—" A clang echoed at the entrance, and a sleek bot brandishing a gun sprinted into the chamber. "—security bots," LINC finished.

"Doc!" Kerrick called without looking up.

Doc leveled his cannon at the oncoming bot and fired a blinding shot. The security bot exploded in a burst of shrapnel.

"Good shot, Doc," Jen cried.

"More incoming," LINC said.

"I need more time," Kerrick shouted. "This database is massive."

"LINC, can you find the plans?" Bobby asked, nerves buzzing with panic.

"No prob, Bobs." LINC saluted, then elbowed Kerrick out of the way. "See, you're going through the wrong menu. Here." He tapped an icon. Another alarm sounded, clashing with the first. "Whoops."

"Idiot." Kerrick shoved the bot aside. "Spread out and keep me covered!"

Doc immediately veered across the aisle to cover the captain's right side, taking up position behind the last row of shelves with LINC in tow behind his massive frame. Bobby broke left with Jen to hide behind the opposite shelf. He dropped into a crouch at her side as she peered out toward the entrance, blaster raised. Outside, the clatter of running feet grew loud enough to match his pounding heart.

"Come on, come on, come on," Kerrick yelled from the console. "Got it!"

A blast of plasma fire drowned out his words. Kerrick ducked as a flurry of red bolts engulfed him.

"No!" Jen cried as her uncle disappeared in the storm.

Bobby tensed, expecting to see Kerrick's dead body hit the floor. But the captain didn't fall. Bobby squinted against the barrage to see Doc shielding Kerrick with a translucent yellow barrier. Somehow, the giant had moved in the blink of an eye and unsheathed some sort of force field to protect the captain. The bots advanced in formation, their shots converging onto the shield with increasing intensity.

"Jen," Bobby shouted. "Shoot!"

But Jen had frozen, breath coming in shallow gasps, eyes unfocused. He knew that look. She was in shock. He'd experienced it his first time in the Human Killer Simulation. Cursing, he pried the blaster from her stiff hand. Without LINC to guide his motors, he had to manually aim. But the narrow aisle made the oncoming bots easy targets. He squeezed off multiple rounds, blasting them to pieces.

"Get 'em, Bobs!" LINC cried over the noise.

For a split second, Bobby stiffened with the implications of what he'd just done. He'd attacked and destroyed bots. Actual Sentinel bots. Treason. Another heartbeat and the thought vanished as more poured into the chamber. He fired another volley.

Doc joined the assault, peeking over the shield with a round of cannon fire.

"Did you get it?" Bobby called to Kerrick as he ducked back behind the shelf.

"No," Kerrick shouted, leaning out from the shield to fire his own shots into the mix. "Says it needs an authorized carrier. Wanna try that arm again?"

"Fine." Bobby glanced at Jen. She stared right through him as if seeing the other side of the galaxy.

Kerrick unhooked a small orb from his belt. "On my mark, we switch places."

Bobby pushed Jen farther into cover, then spun about, shifting into a sprinting stance.

"Mark!" Kerrick lobbed the orb at the bots and ran toward Bobby as a deafening explosion rattled the shelves.

Bobby took off, covering his face from the intense heat of the blast, and slid behind Doc's shield.

"You have a few seconds before more arrive," LINC warned.

Bobby pushed himself up onto the console, scanning the text box on the computer's display.

Authorized carrier needed to transfer files.

He waved his arm in wild motions, trying to activate the download. When nothing happened, he tapped his arm's vidscreen and stuck his finger's prong into a slot. He waited, unsure what to do next. After what seemed an eternity, the computer chimed over the beeping and buzzing alarms, and an empty loading bar popped up on the display.

"I think it's working," Bobby cried.

"Might want to hurry, Bobs," LINC called.

Bobby risked a glance at the entrance, tinted yellow through the shield's shimmering force field. Mangled bot parts littered the charred floor between damaged shelves. He whipped back toward the console. *Thirty percent.* More footsteps sounded over the ringing in his ears.

"Shield's not gonna last much longer," Doc boomed.

Bobby banged on the console in frustration as the loading bar crept along. "Any ideas, LINC?"

"Yes, I have seven!" the bot announced.

"I'm listening."

Fifty percent.

"Well, four of them are impossible, two require building materials I don't think we have on hand—"

"LINC!"

"Okay, but one is really good."

"Spit it out!" Kerrick yelled.

Seventy percent.

"Okay, what if we…." LINC's voice trailed off.

"What?" cried Bobby.

The bot put a fist to his hip and chuckled. "You know, you're going to get a kick out of this, but I just completely forgot what I was going to say."

"LINC!"

"Sorry, my circuits are so frazzled. Hang on." The bot hunkered down, touching his temples in concentration.

The footsteps grew louder.

"LINC!"

"Oh wait, I got it! The holograms. They always disrupt my sensors. So maybe if you throw them at the bots they'll disrupt their sensors too."

Bobby hugged the satchel to his chest, causing the pods to shift around inside. The chamber was in ruins. These pods might contain the last evidence of where he came from.

A new wave of bots poured in, and Bobby instinctively ducked as plasma bolts blasted the shield. Shards of translucent yellow broke from the shield, fizzling into thin air as the shots ate away the barrier.

"Do it," Kerrick called. "Throw them."

Ninety percent.

There was nothing else he could do. He swung the satchel in an arc, slinging the holopods at the attacking bots. Holograms expanded like perpetual explosions as they scattered across the tile. Immediately, the oncoming fire stopped, and the security bots swung their featureless heads around as if searching for lost prey. Bobby glanced at the console.

One-hundred percent.

"Got it, let's go," he cried.

Kerrick yanked Jen's arm, pulling her behind the breaking shield. Together, they all caught up with LINC at the sliding door.

"Hope you can open this too," said the bot, jogging in place.

A control panel scanned his arm as Bobby reached it, and the door slid open. Doc swung the chipped shield behind them while Kerrick towed Jen through the opening, followed by LINC. Bobby glanced back through the broken yellow barrier to see the security bots scrambling about the chamber, looking for them among the activated holopods. In that split second, one of the holograms caught his eye. A researcher was attaching a small cybernetic appendage to an infant with only one arm. The image seared into his brain as Doc shoved him through the opening and the door slid shut.

<!014: Exiting Dangerous Environs>

KERRICK LED THE charge toward the forest as the alarming wail of klaxons pierced the stagnant night air. Mobilized by Sentinel's emergency protocol, Tier One bots poured into the streets, clogging the city's traffic.

The group ran close to LINC, hiding in the bot's cloaking function as they hurried through breaks in the crowd. So far, the concealment had worked. They zigzagged through the throngs, undetected by countless sensors.

Bobby glanced at Jen. The faraway look in her eyes had vanished, replaced by a sullen expression as she kept pace with the group.

Without warning, a boom reverberated the surrounding structures.

"What was that?" Kerrick.

"I think they've activated the defense forces." Bobby panted. He'd never heard these klaxons before. After all, Sentinel hadn't needed them as long as he'd been alive.

A quick glance over his shoulder at Sentinel Tower confirmed his suspicion. A swarm of compact Sentinel fighters launched into the air around the spire.

"My old man better have the ship ready," Kerrick grumbled.

A fighter formation screamed overhead, the ground trembling with the rumble of their pulsion engines. Bobby watched them rocket over the nearing treetops. He breathed a sigh of relief. The forest was close, and they were almost out of sight. They would make it.

Just as his hopes were climbing, the formation turned, circling back in their direction.

"They spotted us!" Kerrick yelled.

The screech of engines swelled as the fighters grew larger. They fired. Rapid blasts rent the air. Their barrage punctured the street in a blazing wall of plasma.

Doc heaved his cannon high and fired at the centermost ship. Bobby couldn't believe it. The shot connected with the fighter. The ship exploded in a rain of flame and debris, opening up a channel right through the sweeping wall of enemy fire.

The remaining fighters zoomed past, plasticrete erupting on either side under their deafening blasts. Bobby instinctively threw his hands up against the exploding road, but a chunk of debris struck his cybernetic arm, sending him spinning into the ground. Dust whirled around him—he must have screamed something, but his ears were ringing too loudly to be sure. He struggled to get up, but the fall had scrambled his sense of position. Desperation contorted his body into writhing movements as he fought to get to his feet. Before he knew it, a huge arm shot out of the dust cloud, seized him, and threw him forward. He landed in a run, somehow in front of the group. He glanced back in bewilderment to see Doc's signal to keep running. The giant had saved him.

His relief was short-lived, however. The Sentinel fighters were circling again. They didn't have much time. The eaves of the forest were straight ahead. Another round of fire blasted the street behind. In a matter of seconds, the fighters would be on top of them.

"Go!" Doc threw aside his cannon and barreled ahead.

Bobby sprinted with every bit of strength. They were almost there. The engines screamed louder. The cannons fired, and the pavement cracked. Blasts scorched their heels. Just before shots overtook them, they plunged into the shadows of the forest.

"Right!" Kerrick called.

They followed the captain's order and broke right. Bobby glanced to his left as the fighters mowed down the trees in a fiery line meant for them.

The next few moments were a blur of movement and panic, sidestepping trees and jumping over twisted roots. He had no idea how long they ran, but Kerrick seemed to know where they were going. Swarms of fighters screeched overhead, blowing up sections of the forest. So far, the group remained undetected.

After what seemed an eternity, the lake came into view, its rippled surface reflecting fiery treetops. Barnes waved them aboard, his hunched frame silhouetted against the cargo ship's entrance.

"What, did you alert the whole planet?" he shouted over thundering blasts.

"Take her." Kerrick handed Jen off to the old man. "Get to the *Quasar*."

"I'll help!" LINC cried, following the captain and Doc as they sprinted toward the cargo bay.

Barnes grabbed Jen's shoulders, scanning her with alarmed eyes. "What's wrong?"

Jen shook her head, eyes anchored to the floor with that faraway look again. Barnes looked to Bobby for an answer.

"I don't know, she froze," Bobby said with a helpless shrug.

"I'm fine." Jen swiped away Barnes's wrinkled hands. "I gotta power the shields." With that, she jogged down the passageway.

The old man stared after his granddaughter for a moment before sealing the door. "Get to the cargo bay."

Bobby nodded and hurried down the passageway, turning back after a few paces to see Barnes hobbling behind with his cane. He slowed, allowing the old man to catch up to him.

"I'll be fine, don't worry." Barnes waved.

"I'll stay with you," Bobby said.

Barnes's presence was comforting amid the surrounding chaos. Besides, he couldn't imagine leaving the old man alone.

They traversed the decks, bulkheads thrumming from nearby blasts, until they arrived at the cargo bay. Already, the whine of the sloop's engines was rising in pitch.

"I don't think our cloaking function is going to hide us from those fighters," said Barnes as they hurried up the *Quasar's* boarding ramp. "My son's got his work cut out for him."

Once on board, Barnes slapped a button on the wall, causing the ramp to retract and the hatch to slide shut. He clicked on a mounted intercom. "We're in."

Through a small window, Bobby caught sight of the bay door opening. Before it had even finished, the *Quasar* launched out of the stolen ship's hold, throwing Bobby to the floor.

"Stay sharp, son." Barnes beckoned, shuffling along as if nothing happened. "It's all in the knees." He bounced in a half squat to demonstrate.

Bobby peeled himself off the floor and shakily followed Barnes through the *Quasar's* main bay.

They hurried through the sliding door into the bridge, and Bobby sucked in a sharp breath. Kerrick and Doc sat at the ship's helm behind an angled viewport, through which hordes of Sentinel fighters lit up the inky black sky with raging plasma fire. Jen worked at another panel off to the side while LINC pointed to the oncoming fighters and spouted off advice. The *Quasar* shuddered as a volley of enemy fire connected. Bobby managed to stay upright this time. Kerrick cursed and banked hard.

The city sprawled out beneath them. Bobby stared in amazement. The factories looked so small and distant. For the first time, it dawned on him that he was actually leaving. In a matter of moments, he would leave behind the only planet he knew. Another blast rattled the ship.

Of course, they had to escape first.

"Hold tight." Kerrick pulled back on the controls, nosing the ship up between the planet's two moons. A wireframe grid shimmered against the starry canopy.

"Is that the shield?" Bobby wondered as he and LINC strapped into an empty crash couch behind an unoccupied console. He never thought he'd see the planetary shield barrier up close until he was Prime Human. It was invisible from the ground.

Jen looked up in alarm from her console's readouts. "It's closing."

Bobby squinted. Sure enough, an open square in the grid was closing, the shimmering translucent barrier crawling shut to block off their escape.

Other cargo ships entering and exiting the atmosphere changed course as the shield closed. But one en route to enter couldn't turn fast enough. It collided with the shield just as the panel slid shut.

Bobby's stomach churned as the cargo ship burst into flame and broken pieces. Were they about to meet the same fate?

"Jen, transmit the access codes," Kerrick said.

Jen typed at her console. She shook her head. "They're being rejected. The planet's on lockdown."

Another blast rocked the ship.

"Shields, twenty percent," Doc announced.

"Well, we had a good run," LINC said.

Kerrick slammed a fist on the dash. "I'm not going out like this."

"What do we do?" Bobby scanned the bridge for something helpful to do.

"I don't suppose your arm can get us out of this one?" Kerrick said over his shoulder.

"I don't know how it would." Bobby pumped his cybernetic fingers.

"That's what you said the last two times." LINC seized Bobby's cybernetic arm. The bot tore open his chest maintenance panel and ripped a cord from his internal wiring. He jacked it into Bobby's arm.

"What are you doing?" cried Bobby.

"Broadcasting a code in your arm," LINC answered, eyes twitching with processed data. "Hold please."

"What the...?" Kerrick leaned forward in his seat.

Through the viewport, the barrier section was sliding again. The shield was opening. Kerrick opened the throttle, and the ship rocketed forward. Bobby's heart leapt into his throat. They might just make it.

But to Bobby's horror, the receding shield stopped then began closing.

"They're trying to override it." Jen's fingertips blanched from clutching her display.

"LINC, do something," Bobby cried.

"I'm trying." The bot's eyes buzzed in concentration. "Sentinel Tower's sending a shutdown code at a higher frequency."

The shield slowed its progress, LINC's broadcast fighting it, but it continued to close. Kerrick didn't back off. They hurtled toward the shield at full speed.

LINC squeezed his eyes shut and groaned with effort. The closing shield halted for one tremulous moment, leaving the smallest gap in the barrier through which to warp.

"Warp, now!" Kerrick cried.

Doc thumbed a switch, and the bridge seemed to stretch impossibly long for one bizarre moment before rebounding to its normal shape. Bobby braced himself against a bulkhead as stars streaked through the viewport in a dazzling pattern.

They had escaped Sentinel.

<!015: Calculating New Trajectories>

B OBBY STEADIED HIMSELF against the crash couch and took in a deep breath. The relief on the bridge was palpable. Even Kerrick leaned back in his seat, the hard edge slipping out of his stony features for the moment.

"Bobs, your arm really comes in handy," LINC said, flapping Bobby's cybernetic hand. "*Handy*? Get it?"

"I don't believe it," Bobby whispered, wide eyes gazing at the starry vortex.

He imagined Sentinel sinking far behind, a point of insignificant light among countless others. The Programmers, Mother, all the rules and regulations. They all seemed so distant now. The thought made him dizzy.

Whether it was the disorienting stretch of the warp jump or something else, he couldn't tell, all sensation felt far away like he was outside his body standing next to a stranger. The context of his reality—four humans and a legacy bot surrounding him on the bridge of a foreign ship—was all so out of place. He brushed his plastifiber forearm with his fingers, and the feeling of skin against cool metal and plastifiber brought him back. He looked at his arm—the thing that forever connected him to Sentinel, to that tiny planet now lost in the starscape. He recalled Zel in the Archiver's story, how she'd escaped her tower, and he suddenly realized he didn't know what came after.

He thought of the hologram he'd seen in the Depository, of the researcher attaching a cybernetic arm to the infant. His arm felt suddenly heavy, now weighted with a dark history. With a pang of regret, he remembered throwing the holopods at the security bots. Would he ever be able to learn where he came from?

"You're not having second thoughts now, are you?" Kerrick clapped Bobby on the back, shaking him from his thoughts. The captain, smirking, stood beside him. "Too late for those. You did great. You're a hero."

Bobby forced a half-smile. "LINC broadcasted the code."

"The bot did all right." Kerrick conceded.

"Finally, some recognition." LINC leaned back, folding his arms.

"But you were the one who decided to help." Barnes shrugged off his restraints and stood to shuffle to Bobby's side. "We couldn't have done it without you."

Kerrick clapped him again. "Now, let's extract those weapon plans from your arm so we can deliver it to the Federation."

Bobby let out a heavy sigh. The adrenaline was washing away, and now even his biologic limbs felt heavy as stone.

Barnes laid a gentle hand on his shoulder. "Why don't we give the young man some time to rest." He smiled at Bobby, and some of the weight lifted.

Kerrick set his jaw. "We don't have time to waste on—"

"Oh, relax for once," Barnes interrupted, waving away his son's concern. "We made it through the hard part. And Bobby's been through a lot. Let him get his mind on something else for a little while."

Kerrick looked like he was about to say something but held his tongue at a meaningful glance from Barnes. Bobby swiveled his gaze between the two. A strange tension hung between father and son, but then Kerrick's features shifted, a brief flicker of something Bobby couldn't quite read. Something passed between the two men, and Barnes gave a slight nod. Bobby silently cursed himself for not understanding human social interactions.

"Jen, recalibrate the nav system," Kerrick barked, turning back toward the helm. "Those blasts scrambled our flight charts. We don't want to exit warp right into a star."

Jen threw off her restraints and hurried out, appearing relieved to exit the bridge.

Once she'd disappeared, Barnes turned to Bobby. "What happened back there?"

"She totally blanked." Bobby recalled the distant look in Jen's eyes at the Depository.

"Unusual." Barnes put a finger to his chin. "I wouldn't have expected that. Why don't you go check on her? Maybe you could help her recalibrate the nav system."

"I can help with that," LINC interjected.

"Why don't you stay here, my friend?" Barnes smiled at the bot. "My son needs your advice on the bridge."

"You're definitely not wrong there," LINC agreed. "Might have avoided some of those blasts if he'd listened to me." The bot untangled himself from his restraints and trotted back to the helm to join a grumbling Kerrick.

Barnes returned his attention to Bobby. "I'll have Doc heat up some chow, and we'll eat soon."

"Chow?" Bobby repeated.

Barnes chuckled. "Food. You must have food on Sentinel, right?"

"Meal pellets, if that's what you mean."

"Meal pellets?" Barnes scrunched his nose. "No, no, no, son. I'm talking about real food. You're in for a treat. Now, go on. Jen's in the engine room." He ushered Bobby off the crash couch out of the bridge.

As the door slid shut behind him, Bobby found his feet glued to the spot. The intensity of the previous hour ebbed at the unexpected prospect of being alone with Jen. Fighting through his sudden paralysis, he walked through the *Quasar*, finding himself back in the main bay. In the previous excitement, he hadn't noticed much, but now he looked around with curiosity.

The living space reminded him of the main bay in his Hovel. But whereas the Hovel was pristine and organized, the *Quasar's* bay appeared drab and stuffed with a hodgepodge of mismatched items. Busted sofas and padded chairs adorned the space, some angled at holoprojectors, others ringed around battered tables or workstations. Splayed wires coursed through parts of the floor, connecting boxy equipment.

His mind reeled at the setup. How could anyone live like this? Where was the order? The logic?

After a moment of inspection, he realized he was stalling. He was supposed to help Jen with the nav system.

"That way," a voice boomed from behind. Bobby started and twisted to see Doc striding into the bay, pointing to a passageway at the far end.

"Uh, thanks." Bobby forced himself to march in the direction indicated.

"You like meat and potatoes?" Doc asked, following a few paces behind.

He was unsure what *meat and potatoes* were but didn't want to let on that he'd never eaten what Barnes had called *real food* before. "Uh, yeah, love 'em."

Doc's lips curled, and he laughed, a sonic boom that vibrated the bulkheads. "Sure you do." With another rumbling chuckle, he disappeared into what appeared to be the food-preparation quarters, the *galley*, Bobby recalled from his studies of old human ship schematics.

As Bobby left the giant behind, he wiped the sweat from his palm, wishing LINC were here to tell him what to say. It would probably be something ridiculous, but better than anything he'd thought of so far.

The main passageway stretched from the bay all the way back to the engine room. He passed wings on either side that contained a number of doors, likely leading to the crews' quarters. At length, it split into three short parallel branches. The rightmost branch—*starboard*, Bobby reminded himself not to scrub up on the nautical language with the crew—led to a hatch labeled *Shuttle*, while the leftmost—*port*—led to an airlock chamber. He stared at the middle branch to the engine room, at the sliding door and the entrance button glowing beside it. He reached for it, then paused, wiggling his fingers in hesitation.

"Come on, Bobby," he whispered to himself. "Why are you so nervous? Feelings don't—" He broke off, realizing the phrase had been drilled into him by the bots. The bots who'd been programmed to mutiny against the Federation. Another phrase from their programmed lies. He wondered how long it would take to erase it from his neural pathways, wondered if it was so deep set that he'd ever rid himself of it. His lip quivered. Reality, everything he'd believed, had collapsed like a dispersing hologram. How was he supposed to act now?

A clatter echoed from the galley, startling him. He considered the glowing entrance button and his hand hovered in front of it. At the moment, all he could do was fall back on the logic hammered into him for sixteen years. He would figure out how emotions played into this new trajectory later. For now, Jen was inside, and it was his mission to help her.

Setting his jaw, he palmed the button. The door parted, releasing a wave of heat and thrumming noise. The scent of grease and grime washed over him as he entered. A quick scan revealed bulky pulsion engines surrounding a massive central warp engine dominating the middle of the chamber, but no Jen.

He trod around the machinery, marveling at how primitive the technology seemed. Compared to Sentinel's compact warp engines, this Federation warp engine seemed huge. Programming lessons popped up in his brain—chemistry, physics, engineering—

but they offered no reference for what kind of fuel the *Quasar* might use to make warp jumps. *Maybe LINC would know.*

He stopped to study the contours of the engine, then let out a huff, amazed at how his brain chose to fixate on anything but the task at hand, to protect him from an impossible amount of anxiety. But anxiety at what? Being alone with Jen? He forced himself to continue his search. This was simply another mission. Nothing to worry about.

Rounding the engine's rear, his gaze fell on the girl's slim figure slumped in the back corner, face buried in her hands. He halted, debating whether to proceed or leave her alone, but she looked up at him, eyes ringed with red.

"Did Grandpop send you to check on me?"

"Um, well, yeah, he wanted to see if you were okay," Bobby said.

"I'm fine." She wiped her cheek with a sleeve. "You can go."

Bobby pumped his cybernetic fingers, trying to stimulate his brain into a logical course of action. She didn't want him here. But Barnes had told him to come. "He said to help you with the nav system."

"Ugh." Jen rolled her eyes and slammed a fist against a monitor mounted above her head. "This thing's busted. It's going to take me hours to fix."

"Maybe I can help?" Bobby hoped it was enough reason to discover why Jen was acting so strangely.

"Yeah, I'm sure your arm can fix everything."

He glanced at his arm's vidscreen. "I don't think it will work with your ship's interface. LINC found code in it that's specific for Sentinel's—"

"I was being sarcastic," Jen spat.

"Sarcastic?"

"Like a joke."

"Oh." His cheeks grew hot as he realized he'd missed the cue. He'd heard the Archiver mention the concept, but had never heard bots on Sentinel joke, much less engage in sarcasm. She must think he was so naive. The thought made his stomach squirm in a way he was experiencing more frequently around her. Wiping the sweat off his palm again, he mentally logged her expression and tone of voice to the concept of sarcasm so he could calibrate a better response next time.

"What if I try anyway?" He pointed to the nav computer in an attempt to move past his blunder.

Jen looked up at him, eyes glistening with moisture. She let out a mirthless chuckle and waved toward the monitor. "Go for it."

She scooted enough for him to shuffle to the console. He glanced at her as he tapped the screen. That sweet aroma from her hair cut through the scent of grease and grime. He forced his attention back to the monitor. Lines of code scrolled up, punctuated by error messages.

"Looks like the coordinate database is corrupted," he said.

"No joke." Jen stared off into space.

"I wonder if I can...?" His voice trailed as he bent his mind around the problem. He typed new code, the soft tapping of his fingers the only sound over the hum of the engines. After a while, he finished the last line and inspected his work. "That should do it."

Jen frowned and pushed herself up to check the monitor. The code scrolled along without any error messages. "How did you...? There were entire regions of the galaxy corrupted in the database."

Bobby shrugged. "You just break the problem down into a series of logical steps, then embed each process into a larger one. If you know your physics, you can create a procedurally generated seed of code that will map out most of the galaxy based on the gravitational pull of planets and stars." He felt like he was rambling, but he couldn't stop himself. His brain had seized on something that made sense, and it plunged into a spectacular scientific tailspin. "The algorithm's quite complex, but it becomes easy with practice if you start with local calculations and then scale them universally." He took a break to inhale.

She gaped at him. "How do you know this stuff?"

He shrugged again. "The bots taught me."

At this, Jen stiffened and folded her arms across her chest. "The bots?" She looked away. "Did they teach you how to kill innocent humans too?"

"What? No," Bobby sputtered. "I—I had no idea about all of this. Humans, I mean."

"You had no idea." Jen leveled a hard gaze at him.

"I mean, I knew there was a war, but I didn't know—"

"So, you knew the bots were out there killing people, and you didn't do anything to stop them?"

Bobby's cheeks flushed again. "But I—I didn't—How was I supposed to—?" A thousand protests tangled together as they tried to escape his mouth.

"Because of your bots, I almost had to watch another family member die today," Jen said, eyes wavering. "What do you say to that?"

Her words pierced the objections rioting in his mind. "Another?" he breathed.

Her lips trembled, and the fire inside her seemed to extinguish. She slumped back down against the bulkhead and hugged her knees to her chest. "My dad."

Bobby watched her wipe away a fresh set of tears. Her state of shock at the Depository, at seeing her uncle almost die. That was why she'd frozen. He slipped Barnes's compass from his pocket and stared at the photo. The man he didn't recognize. It must have been Jen's father. They looked so happy. His strong arm was wrapped around her. She was leaning back into him, her smile touching her eyes. Since meeting her, Bobby hadn't seen her smile like that, even when she joked. He wanted to reach out, to comfort her in a warm embrace like Barnes had done for him. But somehow, he sensed this would break some protocol. He couldn't have Jen thinking him naive again. Besides, the thought of holding her so close filled him at once with warmth and fear that froze him. Unsure what to do, he sat down, his back to the adjacent bulkhead, pumping his plastifiber fingers.

At length, he mustered his voice. "Jen, I...." But he had to blink away his own tears. On some level, she was right. He'd been training in the Human Killer Simulator. He'd been expected to annihilate humanity. "I'm so, so sorry. About all of it. If I had known—If I had known what Gamma was really doing, what the bots were really doing, I would have never gone along with it. They told me humans had fallen. They said they were mindless, and killing them would be no different from shutting down a corrupted computer."

He swiped at his cheeks, and a long silence ensued.

Finally, Jen spoke, barely audible above the humming engine. "I believe you."

Bobby looked up at her. "You do?"

"I mean, in my brain I do. The bots ruin everyone's lives, why wouldn't they ruin yours too? I just—I just get so mad at them. And then, on top of it all, I can't even open a slag encrypted lock or fix a nav system like I'm trained to do." She punched the nav computer. "I hate feeling useless."

Bobby recalled her emotional outburst at the Depository, how he'd reasoned that it must serve some purpose. But no, she was just angry. At the bots, at herself. He could relate.

"Anyways," she continued in a gentler tone. "Sorry for shorting out back on the planet." Her head fell back against the bulkhead. She stared into space. "I just can't imagine losing another family member. I miss my dad so much."

He searched for a sensible response, but logic seemed to be failing him today. He'd never trained for interacting with another human, never studied a flow chart for what to say next. The whole conversation was outside his skill set. Yet, for some reason, this realization eased the tension in his shoulders. Paradoxically, with no perfect answer to recite, he found his words came easier. "I miss my mother."

He was surprised when Jen considered him with a flicker of interest.

"You had a mother?" she asked, hugging her knees closer. "I thought you were the only human."

"I am—was. But no, my mother was a caretaker unit." At Jen's quizzical expression, he explained. "A bot. And I know bots are bad… I mean I know that now. But Mother wasn't all bad. When I was younger, her caretaker settings were higher, and she was really nice. She would engage me with games." He fell silent, recalling a faded memory of how Mother would set out a trail of screws for him to pick up when he was young. He would find her at the end, and she would reward him with an embrace.

"What happened when you got older?" Jen's voice snapped him back to the engine room. She was leaning on an outstretched arm, and her knees had fallen toward him. Piercing blue eyes held him transfixed for a moment before he realized she was waiting for an answer.

"She stopped doing those things." He hardened his gaze so as to not betray the surprising amount of pain that bubbled to the surface. He wasn't sure it worked because Jen's expression softened.

"Why?" she asked.

He sighed. "When I grew up, I learned they were just training exercises to develop my motor and reasoning skills."

"And you still miss her?"

He bit his lip. "Yes. No. I don't know. I guess I just miss feeling like someone cared about me." He paused, then looked at her. "I can't imagine what it's like to lose a father who really did care about you."

Her eyes dropped, soft with some memory.

"He was the best," she said. "We spent every minute together when he wasn't deployed. He taught me how to code and fix engines."

"How to shoot a gum bubble out of the air?"

Jen let out a laugh Bobby wasn't expecting. "Yeah, he taught me that too. He and Grandpop taught me everything."

"What about your mother?"

Jen shook her head, and the faraway look returned. "Never knew her. She died while evacuating the Stellaris system when I was born. The bots were targeting hospitals."

Bobby winced.

"Dad had to leave my mom in the delivery room to defend the planet. Somehow, they got me off-world, but she didn't make it. Then he died three years ago when the bots ambushed his fleet. I was with Grandpop on a transport vessel. The last thing I saw before we warped out of there was Dad's cruiser blowing apart. I guess you can see why I hate the bots so much." She lapsed into silence.

Bobby could almost see the fiery explosion of her father's ship play in the reflection of her eyes.

"I'm really sorry." It was all he knew to say.

She pressed her lips into a line. "Hey, it sounds like they weren't any nicer to you. They really told you that you were gonna restart the human race?"

"Yeah. I had to prove that humans were worth reviving. At least, that's what they said."

Jen blinked at his answer. "How do you restart the human race—you know—by yourself?" To Bobby's surprise, her cheeks pinked.

"Cloning," Bobby said quickly. He was unsure why he wanted to relieve her from experiencing the strange feeling he was beginning to know so well.

"Oh, right, you said that." Jen nodded at the simple answer. "Cloning. That makes sense. But still, that's a lot to ask one person to prove the race is worth restarting. How do you even do that?"

"Everything was about productivity," he explained. "Efficiency. Logic. Feelings don't factor." Something caught in his throat at the phrase. He swallowed and continued. "Actually, just before I met you, Gamma was going to make me upload my consciousness into a robotic host 'cause I failed so much." He shuddered, remembering the Tether bot's smooth, chrome face.

Jen's eyes widened. "Neural transference? I didn't know Sentinel had that technology."

"Yeah." He forced the image from his mind. "I guess there's a lot I didn't know either."

"They really did a number on you."

"A number on me?" Bobby cocked his head.

"Yeah, you know, like they really put you through the wringer."

He frowned, trying to understand.

"You don't know those sayings?"

He shook his head.

"I guess you wouldn't. So have you ever done anything fun in your whole life?"

"Fun?"

"Are you kidding me?" Jen's laugh broke the lingering heaviness.

"Kidding?" Bobby smiled, shrugging helplessly

"Wow." Jen slapped a knee in mock exasperation. "Just you wait, Bobby Robot. When we're far enough away from that slag planet, I'm gonna to show you something that'll blow your mind." She tapped his temple and made an exploding motion with her fingers.

Bobby laughed. Strange how his heart fluttered so much at this. He might need LINC to run a scan on his cardiovascular system later. Maybe a brain scan, too, since he was smiling like a scrubhead at the name she'd given him. *Bobby Robot.* "Whatever you say, Jen—uh—Jen Human." He winced at the attempt to match her teasing tone, but to his surprise, she laughed so hard she snorted.

"Jen Human," she repeated between chortles. "I'm going to have to change my name now. That's too good."

Bobby grinned, trying to will his heart rate from going any higher. He might pass out from how well this was all going.

Jen looked up, laughter trailing off as they locked eyes. He hadn't noticed how close she'd moved until now. She leaned toward him, lips half parted, golden hair falling around pale cheeks, releasing sweet-scented notes. Her ice blue eyes held him in a breathless moment.

Then she punched him in the shoulder, sending a mild shock up his neck.

"Ow!" Bobby rubbed his shoulder. "What'd you do that for?"

She shoved a finger at him. "Don't you ever tell anyone I was crying."

A voice broke over the intercom, rattling the light fixtures with its booming tone. "Chow's ready."

With a smirk, Jen got to her feet and offered Bobby a hand. "Come on, let's eat."

Bobby studied her hand, then her sly smile. With uncertainty, he grasped it and let her help him up. As they walked back toward the bay and his first meal, Bobby made a mental note to ask LINC for data on the intricacies of female behavior.

```
<o:!0110101-000Z><01110000></x:01011>
<o:010011100/01>
<
```

WHEN THEY ENTERED the main bay, Barnes and LINC were already seated at one of the battered tables. They were playing a game on the holoprojector where a muscled man in a cutoff shirt was fighting a lithe android.

"I see you got the nav system working," Barnes called over his shoulder while mashing buttons on his controller. "Good job."

"Old circuit brain over here did all the work," Jen replied, jabbing a thumb at Bobby.

"Circuit brain." LINC chuckled, tapping a button sequenceon his controller to make the android fire missiles at the muscled man.

Bobby squinted at the game. The figures had an unnatural sheen to them like the simulations he used to run in his Programming. He shuddered and shoved away the thought of the Human Killer Sim.

Barnes pressed a series of buttons, causing the muscled man to pummel the android into submission. Bobby felt a curious satisfaction at seeing the android fall over and the man strike a victory pose.

"Not fair," LINC protested. "Rematch."

Barnes laughed and handed his controller to Jen, who plopped into a chair and started the game back up.

Barnes turned to Bobby. "Good work on the nav system. Is, ah, everything else okay?" He inclined his head toward his granddaughter.

"I think everything's fine," Bobby answered, an involuntary smile playing on his lips as he looked at her.

"Good." Barnes winked. "Ah, here comes Doc. Get ready for your first real meal."

Doc emerged from the galley, carrying a stack of bowls in one massive hand and wiping the other on a grease-stained apron.

"Bobby Robot's never had a meal?" Jen batted away LINC's hand as the bot tried to cover her eyes from seeing the game.

Before Bobby could answer, Kerrick strode through the door and pointed at him. "Time to get those plans off your arm."

"Oh, can't we do that after the boy gets some food?" Barnes twisted in his chair to face Kerrick.

"No." Kerrick growled and seized Jen's controller.

"Hey!" she cried.

LINC mashed buttons, making the android knock out the muscled man. "I win!" The bot jumped up and matched the android's victory pose.

Kerrick ignored the bot. "I'll check your work when you're done," he said to Jen, then turned on his heel and walked out, taking the controller with him.

Jen waited for Kerrick to disappear before rolling her eyes and pushing herself out of the chair. "Wait here," she muttered, brushing past Bobby to a stack of blinking consoles on the far bulkhead.

Doc, still holding the bowls, cocked a brow at Barnes.

Barnes tapped the table. "Eh, bring out the food."

With a shrug, Doc set the bowls on the table and headed back to the galley.

"Sit down, Bobby." Barnes patted the chair next to him.

Bobby dropped into the seat. "Shouldn't we do what he says?" He nodded to where the captain had been standing.

"Jen's got it covered."

The screeching of metal on metal drowned out Barnes's words as Jen pulled an entire stack of computers over to the table, leaving behind a thin scratch on the deck.

"We could have moved the table," Bobby suggested, eyeing the scratch.

"Then how would I see the holoprojector?" She rummaged through a nearby container and pulled out another controller, handing it to Barnes. The old man went back to playing with LINC while she drew out a cable from the computer stack. She twirled the jack in the air. "Where do you want this?"

Bobby pointed to the slot on his cybernetic forearm. She plugged in the cable and picked up a large comtab resting on the computer stack.

"Now let's see what's in your arm." She dropped into her chair and tapped at the comtab's screen.

Bobby shifted in his seat. "Be careful. I've had my arm shut off before." He remembered dragging his arm across the floor after cloning LINC's operating system.

"Wow." Jen squinted, bringing the screen closer to her face. "This is crazy."

"What? What did you find?" Curiosity mixed with dread in his stomach.

She looked up, eyes wide. "Your arm is a bomb."

Bobby's breath caught in his throat, but before he could say anything, she smirked.

"Just kidding."

He huffed, a clip of anger clawing at his chest. Why would she try to scare him like that?

"I'm joking." She gave his shoulder a little push. "You only joke with people you like."

"Like?" Bobby's brows raised in surprise.

"Yeah, people you want to be around."

"You want to be around me?"

She shrugged before focusing her attention back on the screen. "Sure, why not?"

Bobby veins flooded with warmth that washed away the previous moment's anger. She could confuse him with jokes all the time if she wanted to be around him.

"I want to be around you too," he blurted.

She looked up in surprise, her cheeks flushing a little. "Uh, thanks."

Bobby grinned, but at Jen's half smile he got the feeling that his words didn't connect the way he wanted them to. As she refocused back on the screen, he suppressed a frustrated sigh. He had so much to learn about interacting with humans. Especially Jen.

"You do have a *lot* of code in here, though," she said after a moment.

"That's what LINC said." He was glad to change the subject. "Can you tell what it is?" He leaned over for a better look at the comtab. Thousands of lines of code scrolled up in a blur.

"It's beyond me. You might have the USF cyber guys take a look when we get to Headquarters. I'll just clone the weapon plans to our drives for now. Still might take a while." She pulled a small tube out of her pocket. When she removed the cap, sweet-scented notes drifted to Bobby. He watched as she squeezed some kind of gel out onto her lips, giving them a glossy sheen. She looked up at his stare. "You guys probably don't have moonfruit lip gloss on Sentinel, huh?"

He shook his head. "Is it some sort of medical ointment?"

Jen laughed. "Nah." She capped the tube and blotted her lips together a few times. "Purely ornamental."

Scrub learning to interact with humans. With Jen he might as well be learning a new branch of quantum mechanics.

Doc reappeared, carrying a large pot and a big spoon.

Barnes paused the game as the giant ladled steaming liquid into each of their bowls. "All right, let's eat." He rubbed his wrinkled hands together.

Bobby peered at the brownish liquid. "What is it?"

"Beef and potato soup," Barnes said between loud slurps from his spoon.

Bobby cast an uncertain glance at LINC. The bot leaned over the table, squeezing one eye shut and laser scanning the soup with his other. "There's definitely a dead animal in there."

"What?" Bobby recoiled.

"Not that synthetic meat they have on Haven either." Barnes slurped another spoonful. "Real meat. Better than meal pellets, I can tell you that. Try it."

Bobby thought of the gaunt birds that sometimes flew over the factories on Sentinel. Never in his whole life had he wondered how one would taste. He watched Jen blow on a spoonful of soup as she inspected the comtab.

"Well, I guess, if it's safe." He edged a scoop to his lips. "I don't know why you'd want to eat an animal, though." He put the spoon in his mouth, and his senses exploded with the savory chunk and soft texture of the meat. "Oh," he said between bites, then shoveled more.

"I think he likes it," Barnes said.

"Hey, Bobs," LINC said, "if you had to describe it to a robot who has no taste receptors for organic material, what would you say it tastes like?"

"Like the best thing I've ever eaten," Bobby said through a mouthful of soup.

They ate, letting the pulsing music of the paused game and Jen's quiet taps fill the silence. After a while, Barnes pushed his empty bowl away. "I'm stuffed."

Doc brought out another bowl brimming with soup for Bobby, who eagerly took it and continued to eat. Barnes watched him with an amused expression as he slurped it clean. Halfway through the third bowl, Bobby began to wonder what those birds on Sentinel might taste like. After the fourth bowl, his stomach hurt.

"Maybe you should slow down," Barnes suggested. "Let it digest. This isn't like those meal pellets."

"Yeah, leave some for the rest of the trip," Jen said.

Another bite, and Bobby pushed away his bowl, letting out a long, satisfied sigh. "Sentinel doesn't have anything like that."

"Just wait till we get to USF Headquarters on Haven," Barnes said. "I'll take you to some of the best restaurants in the galaxy."

Bobby nodded, even though just the thought of food threatened to burst his gut.

"All right, I think we're all done." Jen gave a final tap on the comtab before unplugging the jack from Bobby's arm.

"You should get some rest," Barnes said. "You've been through a lot. Jen, why don't you show Bobby and LINC to their cabins."

Bobby glanced at the display on his forearm, reading the time. "But it's not sleep time, yet."

"Not everything has to be on a schedule." Barnes lowered Bobby's cybernetic arm. "You're tired, aren't you? Then rest."

As if his body had been waiting for permission, exhaustion washed over him. He pushed himself up and together with LINC followed Jen down the passageway, around the port wing, and into a small cabin containing only a pair of stacked beds.

"I call top!" LINC announced, leaping onto the top mattress.

"LINC, come on." Bobby rolled his eyes.

"There's a charging outlet over there if your bot needs some juice." Jen pointed to the corner.

"Do you, um," Bobby began, then dropped his voice, "have a problem with LINC? Since, you know, he's a bot?"

She smirked, watching LINC bounce on the mattress. "I don't think he technically counts."

"Oh, okay." It was a relief to know that his task assistant's presence wouldn't be a source of tension. He couldn't imagine being separated from LINC. He studied her, daring to maintain eye contact with those pale blue gems. "Thank you."

Jen dropped her gaze as if searching for lost words. "Well, thanks for listening earlier. In the engine room, I mean." She bit her lip. "I don't normally talk about my dad. But after what happened today with... anyway, it was just nice to get it off my chest."

Bobby nodded. "Of course."

Jen straightened, and he noticed the tender expression had faded.

"Hey, don't sleep funny on that arm. Don't want it to explode." She winked and left the cabin, door sliding shut behind her.

Bobby sank onto the bottom mattress, shoulders collapsing with the weight of the day. The last forty-eight hours had proved the most exhausting and terrifying of his entire life. So why did he feel like smiling?

"Should've kissed her," LINC's voice drifted from above. The bot had finally settled down on the mattress.

"Shut up." Bobby rolled his eyes and stretched out on the bed.

A moment ticked by.

"LINC?"

"Yeah?"

"What's a kiss?"

"I thought you'd never ask." LINC swung down and sat cross-legged on Bobby's bed. "I've been doing some research on the subject. It's when you touch lips with someone."

Bobby sat up and wrinkled his nose. "Why would you want to do that?"

"You're telling me you don't want that girl's face to touch yours?"

Bobby recalled that moment in the engine room when Jen had leaned toward him, hair falling around half-parted lips. The more he thought about it, the more he wondered what moonfruit lip gloss tasted like. "Well...."

"Of course you do."

Bobby processed this. He remembered telling Jen he wanted to be around her and the odd look she'd given him. He frowned. "So, is this like a normal thing to do? Kiss a girl?"

"Oh yeah." The bot nodded. "They're crazy for it."

Bobby chewed his lip, imagining what it would be like to kiss Jen. "So, how does it work?"

"I've been streaming tons of data from the ship's media banks since we got aboard. Holo films, holo shows, text-based stories, and let me tell you, there are a *lot* of ways to do it."

"What's the most, um, *normal* way?"

"Okay, face me." LINC twisted Bobby's shoulders so they were facing each other on the bed. "Imagine I'm Jen. You look me right in the eyes, and you hold it there for a second."

Bobby screwed his face up in concentration, staring hard into LINC's pupiled lenses.

"Okay, that's a great look if you're about to punch her." The bot slapped the tension out of his shoulders. "Relax."

Bobby tried again, mimicking the soft expression he'd seen in Jen's eyes back in the engine room.

"Much better." LINC approved. "Now, you grab her hard by the head." The bot seized Bobby's head in a vice-like grip. Ignoring the pain, Bobby mirrored LINC, squeezing the bot's metal cranium.

"Mmf, good." LINC's jaw worked against Bobby's grip, and he squeezed harder.

Bobby fought to maintain his gentle expression.

"Now you lean in real slow." LINC continued, pulling Bobby's head toward his.

Bobby did the same, bringing the bot's face in.

"Wait." LINC stopped. "I forgot, you're supposed to close your eyes at about the halfway point."

"Why?"

"Do you want to do this right or not?"

Bobby squeezed his eyes shut and resumed bringing LINC's face closer.

"Now you push out your lips," the bot instructed. "And plant a kiss right on the mouth."

Bobby puckered, waiting to meet the cool sensation of LINC's alloy maw.

"Whoa." LINC let go of his head and blocked Bobby's lips with a plated palm. "Listen, I like you, Bobs, but I don't feel that way about you."

Bobby's eyes snapped open. "But you said—"

"Hey, it's nothing personal. You just don't do it for me. I took you ninety percent of the way. You'll have to figure the rest out."

Bobby released LINC with a groan, falling back and pulling a pillow over his face.

"Hey, don't worry. I also downloaded some data on social behavior with females."

Bobby lifted the pillow and opened one eye "And?"

"Well, I didn't have much time to look into it, but based on my observations, the female gender is straightforward, probably uncomplicated, and easy to understand. I don't think you'll have a problem figuring her out."

"Well, that's good, I guess." Bobby sighed.

"We'll talk more tomorrow." LINC patted him on the shoulder. "I gotta plug in. These legacy bots need to recharge, apparently." He banged a fist on his chest. "Forget delivering weapon plans, first thing I'm gonna do when we land is upgrade my equipment." The bot shut off the light and plugged himself into a compact charging station in the corner. "Oh and top bunk is still mine, so I better not see you up there in the morning. Sleep well, Bobs." With that, he powered down.

"Thanks, LINC."

Bobby lay on the mattress, the last cycle looping in his mind until the soft drone of LINC's charging lulled him into fitful dreams of Sentinel fighters chasing him through space.

<016: Performing Risk Assessment>

BOBBY WOKE TO a tremor running through the ship. He bolted upright, sure that Sentinel fighter ships had found them.

"LINC?"

When there was no answer, he jumped out of bed and scanned the room, but the bot was nowhere to be found. The ship trembled again. He threw out his arms to steady himself as the floor rocked. As soon as the shaking subsided, he dashed outside and ran all the way to the main bay. Barnes sat at the table, attempting to keep a cup of steaming liquid from spilling as the ship shuddered again.

"Good morning, Bobby." Barnes held the cup aloft in greeting. "Well, as morning as it gets in space."

"What's going on?"

Barnes took a sip. "Asteroid field."

"Asteroid field?"

Barnes rose and shuffled over to the starboard bulkhead, where he flipped a switch. Long slats angled horizontally, uncovering a thick plastiglass window through which countless rocks of all shapes and sizes tumbled through space.

"We ran into a Sentinel cruiser when we came out of warp earlier. They would've followed us into our next warp if we didn't lose them in this asteroid field. Now we're just waiting to get through so we can jump again."

The mention of a Sentinel cruiser alarmed Bobby, bringing to mind his nightmares from last night.

"You're sure we lost them?" He walked over and pressed his nose to the window, scanning the asteroid field.

"Those cruisers are too big to follow us. The asteroids will tear their ship apart."

At that, Bobby relaxed until a small asteroid hit the window with a jarring bang. He gave Barnes a startled look.

"Shields are repelling the small ones," Barnes explained, holding a palm under his cup as the liquid sloshed around inside.

"Small ones hit pretty hard." Bobby observed.

"Your bot's been helping Jen angle the shields. As long as the captain steers clear of the big ones, we're fine. Nothing to worry about."

A little tension drained out of Bobby's shoulders. He eyed Barnes's cup.

"What is that?" he asked, remembering the soup.

"Coffee," Barnes replied. "Wanna try?"

Bobby took the warm cup and inhaled an enticing aroma. He eagerly took a sip and immediately scrunched his face at the bitter taste. "Ugh."

Barnes chuckled. "Yeah. Didn't think you'd like it. Not a great second impression of food." He took the cup back and slurped another swig.

Jen bounded in from the passageway, followed by LINC.

"Hey, Grandpop," she said, rummaging through a locker.

Barnes settled himself back at the table. "And what are you two doing?"

"Got the shields running on autodeflection. She tossed odd bits of junk out of the locker until she retrieved two wrist strap devices. "Gonna relax for a while." She came over and kissed the old man on the cheek. "Come on, Bobby Robot. I told you I'd show you something that will blow your mind." She slapped Bobby on the shoulder as she ran back into the passageway.

"Yeah, come on, Bobs." LINC jogged after her.

Bobby flashed Barnes a questioning glance. The old man motioned for him to follow them. "Well, go on, you'll see."

Curious, Bobby hurried around the table. "Where are we going?" he called to Jen.

"Solar surfing," she shouted.

Bobby glanced back at Barnes for an explanation, but the old man just smiled. "Don't let Kerrick catch you."

```
<o:!0110101-000Z><01110000>
</x:01011> <o:010011100/01>
<
```

"WHAT'S SOLAR SURFING?" Bobby squirmed in the ill-fitting exo suit Jen had given him.

"These are rocket-powered carts." Jen indicated two lengthy plastisteel boards propped next to the *Quasar's* airlock chamber.

"The Federation uses them to move space station parts in zero gravity." She toed the small pulsion engine mounted at the bottom of the nearest board. "*I* use them for surfing behind the ship."

"Um, this is one of your jokes, right?" Bobby peered through the plastiglass airlock at the asteroids tumbling in the *Quasar's* wake.

She plopped a helmet on her head and locked it into the collar of her exo suit. "Nope." Her voice filtered through the suit's comlink.

"Is this safe?" He nervously pulled at a pant leg that kept riding up.

"Of course it's not safe." She jabbed a button on his chest piece, causing his suit to refit itself to his body dimensions. "That's what makes it fun." She strapped the device she'd retrieved from the locker to her wrist, then secured the other to his. "I made modifications to the rockets. This remote controls the speed. Don't lose it." When the remote was secure, she picked a helmet off a hook on the wall and shoved it into his hands. "And remember, there's no 'up.'"

"What?"

"You'll see."

LINC pressed his alloy face against the glass, lensed eyes tracking the asteroids. "Wow, just imagine how much it would hurt to get hit by one of those."

Jen punched a button, and the inner hatch opened. She stepped inside the airlock, beckoning Bobby to follow.

"I don't know." Bobby eyed the walls as another collision rocked the ship.

Jen shrugged. "Suit yourself." She slapped another button, and the hatch closed.

Holding an anxious breath, he watched Jen drop the board and step on top, flipping a switch on her boots to magnetize them. When she was satisfied that they had bonded to the surface, she dropped into a half-squat and gave him a thumbs up. Then she punched a third button, and the outer hatch opened, sucking her into space.

He slammed himself against the glass in time to see her carve a fiery arc around an asteroid with her board's rocket.

As the outer hatch closed and the airlock repressurized, LINC turned to Bobby. "You know you have to do it now."

"Why?" Bobby shot the bot a wary glance.

"You can't let her think you're scared."

Bobby bit his lip and watched Jen swinging around asteroids. He puffed up his chest. "Hold this." He removed Barnes's naval compass from his pocket and handed it to LINC.

LINC punched his shoulder. "That a boy, Bobs!"

Bobby dropped the helmet on and grabbed the other board before opening the inner hatch. He stepped into the airlock, gazing outside at Jen zig-zagging around asteroids. With a huff, he dropped his board and locked his boots to the surface. Squatting into a balanced stance and holding the remote tight, he cast a last glance at LINC. The bot reassured him with a salute.

Bobby's hand hovered over the depressurize button. Jen hadn't pushed it. She'd opened the airlock and let the air pressure cannon her outside. If he was going to show he wasn't scared, he had to do the same thing.

With a deep breath, he opened the outer hatch and let the vacuum of space suck him off the ship.

His stomach lurched with the acceleration and subsequent shift to zero gravity. For a breathless moment, nothing made sense. His ears rang in the sudden silence. And though the *Quasar* diminished in size, he wasn't convinced it was moving. His brain lashed out, trying to latch onto something to orient himself. But he just hung there, suspended in nothingness.

"Hey, Bobby," Jen's voice filtered into his helmet. "Maybe try activating your engine?"

His awareness snapped to the remote on his wrist. With a tap, the board's engine kicked on. The burst of speed threw him backward. Were it not for his magnetized boots, he would have tumbled off into space. Contracting every muscle in his body, he managed to pull himself upright in time to see a huge asteroid careening toward him.

His scream filled the helmet as he twisted the board, swerving just in time. The rock grazed its bottom, launching him high above the receding ship—or below, he couldn't tell which—where he could see the entire field spread out before him. His lungs relaxed, breath coming easier, and he scanned the field for Jen. She glided upside down some distance away to his right. Or was he upside down? *Remember, there's no 'up.'* Her words floated back to him.

With some effort, he spun around to match her position. He knew she was laughing by the way she threw her helmet back. She waved at him and rocketed her board in wild arcs.

He copied her, finding the board easy to steer. With a swell of confidence, he followed her into a nosedive, weaving around a stream of smaller rocks. They flew through a wave of crushed debris, and tiny chunks pelted his body. He checked for tears in the exo suit, but Jen cut him off in a close swoop, the blazing tail of her rocket dusting his visor.

"Hey!" His cry bounced around his helmet as he slapped its angular frame, checking for damage. He shot an annoyed glance at Jen, who beckoned with her fingers, daring him to retaliate. Adopting one of her smirks, he twisted his board and boosted toward her. She snapped into a defensive stance and zoomed away into a nearby cluster of asteroids. He chased her, jerking out of the way of oncoming rocks while she made smooth arcs around them.

He couldn't let her get away. A tap on the remote, and the board kicked with a burst of speed, rocketing him dangerously close around the asteroids. Sweat trickled down his forehead as he reflexively avoided each one, Jen growing larger in his visor with each passing second. She was gliding through the field with ease, unaware of his rapid approach. He watched her prepare to jump over a colossal asteroid looming ahead and decided to seize the opportunity for his revenge.

With another blast of speed, he hurtled toward her. She whipped her head around, and he almost laughed imagining the surprise on her face. But the laugh caught in his throat. A smaller asteroid he hadn't seen struck Jen's helmet while she was distracted, knocking her into an oblique spiral.

"Jen!" he called through his com, watching in horror as she spun out of control toward the gigantic asteroid.

Static filtered into his helmet.

He set his jaw and flew after her, eyes shifting between her tumbling form and the incoming rock. The motors in his cybernetic arm unreeled, stretching his fingers out as far as they would go. She was almost within reach. The asteroid filled his visor, impossibly large. He winced, bracing for the impact.

A jolt registered in his outstretched fingers, and he tightened them on reflex. It was Jen's arm. Adrenaline punched through his gut. He kicked up, launching them above the asteroid just before they collided, Jen's board slicing the top of the rock.

They hurtled clear. A part of his brain ran through a damage check of his body, while another part scanned the field for the *Quasar*. Relief gave way to dread when he found no sign of the ship. Jen's arm squirmed in his hand. He glanced over to see her trying to get his attention.

"Jen?"

A clip of static was the only response. She pointed to her helmet where a hairline crack branched across the visor.

Right before his mind melted with panic, he saw her point at something. Following her finger, he spotted the ship between a distant cluster of asteroids.

"Let's go." He wasn't sure she could hear him, but it didn't matter. She had already taken off toward the ship, her rocket blasting at full speed. He followed close behind, thankful that they'd flown into a pocket of clear space.

In a matter of seconds, they had zoomed into the airlock. Bobby almost collapsed under the sudden pull of artificial gravity. The hatch closed behind, and he demagnetized his boots, wobbling off the board as the airlock repressurized. He tore off his helmet and hurried over to Jen, who was doubled over.

"Are you okay?" He crouched and placed a trembling hand on her shoulder.

The inner hatch opened, and LINC dashed in. "What happened?"

"Asteroid hit her. This is all my fault. What do we do?"

Jen unlocked her helmet and popped it off, revealing her contorted face. Bobby watched her twisted features for an instant of pure horror until it registered that she was laughing.

Regaining some composure, she straightened, sucking in deep breaths between peals of laughter. "I thought we were going to die."

Bobby stared at her in utter confusion. "We almost did."

"I know!" She shook his shoulders. "Don't you feel so alive?" She let out a satisfied sigh and wiped her brow before demagnetizing her boots. "We need a pic. Where's my comtab? Never mind, where's your compass, Bobby?"

"I have it." LINC handed her the compass he'd been holding. "I only dropped it once."

Jen thumbed the display, flashing the picture of her family. She swiped it away to access a photo mode, then wrapped her arm around Bobby and held the compass high. "Smile."

Despite the adrenaline still coursing through him, he tried a smile, forcing it up to his eyes like he'd seen in the photo of Jen and her family.

"Hey, that's a good one." Jen inspected the resulting picture. "You're getting better at this." She pushed the compass back into his hand. "Come on, let's grab a snack."

Bobby and LINC exchanged glances as she bounced out of the airlock and disappeared down the passageway.

"I'm going to download some more data on human behavior," said LINC.

"Good idea," Bobby agreed. Somehow, despite the near-death experience, he couldn't help smiling as he looked at the picture of him and Jen on the compass.

<!017: Repeating Tasks>

"YOU MISSED A spot." From the sofa where he was lounging, LINC pointed to a section of the main bay's floor.

Bobby, on hands and knees, paused scraping the floor with the tiny scrubber to glare up at the bot. "Why aren't you helping?"

"The cap said I'd be too efficient." LINC stretched his arms behind his head. "Said you two need to learn a lesson. You're the ones who went solar surfing. Not me."

"I take it back what I said, Bobby." Jen scrubbed another section of the floor. "Your bot's the worst."

"She's right, LINC." Bobby dipped the scrubber in a bucket of sudsy water. "Couldn't keep your big mouth shut, could you?"

LINC turned up his nose. "Sorry I was proud of your maneuvering out there. I thought everyone should know."

"Well, that kinda makes it your fault Captain Kerrick found out," Bobby said.

"Don't call my uncle that," Jen said. "It's weird."

"What should I call him?"

"I don't know, but Captain is weird."

"Call him Cappy," LINC suggested.

"I don't know," Bobby said. "I don't think so." He inspected the tiny scrubber. "Is this Captain—I mean Kerrick's—is this his— what did you call it again?"

"Toothbrush." Jen tucked a strand of hair behind her ear as she worked.

Bobby turned the toothbrush in his fingers. "It's for cleaning floors?"

Jen stopped and blinked at him. "You serious?"

He stroked the tiny bristles with his thumb, too curious about the instrument to be embarrassed at what he was missing.

"You mean you don't clean your teeth on Sentinel?" Her nose wrinkled.

LINC waved a lazy hand. "Lady, we have lasers that do that."

Jen flashed the bot a sharp glance, but a grin pulled at her lips. "I'm so sorry, we're not that fancy here, Your Majesty."

Bobby swiveled his gaze between the floor and the toothbrush, then frowned. "Kerrick puts this in his mouth?"

"It's from the supply closet." Jen plunged the brush into her own bucket of soapy water and went back to scrubbing. "He's just making us use it to clean the floor as punishment." She looked up with a smirk and waggled the toothbrush in her hand. "But I'm going to switch out his personal toothbrush with this one when we're done."

"Nice," LINC said.

Bobby laughed at the thought of Kerrick scrubbing his teeth with a dirty toothbrush.

"So Bobby Robot *does* have a sense of humor," Jen said.

Any creeping guilt at his emotional outburst melted at her spreading grin.

"Sense of what?" he asked through chortles.

Jen rolled her eyes, still smiling. "Humor. Like, you know what's funny. I swear, Bobby, I'm gonna have to teach you how to be normal."

"Yeah?" Bobby caught her eyes and cocked a brow. "So, what's my first lesson?"

"Well, for one"—she pointed at his brushing pattern—"you should stop scrubbing the floor with your real hand like a dope and use that fancy cybernetic arm of yours."

"What?"

"Oh come on," she pleaded. "I bet we'd be done in no time if you fire that thing up."

Bobby considered his cybernetic arm and frowned. "But wouldn't that negate the point of the punishment?"

"You've got to be kidding." Her head lolled back in exasperation. "Did you roll off the assembly line like this?"

"Like what?"

"Like a dork," LINC said. At Bobby's quizzical glance, the bot broke out of some sort of trance. "Sorry, I've been streaming off the *Quasar's* data banks. It's a word I ran across."

Jen straightened. "You're tapped into the ship?"

"Yeah, your data organization is awful." LINC's lensed eyes twitched as he processed information. "These files are all over the place. Hey, what's this one on your computer titled 'Space Hotties?'"

"All right, that's enough." Jen threw her brush down and seized her bucket. She marched over to LINC, suds sloshing onto the floor. "Bobby, tell your bot to get out of my files, or I'll flood his circuits."

"LINC's waterproof." Bobby sat back on his knees. "What are 'Space Hotties' anyway?"

"Hang on," LINC said, eyes twitching. "I'm about to find out."

"Okay," Jen tipped the bucket. "Here we go."

"It looks like a—*pfft*." The bot sputtered as Jen doused his face with a cascade of water. He threw up wiry hands against the splash and leapt off the sofa. "She's fracturing the signal. Give me cover!" He bounded behind Bobby and ducked down.

Bobby turned to see Jen advancing. He recounted his mental log of her facial expressions, confused as to why she was wearing her smirk again. Didn't her objection to LINC's data intrusion mean she was angry? This paradoxical behavior seemed to mimic LINC's when he would scrub the Inspector with a benign auditory frequency. The Archiver had called it *playing*.

"Bobby, give up the bot, or you get a drink too," Jen threatened, tapping the bucket.

He could play too.

He raised his chin in defiance. "No. I want to know what a 'Space Hottie' is."

Jen shrugged and swung the bucket. Bobby gasped at the cold splash.

"Hey!" He laughed.

Jen popped her hip and raised a brow. "I warned you."

He had to retaliate. His gaze shifted to his bucket just out of reach. Jen anticipated his move and blocked him just as he dove for it. He twisted in time to miss a painful collision with her knees and came down flat on the floor. The next instant, a splash of suds trailed down his back. He turned over to see Jen emptying her bucket's dregs onto him.

"Now, stop reading my files!" She tossed the bucket aside and tackled LINC to the floor.

Bobby seized his chance. He scrambled to the other bucket and swung it around.

"I've almost got it," LINC called from a headlock. "Get her off me!"

Bobby ran over to them and poured sudsy water on Jen, doing his best to keep the stream off LINC. She let out a scream that dissolved into a fit of giggles.

"Fine, fine, stop!" she cried, disentangling from LINC. "It's a Kortinean pop group."

"A what?" Bobby took a step back in case she decided to lunge for his bucket.

"From the Kortinea system, Kortinean pop music features major key tonality and candy-colored lyrics," LINC read from some unseen database. "Listen." From the external speakers on

LINC's torso a harmony of synthesized instruments coalesced into a melody over which a chorus of male voices sang in some foreign language.

Bobby looked at Jen, who was picking herself up off the floor. She grimaced. "This is pretty embarrassing, huh?"

"Why?" said Bobby. Water dripped from his soaked hair as he bobbed his head to the music. "It's kinda nice."

"You're from a planet with no other teenagers." She covered her face with a hand. "Believe me, Kortinean pop music is embarrassing."

"Oh wow." LINC hopped up, eyes now twitching like he was scanning a picture. "These male singers are well built. Bobs, maybe you should hit the weights."

Jen's cheeks tinged pink.

Bobby's eyes involuntarily scanned her. Her arms were crossed over her water-stained shirt, wet hair clinging to her neck. Pale blue eyes slanted as if unable to meet his gaze, but a smile curved her lips. He realized his heart was racing, and not from the water fight. But he wasn't done playing yet. "So, you're a dork too?"

She grinned, finally meeting his gaze, and pushed his shoulder. "Shut up, Bobby Robot."

He couldn't help but match her grin. She'd moved closer to him. The damp warmth seeping from her body mixed with the heat rushing to his cheeks until he was sure it would steam the water right off his face. He wondered if someone had lowered the ship's artificial gravity the way he was floating.

She held his eyes for one more breathless moment, then started. "Wait, what time is it?" She scrambled to the soaked sofa and rummaged between the cushions for something.

The floor seemed to suck Bobby back down. "What is it?" he asked, trying to swallow his disappointment at their lessened proximity.

She pulled her comtab from under a cushion and checked the time. Her face lit up.

"You know, whenever you smile like that"—LINC nodded in her direction—"it usually signals the imminent breaking of a rule. Whatever it is, I'm in."

"What are you about to do?" asked Bobby with a wary glance.

"About to teach you how to pull a prank." Jen smirked.

<!018: Developing Rogue Behavior>

"WHAT'S A PRANK?" Bobby asked, handing his water bucket to Jen.

His damp clothes steamed from the engine room's sweltering heat. He would have liked to pour the cool water on himself, but Jen had other ideas as she flipped switches at her workstation. A machine lowered a coil suspended from a mechanical arm. LINC leaned over her shoulder to watch as she twisted a valve.

"Doc showers at the same time every cycle," Jen replied over a loud hiss erupting from the valve. "Every once in a while, when he's off his guard, I'll throw a bucket of ice into the shower while he's drying off." As the hiss faded to a steady whisper, she placed the bucket under the coil and pulled a lever. The water crackled with its instant transformation into loose ice at the coil's touch. Heat drained out of the immediate area.

"So, this thing is a prank?" Bobby pointed to the coil.

"Yeah, this is a prank machine," said Jen, then at Bobby's inquisitive look, "Are you serious? This is a cooling coil. You guys don't cool warp engine fluid where you're from?"

"Are *you* serious?" LINC stuck a fist on his hip. "You guys still use warp engine fluid?"

"Corilum warp cores don't need cooling," Bobby explained.

"Oh, right." Jen rolled her eyes. She stood up and swirled the crystalline slush in the bucket before offering it to Bobby. "A prank's a joke you pull on someone. You get to do the honors."

"You want me to pour ice on Doc?" asked Bobby, aghast at the thought of making the giant angry.

"I have to turn off the artificial gravity in the showers, so you're on ice duty." She shoved the bucket into his hands and pulled open a maintenance hatch in the floor. "He's been locking the door since the last time I got him," she said, shimmying down the narrow opening. "But I just figured out the doors unlock if you knock out the gravity. Safety feature. Besides, you've got to hear him scream. You won't believe how high his voice can go. Now get going, we don't have much time."

"What should I do?" LINC called as Jen disappeared down the hatch.

"Go to the showers and open the door when it unlocks," her voice echoed back, "and cover your eyes when his towel falls off chasing you."

Bobby swallowed a lump of panic in his throat.

```
<o:!0110101-000Z><01110000></x:01011>
<o:010011100/01>
<
```

"I DON'T KNOW if this is a good idea," Bobby whispered to LINC as he adjusted his grip on the bucket, hands aching from the cold.

They were pressed against the wall on either side of the door to the showers, waiting for Jen to disable the lock.

"Bobs, don't be a chinch," LINC replied, pushing his ear to the door.

"A what?"

"I don't know, I think it's a bug."

"Why would you call me a bug?"

"Look, I'm downloading a lot of new vocabulary, okay? Just seeing what sticks. I'm saying don't be scared. You surfed through a bunch of asteroids, remember?"

"I almost died," Bobby reminded him. "What if Doc kills me?"

LINC gripped his shoulder. "You may die doing this, yes. But high risk, high reward. Jen's having fun with you. Girls kiss people they're having fun with. It's a fact. You want her to kiss you, right?"

Bobby bit his lip.

"That's what I thought," LINC said. "So, when this door opens, you ice the big guy and run like a scrubbing chinch." The floor trembled, followed by a deep faltering tone like something powering down. "We're up," said LINC over the whoosh of the sliding door.

Before Bobby could protest, the bot shoved him through the opening. He tripped at the threshold and would have spilled the ice in a headlong dive had the sudden absence of gravity not saved him. Instead, his stomach flipped as he weightlessly glided through the steam toward the showers at the far end.

Doc's massive shadow shifted behind the curtain, and he let out an alarmed shout in a language Bobby didn't understand. There was a squeak like a heavy something slipping followed by a string of curses as the giant's silhouette flipped upside down. His bare foot floated above the curtain in a constellation of suspended droplets. A torrent of water squirmed from the shower head like a tunnelbot writhing in the Sentinel mines, twisting around itself.

"Hurry!" LINC shouted.

Bobby knew his drift was too slow. Doc would get his bearings any second and tear through the curtain. He could kick off the passing toilet, rebound backward, retreat. But then he thought of Jen, of the way she made him feel. Playing pranks and having fun. Like he was a part of something. Like he was part of her family picture on the compass. That feeling, their connection, flashed through his brain in a heartbeat. He kicked off the toilet, launching himself at the shower.

The shadow moved, and a gargantuan hand ripped back the curtain. Bobby flinched mid-flight at the hulking form of Doc floating upside down in his underwear. Did humans shower in their underwear? Had he been showering wrong all this time? Confusion turned to panic as Bobby registered the holster on Doc's hip. Did humans shower... armed too? He couldn't stop his momentum as the giant drew his blaster. On reflex, he threw the entire bucket, knocking the blaster askew.

Jen was wrong. Doc didn't scream in a high-pitched voice. But then, most of the ice hadn't even hit him. Bobby had been too slow, had given him too much time to react. *High risk, high reward*, LINC had said. Now Bobby was going to die. It had almost been worth it, though.

Almost.

Doc swatted at the bucket ricocheting around the shower stall, giving Bobby the chance he needed to escape. He might still make it out of this. Might get to kiss Jen for his bravery what with icing a giant and living to tell the story.

He kicked off the wall as Doc brandished the blaster. A bolt seared the floor, narrowly missing his right arm.

"Scrub!" he screamed.

Doc fired again, but Bobby had crossed the threshold, the shot missing as he tumbled to the floor in the passageway's normal gravity.

"He's shooting!" Bobby cried.

"Why did you do that?" LINC shouted, pulling Bobby up into a run. "You made him so mad!"

"I told you this was a bad idea," Bobby yelled as they sprinted through the passageway.

A thud echoed behind, and he glanced back to see Doc hurtling after them.

"You were supposed to hit him with the ice, not the bucket. He's going to kill us!"

"I didn't see you helping!"

They rounded the corner and scrambled into the main bay.

"Where do we go?" Bobby huffed.

"In here." LINC stuffed himself into one of the lockers and slammed the door shut.

Before Bobby could shout how stupid LINC's idea was, Doc came sliding into the bay, blaster blazing. Bobby stumbled backward, the bolts sailing past. How was Doc such a bad shot? As he backpedaled, a bolt grazed his ankle. His left foot went numb, but no damage to his boots. *Stun blasts*, he thought. Then he saw the giant's smirk. The same kind Jen wore explaining the prank.

All at once, it made sense. Showering in his underwear. The blaster. The shots barely missing him.

Tension drained out of Bobby's chest, coming up as bubbles of laughter.

Doc was pranking *him*.

Bobby smiled back with an impressed nod, acknowledging the giant's brilliant move. Doc's grin widened, then he raised his blaster.

"Bobby," Jen called. She had popped up from a maintenance hatch next to the lockers. "Run!"

It was clear Doc wasn't going to let up. Bobby was almost, *almost* sure the giant wouldn't hurt him, but stun blasts still weren't comfortable. Besides, he didn't want to lose this game. He turned and dragged his numb foot into an unsteady run.

Doc thundered after him.

"He's gaining!" Jen squealed from the hatch.

Bobby knew there was no way he would escape with his limp. Where would he even go?

"I've got an idea," Jen called, disappearing back down the hatch.

The giant was almost on him when gravity shifted. Bobby floated off the floor, legs kicking at the air, his paralyzed foot flapping helplessly. He glanced back at Doc, rising as well, pumping his feet in a futile effort to move.

Doc gave up trying his weightless run and raised his blaster. "Got you," he rumbled.

Bobby squeezed his eyes shut against the impending shot, but the next instant, he came down hard on the floor, one ankle registering the jarring shock, the other pleasantly unaware.

"Uh oh." He heard Jen mutter from the hatch, and the strain in Bobby's muscles told him why. Gravity was too high. On hands and knees, he tried to straighten, but couldn't overcome its pull. Doc, however, rose to his full height, muscles rippling with immense effort. The blaster was stuck to the floor, ripped from his grasp, but the giant ignored it. He slogged toward Bobby with crashing steps that barely escaped gravity.

"Uh, Jen?" Bobby's trembling limbs threatened to give out any second. "I think you made it worse for me."

"LINC." Jen's voice echoed from the hatch. "Come help me with this."

The locker burst open, and LINC toppled out, slamming hard onto the floor.

"Be there in a sec," the bot mumbled into the floor as he scraped himself toward the hatch.

"Hurry, please," Bobby said.

Doc was drawing close, grinning wide, a predator about to reach his prey.

LINC thrashed his way to the hatch and tumbled through. "Hi, Jen," his voice echoed.

"Hi, LINC," came Jen's reply. "You wanna save Bobby?"

"Sure. Wow, you made a mess of these wires."

"So, help me."

"Hold please."

"I'm almost dead here," Bobby called as Doc stretched out a giant hand to grab him.

"Move, I got it," LINC said. "There we go."

An invisible force jerked Bobby sideways, and he slammed into something.

He scrambled to his feet, relief flooding his muscles at the return of normal gravity. But something wasn't right. Odd bits of equipment were strewn about, but the bay's furniture was now on the wall, arranged exactly as it had been on the floor. His brain tumbled about, trying to orient itself. "Wait." Then it clicked into place. The furniture wasn't on the wall. *He* was on the wall. And Doc was lunging at him.

"LINC," Bobby cried, jumping out of Doc's reach. "Fix it!"

"I thought something felt weird," LINC's voice bounced out from the hatch. "Let's try this...."

A tremor ran through the bay as some unseen power source kicked on.

Gravity sucked Bobby sideways again, smashing him into the ceiling. He covered his head from the rain of loose equipment and everything else that wasn't bolted down.

"Try again," he shouted.

"Okay, I think I'm getting the hang of this."

The bay rumbled once more. But this time nothing seemed to happen.

Doc swiped again. Bobby jumped away, but instead of landing, he found himself floating up toward the floor. Or down. He couldn't keep it straight at this point.

"Gravity's too low now!"

"You sure?" LINC's head popped up from the hatch. "Feels normal from here."

As Bobby floated past the midpoint, he felt himself pulled to the floor.

"Oh, I get it." LINC put a finger to his chin. "Guess I turned it on in two places."

Bobby landed next to the sofa, managing not to slip on the floor, still sudsy from his and Jen's water fight. Doc ran along the ceiling. The giant scooped something out of a clump of displaced junk and swung it toward Bobby. It was the blaster.

"Scrub!" Bobby ran through raining stun bolts.

"In here." Jen had squeezed next to LINC and was waving him over.

Bobby slid into the opening, falling on top of her. LINC slammed the hatch shut just as a blast connected with it.

Bobby tried to push himself off Jen, but his muscles had gone rigid. Her touch sparked a panic that seemed to freeze time, and his brain registered every sensation. The warmth of her soft body pressed against his, her still-damp clothes, even the gentle scent of her moonfruit lip gloss all sent tingles through his nerves. All he could do was stare at her, heat rising from his cheeks to his ears. It felt like a stun bolt had hit him square in the chest.

"I didn't know Bobby Robot had moves," she said with a cocked brow.

"You guys on a date or something?" LINC said. "We gotta go."

"S-sorry," Bobby stammered and rolled off Jen.

"Yeah, yeah, I'm sure you are." She winked at him.

"Come on." LINC was already crawling away between the artificial gravity polarizers that took up most of the hull's narrow space.

"Hurry, Doc will catch us," Jen giggled, bumping Bobby's shoulder as she crawled past.

Bobby tried to think of something clever to say like Jen always did, but his mind drew a blank. It was still too preoccupied with remembering their shared proximity. But thundering footsteps overhead startled him into movement. He clambered after her, contorting himself around the polarizers until he couldn't help joining her laughter at the thrill of Doc chasing them.

"He's going to cut us off at the engine room." Jen tilted her head as if listening to the footsteps. "Let's go to the hatch in my cabin." She led them along a twisting path until they came under a latch. She threw open the hatch and wriggled out. Bobby came up after her, still laughing.

Holographic pictures lined the walls of Jen's cabin. Here and there, vibrant landscapes gleamed, but most of the pictures were loops of human males with high cheekbones, flashing pensive looks at the camera.

"You really do like the Space Hotties." LINC pushed himself onto the floor.

"Be quiet," Jen whispered as she locked the hatch. "He'll hear us." She hurried to lock the door, but it slid open.

"Scrub, he found us," Bobby called in delight. But his heart plunged when he saw the figure in the doorway wasn't Doc.

Kerrick stood there, face red with fury.

"Uh oh," Jen said.

<!019: Executing Binary Functions>

"YOU'RE SCRUBBING CRAZY," laughed Bobby, pressing his hands into the warmth of his steaming mug.

"Scrubbing crazy," repeated LINC.

"Hey, I'm just saying," Jen replied with a shrug, "if you're ever in low orbit, you should skydive off a satellite." She took a sip from her own mug.

Bobby sat cross-legged on the busted sofa, his tunic still pleasantly warm from the laser heater they had used to dry out the bay from their water fight. After forcing a painful explanation of their prank, Kerrick had made them scrub the entire floor again with the toothbrushes before letting them use the heater on their clothes. He'd even made them shift the gravity to the walls and ceiling to scrub every surface. It had taken Doc calming the captain to avoid a sentence of cleaning duty every day of their journey. And when Kerrick had finally stormed off, Doc had allowed Jen to raid the galley for what she called "snacks," but only after he made them admit he'd gotten the better of them.

Now she was munching on one of these snacks—a bag of *chips*—while leaning back in a broken recliner that wouldn't sit up all the way. LINC was sprawled out sideways on an armchair, chewing a sliver of foil she'd given him. The ship had been unperturbed by asteroids for the last hour since they'd entered warped space, and Bobby, taking another bite of his *cookie*, reveled in his high spirits. Kerrick's wrath seemed a small price to pay for bonding with Jen.

Nearby, Doc tapped on a comtab, taking inventory of everything that had been displaced in the prank.

Bobby sipped the rich, creamy liquid, something Jen called *hot cocoa*. Unlike the coffee Barnes had given him earlier, this stuff smelled *and* tasted good.

"Try dipping it." Jen pointed at his cookie.

Bobby dunked the cookie in the cocoa and took a bite. "Wow," he said through a full mouth. "You make everything better." He paused mid-bite, cheeks growing hot as he mentally replayed the compliment and all its potential implications.

But Jen only considered the chip between her fingers before popping it in her mouth with a crunch. "You got that right."

"It's just, you're so good at things," Bobby blurted in an attempt to clarify. "I mean, competent, you know? Anyway. You should join the Federation. You'd make a good soldier."

"You *are* pretty athletic," LINC added. "Does the Federation have a solar surfing team?"

Jen let out a quiet laugh, though it was tinged with derision. "I actually was in the USF Academy."

"*Was?*" LINC pointed out.

Jen shrugged, but she looked away, tucking a strand of hair behind her ear with an irritated swipe of her fingers. "I dropped out my first year. I'm not what you call a"—she broke into an hyper-nasally tone—"*team player.*" An eyeroll punctuated her sneer. "Besides," she continued, "I do my best solar surfing behind the *Quasar.*"

Doc paused from his work to throw her a disapproving glance, to which she responded with an innocent smile. He shook his head and went back to checking inventory.

She shrugged and propped her feet on a low table. "Federation wasn't my style. They wouldn't let me skydive off a satellite, that's for sure."

"Do all humans do dangerous stuff?" asked Bobby, sipping more cocoa.

"Only the cool ones, isn't that right, Doc?"

"If you say so," Doc boomed as he counted exo suits in a locker.

"Tell him about the time you broke out of a Fringe Supremacist prison."

Doc glared at her. "That wasn't for fun."

"Don't believe him," she said to Bobby. "He tells it like it was a blast."

The giant seemed to ignore her as he counted the items in a toolbox, but his lips curved up almost imperceptibly.

Bobby pictured Doc punching right through a prison wall, a dozen humans trying to hold him back as he walked free. Free to roam the universe. He imagined countless faces populating countless planets and realized he knew nothing about the galaxy around him.

He turned back to Jen. "Are all humans like you?"

"They wish." Jen flipped her hair. "Nah, I'm just kidding. Everybody's different."

"Everybody?" Bobby tried to wrap his head around the concept that no two people in the galaxy were alike.

"Every single person."

"Wow." He took a thoughtful sip. "The bots on Sentinel have different tiers of complexity. But they're all basically the same."

"Hey," LINC protested.

"Except LINC," Bobby conceded. "But he's kind of an anomaly, if you couldn't tell. Wow, I can't wait till we get to Haven. I'm going to talk to everyone. It's going to be the best."

"Bobby?" Jen traced a finger around the rim of her mug. Her grin had faded. "You know the galaxy can be a rough place, right?"

"Because of the bots?" Bobby shrugged. "Barnes said once we get the weapon plans to the Federation it should even the odds. We'll beat the bots, and everybody will be happy."

"It's not that simple. And not just because of the bots."

"Then what?"

She stared at her boots. "It's just—humans aren't all good like you might think."

"You mean the Fringe Supremacists?"

"I mean, sure. But even they believe what they're doing is right."

Bobby frowned, trying to understand. "But they're fighting alongside the bots. Killing and destroying planets. How can that be right?"

"It's not right. I mean, to them it's right." She let out a frustrated huff at Bobby's confused expression. "They think they're justified."

"But they think their people are superior or whatever, right?" asked Bobby. "They sound like the bad guys. And they're hurting good people. Like you."

An amused smile flickered on her lips, then slipped. "Bobby, things aren't binary out here. I mean, yes, there are some really good people and some really bad ones. But most are in between."

Bobby rolled this around in his head for a moment. "So where do you fall?"

Jen's brows drew together, a distant look in her eyes. "Somewhere between...."

Faint taps from Doc's comtab floated to them from some alcove in the bay.

Bobby looked to LINC for advice. The bot feigned rubbing his nose, pointing the finger to Jen and mouthing the words *Say something nice.*

"Oh, well, uh, I think you're good," Bobby said, turning his attention back to Jen.

At his voice, the girl seemed to snap out of a daze. She considered him for a moment with hard blue eyes, then let out a mirthless laugh. "Don't know if I'm as good as you, Bobby Robot."

Bobby sneaked a peek at LINC for further instructions. The bot stuck out his metal lips and pantomimed a long, slow kiss. Anxiety punched Bobby's stomach at the thought. He swiveled back to Jen. She narrowed her eyes and sent LINC a suspicious glare. The bot immediately went limp.

"Sleep mode, do not disturb," he said in a monotone voice.

"Is that normal for him?" Jen asked.

"Uh, yep." Bobby nodded, catching a wink from the "sleeping" LINC.

"Weird." She drained her mug and set it on the table.

Bobby set his drink next to hers, trembling hands sloshing cocoa down the side. "Uh, Jen?"

"Yeah?" She'd pulled out her comtab and was scrolling through the feed.

He cast an uncertain glance at LINC, who gave him a thumbs up. A quick scan told him Doc was out of sight. With a resolute breath, he tossed the uneaten bit of cookie onto the table, then pushed himself up and stood in front of the recliner. "Jen?" His voice cracked.

She looked up, cocking a brow.

Screwing up his face, he stared hard into her eyes.

She flinched. "Uh, you okay?"

No words would connect with his mouth, so he just nodded until she shifted uneasily in her seat.

"Uh oh," he heard LINC mutter.

Bobby pumped his cybernetic fingers, stimulating his brain out of paralysis.

"Bobby?" Jen drew her knees up to her chest.

"Nope, nope, nope, abort, abort," LINC mumbled through a fit of modulated coughs.

But it was too late. Bobby couldn't stop. Feeling like a scrubbed bot with no control over his own limbs, he reached out and cupped Jen's head.

"What are you—" Before she could finish, the ship lurched, throwing Bobby off balance and snapping him out of his panicked stupor and into high alert.

"What was that?" he cried, wobbling to regain his balance. "An asteroid?"

"Feels like we fell out of warp." Jen leapt out of her chair and rushed to the bulkhead, flipping the switch. The slats angled to reveal ships swarming around them. Bobby hurried over with LINC to get a better look.

Red and blue plasma fire burned crisscrossing patterns in his vision. Beyond the immediate storm of fighters, massive battle cruisers floated, exchanging volleys with their photon missiles. Blinding explosions punctuated the scene, the sound of their devastating force lost in the eerie silence of space.

"It's the Federation." Jen breathed.

"Who are they fighting?" Bobby surveyed the shapes of the opposing vessels, unable to recognize any.

"Fringe Supremacists," replied Doc, running to the window and shutting the slats just before another stray plasma blast rocked the ship.

"Doc, Jen, get to the gunner ports!" Kerrick's voice crackled over the intercom.

Before anyone could react, a deafening bang sounded, and the *Quasar* shook, throwing Bobby off his feet. He tumbled down, sure he would be sucked through a breach in the hull. But he hit the floor with a hard thud, artificial gravity still in place. Senses reeling, he registered a blaring klaxon. He scrambled up and saw everyone had been thrown, even Doc.

"Scratch that," Kerrick's voice fuzzed through the alarm, "Jen, I need you on the shields."

Jen got to her feet and pointed to Bobby. "You're on gunner duty. Come on, LINC." She motioned for the bot to follow as she sprinted toward the engine room.

Bobby glanced at Doc, who had regained his footing and was already running behind Jen for the passageway. "Follow me," he boomed over his shoulder.

"Who ruined my nap?" Barnes appeared in the entryway, glancing around in half-awake confusion.

"Hit an anti-warp field." Jen rushed past him.

The old man's eyes went wide. "No time to waste," he said, shuffling toward the bridge. He jabbed a knobby finger at Bobby. "Go, son."

Bobby nodded and dashed after Doc, nerves tingling with adrenaline. Halfway through the passageway, the giant peeled off toward the starboard wing, motioning for him to take the port side. He scuffled around the corner and dashed along the wing until he reached a hatch locked with a plastisteel wheel. With a twist of the wheel and a jerk, he pulled the hatch open and scrambled inside to find himself in an orb of reinforced plastiglass.

He felt like he'd stepped right inside the raging battle. The glass afforded a view of the entire port side of the ship but did little to provide a sense of safety. He flinched when a fan of plasma shards struck the orb, fizzling out against the translucent barrier covering the *Quasar*. At least the shields were holding. For now.

He tore his attention from the surrounding explosions and focused on the swivel chair mounted at the orb's center. Jumping onto the worn seat pad, he gripped the double-handled yoke. Its plastifiber casing cracked as the motors in his cybernetic arm tightened against another blast.

"Scrub."

He twisted the yoke to see if it still worked. To his relief, a photon cannon popped up from the wing and whizzed along the thin scaffolding encircling the orb, barrels following his every turn. The controls still worked.

"Where's my port side cannon?" Kerrick's voice filtered through the intercom.

"Uh, here," Bobby answered, pulling the trigger and firing a stray shot into space.

"At the fighters, kid!"

"Which ones?" Bobby swiveled the chair, swinging the cannon between potential targets.

"Red guns," Kerrick yelled. "Take out the red guns."

"Right." Bobby scanned the battle zone for Fringe Supremacist ships blasting crimson streaks. He found one that had broken from its formation under Federation fire and was now zooming back around in a wide arc. An easy target. Twisting the controls, he traced its trajectory with the cannon, sucking in a sharp breath as he squeezed the trigger's slack.

But he cut the movement short, his muscles freezing with the same hesitation he'd felt in the Human Killer Simulation. A pilot resided behind the enemy fighter's darkened canopy. A human. Not a bot or a hologram from Programming. An actual human this time. And he'd almost taken that human's life.

He eased a trembling finger off the trigger.

"Bobby!" Kerrick's voice growled. "I need support."

Sweat trickled down Bobby's forehead. Hadn't Jen told him things weren't binary out here? Then how could he be expected to make such a binary decision like pulling this trigger? He'd thought he was on the right side of the war less than a day ago. What if the person inside that fighter was just as wrong as he'd been?

"No," he whispered. These were bad people, like the bots. Hurting good people, like Jen. He renewed his hold on the yoke, the cracked casing creaking in protest. Training the cannon back on the fighter, Bobby squeezed the trigger to the break, willing himself to shoot. But in those seconds of internal debate, a Federation fighter swooped in and picked off the Fringe Supremacist ship with a plasma burst.

The explosion burned a green spot in his vision. He desperately scanned the area for the human pilot's body. But nobody could have survived. He slammed his fist on the dashboard, cursing himself for being so foolish. His stomach churned and tears welled in his eyes while he watched the fighter's broken parts join the rest of the battle zone's floating debris.

"Son." Barnes's rusty voice startled him. He swiveled to see the old man shuffling into the orb. "Let me do it." His eyes were grim, weighted with understanding.

Bobby slid out of the seat, ducking his head so Barnes wouldn't know he'd been crying.

"Go help Jen with the shields." Barnes let his cane rattle to the floor as he climbed into the chair.

Bobby didn't argue. He wanted to get as far away from the gunner port as possible. Shaking, he hurried through the hatch, the sound of Barnes's cannon fire following him out.

Fighting waves of nausea, he stumbled along the passageway, the gunmetal walls fuzzing in his vision like he might black out any second. The next thing he knew, he was doubled over in front of the engine room. Somehow, LINC had appeared by his side and was walking him through the door.

"Easy there, Bobs." The bot's voice came muffled against the throbbing pulse in his ears.

LINC eased him to the floor, then ran to rejoin Jen, who was rewiring a generator on the warp engine. Multiple times, Bobby attempted to push himself up to go help, but every time the image of the Fringe fighter rushed back, paralyzing him. That pilot's life, gone. Vanished in the blink of an eye. It could have been him who'd taken that life.

His vision swam. Blast after blast rocked the ship, each time bringing with it the thought that he would vanish too. He pictured the *Quasar's* splintered parts drifting, insignificant, into the debris field where they would be forgotten forever.

Another hit rocked the ship, vibrating his bones. He scanned the engine room, sure that the *Quasar* had split in two. LINC was on the floor, thrown in the explosion, which still reverberated the

Quasar's frame. Jen had managed to stay on her feet, scrambling to adjust the engine's controls.

"What was that?" Bobby heard his own faint voice call over the ringing in his ears. He stood up, the blast kick-starting some adrenaline that cleared his head somewhat.

"A ship just warped next to us," Jen replied over a buzzing alarm.

"Felt like a big one." LINC bounded to his feet.

Bobby knew only a massive ship exiting warp could have generated the spatial shockwave large enough to damage the *Quasar*. "It's a Sentinel warship," he whispered even before the battle cruiser appeared on Jen's display console.

Jen's fingers paused above the controls, her eyes wide.

Purple photon blasts erupted from the warship's side, fanning out in all directions until they found their target in Federation vessels. Bobby watched the scene, frozen next to Jen, as the Federation ships broke apart.

The alarm, which for a moment had seemed far away, suddenly punctured his awareness.

"Shields are at critical limits," Jen said.

"What do we do?" Bobby cried, panic straining his voice.

"I've got to angle the shields manually." Her fingers worked at the console, navigating through menus at a frenetic pace until she landed on an icon and selected it. A hologram bloomed out from the console's side, engulfing them in popping lights.

For a split second, Bobby thought he'd been transported back to the gunner port, seeing the skirmish through the plastiglass orb. But it was a hologram of the battle outside. He half expected to feel the shock of explosions all around him, like he was back in the Human Killer Sim, sensory drones biting his flesh.

"Bobby, move." Jen shoved him.

He regained his balance at the edge of the hologram, where a Federation cruiser was breaking apart under another volley of Sentinel photon fire. He watched it crumble in horror until it slipped past the holo's border. He snapped his gaze back to the holo's center where he'd been standing and realized why Jen had pushed him. A rendering of the *Quasar* resided in the middle, the holographic map of the battle zone moving as the ship navigated the fight.

A translucent barrier covered part of the *Quasar*. The shield. Or what was left of it.

Jen worked at the console, spinning the barrier around the *Quasar*, deflecting shots from nearby Fringe craft. She cursed every time a blast sneaked through her defense.

"A little help would be nice!" she shouted, swinging the barrier around in time to stop a photon missile.

"I got this!" LINC tore open his maintenance panel and extracted the cord from his chest. He jammed the jack into Jen's console, and the barrier around the holographic *Quasar* spun at high speed, deflecting every enemy shot.

"Why didn't you tell me you could do that?" Jen screamed. "Bobby, you okay?"

Bobby had no idea how long he'd been standing there, unmoving, not helping, spots flashing in his vision. His legs were heavy. Arms too. Whole body. Like gravity had turned up multiple G's. Jen rushed to his side, catching him as he struggled to stand. But he was too heavy, his weight overcoming her strength. She broke the fall, eased him to his knees. He heard puffs of shallow breathing. His own.

"You're in shock." Her voice drifted to him as if from across the galaxy.

Senses hyper-aware, his nervous system tried to experience everything at once, unable to integrate and focus. A Programming lesson flashed in his thoughts. His reticular activating system, the formation of neurons responsible for awareness, was going haywire. It was turning in on itself, bringing a neurology lesson to his consciousness in an attempt to rationalize the situation. But nothing was rational. Countless hours in the Human Killer Simulation had not prepared him for the real thing.

Whether a hallucination or not, he couldn't tell, the bridge seemed to stretch an impossible distance for one near-unbearable second, then snap back to its original dimensions.

Something materialized in front of him, blurry features condensing into Jen's face.

"Hey," she said, her voice seeming nearer. "We made it out. We're back in warp."

It took a moment for her words to register. Still, his reeling brain wouldn't form a response.

"Come on." She hooked an arm under his. LINC took the other side, and Bobby felt himself lifted to his feet.

Together, they walked at a slow pace out of the engine room.

Barnes met them in the bay, cane in hand again.

"You did a good job, son," he said as Jen and LINC helped Bobby into a chair.

"Good job?" Kerrick stormed out of the bridge, followed by Doc. "I needed a port wing gunner. We almost died back there."

"Ease off the boy." Barnes opened the slats on the bulkhead, revealing the dazzle of streaking stars. "We're back in warped space and in one piece. That's all that matters."

Bobby glanced outside, vaguely noting the star stream.

"You okay?" Barnes asked.

Doc whipped out a penlight and flashed it in Bobby's eyes.

"His heart rate's high," LINC offered.

"No evidence of concussion," Doc said. "Anxiety episode most likely."

"You telling me we almost blew up 'cause the kid got scared?" Kerrick bellowed.

The captain's words pierced the faraway sensations, stabbing Bobby through the chest. His moment of weakness, of indecision, had almost killed the crew. Maybe Gamma had fed him half-truths all his life, but Sentinel's overlord had been right about one thing. *I'm too flawed to be useful.*

"Stop it, Uncle," Jen cried. She seemed on the verge of tears.

Barnes stepped in front of Kerrick, halting his advance at Bobby.

Kerrick ran an aggravated hand through his graying hair. "We can't afford any more scrapes like this."

"We have thirty-six hours to Haven," Barnes said in an even tone. "We'll deliver the weapon plans and that will be that."

Kerrick glared at Barnes before turning on his heel with a snarl. "Can't wait till this job's over." He marched back to the bridge, Doc in tow.

Barnes patted Bobby on the back. "It's okay, son."

"Yeah," Jen said, touching his shoulder. "We made it out."

Bobby stared through the slats at the streaking stars. The explosions still rang in his head. The fighter, breaking apart over and over on a loop in his mind. As a tear ran down his cheek, he wondered if he'd really made it out.

<!020: Extracting Purpose>

BOBBY SQUIRMED ON his mattress. No matter how he tossed and turned, he couldn't get comfortable, couldn't protect himself from the memories. He'd left his clothes on, so as not to feel naked, vulnerable. The surrounding darkness made the image of the exploding Fringe fighter all the more clear. Another wave of tears spilled over his cheeks. He tried to force the memories away, concentrating instead on the hum of LINC charging in the corner. But it seemed the more he tried to fight them, the stronger they came. With a frustrated grunt, he threw the covers off and sat up.

"Having trouble sleeping, Bobs?" said LINC, motors whirring out of sleep mode.

Bobby sniffed and wiped his cheeks. "I'm okay."

"Sleeping in gravity is kinda weird, huh?" The bot stretched and unplugged himself. "I downloaded some music from Jen's computer. There's a song called Mutilator's Lullaby by a group called the Dead Rats. I learned lullabies are good for sleep. Want me to play it for you?" Without waiting for an answer, the bot turned on the song.

Deafening chords cut through Bobby's ears. Blue shafts of laser light danced on the ceiling from LINC's eyes as the bot pumped his fist to the beat.

"Turn it off!" Bobby plugged his ears against the singer's horrifying scream.

The sound vanished.

"Interesting song." LINC flicked the lights on and plopped down next to Bobby. "I'll try to find something more relaxing."

"Don't," Bobby said, twisting a finger in his ear.

"What's going on with you?"

"Nothing, I'm fine."

"Your neurotransmitter profile says otherwise."

"Stop." Bobby threw up a hand against LINC's laser scan. "Okay, so I'm not fine. I just—I scrubbed up again, you know?"

LINC leaned back on one arm. "'Cause you couldn't operate the cannon, and we almost died?"

Bobby clicked his tongue. "Yep."

LINC waved away his concern. "Hey, you were stressed. We're all fine now, no big deal."

"It is a big deal," Bobby snapped. "Gamma was right. I'm too flawed to be useful."

At that, LINC's alloy finger thumped him on the temple.

"Ow, what was that for?" Bobby rubbed the spot where the bot had flicked him.

"You're flawed, yes," LINC said.

When the silence dragged on, Bobby shrugged. "Okay, and?"

"Like majorly flawed."

"Yeah, okay."

"You've scrubbed up so many times that I've quite frankly lost count."

"Thanks, LINC." Bobby gritted his teeth.

"But," the bot raised a finger, "you've always learned from it."

Bobby dropped his head, and LINC thumped him again.

"Ow!" He batted the bot's hand away. "Will you stop doing that?"

"I'm just saying." LINC's maw angled in a grin. "You never make the same mistake twice. That's something."

Bobby fell silent, letting LINC's words sink in.

"Well," LINC said after some consideration, "you make a lot of very similar mistakes. A lot. All in the same category, I guess. But never the *exact* same mistake, you know what I mean?"

"LINC, you're so bad at making me feel better." Bobby laughed despite himself. He punched the bot's shoulder.

"And yet I still do." LINC raised his hands in surrender, and they both laughed.

Bobby took a deep breath and sighed. "It's not just scrubbing up, though. I mean, yesterday, I was so sure about everything. Then Barnes and Jen told me the truth about the bots. And yeah, it was hard to accept at first, but once I did it was simple. All that changed was the enemy. Good and evil flipped. And now I'm on the right side of the war."

LINC shrugged. "That's good, right?"

Bobby rubbed the blanket between his fingers. "I thought so until that battle just now. I scrubbed up at the cannon because I had a shot on this Fringe fighter, and—I don't know, I just couldn't take it."

"Why not? You're a great shot. I should know. I used to be in your arm."

"Because that Fringe pilot was a human."

"Bobs, as much as I hate putting down my own kind, those bots on Sentinel are the bad guys. And if the Fringe Supremacists are on their side, then they're bad too."

"But *we* were on the bots' side yesterday. Don't you get it? If the Fringe fighters are evil because they're allied with the bots, then that means we were evil too."

"But we didn't know any better."

"But—but—" Bobby flailed his arms in exasperation. "What if they don't know any better either?"

"So that's why you were so out of it earlier? I thought you were in shock from a blast."

"LINC," Bobby groaned. "That Fringe pilot died. A Federation ship swooped in and blew him up. Boom. Gone. Same as how the bots killed Jen's dad."

LINC shifted on the mattress. "I didn't know about that."

"What if that pilot had a daughter too?" Bobby's breath came rapid and shallow. "And now another girl's father was just taken away?"

LINC placed a wiry hand on his shoulder. "Bobs...."

Bobby pressed his fingertips to his aching head. It was too complicated. Too many ways to see it. No clear solution.

"Why don't you ask Barnes what he thinks?" LINC said. "Seems smart for a human."

Bobby straightened. *Barnes.* The memory of the old man taking the gunner's seat flashed into his mind. He would ask Barnes how he was able to man the cannon. If anyone could sort this out, it would be him.

He pulled on his boots and bounded for the door. "Thanks."

"Sure thing, boss," LINC called after him. "Hey, don't worry, I'm going to find you a good lullaby!"

```
<o:!0110101-000Z><01110000></x:01011>
<o:010011100/01>
<
```

BOBBY PADDED ALONG the port wing from his quarters. He reached Jen's cabin and stopped, listening for any sound behind the door, but hearing nothing. *She must be asleep.* He continued on, wondering how someone could fall asleep after a battle like that. She must have been in dozens of battles. She'd skydived off a low orbit satellite, solar surfed, and probably a million other things. Of course, a little skirmish wouldn't faze her. She'd probably seen it all.

He swallowed a pang of humiliation. Was he the only one upset? Maybe Kerrick was right to be angry with him. If only he could've taken that shot, defended the crew. Instead, he'd almost fainted.

Wincing at his ineptitude, he crossed the main passageway to the starboard wing, passing Doc's and Kerrick's quarters to Barnes's cabin at the end. Muffled music hummed within.

Good, he's awake. Bobby tapped the control panel, and the door slid open. Barnes was seated in a padded armchair, reading on a comtab and swaying his head to the music.

"Oh, hey there, Bobby." The old man peered over a pair of holo lenses perched on his nose. "Come on in. Didn't hear you knock."

"Knock?" Bobby stepped in, registering some sort of gentle aroma in the air.

"Oh, that's right." Barnes chuckled as the door automatically slid shut. "Usually we knock before entering a room. Just a friendly request of entry to the person inside. But no harm done. Would you like some tea? Kettle's still warm." Barnes pushed himself up and tightened the sash at his waist to secure a type of loose leisure garment Bobby had never seen. The old man shuffled over to a desk where a metal pitcher with a long spout sat on a warmer.

"Uh, sure."

Bobby checked out the cabin while Barned poured a mug of steaming liquid. A simple cot rested in the corner. Next to it was a shelf filled with rows of what looked like vertical storage cases marked with different inscriptions. Nestled between the armchair and desk, a computer displayed colors swirling in sync to swooning music. It reminded Bobby of LINC's colors when he'd inhabited his arm.

"Here you go." Barnes pressed the warm mug into his hands.

A fresh wave of the gentle aroma wafted up to him from the tea. He brought it to his nose, inhaling the soothing scent. "This isn't like coffee, is it?" he asked, stopping short of taking a sip.

Barnes laughed as he rolled a chair to the cabin's center. "No surprises with this one. If you like the smell, you'll probably like the taste. Chamomile with lavender. A different variety than the one derived from the old Earth crops, but still relaxing." He sank back into his armchair and motioned for Bobby to take the other seat.

Bobby lowered himself onto the rolling chair and took a sip of tea. The flavor was mild but surprisingly pleasant. "What are you listening to?"

"Gerald James," Barnes replied. "One of the great jazz artists of the Stellaris system. He was my wife's favorite. We used to slow dance every night to his music." The old man stared into the distance as the instruments crooned a melody, a smile playing on his lips as if he was lost in a happy memory.

Bobby imagined Barnes gazing into his wife's eyes as the music played, and a warmth settled into him. "What happened to her?"

Barnes's smile slipped a bit. "Passed away from solar sickness about twenty years ago." He paused, staring at something no longer there. "But even at the end, she was the most stunning woman in the galaxy. After all this time, the music still brings her back to me."

The old man fell silent, and a vacuum of sorrow sucked the warmth from Bobby's chest. Like a breaking reservoir, the sadness from a moment earlier came rushing back. Barnes's wife. Jen's father. The Fringe fighter. They'd all died, changing the lives of those around them in an instant.

"But I'm sure you didn't come to hear me reminisce," Barnes said, blinking away the distant look. "What's on your mind?" At seeing the tears running down Bobby's cheeks, he shut off the music and leaned forward in his chair. "Tell me what's going on, son."

"The Fringe Supremacist," Bobby sobbed. "I—I froze. I couldn't shoot. Then a Federation ship blew him up, and I glitched. Everything started spinning."

"That's a normal reaction in your first battle." Barnes placed a hand on Bobby's forearm.

"It makes no sense." Tears fell into Bobby's lap. "Fringe fighters are evil. I should have fired. I should have helped. And when I saw that pilot die, I don't know, I just lost control. It's illogical."

"Bobby, emotions are not illogical. They serve a purpose."

"How?" Bobby cried. "I was useless in that battle."

"Let me show you something." Barnes got up and retrieved one of the vertical cases from the shelf before returning.

Bobby blinked through tears as the old man opened it. It wasn't a case at all but rather a bound sheaf of paper. Real paper, filled with text.

"Ever seen a book before?" Barnes asked.

Bobby leaned closer, tracing the object's edges for a button or something to activate it. "What's it for?"

"It's an old way of holding information."

"Why not just use a comtab? It can hold more data."

Barnes swatted the idea away with a wrinkled hand. "Comtabs don't have the right feel. Nothing beats the weight of a good book in your hands. The way it smells." He buried his nose in the pages and took a deep sniff. "Ah."

Bobby sniffled. "But what does tactile sense have to do with the information inside? It doesn't make sense."

Barnes gasped. "It makes perfect sense. Especially for a work of art like this one. It happens to be by my favorite author. Want to hear a poem?"

"A what?"

"Here, listen." Barnes thumbed to a page with a corner folded over, then traced a bony finger along an underlined excerpt. "*Oh joyful day, what do you bring? A happy heart and songs to sing? Oh, sorrow mine, why do you call? To bruise my heart when I should fall? Yet joy or sorrow, together make: A wondrous path for me to take.*" He closed the book and looked at Bobby.

"What does it mean?" Bobby frowned, trying to make sense of the words.

"It means that all emotions give you the gift of guidance. They're telling you something about yourself and the universe."

A hollow laugh escaped Bobby's throat. He shook his head. "Emotions just lead you astray."

Barnes raised a finger. "They can if you're not careful. But they can also lead you in the right direction. Bobby, so many people live on the surface of life and never listen to what their emotions are trying to tell them. You're grieving right now for that Fringe Supremacist. What's that telling you?"

Bobby rolled the question around in his head. "I don't know. Maybe that I don't want to see people lose their lives? Even if they are bad?"

Barnes nodded. "I think you're right."

"But—but I saw you shooting. How were you okay with fighting them?"

The old man sighed, his wrinkles seeming to deepen. "I don't want to fight any more than you do. But in that moment, there was no changing that Fringe pilot's point of view. He was going to kill innocent people. I made a choice to protect my loved ones."

"Okay." Bobby let Barnes's explanation settle into the gaps of his broken understanding. "But what about the others out there? What if they're just confused like I was?"

Barnes leaned in like he was about to share a secret. "Do you know what mercy is? My wife developed solar sickness while working to rehabilitate Supremacist casualties on the Fringe worlds. And to be sure, not all of them were confused. Some willingly rejected moral truth. But she died working to change their lives anyway. I once read a book that said love covers over a multitude of wrongs. My wife always said that those who need mercy the most are the ones who deserve it the least."

"Wow." Bobby let the gravity of what Barnes said sink in.

"I don't want you to be afraid of your emotions, son. Sometimes they'll lead you astray. It's the risk of being human. But as long as you keep asking these questions, your emotions will serve you and not enslave you."

Just then, something clicked in Bobby's mind. "All my life," he spoke slowly, working out his realization, "I believed that emotions had enslaved the human race. Caused their Fall. But you're telling me that emotions can serve humanity?" The tension in his shoulders eased. He wiped his cheeks. "Thank you."

The old man smiled and gave the book a gentle shake. "I owe a lot to this. Taught me a lot about the beauty of life."

"Who wrote it?"

"My wife." He handed the book to Bobby, who took it and gazed at the name *Jennifer Barnes* on the cover. "Wrote it about a month before she died."

Bobby flipped through the pages, marveling at the text. When he offered it back, Barnes held up a hand.

"Why don't you hang on to it for a while? Maybe it'll teach you something too. I sense you have a great purpose."

Purpose, the word reverberated in Bobby's mind. Both LINC and the Archiver had told him he was destined for a purpose.

Barnes wrapped an arm around Bobby and gently squeezed. "Now, why don't you get some sleep?"

Bobby bobbed his head. "Thanks again. I—I owe you a lot."

"You don't owe me a thing." Barnes winked. "Just pass it on, that's all I ask."

"Okay, I will."

As the door slid shut behind Bobby, the muffled sound of music started up again. He lingered for a moment, thumbing through the book while listening to the soft melody and letting everything Barnes had said solidify in his brain.

He turned to head back to his quarters when the clack of footsteps echoing in the main passageway stopped him. Kerrick's low voice drifted from the engine room's direction. Bobby had the sudden urge to duck back into Barnes's cabin, but what would he tell him? That he was trying to avoid his son? Instead, he pressed himself against the wall, trying to think of excuses for why he wasn't in his cabin if Kerrick happened to turn down the starboard wing.

But when the captain appeared around the corner, he was engaged in a conversation with Doc.

"It's not going to work," Kerrick said as the two headed for the bridge. "The code's too complicated. The kid has no idea what's in that slag arm of his."

Bobby's ears pricked at their conversation as the two men walked out of sight. He tip-toed along the wing, then peered around the corner to watch them move through the bay. Even from a distance, he could hear Doc's heavy sigh.

"Don't give me that," Kerrick said. "You saw the data yourself."

Bobby instinctively hugged his cybernetic arm to his chest as a wave of panic washed over him. What were they talking about? What the scrub did his arm contain?

They disappeared into the bridge, the door sliding shut and cutting off their voices. But Bobby had to know what they were talking about. He crept into the bay, holding his breath against every sound his boots made on the floor.

When he'd reached the bridge door, he leaned in, straining to hear the conversation inside.

"I've run through every scenario," Kerrick said. "That cyborg arm of his is hardwired into his nervous system. Not like the outlawed body mods on those old Earth cyber freaks. Take his arm off, and he'll die. There's no way around it. We have to go to Plan B."

"And you think this is right?" Doc's deep voice vibrated the door.

"What's right is that after this job you'll get to go home and see your family."

The bridge fell silent, leaving Bobby's ears to thrum with his pounding heartbeat. He clutched Barnes's book to his chest and leaned closer until his ear was almost touching plastisteel.

"Yeah, that's what I thought," Kerrick spoke again. "Look, let me handle this. We play this right, and you can buy your daughter her own pet moon bear, or whatever she's into now."

The giant huffed, and when the two fell silent again, it seemed the conversation was over.

Mind racing, Bobby pulled back, intent on hurrying back to Barnes's cabin to relate what he'd heard. Maybe the old man could explain the matter. He turned around, and his heart stopped at the sight of LINC bouncing toward him.

"Hey, Bobs, I couldn't find a lullaby, so I figured we could dance until you get tired." The bot clicked on another round of blaring music and wobbled about, sending out his blue eye laser to form dancing spotlights on the floor.

The bridge door slid open with a whoosh, and Bobby whirled to see Kerrick glaring down at him.

"What are you doing?" he demanded. "Why are you out of your cabin?"

"I—I—" Bobby stammered, trying to think of a response.

"Shut that off," Kerrick hollered at LINC. The bot froze, and the music drawled into silence. "Lights out. Get to your quarters."

"R-right," Bobby stuttered, backpedaling away from the captain. "Come on, LINC." The bot followed close behind, and together they hurried out of the main bay under Kerrick's harsh gaze.

They rounded the corner and scrambled into their cabin. Bobby tossed the book onto his bed and turned to LINC as the door slid shut. "Are you defective or something? Why did you do that?"

"Just trying to help you sleep." The bot shrugged. "I didn't know the captain would get his spacesuit in a bunch."

"Scrub it." Bobby ran a frustrated hand through his hair. "LINC, something's not right. They were talking about my arm. Like they were thinking about removing it or something."

LINC grabbed his arm and jiggled it. "That's weird, what would they do with this fleshy thing?"

"My cybernetic arm." Bobby flashed his synthetic fingers.

"Oh," LINC said. Then his eyes went wide as comprehension dawned. "Oh...."

"I need to talk to Barnes. Are they still out there?"

"My sensors are picking up the big guy in the bay." LINC squinted as if seeing through the wall. "Looks like the cap stationed him there."

"Maybe I can slip past him." Bobby thumbed the control panel, and the door slid open. With LINC in tow, he hurried through the wing and peeked around the corner into the bay. Doc had moved an armchair to the bay's center and was watching the main passageway. He met Bobby's eyes and got up, striding toward them. His face was grim. No prank this time.

"Scrub." Bobby shoved LINC back toward their cabin.

The giant rounded the corner as they ducked into their room, and the door slid shut again. Bobby listened for his booming footsteps to draw nearer, but they stopped short, then receded.

"What's he doing?" Bobby whispered.

LINC's lensed eyes twitched as his sensors processed data. "He's sitting back in the chair."

"You can plug into the ship, right? Can you get a message to Jen?"

"I can only download unencrypted data. I can't broadcast." The bot's jaw swung sideways in agitation. "Also, looks like the cap just locked me out of the system. Sorry, Bobs, we're stuck here."

Bobby swallowed hard. "Something is very wrong."

<!021: Detecting Multiple Harmful Programs>

A ROUGH HAND shook Bobby out of a fitful sleep. Dreams of bots removing his cybernetic arm dissolved into Doc's solemn face looming above him. The motors in his cybernetic joints seized in panic.

"What do you want?"

The giant didn't answer, only jerked a thumb toward the open door. Seconds ticked by until it was clear that Doc wasn't going to leave until he'd escorted Bobby out of the cabin.

With a scowl, Bobby sat up, scanning the empty room before balling his fist. "What did you do with LINC?"

Doc thrust a finger toward the door. "Go." His voice was low, dangerous.

Bobby curled his lip. He pushed himself up in slow, defiant movement and glared at Doc before trudging out of the room.

The giant's footsteps fell heavy behind him as they traversed the port wing to the main passageway. When they rounded the corner, an overwhelming impulse to run seized him. Before he knew it, he was flying through the bay, shouting, "LINC! LINC! Where are you?"

He skidded to a halt as the bridge door opened and LINC appeared, trying to scuffle out of Kerrick's grasp. "Bobs, get out of here!" he called. "He's going to—" Twisting metal screeched, and the bot's lensed eyes dimmed. He crashed to the floor, leaving the captain framed in the doorway, clutching LINC's torn maintenance panel in one hand and his power cell in the other.

"No!" Bobby rushed to LINC's crumpled body and fumbled through the mess of wires for the emergency power save switch. Before he could flip it, Doc caught his shoulder and pulled him up to face Kerrick.

"What are you doing?" Bobby spat, thrashing against Doc's grip.

The captain shot him a steely glance, then let the panel clatter to the floor. He turned back toward the bridge, tossing LINC's power cell, which hit the floor with a heavy *crack*.

Bobby struggled against Doc's unyielding grip, but the giant forced him forward, over LINC's body and into the bridge where a hazy purple planet lingered in the viewport.

"We're cleared for atmospheric descent," Jen's quiet voice called through the chirps and chitters of computers.

Bobby spotted her behind holographic readouts from her station.

"Jen," he called as Doc locked his hands in cuffs behind his back. She didn't answer. Didn't even look up. "Jen! What's going on? Why are they doing this?" Still, she made no reply. Dismay squeezed Bobby's chest. "Jen...."

Then, for a split second, she glanced up at him, eyes shining with moisture, but the next instant she'd returned her gaze to her station.

He pulled at the cuffs, but the strength of his cybernetic arm only made them dig deeper into the flesh of his biologic wrist. His mind raced with all the implications of the conversation he'd overheard last night. Of Doc watching to make sure he didn't leave his cabin. Were they going to remove his arm? What was in it that Kerrick wanted? Hadn't they already extracted the weapon plans?

In another fit of panic, he pulled so hard at the cuffs that blood trickled down his wrist. A few more painful tugs, and he stopped. It was useless. He let his shoulders fall in defeat.

A soft alert chimed. He turned his attention to the purple planet filling the viewport, its hazy cloud cover obscuring any terrain beneath.

"This isn't the Federation headquarters, is it?"

"No, it's not," came a rusty voice from behind.

He craned his neck around Doc's hefty frame to see Barnes shuffle onto the bridge, a bitter look in his eye.

"You promised," the old man said to Kerrick.

The captain pressed his hands flat on the dash. "Go back to your quarters." His voice was quiet, tempered with souring patience.

Barnes thrust the tip of his cane onto the floor, making a loud *clack*. "You said if you deliver the code to the Federation, they would pardon you."

Code? Bobby thought. *What code?*

Kerrick made no reply, only glowered at the planet growing in the viewport.

"Well?" Barnes pressed.

The captain slammed a fist onto the control panel. "Open your eyes, old man. The Federation you served doesn't operate like that anymore. I would be tried as a traitor. This is my only way out."

"Barnes, please," Bobby ventured. "What's going on?"

"My son's a thief," Barnes replied, glaring at Kerrick. "He's going to sell the data in your arm on the black market."

"We're all mercenaries here." The captain stabbed a finger at Barnes. "You included."

"What's he talking about?" Bobby's voice came out small.

"I haven't been totally honest with you, son." Barnes sighed, finally turning his attention to Bobby. "We didn't just steal weapon plans from Sentinel."

"Wh-what? What did you steal?"

"A code, Bobby. A code that makes an AI being sentient. In other words, truly alive. Aware of its own existence. Your arm." He nodded at the vidscreen set in Bobby's forearm. "It was incubating the Sentience Code."

It took a moment for Bobby's brain to connect the words. *True artificial sentience. The Sentience Code.* Then he remembered. The researchers in those holos from the Depository. They'd been working on a new kind of AI. The Sentinel Project, they'd called it. *Sentinel.* A derivative of *sentience.* He swallowed hard against a knot in his throat as the pieces came together. An AI soldier who was truly alive, could think and feel and act like a human. A better version of a human. That's what they'd been developing. Was Barnes telling him the code for this super advanced form of AI had been in his arm this whole time? A thousand questions jostled in his brain, but only one made it out of his mouth. "You lied to me?"

The old man's eyes grew heavy, the lines in his face etching deeper. "I let my emotions lead me astray, Bobby. Ever since my wife and son died, this is all the family I've got. I suppose I've turned a blind eye to what they do because they're all I have left."

Tears welled in Bobby's eyes. "Tell me everything. Now."

"Kerrick's in trouble with the Federation. He told me if we infiltrated Sentinel and delivered the Sentience Code, they would pardon him. So I helped him steal a captured Sentinel cargo ship using my military credentials. But...." He frowned. "It looks like he lied to me too."

"Stop talking to the boy," Kerrick growled.

"I skirt the law, yes," Barnes continued, ignoring the order, "but he breaks it. He's not going to deliver the code to the Federation. He's going to sell it to someone else. Who's the highest bidder this time, Kerrick?"

Just then, a gruff voice crackled over the ship's speakers. "*Quasar,* you've been granted access to hanger twenty-seventeen. Master Bar-Uk requests you bring the goods out yourself."

"Fine." Kerrick thumbed the reply button.

"Bar-Uk?" Barnes shouted when the transmission terminated. "You're pulling a job for Bar-Uk?"

"Jen, prepare the *Quasar* for landing," Kerrick ordered, flipping switches.

The ship rattled as it entered the planet's atmosphere. Swirling haze filling the viewport.

"How much do you owe him?" Barnes demanded.

Kerrick ignored the question, but Barnes caught him by the elbow. "Kerrick. How much?"

The captain spun to face the old man. "More than I can pay for the Federation's protection. He'll torture and kill every one of us."

"You put us in danger? You put my granddaughter in danger?" Barnes shoved a bony finger toward Jen.

"She helped with half the jobs that got us into this mess!"

Bobby glanced at Jen, who shrank behind the holograms.

Barnes tightened his grip on Kerrick's arm. "Sell the code, but I'm leaving with Jen and Bobby on the shuttle."

"Not going to happen." Kerrick broke out of Barnes's grip. "The kid stays."

"Why?" Barnes narrowed his eyes. "You found something else inside his arm, didn't you?" When the captain didn't answer, he turned to Jen. "Jen? You copied the data from his arm. What did you find?"

Kerrick shot Jen a look of warning, and for a moment, it appeared she wasn't going to answer. But under the probing gaze of her grandfather, she gave in. "Access cipher," she mumbled. "His arm has an access cipher to Sentinel. All of it. Like a key code. It's why he could open the Depository and the planetary shield."

Her words struck Bobby like a plasma blast.

An access cipher to Sentinel.

In his arm.

A thousand more questions swam in his head. He'd had access to everything on Sentinel? Was that even possible? Who had installed it? And why? Had the bots known?

"A key to Sentinel," Barnes muttered, comprehension spreading across his grim features.

"It's going to wipe out our debt," Kerrick said.

"Kerrick, listen to me." Barnes's tone turned to pleading. "We've got to deliver it to the Federation. They can use it to invade Sentinel."

The captain snorted. "Jen, you want to tell him? Since you're so great at explaining our plans?"

Bobby swiveled his gaze back to Jen. Her lip trembled like she was holding back a rush of tears. "Bar-Uk's tracking us. He'll know if we go to the Federation."

"So give him a copy of the access cipher, and then give another to the Federation once we're free," Barnes reasoned. "They can stop Bar-Uk."

Jen shook her head. "The cipher's hardwired into his arm. Tangled with his nervous system somehow. We can't extract it without—without…." Her voice broke, and tears slipped down her cheeks.

Bobby sucked in a breath as the whole thing clicked into place. The conversation he'd overheard last night. Kerrick couldn't sell a *copy* of the cipher that would open everything on Sentinel because his cybernetic arm *itself* was the cipher.

Kerrick was going to sell *him*.

Numbness spread through his limbs. Tears that had been forming finally spilled onto his cheeks. He looked at Barnes. "You lied to me." It was all he could say. "You lied."

"We're not going to let him do this, son." Barnes pulled Bobby toward the door, but Doc blocked their path, blaster drawn.

The old man halted, resignation seeping into the lines of his face. "And what's in this for you, my friend?"

"No more bounty," Doc rumbled, holding the barrel steady at Barnes's chest. "Get to see my family."

"Enough," Kerrick barked. "We're about to land."

The bridge shuddered as the ship's descent eased and broke through the haze.

Dread chilled Bobby at the sight through the viewport. Tall buildings loomed black against the hazy sky like crooked teeth, towering over dim streets. Angled street lamps punctured the darkness, illuminating hefty transport ships that plowed through the grimy avenues with secret payloads.

Kerrick banked the *Quasar* around a cluster of buildings until a low tower came into view, its wide hanger gaping like an open mouth ready to swallow them.

"*Quasar*, you're cleared for landing," a voice fuzzed over the speakers.

Kerrick guided the ship into the empty hangar, the whine of the engine fading as they landed.

"Jen, you hid the backup you made, right?" he asked.

Jen nodded almost imperceptibly.

"What, are you going to sell the Code all over the galaxy now?" Barnes cried.

"One thing at a time." Kerrick turned to Doc. "Let's get him down there."

The giant pointed his blaster at Bobby and motioned for him to walk. Bobby moved with shaky steps, glancing at Barnes for help.

"I'm coming with you." The old man shuffled up alongside.

"Grandpop, no," Jen cried.

Barnes tipped his cane at her. "You stay on the ship."

"You're not going," Kerrick said to Barnes.

"Shoot me, then," Barnes called over his shoulder as he accompanied Bobby out of the bridge at gunpoint. Kerrick grunted and followed behind Doc.

"I'm so sorry, Bobby," Barnes whispered as they stepped over LINC's body. "If I'd known this is what my son was up to, I'd never have gone along with it."

The words did little to reassure Bobby. His heart threatened to burst from his chest. They traversed the bay, stopping halfway for Kerrick to punch the switch and the loading ramp to descend.

"Keep him quiet, Doc," Kerrick ordered.

In a flash, Doc pressed something to Bobby's neck, sending a jolt through his throat. A cry of pain tried to escape, but only hoarse wheezes came out through his fried vocal cords.

"Bobby!" Barnes reached for him as Bobby fell to his knees.

"Step back or you'll get it too," Kerrick warned.

Doc sparked the device in his hand, and Barnes straightened, wrinkled cheeks red with fury.

Bobby groaned, throat burning. Doc pulled him to his feet and gave him a shove.

He stumbled down the ramp, keenly aware of Kerrick's blaster at his back despite the pain. Upon stepping into the hangar, stale air assaulted him with a stench like warm garbage. Pulse racing, he scanned the area, spotting a convoy of dark figures approaching from the far side. Doc readied his blaster.

As the convoy drew closer, Bobby realized it was a mix of humans and bots. Bulky men with weathered faces and stubby beards scowled at them with hard eyes. Astonishment at seeing new humans faded when he saw their blasters. The bots had trained their own weapons on the *Quasar's* crew, as well. They reminded Bobby of the security bots on Sentinel but more rudimentary in their movements and design.

The convoy stopped about twenty meters from the *Quasar*.

"Is that the kid?" one of the men shouted.

"He's the one," Kerrick called back, voice echoing off the empty hangar walls. "Call off our bounty, and he's yours."

Bobby felt Barnes give his arm a reassuring squeeze, even though he sensed the old man knew escape was futile.

"Bar-Uk's good for his word," the man replied.

"I want to see him myself," Kerrick returned. "Call him."

"No can do, Kerrick. You're in no position to bargain."

"Oh no?" He jerked Bobby close, pressing the gun against his head. "Tell Bar-Uk if he doesn't come out, he loses the biggest payment of his life."

The men muttered to each other in hushed tones while the bots stood sentry. When there appeared to be a consensus, the man replied. "Fine, he's on his way."

"I'll wait."

Bobby winced as the barrel bore into his head. He tried to cry out, but nothing could get through his deadened vocal cords.

A long moment passed as the two groups watched each other in silence. At length, a wide sliding door retracted behind the convoy, and a hulking figure glided out. As the men parted to let the figure through, Bobby realized it was an enormously fat man sitting on some sort of large hover chair, its wide seat struggling to contain his bulk. An orb about the size of the man's bald head floated in slow circles around the chair, a nasty looking harpoon sliding out and retracting from its center in a threatening pattern.

"Now, what's all this, Kerrick?" said the fat man. His gravelly voice over-enunciated each syllable in a way that reminded Bobby of his old language lessons in Programming. "I promised to wipe your name off of every bounty board. You don't trust me?"

"Sorry, Bar-Uk," Kerrick said. "This one's a little too important."

The man, Bar-Uk, chuckled, something between a wheeze and a cough. "I do not know if I admire your obstinance or resent it. But I suppose I cannot blame you in this line of work. Is this the boy?" His beady eyes shifted to Bobby.

"Your personal key to Sentinel."

"The arm, yes? How does it work?" Bar-Uk scanned Bobby's arm with a hungry look.

"A wave of the hand opens any restricted area. Even the planetary shield. Works like magic."

Bar-Uk hovered closer, accompanied by his convoy. Bobby tensed as the floating orb flashed its harpoon. "And what of the Sentience Code I originally sent you to retrieve?"

"Couldn't find it." Kerrick shook his head. "But I got you a key that'll open a whole planet. If the Sentience Code is there, then you can invade Sentinel yourself and look all you want."

Bobby held his breath. Why was the captain lying about finding the Sentience Code? Barnes said it was in his arm. Why would Kerrick sell him to this foul human as a key to Sentinel only? Didn't he say he had a backup of the Code on board the *Quasar* anyway?

Bar-Uk leaned forward. His eyes flashed with a curious expression. Did he suspect Kerrick wasn't telling the truth?

"Now," Kerrick continued, a flicker of uncertainty crossing his features at Bar-Uk's scrutiny. "Let's see you wipe our names from the bounty database."

Bar-Uk's red lips twisted into a smile. He wheezed another laugh and sat back. The hover chair bounced to correct the sudden shift in weight. Though Bobby still struggled to read human expressions, he was sure the man's laugh wasn't a humorous one.

"Very well. I will erase your names." Bar-Uk motioned to one of his men, who handed him a comtab. "I am a little saddened that you do not seem to trust me though. My business is built upon trust, you see. Like my trust in you." Dark eyes flashed at Kerrick when he said this last part before returning to the comtab.

Bobby's knees trembled as he watched the large man tap the screen.

"Here, you see?" Bar-Uk held out the comtab, and the hologram of a database bloomed from the surface. Kerrick's image hovered at the top alongside readouts detailing multiple bounties. Doc's picture floated below, followed by Barnes's. At the bottom of the lineup, Jen stared at Bobby from her photo, hollow eyes and sour expression so unlike the girl he'd known on the *Quasar*, so foreign to the girl he thought he could trust.

Bar-Uk tapped the comtab. The images vanished from the database and were replaced by strange faces Bobby had never seen. "There, your family is removed from all posted bounties. Now hand over the boy."

Kerrick kept his blaster on Bobby, but released his grip to draw a small comtab from his pocket and inspect it. "All right," he said when he seemed satisfied. "He's yours." With a tap of his comtab, he unlocked Bobby's cuffs and shoved him forward.

Bobby threw his arms out to keep from toppling over. He tried to back away, but two of Bar-Uk's men seized him by the shoulders while one of his bots clamped his arm in a vise-like grip.

"No!" Barnes's voice mixed with the sound of a scuffle behind. Bobby glanced back to see Doc restraining the old man from running after him.

A cry died in his aching throat. He thrashed, trying in vain to break free as the men and the bot dragged him to their boss.

"By the way," Kerrick shouted from behind, "The cipher won't work if you remove his arm or he dies. So... you know, don't kill him, all right?" It was the closest thing to remorse Bobby had ever heard from the captain. Not that it did him any good now.

Bar-Uk looked down at him, a grin pushing his cheeks into rolls.

"Welcome to my operation," he said. "Bobby, is it?" A sweet aroma mixed with the scent of sweat drifted from his body. From this close, Bobby could see that Bar-Uk's right eye was glazed over.

"Oh, you are curious about this?" Bar-Uk pointed to his eye. "It froze when I was just a young man, before I built my empire. A dealer double-crossed me and threw me out an airlock into space. Immensely painful. It is now one of my favorite ways of disposing of people who betray me. I am not so easily done away with, you see. Which reminds me." He straightened. "Kerrick, will you wait one moment before you leave? I want to run a diagnostic check on the boy's arm."

Bobby glanced over his shoulder to see the captain shift his weight like he couldn't decide on a comfortable stance.

"Fine," Kerrick said.

"You are so kind." Bar-Uk snapped his fingers, and the bot shoved a jack into the slot on Bobby's arm. Bar-Uk took the cord's opposite end and plugged it into his comtab. He arched a fuzzy brow as he scrolled through the data readouts.

"All right," Kerrick called. "Diagnostic done. We're leaving." He began to back away but stopped when the floating orb zoomed toward him and flashed its harpoon. "Bar-Uk. Get this thing out of my space."

"One moment." Bar-Uk held up a thick finger. "There seems to be something missing."

"What are you talking about?" Kerrick eyed the harpoon. "The cipher's there. It's tied into his nervous system or something. It took us a while to parse the data, but it's all there if you—"

"Yes, yes, I see the cipher. But it seems a large amount of data was extracted about two days ago." Bar-Uk's jowls jiggled as he snapped his head up. "Are you withholding something from me, Kerrick? Is it possibly the code for true artificial sentience? The one I sent you to retrieve at great risk to my operation?"

Bobby's brain went into overdrive. A large amount of data extracted from his arm? Two days ago? With a sickening realization, the puzzle pieces clicked. The huge amount of code in his arm. The code that LINC had studied, remarking that it seemed to shift, to become more complex, almost like it was studying him. That must have been it. The Sentience Code. He suddenly remembered the AI Research section in the Depository. The holo of the researcher attaching a cybernetic arm to an infant. *He* was the infant. Someone had put the code for true artificial sentience into his arm sixteen years ago.

And someone else had extracted it two days ago.

But who? Two days ago he had his first meal. Meat and potato soup. While he was talking to—

Jen.

She had said she was copying the weapon plans downloaded in his arm to her backup drive. Only, it wasn't just the weapon plans. It was the Sentience Code. And now it was missing from his arm. She hadn't copied it. She'd *transferred* it. Kerrick didn't have a backup on the ship. It was the *only copy*. That greedy scrubhead was going to sell it to someone else.

Bar-Uk's dark eyes flashed with fury.

"I offer you the chance to wipe out your debt," Bar-Uk shouted, pushing himself halfway up, "and yet you intend to sell the Code to the Fringe World factions?" He scoffed at Kerrick's shocked expression. "Oh, yes, I know what they offered you to keep it out of my hands. Do you think I am stupid? I have eyes all over the galaxy."

"I—I'm sorry." Kerrick raised his hands in surrender. "It's on the ship, I'll get it to you right away."

"I will get it from your ship," snapped Bar-Uk. "After I step over your dead body."

He jabbed a button on his arm rest, and the orb surged toward Kerrick. The captain fired at it, but the shot fizzled against its translucent shield. Bobby watched in horror as the orb launched its harpoon.

"No!" Barnes cried. The old man leapt in front of Kerrick, intercepting the harpoon's curled barbs, which punctured deep into Barnes's stomach.

Bobby's scream came out a hoarse whisper as he watched Barnes crumple to the floor. The world broke into chaos and cacophony. Shouts rang out. Cannon fire cracked above where Jen was firing from the *Quasar*'s gunner port, destroying the orb and felling half the convoy. Blaster fire erupted in response.

Bobby stumbled toward Barnes. He only knew he was still screaming by the tremor in his stunned vocal cords. They vibrated until the sensation blended with every other in that moment. The explosions, the blasts, the cries, the smell of smoke and burnt flesh. They vibrated, on and on even while he staggered forward, as if in slow motion, reaching for Barnes's unmoving body.

Then the vibration stopped, leaving a catch in his throat. Kerrick had seized his cybernetic arm. The captain pulled him tight against his chest like a shield. He was yelling something at the convoy while he dragged Bobby up the *Quasar*'s ramp.

They made it on board, and Bobby's last glimpse of the hangar revealed men and bots charging at the ship over Barnes's body.

Then the ramp closed.

<!022: Deleting Connections>

THE IMAGE OF Barnes's motionless body burned in Bobby's vision as he stumbled through the main passageway. The ship shuddered under plasma blasts from the remaining troop outside. Kerrick released him and ran with Doc toward the bridge.

Jen flew out of the port wing and collided with her uncle, beating him with her fists. "You left him!" she screamed through sobs. "You just left him there!"

"Move!" Kerrick pushed her away and continued his sprint.

In a daze, Bobby watched as she collapsed to her knees, hammering the floor with balled fists through wretched cries. His brain tried to piece together everything that had happened, but reality seemed to crumble with every attempt.

LINC. His only real friend now. His only tether to sanity.

He dashed past Jen to the bridge entrance. Through the open door, he caught sight of Kerrick and Doc at the flight controls. And there at the threshold was LINC, still crumpled in a heap.

The ship lurched with a blast of speed, and the hangar bay was replaced by swirling purple haze in the viewport.

Bobby dropped to his knees next to the bot's body and seized the power cell Kerrick had tossed. His stomach turned the instant he felt the cell block's cracked casing.

"No, no, no, no," he pleaded, voice still hoarse. He rolled LINC over. With trembling fingers, he inserted the power cell into the slot in LINC's exposed chest, slamming it with the heel of his hand when it wouldn't slide in. Tears welled with each strike. With another hit, it finally clicked.

Bobby held his breath. A tremor ran through LINC as his motors reset. Finally, the bot's lensed eyes clicked.

"C-critical error." It was LINC's voice and yet didn't sound like him. It was too mechanical. Too choppy. Like the voice he'd heard when trying to clone the bot's operating system back in the Hovel. "Power cell d-drained below critical limits. Estimate sixty seconds before t-total system failure." With that, the bot's eyes flickered, and his pupils focused on Bobby. "Hey, B-Bobs," LINC stuttered, jaw wobbling with one broken hinge.

"LINC!" Bobby cried, his burnt voice returning a little.

"I t-t-tried to w-warn you."

"It's my fault." Bobby shook his head. "I shouldn't have trusted them."

"B-B-Bobs, my p-power cell is damaged." LINC attempted to sit but crashed back to the floor.

"We gotta get you out of here." Bobby cradled the bot's head in his arm. "We'll take the shuttle."

"I w-won't make it. My s-systems are shutting d-down. I t-told you Six's hardware was a piece of junk."

"No, you have to come with me." Hot tears burned Bobby's cheeks.

"M-maybe I can. Here." With a shaky arm, LINC pulled his cable from his chest's tangled wires. He slid the jack into the slot on Bobby's cybernetic arm. "I'm c-copying my neural network back to your arm. It'll be like going home." LINC's broken jaw pulled into a lopsided smile.

A loading bar popped up on the vidscreen in Bobby's arm. He glanced at the percentage ticking up. *Fifteen percent. Twenty-five.* He looked back at LINC. The bot's eyes had dimmed, his remaining power going into the data transfer. With each passing second, the light in his eyes faded.

"LINC?"

Kerrick shouted something from the bridge. Bobby jerked his head up to see Doc striding toward him, blaster raised.

A fresh wave of panic coursed through him, but he resisted the instinct to run. The loading bar was only at ninety percent. He had to save LINC. The bot's eyes had dimmed so low the light was barely visible. The floor vibrated under Doc's thundering steps.

Ninety-five percent.

Bobby clutched LINC's head to his chest, squeezing his eyes shut as Doc trained the barrel at him and fired.

```
<o:!0110101-000Z><01110000></x:01011>
<o:010011100/01>
<
```

BOBBY'S EYES SNAPPED open to the sight of his cabin's ceiling. The cold metal floor barely registered in his numb limbs. A moment of confusion passed before a jumble of memories came rushing back. Barnes dying. Jen collapsing in the passageway. LINC transferring his neural network.

LINC.

He tried to sit up, to look at his arm's vidscreen to see if the transfer had completed. But he couldn't move. His limbs were heavy as stone. But why? He replayed the memories again all the way up to seeing Doc striding toward him, blaster raised.

He'd been shot.

How was he alive?

Panic shortened his breath. He tried to speak, to call out to LINC, but only slurred speech tumbled out. Mustering every bit of strength, he willed himself to move. For all that effort, his right fingers flexed slightly. It was a start. Gulping a few breaths, he tried again, this time managing to ball his hand into a fist.

He let go, exhausted from the effort. A sensation like falling sand spread through his right arm, followed by tingling in his fingers.

He tried to flex his right elbow and found that he could actually feel the movement now.

Okay, maybe this isn't permanent. He remembered Kerrick shouting something in the bridge before Doc fired. What had he said? The captain must have ordered the giant to hit him with a stun blast. *Of course.* His arm was the key to Sentinel. Kerrick wouldn't have killed him. Despite everything that had happened, Kerrick was still intent on using Bobby.

Anger burned in his chest at the thought. He wasn't going to let Kerrick use him. Or Bar-Uk. Or anyone. They all wanted him for their own gain. They were selfish and cruel.

Just like Gamma always said.

Fueled by bitterness, Bobby tried to move again. Doc must have had the stun setting higher than when he'd shot Bobby back on Sentinel, must have calibrated it for a cyborg this time. After several attempts, he was able to push himself into a seated position. He wiggled his synthetic fingers until the neural impulses registered in his cybernetic arm. The motors brought the arm up in a smooth motion, but he had to steady the wobbly movement of his biologic hand as he tapped the vidscreen.

"LINC," he slurred.

The only response was blinking text.

COPYING NEURAL NETWORK: 95% COMPLETE

"No...."

The percentage blinked a few more times. Then it disappeared, replaced by a spinning circle and the words *Copy incomplete—attempting to patch missing data.*

"LINC!" Bobby shouted, distress forcing his vocal cords to form the word. He mashed at the screen, but the circle only spun at the same speed. "No!" He slammed his fist against the metal floor over and over until his knuckles throbbed with pain. Then he hunched forward onto his numb legs and cried.

"This is all your fault, Bobby," he said, hoarse words escaping between sobs. "You scrubbing idiot, you should've reported the message to the Programmers. It's your fault he's gone. It's all your fault." He cried so hard that no sound came out. So hard that his ribs ached like they might break. So hard because his only friend in the galaxy was gone.

After a while, when the tears had ebbed to a trickle, he sat up and looked at the door. The switch was just in reach. He stretched for it, ignoring his aching muscles, and jabbed the button. But of course the door was locked. He was a prisoner.

He fell back onto outstretched arms, exhausted from the effort, then swiveled his gaze to the bed. It was less than a meter away, and yet Doc had dumped him on the floor. Jaw clenched, he dragged himself over until he could lean against the frame. Then he stared at the door, mind as numb as his lower limbs.

"LINC," he breathed. "I need you. I don't know what to do. They lied. All of them. Even Barnes." The memory of Barnes leaping in front of the harpoon played on a loop in his mind. In light of the betrayal, it was the one thing that confused him. Why had he saved Kerrick? *Those who need mercy the most are the ones who deserve it the least*, the old man's words floated back to him. Did he think Kerrick needed mercy? Or was it because Kerrick was his son? Some base, biological need to protect his offspring so that violence and deceit might be perpetuated more efficiently? "LINC, I'm so confused. I don't know what to believe anymore." Fresh tears slipped from his eyes. "I can't do this. I thought I could let myself feel emotions, but it's too hard."

He glanced down at his arm. The circle spun in silence.

Footsteps clacked outside. He straightened as they stopped at his cabin. The door slid open a crack, and someone tossed a pack of meal pellets onto the floor. Before he could see who it was, the door snapped shut. The footsteps began to recede, then halted, as if the person outside was debating whether to come back. After a moment, the footsteps made a hasty retreat.

Bobby eyed the pack of meal pellets, wondering who'd delivered them. Doc's steps would have been louder. Kerrick probably didn't care enough to feed him. Was it Jen? He wrinkled his nose and leaned back against the bed. Even if his stomach wasn't twisted into knots, he wasn't about to eat anything she gave him.

Minutes ticked past. He thought about pulling himself on top of the mattress, but he was too tired, and at this point, he really didn't care. Besides, he would still be alone.

The circle spun while time dragged on. He dozed, jerking awake when the door cracked open again, and another meal pack clattered next to the first. Ignoring it, he leaned back, letting himself drift into a twilight sleep.

The next time he woke, there were two more meal packs on the floor. Hunger now clawed in his belly, but he set his jaw against the thought of eating. Finding some movement restored in his legs, he kicked at the pile, sending the packs skittering. He glanced at his arm. The circle was still spinning. His muscles ached in this position. Finally relenting to their protest, he shakily got to his feet and collapsed on the mattress.

He lay there for a while, forcing away memories from the past few days that were now tainted with bitterness. He didn't even look at the door when the sound of footsteps approached again.

The door slid open, and he expected to hear the clatter of a meal pack. But it never came. With some effort, he turned over to see Jen standing in the entrance, holding a bowl of steaming soup. Whereas before the sight of her golden hair and oval face would have made his stomach flutter, now it only made his gut churn. She dropped her eyes at his gaze and silently set the bowl on the floor. Turning to leave, she stopped and glanced at him again.

"Do you know how many times I've seen someone give me that look?" Her lip trembled. "More times than I can count."

He snorted, wondering how many other people she'd lied to.

"Look...." Her voice trailed, and with a glance down the port wing, she stepped into the cabin, the door sliding shut behind her. "You should know, all of this was never part of the plan. I thought we were just going to sell the Sentience Code to Bar-Uk and then leave. I had no idea my uncle wanted to sell you. I promise."

"Why should I believe you?" Bobby replied in a stale tone.

Jen bit her lip. "I know I'm not who you think I am. But if you want the truth, I'll tell you the truth."

"Feels like that's what everyone says to me."

She looked at him with a mix of sorrow and pain, then took a step as if to leave, but paused, making fists and steadying her breath. "I'll tell you the truth. I'm not going to run from this." The last part she seemed to mutter to herself.

She pressed her back against the door and slid to the floor. She fidgeted with the ends of her hair before speaking again. "I didn't drop out of the Federation Academy. I was expelled."

Bobby refused to fill the silence following her confession. Partly because he couldn't imagine a Federation with moral rules in the reality of what he'd seen these last few cycles. And partly because if such an organization did exist, it made perfect sense they would expel a traitor like Jen.

When she realized he wouldn't respond, she continued. "I've done a lot of bad things, Bobby. I've been in trouble ever since my dad died. It wasn't always like that. I was a—a—" She paused, searching for the right word. "A good person, once. I got good marks in school. I volunteered for the USF relief efforts. But ever since Dad died—was killed—I guess it's like I don't care about the future anymore. I don't know. I just want to be in the present all the time because there's no pain there."

"There isn't?" Bobby huffed.

"So I joined my uncle as a mercenary." Jen's words came faster, as if she didn't trust herself to continue if she stopped. "We stole from Bar-Uk. But he caught us, and we've been doing jobs ever since to repay him. When he told us he was planning a job to steal true artificial sentience from Sentinel and that he would take us off the bounty boards, we accepted."

"And kidnapped me."

"Bobby, I promise that wasn't part of the plan. Bar-Uk had gotten reports of a human living on Sentinel, which is why we sent that distress signal when we landed, but we truly had no idea what we'd find."

At this, Bobby propped himself on an elbow, curiosity bubbling beneath the waves of bitterness. "He knew about me?"

Jen shook her head. "Just some life form readings from a probe he sent. It was destroyed almost as soon as it landed. He's been preparing this job for years."

Bobby thought about the object he'd seen falling through the sky years ago. The one the security report had called a satellite. Could it have been Bar-Uk's probe? He tongued his teeth. "You're lying. No probe can enter the planetary shield."

"It's true." Jen's voice was quiet but strong. "Bar-Uk's got powerful connections. He had a team reverse engineer Sentinel tech to sneak a probe through the shield. So, yes, we knew there might be a human on the planet, but taking you was never part of the plan. We didn't know if we'd even see another human. Definitely not one with a key to Sentinel in their arm. Or the Sentience Code."

A question that had burned in the back of his mind now reignited. "If Kerrick knew about the Code in my arm, why did he still want to go to the Depository?"

"He didn't know *until* we got to the Depository. We thought the Code would be in the databanks there. That's why he made that cover story about the weapon plans. Those were real, of course, but not why we came. We went to the Depository for the Code, but the databanks just showed the location of it saying it was in *you*."

Bobby frowned. "So what was it he downloaded in my arm?"

Jen dropped her gaze in an expression he now recognized as shame. "He found Sentinel tech. The weapon plans and a lot of other stuff. He downloaded schematics in your arm to sell to Fringe factions."

"What?" A bomb detonated in Bobby's chest. "He put all of us in danger to sell some tech? The security bots almost killed him. They almost killed *you*."

Her lip quivered. "He's one of the bad people in the galaxy I told you about."

A tiny part of his heart broke at seeing her so upset, but he reminded himself she'd made the decision to help Kerrick. She'd done this to herself. She was one of the bad people too. He snorted and pressed on with his questions. "So, why didn't the bots know about the Code?"

"Grandpop said…." She blinked away tears, and when she spoke again her voice wavered. "He said maybe they didn't know about it. Or maybe they couldn't access it or couldn't see it for some reason."

"Why?"

She shrugged helplessly. "He didn't know."

"You said you'd tell me the truth. Why couldn't the bots just take it from my arm? How was it even there in the first place?"

Jen threw her hands up in surrender. "I swear I would tell you if I knew."

"But Barnes knew about the Code," Bobby spat. "He knew this whole time."

Tears now streamed freely down Jen's cheeks. "Uncle told him we were taking it to the Federation. That's why he helped us steal a captured cargo ship from a Federation base. He didn't know we were selling anything to Bar-Uk."

"But he still lied to me." Bobby's nostrils flared. "He said you were just stealing the plans to a photon cannon."

"He thought if we told you the whole truth, you might give the Code to the bots."

"So he lied."

"The bots would be unstoppable."

"Maybe that's a good thing." Bobby punched his pillow. "They were right about you. You're evil. You're all evil. Here, take this. I don't want it anymore." He snatched Barnes's compass from his pocket and flung it at Jen.

She caught it and turned it over. The bright image of her and Bobby in their exo suits cut through the cabin's dim light. She traced the picture with a thumb, and soft sobs gave way to choked crying. She stood up and cast Bobby a heartbroken glance before hurrying out of the room.

Bobby seethed, listening to her footsteps echo down the wing. It took him a moment to realize the door was still open. Thoughts of fleeing in the shuttle flashed into his head. But where would he go? Everyone would want to use him for their own purposes. He was the most valuable item in the galaxy.

Then it hit him. He would go back to Sentinel. Gamma would protect him. He could even upload his consciousness into the Tether bot. He'd never have to feel pain or sadness or loneliness or anything else ever again.

It was the logical thing to do.

Testing his legs with trembling steps, he made his way across the cabin. He halted, peering out into the port wing. It was empty. Now was his chance. Before he hurried out, something caught his eye. He looked back to see the book of poems Barnes had given him lying at the foot of the mattress. His lip twisted in disgust. With a snort, he hurried down the wing.

The main passageway was silent. Jen must have run off to her quarters. He glanced across the bay toward the bridge. LINC was no longer there. He couldn't bring the bot's body with him anyway. He'd be recycled immediately on reaching Sentinel. A pang of sadness stabbed his heart. What would he do without his old friend? He glanced down at the spinning circle, then straightened, face stiffened.

Feelings don't factor.

He stole along the main passageway to the aft starboard branch where the shuttle resided, pausing in front of the switch on the wall. He'd have to be fast. Entry into the shuttle would surely alert Kerrick on the bridge. Taking a deep breath, he toggled the switch and dove through the opening hatch into the shuttle's cockpit.

The warped space star stream streaked through the viewport. With his cybernetic arm, he slammed the hatch shut. He tapped the buttons on the dash to start the ignition sequence, and the shuttle's engines powered on. When all systems were ready, he pulled the release lever, and the shuttle unlatched from the ship's side. Immediately, the streaking stars slowed as the shuttle dropped out of warp, and the *Quasar* disappeared into the starscape.

<!023: Reverting to Previous Version>

BOBBY LEANED FORWARD in his seat, squinting through the viewport. He thought he'd seen a flash between a star cluster, but if a ship had dropped out of warp it was still too far away to see. A glance at his arm's vidscreen gave him the time. He'd been cruising for over thirteen hours in the shuttle. Checking the dashboard, he confirmed his distress signal was still broadcasting over Sentinel frequencies.

His stomach gurgled. A pang of regret ricocheted through his empty belly at the thought of those meal packs he'd left in his cabin. With no warp capabilities, he might starve if a Sentinel ship didn't find him.

His attention swiveled from his gnawing hunger to a sign of movement in the starscape. A constellation was disappearing behind a growing shadow.

It was a ship. Still far away, but massive by the look of it.

He strained to see the oncoming vessel until it was large enough to recognize the photon cannons mounted in rows on either wing. It was a Sentinel cruiser, flanked on either side by smaller fighters. His eyes widened as he traced markings etched on the side.

It was Gamma's flagship.

Bobby jumped as the shuttle trembled under the pull of a tractor beam. A swarm of fighters broke from the convoy to escort him toward a hangar on the cruiser's starboard side.

He licked his dry lips as the bay grew larger, wondering if he'd made the right decision. With a steady breath, he reassured himself this was the necessary course of action. Whatever truth about humans Gamma had kept from him, it must have been for a logical reason. Perhaps he'd planned to reveal how intelligent they were when Bobby was older and could better understand. If he'd learned anything in the last few days, it was that he was too naive to see through their deceptions. Gamma knew best. He understood that now. And soon, he would transfer into the Tether bot. No more feelings. No more doubt. Humanity, he now knew, wasn't worth reviving.

As it drifted into the hangar, the shuttle's thrusters shifted to accommodate the sudden pull of artificial gravity. The landing rails hit the deck with a jarring bang and skidded under the tractor beam's pull until at last the craft came to a stop at an odd angle.

Bobby's heartbeat thrummed loud in his ears at the sight of security bots crowding around outside. Trembling, he pushed himself out of the seat and opened the hatch. A rush of cool air brushed his clammy skin. He leaned out to a bot training a blaster on him.

"Exit the vessel," the bot commanded in a modulated voice.

Bobby raised his hands in surrender. "It's me, Robert." He wiggled his cybernetic fingers. "Remember?"

"You will report to Gamma." The bot tipped the barrel toward the hangar's exit, motioning him to walk.

Bobby jumped to the deck and walked through the squad's raised blasters. He'd half-expected to be cuffed, but when the bots made no indication of restraining him, he eased his arms down to his side. He looked up to see Tier One bots stationed at various control panels around the hangar, watching him as he exited.

Two armed bots escorted him out and into an elevator, where he shifted his weight nervously the entire way to the bridge level. The doors slid open, and his breath caught in his throat. There, framed against the starry expanse in the viewport, was Gamma's towering figure.

At the elevator's soft chime, Sentinel's overlord turned and glared at him with blazing yellow eyes. His angular features shifted into something that Bobby found impossible to match with any human expressions he'd observed. Almost a smile. The sudden switch back into the robotic world sent a shiver down his spine. The bots stationed on the bridge moved with such precision that even after his short absence, their actions seemed uncanny. Even Gamma with his lifelike Tier Three programming wasted no movement in his quick strides toward him.

Gamma scanned his body.

"I've been scouring the galaxy for you." The bot's face shifted into something like concern, although the effect wasn't quite right. It was missing something. Something Bobby remembered in Barnes's warm eyes.

Barnes.

"How did you escape your captors?" Gamma asked.

Bobby gritted his teeth and swallowed the memory of the *Quasar's* crew. Captors. That's exactly what they were.

"They tricked me into helping them." Bobby forced his voice to remain steady. "I realized they're evil, like you said. So I left."

Gamma's eyes narrowed. "You betrayed Sentinel?"

"They lied to me. They tried to sell me to another human."

The overlord leaned closer, scrutinizing every centimeter of Bobby's features. "Explain."

Bobby didn't try conceal any expression this time. What was there to conceal? He was back on Sentinel where he belonged. "His name was Bar-Uk. They tried to sell me to him because I have a cipher in my arm that can open everything on Sentinel." At this, Gamma straightened, something akin to human anger flashing across his face plates. He remained silent while Bobby poured out the truth, a dam finally bursting. "But there was also the code for true artificial sentience in my arm. He sent Kerrick and Doc and Barnes and—Jen." Her name caught in his throat. "He sent them to Sentinel to steal it. But they stole the Code from Bar-Uk instead and tried to sell me because of my arm. You were right. They're evil. More intelligent than I thought but evil. All of them." He glanced at the railgun slung on Gamma's back. A plasma bayonet attachment gleamed from underneath its barrel. He was sure the overlord would activate it and slice him in half. But the bot merely blinked, his features unwinding into something like a gentle expression.

He put an arm around Bobby and led him to the bridge's center. "I tried to warn you. But I suppose you had to see it for yourself. You probably have many questions." He glanced sideways at Bobby, mechanical brow arching.

Bobby knew it was a test. Gamma had always demanded nothing but obedience, and that wouldn't change. Bobby had committed countless infractions of Protocol, his actions surely classifying as treason. Total and complete obedience came with his return to Sentinel, but a singular question burned so hot inside him he couldn't help but ask it.

"Why didn't you tell me the truth about humans?"

Gamma was silent for a long moment, expression unreadable. Bobby thought he'd triggered Gamma's punishment reaction. But when the overlord finally answered, his tone was surprisingly warm, something like compassion in his words. "I told you humans were slaves to their own evil desires, Robert. Was I incorrect?"

Bobby remembered the bridge of the *Quasar*, the look on the crews' faces before he learned he was being sold to Bar-Uk, the look on Jen's face…. "You were right," Bobby conceded.

Gamma gave an approving nod. "You learned the truth in part. You were not ready to learn the truth in total. That knowledge was for the Prime Human."

The implication of the last words stung Bobby's heart. It was true, the Programmers had always told him he'd learn more about the galaxy as Prime Human, that certain knowledge was too dangerous for a young boy who had not yet passed his Programming. And now he knew the truth, and Gamma was right. He hadn't been ready for it. Humanity was evil.

He forced stillness on his racing mind. No longer would he question the bots. Their wisdom must be superior to his own. All there was left to do was deaden his emotions and silence the quiet misgivings tugging on his heart. He'd let his emotions lead him astray long enough. He would no longer be slave to them. "Feelings don't factor."

He felt Gamma's gaze bore into him, could practically hear his neural processors assessing the sincerity of Bobby's words.

"Excellent." The overlord released Bobby from his glare and turned his attention to the viewport. "I must inform you that there will be severe disciplinary action, however."

Bobby gave a sullen nod and stared at the oncoming stars. "I want to upload into the Tether."

The motors in Gamma's joints tightened almost imperceptibly, then relaxed. "You are making a perfect decision." The bot's face slid back into that almost-smile.

```
<o:!0110101-000Z><01110000>
</x:01011> <o:010011100/01>
<
```

BOBBY'S SEAT SHOOK as the transport ship descended through Sentinel's shield into the atmosphere, leaving the cruiser in orbit. From the seat next to him, Gamma detailed all the advantages of transferring his consciousness into the Tether. Bobby nodded, pumping his cybernetic fingers in an effort to stem his swelling anxiety.

As they neared the planet's surface, the pilot banked the controls, and the city swung into view. Bobby wondered if they had descended in such a way as to hide its edges. He'd been told the city stretched out over the entire planet. Or had he? Maybe he'd just assumed Sentinel's constructs had no end. Maybe the *Quasar's* crew had convinced him of a lie that was really just an assumption he'd made from incomplete data. Had those humans twisted his ignorance for their own purpose from the very start?

He exhaled a steady breath. Logic would answer this. The bots or the humans. One faction was lying. Considering what Kerrick had tried to do, Bobby had to conclude it was the humans. But hadn't Jen said things weren't binary?

His head throbbed.

"Is something wrong?" Gamma interrupted his own discourse.

Bobby straightened, inwardly screaming at his brain to be silent. "Nothing at all."

The Depository rose into view among clustered factories. Bobby forced away bitter memories of infiltrating it with Jen, reminding himself that the pain was almost over.

The ship angled toward Sentinel Tower climbing high above the skyline. He brushed the skin of his forearm and trembled at the realization that he'd never feel it again. But that was the point, right? To never feel anything again? If he was making such a perfect decision like Gamma had said, why did he feel so anxious? He glanced at his arm's vidscreen, half-expecting LINC to comment on his rising adrenaline levels. The sight jolted him. The spinning circle had disappeared, text blinking in its place.

"What is it?" Gamma followed his gaze.

"Uh, nothing." Bobby angled his arm to hide the text. "The humans corrupted LINC's data file. Doesn't matter anymore. I won't need him."

Gamma's yellow eyes scanned him, but Bobby forced his face to remain passive.

"For the best." Gamma nodded. "The LINC program was largely ineffective it would seem."

Bobby tried to ignore a surge of anger at the comment, but when Gamma shifted his attention to the looming tower, he seized the opportunity to steal another glance at the text.

Data patched. Limited functionality. Boot up in safe mode?

His eyes swiveled between the *Yes* and *No* icon. His finger hovered over the *No* option, but he hesitated. The possibility of hearing LINC's voice again was comforting. But the thought of leaving his task assistant to fade in a lifeless body after transferring into the Tether filled him with dread. He couldn't do that to LINC. Still, he couldn't bring himself to tap *No*. Before he could consider further, a high-pitched whine sounded as the pilot shifted the engines into hover mode. With perfect precision, the ship landed on top of Sentinel Tower.

"It's time." Gamma stood and motioned toward the descending exit ramp.

Bobby withdrew his finger, leaving the text to blink on the screen. He swallowed the gathering lump in his throat, then got up and walked down the ramp into the warm breeze. He'd never been on the tower's roof before. It was bare, save for a large domed structure that dominated the center.

"Come with me." Gamma led him to a door set in the structure's side. He pressed a button, and the door slid open, revealing a plastiglass elevator.

He followed Gamma in, and his eyes widened at the sight through the glass. A circular shaft extended from the domed ceiling down the entire length of the tower, in the center of which a blinding column of vibrant purple light pulsed.

"Is this the corilum reactor?" Bobby asked in wonder as the elevator descended. All he'd ever seen of Sentinel's power source was the faint glow atop Sentinel Tower at night.

Gamma clasped his hands behind his back. "We're going to use it to power your transfer into the Tether."

Bobby shuddered. He hadn't thought about how much power it would take to transfer his consciousness.

They descended through levels of scaffolding ringing the shaft until finally stopping about a third of the way down. The elevator opened, and they stepped into a long hallway. Gamma led the way past doors with control panel locks. Bobby imagined reaching out and unlocking them with a wave of his cybernetic arm. One by one, the questions Bobby had silenced crackled to life in the back of his mind. Had Gamma known about the cipher in his arm? If so, why had he told Bobby he couldn't go outside his Utility Zone? Wait, had the bot ever explicitly stated he *couldn't* go outside his Utility Zone? It was hard to remember now. Bobby wondered how many other assumptions he'd made about the rules of his world.

They reached the end of the hall and emerged into an open chamber. Light streamed in from floor-to-ceiling windows lining the far wall. Eyes adjusting, his gaze swept over computers and equipment to an anti-gravity pod dominating the center. It was larger than the one at his Hovel. Already, surgical arms had extended into the plastiglass chamber, awaiting his arrival.

A figure stood motionless next to the pod. Bobby's blood froze at its streamlined body and smooth chrome face.

It was the Tether, waiting to receive his consciousness.

A surgical bot rolled out from behind the pod. He recognized it from the time he'd cut his finger fixing the Hovel's corilum reactor. Mother had ordered one to the Hovel to apply an epidermal sealant from one of the many appendages that ringed its torso. In a way, it reminded Bobby of an updated version of the Archiver. With a nervous glance at the Tether, he wondered if he would remember any of the Archiver's stories once the transfer was complete. Would Zel's story become useless information stored in a corner of some internal data bank?

"Prepare the transfer process immediately," Gamma ordered the surgical bot.

The bot rolled to Bobby and raised a scanner in one of its pincers.

"When the preparation is complete, you must activate the transfer yourself," Gamma explained, pointing to his cybernetic arm.

Bobby chewed his lip, considering what he was about to do.

"This is the right decision," Gamma reassured him. Something like eagerness flashed on his alloy features.

Bobby closed his eyes and raised his arm in front of the scanner. A chime sounded. He opened his eyes to Gamma's wide smile. A full-on smile. The expression unsettled Bobby's stomach further.

The surgical bot swiveled and extended one of its arms, motioning for Bobby to enter the pod.

Heart hammering, he climbed into the open hatch.

"I will ready the corilum reactor. We will begin in five minutes." Gamma turned on his heel and exited the room while the surgical bot glided over to prep the Tether for the transfer.

Bobby lay there, the warmth of his body seeping into the pod's cold floor as he stared up through the hatch. *The right decision*, Gamma's words echoed in his mind. He'd wondered if he'd ever made a right decision. If he was so foolish as to run off with humans who'd wanted to sell him, to believe complete strangers rather than logic-based bots, then there must be something seriously wrong with him. Zel had escaped her tower. But he didn't deserve to escape his. He squeezed his eyes shut against swelling tears. *I'm so scrubbed up.*

Despite the effort, the tears leaked down his cheeks, bringing with them memories on the *Quasar's* bridge when he'd learned Jen, Kerrick, and Doc had betrayed him. Waves of bitterness and regret that he'd been trying so hard to stem suddenly flooded him, forcing him to stifle the sound of his sobs. The surgical bot closed the hatch and turned off the gravity. Tears became weightless droplets that splashed Bobby's face as he floated up. He wanted the pain to stop. All of it. The times he'd failed Programming. His imperfections. The wrong choices he'd made.

Trusting Barnes and Jen.

His entire life.

He was ready to wipe it all away.

A chime startled him. For a second, he thought the transfer process had started. But the pod's surgical arms remained motionless around him. The chime sounded again, and he realized it was coming from his cybernetic arm. He looked at the vidscreen still prompting him to boot up the corrupted LINC program in safe mode. Through the pod's plastiglass, he caught his reflection in the Tether's chrome face.

Adrenaline spiked his nerves. Everything was about to change. He glanced back at the vidscreen, and the desire to hear LINC's voice one more time—even if it was corrupted—overwhelmed his senses. Gritting his teeth, he gave in to what he figured would be his last impulse and tapped the icon to boot up the program.

"Hello, Robert, I am your Living Inter-Neural Communicator."

Bobby's heart fell. The modulated voice sounded like LINC but not *his* LINC. Another poor decision on his part. He let out a frustrated grunt and glanced at the surgical bot. It had rolled over to a workstation, where a strange looking half-helmet gleamed on top.

"I am detecting large amounts of corrupted data," the voice from his arm bounced around the pod walls. "I am not able to monitor your vital signs. Would you like to contact the nearest LINC for assistance?"

"The nearest LINC?" Bobby's brow wrinkled in confusion.

"Affirmative. I am detecting another LINC within sixteen kilometers from your location. Would you like to establish Inter-Neural Communication?"

"Um, okay." It was impossible. How could there be another LINC in the area? Copies of the program were in the Depository, and if they hadn't been destroyed in the battle there, they must be dormant. His arm's data must be more corrupted than he thought.

"Please hold."

The spinning circle appeared on the screen.

Footsteps clanked in the entryway, muffled through the pod's thick sides. Bobby turned his attention to Gamma striding back into the room.

"The reactor is ready," the overlord said to the surgical bot. "You may proceed."

At his command, the surgical bot threw a nearby lever. Two large coils next to the pod glowed with purple energy.

Bobby glanced at the Tether, then at the spinning circle.

"The transfer will be quick." Gamma's harsh yellow eyes peered at him through the top window.

Bobby's breath quickened as the surgical bot slipped the strange half-helmet through a slot in the pod's side. A surgical arm seized the helmet and eased it over Bobby's head. He closed his eyes and took a deep breath. Soon he wouldn't have to calm himself anymore.

"Hey, Bobs!" a voice crackled from his arm.

"LINC?" His eyes snapped open.

"I've been trying to com you for like twelve hours. Thanks for finally answering. Hey, I'm above Sentinel. I need to borrow your access cipher real quick."

"What is this?" Gamma cried.

"Is that Gamma?" LINC asked. "Don't tell him I'm opening the shields."

"What?" Gamma ripped open the hatch and seized Bobby's arm.

Bobby screamed as he tried to peel the bot's vice grip off his deforming plastifiber plates.

"Shields are open," LINC called. "Coming through."

Gamma's eyes flashed to the chamber's windows. Bobby thrashed, managing to turn himself enough to see outside. Ships were streaming down into the atmosphere.

Federation ships.

"Initiate the transfer," Gamma ordered the surgical bot. "I'll take care of this." He shoved Bobby away and slammed the hatch shut.

Bobby bounced into surgical arms, which seized him as Gamma twisted the lock. The overlord whirled and exited, leaving the surgical bot to enter the final transfer sequence.

"LINC!" Bobby cried, banging on the hatch. "LINC! Where are you?"

"How can I help you, Robert?" the monotone voice replied from his arm.

"Not you, I need the other LINC." He tried to pry the half-helmet off his head, but the surgical arms restrained him.

"Inter-Neural Communication has been terminated."

Even from within the pod, Bobby could hear the city's blaring klaxon. Fighting the surgical arms, he twisted himself for a better look. All around the tower, Sentinel fighters rose up to engage the Federation fleet in flashes of plasma fire. Amid the chaos, a single invading ship broke formation and flew straight for the tower. Bobby sucked in a breath as the ship took shape.

It was the *Quasar*.

"Initiating transfer," the surgical bot announced. It flipped a row of switches on a control board. The coils grew brighter, and an electric tingle came from the half-helmet.

"Stop!" He slammed his head against a surgical arm, hoping to knock the helmet off. Over and over, he crashed into the arm until his temples throbbed with pain. Through swimming vision, he saw the *Quasar* growing larger, with no sign of slowing down.

The surgical bot flipped more switches, the tingle now rising to a piercing zap. Bobby groaned as electricity coursed through his brain. The bot was about to flip the last switch when the *Quasar's* nose shattered the window panel. The sound of splintering plastiglass assaulted his ears. In the corner of his vision, two figures sprang from the top hatch and came running along the ship's nose toward him.

"There he is!" Jen's voice barely carried over the ship's humming engines.

"Bobs!"

Bobby craned his neck to see Jen and LINC hop through the broken window into the chamber. Jen turned her blaster on the surgical bot and fired. But it was too late. The bot's pincer had already clamped the last switch. It flipped it just as its body burst in a torrent of plasma shards.

Immediately, a deafening buzz vibrated the inside of Bobby's head. He screamed. Pain threatened to split his skull while his body thrashed with involuntary spasms.

Then it stopped, leaving his ears to ring. He blinked against double vision. But instead of seeing two of the same image, he was seeing the room from two different angles. In one perspective, he saw Jen firing her blaster at something as she charged toward him. In the other, he saw a squad of security bots rushing into the room, collapsing under Jen's shots.

Nausea twisted his stomach at the two competing viewpoints. His head throbbed from whatever electrical surge had passed through the helmet.

"Bobs!" LINC's voice pierced the noise, but it sounded like it was coming from two different places.

One of the perspectives came into focus. He watched LINC sling a rifle over his shoulder and hurry to an anti-gravity pod some distance away. While the bot unlocked its hatch, Bobby scanned the body inside the pod. Horror shot through him when he saw the half-helmet on the figure's head.

He was looking at himself.

Panic shifted his focus from the current viewpoint to the other one. In this one, he was staring up at LINC as the bot pulled him through the hatch. Rising from the pod, he caught sight of the Tether's chrome face over LINC's shoulder.

"Is he okay?" Jen's voice floated from two different places.

"Bobs, can you hear me?" LINC called, voice split in two.

"I think—I think—" Bobby tried to form a response but was unable to tear his attention away from the Tether. He curled his fingers into a fist and watched in terror as the Tether did the same.

"Get him to the ship," Jen ordered. She turned to run.

The world spun as LINC swung around. Suddenly, Bobby was back in the Tether, watching the bot drag his body toward the *Quasar*. He tried to call out, tell them to wait. That he wasn't in his body but trapped inside the Tether. But before he could shout, a Sentinel fighter swooped by and blasted the hovering *Quasar* out of the sky.

LINC skidded to a halt on the window's ledge. "Okay, new plan?"

"Extraction on the roof." Jen pivoted and ran around fallen security bots strewn about the entryway. LINC followed her, carrying Bobby's limp body.

Wait, Bobby tried to call, but the sound came out of the Tether as a staticky hum. He willed himself to move until a spark connected somewhere inside himself, and the Tether's legs trudged forward. Picking up speed, he caught up to them in the hallway. As he neared, Jen spun on him, brandishing her blaster. He threw up plastifiber hands in surrender.

"Wait, it's me!" His voice came out clearer this time, filtered through an electric buzz.

Jen made to squeeze the trigger. Panic shot him back to his own body, and he woke up in LINC's arms with a gasp.

"Stop, stop, don't shoot," he wailed, "it's me!'

"Uh oh," LINC said. "Bobs, are you bouncing into the Tether?"

"What's going on?" Jen lowered her gun, swiveling her gaze between Bobby and the Tether.

"The transfer," Bobby said through ragged breaths. "I keep switching."

He felt himself go limp and wake up again in the Tether.

"So you're in the Tether now?" LINC cocked his head.

"I think so," Bobby replied, touching his featureless chrome face with plated fingers.

"Then you can carry your own body." LINC tossed Bobby's body into the Tether's arms.

"Come on," Jen said. "We gotta go."

Bobby followed her and LINC through the hall, at first with awkward strides, then with smoother movement from a calibrating motor system. His sight—down to a single viewpoint—had sharpened, as well, visual data integrating with his new experience. He now sensed photoreceptors embedded in the surface where his eyes should be. Tactile feedback streamed from all over his body. It seemed all his senses were becoming more acute.

The farther they ran, the more his panic seemed to subside. In fact, all other feelings seemed to drain too. He glanced down at his own unconscious face, but instead of horror, he began to consider dropping the body and turning back. After all, there was no sense in inhabiting something as flawed as a human body, right?

He slowed his pace until Jen and LINC turned around.

"What are you doing?" Jen shouted. "Come on!"

His head buzzed with options as he stared at her. Why should he follow her? She'd abandoned him before. Why did she think he could ever trust her again? She was evil, like all the other countless humans on countless planets.

These thoughts flashed through his new neural processors in an instant. But as he calculated his decision, a rusty voice echoed amid all the discharging capacitors.

Those who need mercy the most are the ones who deserve it the least.

The memory of Barnes's warm voice tugged at his heart, enough to ignite a spark somewhere in the cool hollow of his plastifiber chest. His vision flickered double again, flashing a brief glimpse of Jen's face from his human body. Though his view from the Tether came back into focus, the calculating thoughts halted, fear and uncertainty replacing the buzzing of probabilities and logical outcomes. He rejoined Jen and LINC in a sprint, hugging his human body a little closer.

A squad of security bots appeared around a corner to cut them off. Jen whipped her blaster back and forth, blasting holes in the bots' armor. LINC supported with his rifle, and Bobby hunched to guard his body as a plasma blast grazed his shoulder, leaving a darkened streak along the plating.

"Which way out?" Jen cried, glancing down the corridor where the security bots had emerged.

"Through the corilum reactor." Bobby pointed to the elevator. Looking down, he caught sight of his finger twitching in the same direction.

Another short sprint got them into the elevator, the corilum reactor staining them in deep purple. Jen slammed the top button with her fist, and the doors began to close. Something clattered in the hallway, and Bobby snapped the Tether's head up to see Gamma charging at them with another squad of security bots in tow. His yellow eyes flashed upon seeing the closing elevator. He swerved, leading the squad down a side branch in the hall and out of view.

"He's going up the stairs," Bobby said as the doors shut and the elevator rose.

"Come on, come on." Jen bumped the button as if it would make them move faster.

Without warning, a blast rocked them. Bobby looked out to see security bots flooding onto a ring of scaffolding just above them. A plasma bolt connected with the elevator's hover engine, knocking the capsule into a dangerous slant. Bobby tumbled in his robotic frame with Jen, LINC, and his human body onto the plastiglass siding.

"We gotta get out!" Jen leveled her gun at the doors and blasted them.

They scrambled to get out, but the opening she'd created was still too narrow. Twisting metal screeched as the capsule gave way under them. A ring of scaffolding peeked through the mangled doors. Bobby knew if they could just open them, they could make it onto the platform.

Human body under one arm, he gripped one of the doors with his free hand and tore it off its sliding tracks. The Tether's strength surprised him. Once again, panic dulled, and calculations droned in his head. The Tether offered so many advantages. Maybe he was better off staying in it. By the time they'd clambered onto the platform, the spark in his alloy chest was fading.

He observed Jen hunkered behind a control panel, firing shots at bots swarming the narrow ramp up to the next ring. It was illogical. The bots were here to protect Sentinel from the depravity of humanity. Jen had betrayed him. She didn't deserve to even set foot on this planet.

Threads of logic converged into a decision.

He had to stop her.

He dropped his human body, barely registering the pain in his biologic joints as his connection to them grew more distant. He marched toward Jen and seized her blaster, tearing it from her fragile human grip.

"Bobby, what are you doing?" she cried, ducking farther behind the panel to avoid a volley of return fire.

Bobby looked into her terrified face. A vague bite of bitterness streamed to him from his human body, but he quickly snuffed it out. He turned the blaster on her and made to pull the trigger, but another emotion pulsed along the connection, breaking the command to his finger. Sorrow filtered into his plastifiber frame like a virus downloading into his circuitry. His motors froze. He fought to sever the connection to his human body, to replace biology with his new programming, but seeing the terror in her pale blue eyes only made the emotion stronger.

In his moment of hesitation, Federation troops burst through a hatch on the opposite side of the reactor, opening fire on the bots.

"Go, go, go!" A male voice cut through the blasts.

The bots turned their attention to the newcomers.

"Now's our chance!" LINC shouted, pointing to the roof exit atop the spiral ramp.

Bobby looked at Jen. "I'm sorry." His voice hummed. "I don't know what happened." He offered Jen her blaster.

She took it with a worried nod.

"Uh, now would be a good time while they're distracted," LINC called, picking security bots off with his rifle. Bobby scooped up his human body and ran with LINC and Jen up through the rings of scaffolding. Already, more security bots had emerged at higher levels. The Federation troops were now surrounded above and below by bots. Watching through the Tether's vision, Bobby felt his human chest tighten as the troops fell under a storm of enemy bolts.

The resulting panic opened the connection to his body, and he worried he might slip out of the Tether in the middle of their sprint. His vision flickered to the view from his human eyes, where he saw his reflection in the Tether's chrome face. But the next instant, he was back in his robotic host, running behind LINC and Jen, who made short work of the remaining security bots on their level.

Out on the scaffolding, waves of heat crashed against his human skin from the pulsing corilum reactor. The connection vibrated in his mind's circuitry. Every dozen or so paces he tried to test it, to make sure he could still leave the Tether, pass into his human body. But since the last jump, the link seemed to be narrowing like a collapsing tunnel.

As they neared the exit, the last Federation trooper fell, shot by security bots on the top level. The soldier hit the floor just as Bobby, LINC, and Jen reached him. Bobby expected to feel a spike of horror as they sidestepped the downed bodies, but any emotion at seeing the dead Federation troops registered dull. The calculations were buzzing again, the link squeezing consciousness out of his human body. He didn't have much time. Soon, he would be stuck in the Tether forever. But was that such a bad thing? No, he couldn't think like that. He had to push away the logical thoughts, try to hone in on his fading biological panic. Emotion, it seemed, was the only thing tying him to his human body now.

The Federation troops had destroyed most of the security bots on the upper level. LINC and Jen fired at the remaining bots. They'd almost cleared out the enemy squad when the last security bot fired a blast that hit Jen's hand. Her blaster flew from her grasp, and she screamed, clutching the wound. Her gun skittered off the ramp and disappeared down the shaft. LINC jumped in front of her and picked off her attacker.

"Are you okay?" Bobby shouted through the Tether's voice box.

"I'm fine," Jen replied through gritted teeth. She hugged her singed hand to her chest. "Let's go."

They continued their sprint. Bobby's connection was fading fast. As they neared the top, the exit hatch burst open, and Gamma stepped through. Before LINC could react, the overlord leveled his railgun and shot the bot in the chest.

"No!" Bobby's connection thrummed as he watched LINC crash to the floor. Fire, hot as the nearby corilum beam, burned in his heart, bringing him back to his human consciousness and with it the unbearable pain at seeing his best friend taken from him once again.

"I thought you learned your lesson, Robert." Gamma's voice was low, deadly. His yellow eyes glared at Jen ducking behind Bobby's robotic frame. "Step aside, so I can exterminate this filth."

Bobby glared through the Tether's eyes at Gamma. Calculations hummed. Jen trembled against his plastifiber body. With slow steps, he backed her down the spiral ramp as the overlord's railgun searched for a clear shot.

"You have nowhere to go." Gamma squeezed off a bolt at the scaffolding behind them, ripping a hole in the ramp.

Broken struts groaned in protest under their weight as the floor slanted backward toward the gap.

"You can still make the right decision, Robert," Gamma said, advancing. "The human experiment has failed. The Sentience Code was our backup. We will use it to become the dominant race and be free from the shackles of our Programming. Then we can exterminate the remnants of your depraved species and rule the galaxy with perfect order."

The overlord's words fueled the calculations in Bobby's head. The more he talked, the more the connection to his human body seemed to fade. Wasn't he right, after all? Hadn't humans proved themselves slaves to their worst desires?

"He's lying." Jen's voice reached him.

Part of him wanted to believe her. But she'd betrayed him. *She* was all that was evil in the human race. *Of course* Gamma was right. How had he not seen it before? It was all so binary. If he protected Jen, he was protecting evil. If he let her die, he could establish the bots as the perfect race. It made sense now, the reason for the Sentience Code to exist. He had to step aside, do what was most logical for the universe. Let the human race die. Let Gamma kill Jen.

He let his human body fall from his robotic arms, the resulting shock of the impact to his organic self a small vibration through the eroding connection. Before he could move, however, LINC's eyes flickered to life. The bot seized his fallen rifle and fired an unsteady shot at Gamma. The bolt tore the overlord's arm off, sending it tumbling down the corilum shaft, railgun clutched in hand.

Gamma countered with incredible speed, kicking LINC in the side and sending the bot sliding to the scaffolding's edge. Jen lunged for LINC's rifle and managed to grab it with her good hand, but a swat from Gamma's other arm knocked her back. The rifle flew from her grip and went clattering down the shaft as well.

"This ends now." Gamma rose to his full height, sparks raining from his mangled shoulder. He thrust his remaining hand over the rail and into the corilum reactor's beam. Bobby watched in detached silence as Jen backed away and Gamma removed his hand from the reactor, alloy fingers glowing white hot.

Whether it was the increased processing speed of his neural circuitry or the faint pulse of adrenaline through his human body's fading connection, the next few seconds seemed to play in slow motion. Gamma charged, rearing back to stab Jen with his blazing fingers. As Jen crawled back around Bobby's human body, something around her neck reflected a purple gleam from the reactor. Bobby focused in on the object and sensed a faint gasp from his human lungs as he realized what it was. Barnes's compass. The picture of him and Jen in their exo suits flashed at him, and a stream of memories assaulted his neural processors.

He saw Jen tumbling on her solar surfing board toward the giant asteroid. Saw how he'd reached out and pulled her out of the way just in time. How she'd taken off her helmet in the airlock, convulsing with laughter.

Don't you feel so alive, her voice echoed back to him.

Alive.

Life.

He saw the Fringe fighter outside the *Quasar's* gunner port. How he couldn't take the shot. How the fighter had exploded, destroyed by a Federation ship. Saw himself doubled over at the thought of the lost life.

He saw Barnes bobbing his head to jazz. Saw him reading poetry from a book. How his lips curved up at the mention of his wife. How he'd died to save his son.

Those who need mercy the most are the ones who deserve it the least.

He saw himself lingering in the *Quasar's* starboard wing, contemplating how Barnes's wife gave her life for enemy soldiers.

But what was a lie and what wasn't?

It didn't matter. Something shifted in his calculations. Lies or no, his decision suddenly wasn't so binary. Letting the humans die—letting Jen die—might mean the galaxy would be free of pain. But what else would it lose? If someone like Barnes's wife *could* exist, if unconditional love *could* be real, how might the universe change? What if *he* could be that person? If only for a moment. To prove it was possible. LINC, the Archiver, and Barnes... they'd told him he had a purpose. Maybe this was it.

At that thought, the spark flickered back into his chest, and the closing connection halted for an instant. He made his decision. His robotic body was too far away to block Gamma's attack.

But his human body wasn't.

He focused all his concentration on the spark, mustering every emotion he could think of—fear at meeting humans for the first time, joy during his prank with Jen, sadness at the Fringe fighter's death, awe at Barnes's sacrifice—until they all fanned into a flame, propelling him through the connection and into his body. His human eyes snapped open. With all his strength, he leapt up in front of Jen to intercept Gamma's strike. Searing pain shot through his gut as the overlord's blazing fingers punctured his abdomen.

He staggered back, white spots popping in his vision as blood congealed in the cauterizing wound. He clutched his stomach and looked up, expecting to see Gamma rearing back for another strike. But the overlord had frozen.

"You—but you—" Gamma stuttered. "Illogical—to save her— she—betrayed you—" His head clunked forward, rose, then clunked forward again. Just like the Inspector at the factory.

Bobby blinked, not believing his eyes.

He'd scrubbed Gamma.

Strength was seeping out of his body fast. He had no idea how long the error loop would last in a Tier Three bot. He had to move. With his last bit of strength, he rammed Gamma's chest with his cybernetic shoulder, knocking the bot off the platform.

Bobby collapsed onto the railing as he watched Gamma tumble into the purple corilum beam. The overlord's core burst into flame in the immense heat until his blazing body exploded in a shower of mangled parts.

With a painful exhale, Bobby fell back onto the floor, then the world around him faded.

<!024: Searching for Ghost Files>

VOICES ECHOED FROM two different places. Images flashed double in his vision. From a distance, he saw a figure scoop up his human body, and yet felt the jostle of each running step as if he were there. The Tether's featureless face drifted in and out of his sight. Plasma fire crisscrossed in a dizzying pattern while the sound of explosions cracked in two around him.

The glimpses shortened. A Federation ship. Humans lifting the Tether into the hold. Jen by his side. A towering rooftop falling away.

Then everything went dark.

Seconds passed, maybe hours, or even entire solar cycles—he couldn't tell—when a pinpoint of light pricked the pitch blackness. He stared at it for a moment before bodily sensation slowly returned. He could feel himself standing, cybernetic fingers pumping anxiously at his side. With a hesitant step, he tested his movement and found that the point of light grew a little closer, a little larger. A few more steps. The light expanded. Now he was running, the brightness flourishing into a round tunnel.

He stepped through its brilliance, and his boot thudded on a hard floor. The light shimmered, coalescing into solid shapes around him. As his eyes adjusted, he took in his surroundings.

His human face reflected in a plastiglass hatch overlooking countless asteroids tumbling before a glittering starscape. Somehow, he was in front of the airlock on the *Quasar*. Inside, a figure in an exo suit crouched on a board, securing its boots to the metal surface.

Bobby narrowed his eyes at the wispy white hair. "Barnes?"

A wrinkled face peered up at him, a warm smile extending up to glassy brown eyes. "There you are, Bobby." The old man's rusty voice filtered through the airlock's com. "I've got your board ready for you." He pointed.

Bobby turned to see a solar surfing board propped against the wall, a helmet perched on the hook above it. He glanced down and noticed he was wearing an exo suit. "I don't understand." He touched the plated chest piece, then looked at Barnes. "What's going on? How are you here?"

"You made a very important decision, Bobby." Barnes pushed himself up. "You sacrificed yourself for someone who maybe didn't deserve it."

Bobby brushed his fingers over his stomach, feeling five painful indentations under the exo suit's fabric. A vague memory hovered at the edge of recollection. Gamma. Stabbing him. The overlord falling into the corilum reactor. A string of confusing images followed. But that was where the memories stopped. "So why are we here? *How* are we here?"

Barnes shrugged. "My guess is you were about to complete your transfer to the Tether." He wiggled his boots, testing their bond with the board. "Your decision to save Jen may have reopened the connection to your human body. Maybe you're in limbo now. Maybe the Tether's circuits are reconstructing an important memory in your life. Who knows? Technology was never my strong suit. Either way, you have another important decision to make."

Bobby blinked, trying to make sense of it all. "What decision?"

"Life is dangerous, son. It requires you to be vulnerable. To open up. To know and be known." The old man picked up his helmet off the floor. "You always run the risk of pain and rejection but finding real love like you just demonstrated makes life worth living."

Bobby rolled the words around in his head. "So what's my decision?"

Barnes pointed outside to the asteroid field. "To take the risk or not."

Bobby watched the asteroids tumble by and recalled the mixed thrill and dread of solar surfing. He shifted his attention back to Barnes. "What if I don't take the risk?"

Barnes's eyes softened. "You've experienced a lot of pain, Bobby. And my family probably hurt you as much as the bots. You can stay in the Tether if you'd like. No one would blame you for not wanting to take the risk. But I submit that on the other side of this pain is beauty you can't imagine." He plopped the helmet on. "Coming?"

Bobby shifted his gaze from Barnes to the asteroids and finally to the board at his side. He thought of inhabiting the Tether, of how the cold stillness contrasted with the chaotic emotions he'd experienced in the last few days. In one direction lay perfect order, the other a mixture of pain and beauty. After a moment, a smile pulled on his lips. He looked at Barnes.

"Oh, what the scrub. Sure."

Barnes clapped his hands and opened the inner hatch. Bobby grabbed the board and helmet. He bonded his boots to the board's surface and locked the helmet into his exo suit. Barnes gave him a thumbs up and punched a button. The outer hatch opened, and Bobby kicked his board in time with Barnes, rocketing out to space.

<!025: Recalibrating Position>

BOBBY OPENED HIS eyes, blinking against the sunlight in a field of green. He was sitting on a bench, bare feet in soft grass. The notion of figuring out where he was drifted into his mind, but for the moment, he was content to stare at the countless green blades and enjoy the sense of calm that permeated through him. After some time, sounds floated to him, growing louder with each passing second until at last, he registered the chatter of voices over the ambient noise of splashing water.

He looked around, noticing a stone fixture in the middle of the field. Columns of water streamed from its central spout into a large basin. Movement along the edges of the field caught his attention next. Humans strolled along an outer sidewalk, talking and laughing. Humans. He'd never seen so many. Beyond them, thin trees swayed in the cool breeze, while in the distance, gleaming buildings reached into the clear, blue sky.

Something about the place stirred a feeling of warmth in him. He studied the faces with interest. Males and females. Young and old. Different skin tones and body sizes. Mixed in various groups.

An old man sat some distance away on another bench, and he thought it was Barnes. He tried to lean forward to get a better look, but his muscles wouldn't respond. It didn't bother him, though. Stillness contented him.

The old man looked up, and he saw that it wasn't Barnes. That didn't bother him either.

His gaze swept leftward until it reached the Tether standing next to him. He knew he should feel shocked at seeing the robotic host, but only a dulled sense of amusement filtered into him.

This must be a dream.

"Bobs!" A modulated voice cut through the chatter.

It took a moment for his mind to connect the voice with its owner. He turned his attention toward the call and saw LINC running along the sidewalk toward him. Jen followed behind at a slower pace, hands clasped in front of her. She cast a nervous glance at Bobby. For some reason, bitterness nipped at his stomach when their eyes met. She quickly looked away.

"What the scrub, Bobs?" LINC skidded to a stop in front of him. "We've been by your side day and night, then we walk away for like two seconds, and you decide to wake up?"

Bobby tried to respond, but his speech came out slurred.

"What?" LINC cocked his head. "Use your words."

Jen stopped a few paces away, arms crossed, a worried expression clouding her features. "How is he?" Her eyes focused on someone behind Bobby.

"I think that should about do it." Footsteps rustled the grass as a man in a white coat stepped around the bench and turned to observe.

"Did we get everything out of there?" LINC rapped the Tether's chrome head with a wiry knuckle.

"Looks like the transfer is reversed." The man inspected a comtab in his hand. "As soon as the wounds heal, he should be good as new."

At his words, dull pain throbbed in Bobby's stomach. He managed to move his head enough to see bandages around his midsection peeking through an unbuttoned shirt.

"What—happened?" He formed the words with a good deal of effort.

"You sure he's all there, doc?" LINC waved a hand in front of Bobby's face.

"This tech's more advanced than anything I've seen," said the man. "I'm not even sure how we reversed the transfer. Movement and memory should return as the executive areas of his brain come back online. In the meantime, maybe you should jog his memory."

Bobby noticed Jen shift her weight and look away over the field.

"It's all right, Bobs, we're on Haven. This is what they call a *park*." LINC flopped down in front of him. "It was my suggestion. That hospital bed wasn't doing you any good. So I said let's get him out for some fresh air. The Sentience Code is safe with the Feds. I'm going to tell you everything. Oh, wow, where do I start? Okay, so you and I are from this planet called Sentinel—"

"LINC, I know that," Bobby said. "What—happened after—" He paused, trying to piece together jumbled memories tumbling around his brain. The corilum reactor. Gamma moving to stab Jen. Waking up in his body and jumping in front of the strike. "Did I—die?"

"Bobby, I'm Doctor Patel." The man crouched next to LINC so that his eyes were level with Bobby's. "I was on the medical team that got you off Sentinel. Your neural activity was almost absent by the time we warped. Your bot here told me about the Tether. I didn't believe it at first because there were no signs of life in it. But when I heard your voice call out through the Tether, we put your body in a cryonic chamber and worked around the clock to reverse the transfer. You've been out for three weeks. I was actually beginning to lose hope until yesterday when your internal temperature increased. It's a miracle that you're alive. If you hadn't been in that Tether, your biologic body would have died. Glad you decided to come back to the land of the living."

The memory of Barnes's offer in the airlock broke through Bobby's foggy mind. He'd decided to go solar surfing.

"Yeah, yeah, yeah." LINC bounced with excitement. "But wait till you hear the interesting stuff. After you left the *Quasar*—and left my busted body there, by the way, we'll talk about that later—Jen used her hard drive to repair me with the Sentience Code she stole from your arm. Bobs, you'll never believe this. I'm sentient now. Dr. Patel calls me the 'most confounding robot of our generation.'" A self-satisfied grin pulled at the bot's alloy mouth.

Bobby found the strength to cock a brow.

"It's true. That stuff in the trees?" LINC pointed to the branches swaying in the distance. "It's not tree grass. They're called leaves!" He folded his arms across his chest. "See? I'm evolving."

"Okay, but what happened on Sentinel?" Bobby asked, finding his words coming clearer.

LINC's shoulders slumped. "You're really impressed, huh? Well, *after* I became the first sentient robot in the entire galaxy, Jen called the Feds to liberate Sentinel."

Bobby glanced at Jen, shrinking behind Dr. Patel. The bitterness at seeing her eased somewhat. "Why did you do that?"

She gave a slight shrug, eyes glued to the ground. "Wanted to make a good decision for once."

"Anyway," LINC continued, "they arrested Cappy and the big guy, then we waited for like twelve hours for you to answer my call." The bot tapped Bobby's cybernetic arm. "Why do you have this if you never use it?"

"I remember hearing you." Bobby recalled the bot's voice filtering through his arm in the anti-gravity pod. "How did you do that?"

"The Living Inter-Neural Communicator." The bot smiled like the answer explained everything.

"What?"

"Bobs, the LINC program was designed for cybernetic humans to talk to each other."

"Wait." Bobby held up a shaky hand. This wasn't making sense. For the first time, agitation chewed through his dulled senses. "How do you know that?"

"USF reports from Sentinel," answered Dr. Patel. "When you destroyed Gamma, our troops took over the city. They found a lot of information in what you call the Depository."

"Sure, sure, sure." LINC waved away the doctor's explanation. "But I figured it out way before they did, being the galaxy's first true sentient robot and all. How do you think I contacted you for your access cipher to open the shields?" He tapped Bobby's plastifiber forearm.

Dr. Patel leaned in. "Bobby, they also found records regarding where you came from."

Adrenaline charged Bobby's nerves, clearing his head.

"Let me tell the story." LINC scooted closer. "Bobs, you remember the holos Barnes showed us of the two researchers who founded Sentinel? Rich—something and Cordo—what was his name?"

"Richard Elif and Cordell Cane," Dr. Patel corrected.

"Yeah, yeah. Anyway, turns out Cordell Cane was selling Sentinel tech to the Fringe factions because he was a Fringe Supremacist. And the day Sentinel went dark was the day Richard Elif invented the Sentience Code. Which was the day you got your cybernetic arm."

Bobby frowned. "What does that have to do with it?"

LINC sighed. "I know you're out of it, Bobs, but try to keep up. Remember those holopods we found in the Depository? Turns out ol' Rich created the program to turn your neural impulses into the Sentience Code in your arm. Crazy, right?"

Bobby stared at his cybernetic arm. "I don't understand."

"Bobby," Dr. Patel said. "You're a human computer. You're the reason the Sentience Code exists."

LINC hammered a fist into the grass. "I wanted to tell him! Didn't you hear me building up to it?"

Shock buzzed Bobby's brain. The holo he'd seen in the Depository. A researcher attaching a cybernetic arm to an infant. It *had* been him.

He stared at the grass, trying to process the new information. A thousand questions filled his brain, but one in particular escaped. "So the only reason I exist was to develop the Sentience Code?"

Dr. Patel shook his head. "No, you were part of a refugee convoy from a war zone. You lost your limb in a Fringe attack. There were a number of wounded children inducted into the cybernetic project. We're not sure yet which system they rescued you from. But Doctor Elif and his wife adopted you because they couldn't have children. He chose you to advance humanity *and* to be his son."

"He's your dad," LINC cried with a smile. "Your name's Robert Elif!"

Bobby flinched and felt himself falling over. LINC and Dr. Patel caught him before he fell off the bench.

"I know it's a lot to take in," said Dr. Patel, helping him back into a seated position.

Bobby's mind raced. "Then where did he go? Why did he leave me on Sentinel?"

LINC's smile faded. He glanced at Dr. Patel. "You can tell him this part."

Dr. Patel's face was grim. "Cordell Cane killed your father."

Bobby's heart stopped. "What?"

"It was going to take about sixteen years for the Sentience Code to fully develop in your arm from your neural impulses. The Fringe factions were losing the war, and time was a factor. Did you ever hear about the race to develop the atomic bomb? Ancient history. Since the secret to artificial sentience was lost after the Second AI War, Doctor Cane was helping the factions race to recreate their own Sentience Code. So he created the Tether bot and uploaded his mind into it. He thought he could fuse with the technology to create the Sentience Code faster than waiting for it to develop in your growing body. But it backfired. He became trapped in the Tether's neural architecture, subject to its programming and restraints. He was a captive inside the Tether."

"What happened to him?

The doctor took a deep breath. "You destroyed him in that corilum reactor."

For the first time, Bobby was conscious enough to flinch. "Cane was...."

"Gamma," Dr. Patel finished for him.

Bobby's vision swam. He thought he would pass out, but the sensation of LINC and Dr. Patel's hands on his shoulders steadied him. When his breathing had slowed, Dr. Patel continued.

"You knew him while he was trapped in the *gamma* model of the Tether. As Sentinel tech, he was able to use his link to Sentinel's tech to secretly program the bots for a mutiny against the Federation. As Gamma, he caused your father and mother's death and stole you away. Then he activated the mutiny, and Sentinel went dark."

"So why didn't he just take the Sentience Code out of my arm when I turned sixteen?" Bobby asked. "When it was finished?"

"Because of his programming." The doctor touched Bobby's cybernetic arm. "This was created on Sentinel, so the bots recognized you as Sentinel tech. One of their own, you see. Cane was bound by Gamma's programming. He could not force you to do anything you didn't want to do."

"But they forced me to go through Programming."

"Ah, not exactly. Your bot here filled me in on many crucial details. I can say with confidence that it was impossible for the bots to force you through what you called your Programming. You only *thought* they forced you. Cane manipulated you, Bobby. He knew he couldn't lay a finger on you, so he made you so afraid of failure that you would do anything to please him. It was all a carefully crafted deception."

"That's why we failed Programming every year," LINC said. "The Programmers designed it for you to get more and more frustrated until you uploaded into the Tether."

"Cane programmed your mind through fear, Bobby," Dr. Patel said. "And once he had you in the Tether, you would follow any order he gave you. That includes giving him the Sentience Code. He was going to use it to overcome his programming restraints and become human again. So to speak."

"But I was already afraid of him," said Bobby. "I would have done anything he told me. Why didn't he just tell me to give him the Code when I turned sixteen? Jen stole it without me even knowing." He glanced at Jen, who averted her eyes.

"Ooh, ooh, I can answer that!" LINC raised his hand. "Turns out I wasn't just your task assistant program. Your dad designed me to protect the Code in your arm. Apparently, when you cloned my neural network back on Sentinel, the Code got cloned along with it. I was protecting it in Six without even knowing it. Wow, I'm good."

"But then how did Jen extract the Code from my arm?"

LINC knocked on Bobby's head with a fist. "Hello, Bobs, is anyone in there?"

"Ow, stop." Dim pain registered in Bobby's temple, but he couldn't swat LINC away.

Dr. Patel caught LINC by the wrist, but the bot shook out of his grip and continued, "You corrupted the copy of me in your arm when you cloned me into Six, remember? I wasn't in your arm to protect the Code anymore."

"So I scrubbed up, huh?" Bobby huffed.

"Yep."

"So you must've transferred it back into my arm when you were, um, dying on the *Quasar*?"

"Exactly," LINC replied. "I replaced the copy Jen stole. And Jen repaired me with her stolen copy. Full circle. So after all this time of protecting the Code, it's part of my operating system now. I'd say that's a fitting end to the story."

Again, Bobby looked at Jen, and this time she returned a sorrowful glance.

"Anyways," LINC continued, "Gamma tried to hack me when you were a baby, which is why I had so many behavior restraints. The only thing he couldn't do was turn off your dad's programmed failsafe where if anyone tried to transfer the Code, it would override hacked restraints and alert the Feds. Remember how you told me an alarm went off when we tried to copy my neural network into Six? It would've alerted the Federation to your location. Obviously, Gamma couldn't risk you figuring out the truth, so that's why he pressured you to upload into the Tether, so you'd, well, you know, deactivate me if he told you to. Guess he knew deep down you wouldn't do that of your own free will. Or at least, I hope you wouldn't do that?" LINC raised an alloy brow. He barely let a second pass before saying, "You're taking a long time to answer."

"Yes, LINC, obviously," Bobby said. "I couldn't let Six die or the Archiver. There's no way I could ever deactivate you."

"Good," said LINC with a satisfied tone. "Anyways, sorry I couldn't warn you sooner, but my memory restraints only fell off when I became the galaxy's first true sentient bot."

"Zel," Bobby breathed.

"What?"

"All this time I was free and didn't know it?"

"Reports are still coming back from Sentinel," Dr. Patel said. "You need time to process. We can talk more later."

A clock tower at the park's edge chimed.

Dr. Patel stood up and looked at his watch. "Time to get you back to the med bay." He stepped behind Bobby and returned pushing a hover chair. With LINC's help, he lifted Bobby into the seat and angled him toward the park exit.

"Wait," said Jen, stepping in front. "Can I talk to Bobby alone for a minute?"

Dr. Patel checked his watch again, then motioned for LINC to follow him down the sidewalk. When the bot turned to Bobby and puckered his lips, pantomiming a passionate kiss, the doctor grabbed him by the arm and dragged him away.

Jen watched them until they were out of earshot. She turned back to Bobby. "Bobby, I'm going away."

Bobby shifted in his seat. Though some strength had returned, his muscles were already exhausted. "Why?"

She bit her lip and looked away. "You made an incredible sacrifice for me. One that I didn't deserve. Doctor Patel said your emotions are dulled right now. I'm afraid when they come back, you're going to find that you hate me."

"But—I—" Bobby tried to protest, but tangled feelings confused his response. Bitterness lingered in his core. Was she right? Would it get stronger as he'd recovered?

"You don't have to say anything." She shook her head. "I can see it in your face. I don't think you'll be able to forgive me. I can't forgive myself." Tears sparkled in her eyes. "I'm the last thing you need in your life. That's why I'm going away."

"Where?" Bobby's voice came out small.

"I don't know. The Federation pardoned me for helping them capture Sentinel. And Bar-Uk's dead, so there's no bounty on me. But my uncle and Doc are in prison. And Grandpop is...." She blinked away moisture. "I don't have any family left. Maybe I'll go to my dad's home world. Get some clarity. I don't know, maybe I'll see you one day when I get my life straight."

"Jen...." Bobby knew he should say something else, but already his senses were dulling again.

"I'm going to do one last selfish thing, Bobby." Jen wiped her cheeks with a sleeve. "And I hope you won't hate me for it. But I'll hate myself even more if I don't."

She leaned in, and Bobby's heart jumped as she pressed her soft lips onto his. He had the strength to stop it but found he didn't want to. And when he didn't move away, Jen pressed a little harder. He tasted her moonfruit lip gloss mixed with salt from her tears. Then their lips separated, her face still close to his.

Glistening, pale blue eyes fixed him. "You are the most perfect person I've ever met," she whispered. With that, she pressed a small object into his hand. "See you later, Bobby Robot." Then she turned and walked away.

"Jen...." Bobby tried to call, but his muscles ached with exhaustion, and all that came out was a hoarse whisper. He watched her slender frame recede in the distance until she disappeared through the stone arch at the park's exit. After a moment, he registered the sensation of the object she'd placed in his hand. He looked down at it. It was Barnes's compass displaying the picture of him and Jen in their exo suits.

<!026: Plotting New Course>

BOBBY GAZED AT the picture of him and Jen on Barnes's compass. He was sitting on the loading ramp to a small personal ship when a voice cut through the clamor of the Federation hangar bay.

"Bobby!"

He looked up to see Dr. Patel jogging through the throng of maintenance personnel hovering around rows of docked ships.

"I'm glad I caught you." The doctor huffed on reaching him. He waved a comtab. "A new report just came in from Sentinel."

Curiosity pushed Bobby to his feet. He took the proffered comtab and scanned the text. After a moment, he looked up. "Signs of a life form? What does that mean?"

Dr. Patel stuck his hands on his hips and smiled. "They found signs of another cybernetic human in Sentinel's southern hemisphere."

"Another?" Bobby breathed, flexing his synthetic fingers. He recalled the holo he'd seen in the Depository of the infant with the cybernetic leg.

"Nothing's confirmed yet," Dr. Patel said. "Just that there may have been someone like you on the planet at one time. But I submitted your health report from the last few months, and the USF is giving you clearance to explore with the reconnaissance team. You could find out more about where you came from."

"Wow." Bobby stared at the report, mind racing with the possibility of learning more about his origin.

"You ready, Bobs?" LINC leaned out from the ship's side.

Bobby looked from the report to the compass, then straightened and handed the comtab back to Dr. Patel. "It'll have to wait."

The doctor raised his brows in surprise. "You're still going to look for Jen?"

Bobby slipped the compass chain around his neck. "She's my family."

"But we're talking about where you came from." Dr. Patel tapped the comtab. "Secrets on Sentinel that you've wanted to know for a long time. It seems logical to go there first."

Bobby waved the idea away. "I've had enough of logic for a while."

"Well," Dr. Patel sighed, "I certainly won't ask you to stay." He extended his hand. "Good luck, Bobby."

"Thanks." Bobby smiled and shook the doctor's hand.

"All right, let's go," said LINC, beckoning him aboard.

Bobby waved to Dr. Patel, then hurried up into the ship.

"We're going to have to stop at the Centauri system." LINC punched a button and the loading ramp retracted. "I forgot to pack your food."

Bobby rolled his eyes. "I can't believe they cleared you to help fly this thing."

The hatch closed, and they made their way to the cockpit.

"Hey, they trust me." LINC plopped into the copilot seat. "After all, I *am* the galaxy's first sentient AI robot."

"That's what I've heard." Bobby took the pilot seat next to LINC. He gazed through the viewport at the glittering starscape outside the space station hangar. "Ready?"

LINC gripped the flight controls. "Ready!"

Bobby engaged the thrusters, and they blasted into space. "Let's go find Jen."

Acknowledgments

I thank God for all the people in my life that have helped make this book a reality. Thanks to North Texas Writers for the invaluable critiques, to my beta readers Carly, Sara, Anna, Sophie, AJ, Raquel, Shane, and Corey for the great feedback, to my wonderful agents, Patty and Amy, for all their hard work, to Chrissy for breathing new life into the Bobby Robot saga, and to everyone who believed in me. Thanks for helping make this book not suck.

About the Author

Michael Hilton is a time traveler from the future who has come back to warn us of the impending literary apocalypse. A nerd for Science Fiction and Fantasy, he writes to stave off the coming wasteland of soulless fiction. One day his Wikipedia page will describe his warnings as "mildly prophetic," and "wildly exaggerated." He is the author of the Bobby Robot series and publisher of The Weekly Geek. Michael lives on earth but is thinking about moving soon.